SHAKEDOWN

ALSO BY NEWT GINGRICH

Trump vs. China
Trump's America
Understanding Trump
Electing Trump

MAYBERRY AND GARRETT SERIES (COAUTHOR PETE EARLEY)
Collusion

THE MAJOR BROOKE GRANT SERIES (COAUTHOR PETE EARLEY)
Duplicity
Treason
Vengeance

THE GETTYSBURG SERIES (WITH WILLIAM R. FORSTCHEN)
Gettysburg
Grant Comes East
Never Call Retreat

THE GEORGE WASHINGTON SERIES (WITH WILLIAM R. FORSTCHEN)
To Try Men's Souls
Valley Forge
Victory at Yorktown

THE PACIFIC WAR SERIES
Pearl Harbor
Days of Infamy

To Make Men Free (with William R. Forstchen)
A Nation Like No Other
Real Change
5 Principles for a Successful Life (with Jackie Gingrich Cushman)
To Save America
A Contract with the Earth (with Terry L. Maple)
Breakout
Drill Here, Drill Now, Pay Less

SHAKEDOWN

A NOVEL

Newt
Gingrich
AND PETE EARLEY

BROADSIDE BOOKS
An Imprint of HarperCollinsPublishers

HarperCollins books may be purchased for educational, business, or sales promotional use. For information, please email the Special Markets Department at SPsales@harpercollins.com.

Broadside Books™ and the Broadside logo are trademarks of HarperCollins Publishers.

FIRST EDITION

Library of Congress Cataloging-in-Publication Data has been applied for.

ISBN 978-0-06-286019-4

20 21 22 23 24 LSC 10 9 8 7 6 5 4 3 2 1

Newt Gingrich dedicates this book to his wife, Callista Gingrich, who is tirelessly serving her country and working to end human trafficking and expand religious liberty.

Pete Earley dedicates this book to his granddaughters, Maribella Earley and Audrey Morton.

Shake down (v.): to obtain money from in a deceitful, contemptible, or illegal manner. As in: *racketeers shaking down store owners for protection.*

—Merriam-Webster's Dictionary

CONTENTS

CAST OF CHARACTERS

Brett Garrett . . . . former Navy SEAL

Valerie Mayberry . . . . FBI counterintelligence agent

Gelleh Peretz, aka "Esther" . . . . Mossad operative

Saeedi "The Roc" Bashar . . . . Palestinian assassin

Taras Aleksandrovich Zharkov . . . . billionaire oligarch

General Firouz Kardar . . . . Iranian intelligence

Julian "Big Jules" Levi . . . . Mossad director

Connor Whittington . . . . CIA director

Thomas Jefferson Kim . . . . cybersecurity expert

Boris Petrov . . . . submarine commander

PART I

Life is either a daring adventure or nothing.

—*Helen Keller*

ONE

The old man bent down. Tried, but couldn't slip the envelope under his neighbor's door. Checked the empty hallway. Turned and began walking toward the floor's elevator while pulling a pistol from under his jacket. Pressed the call button and took a deep breath to calm his nerves. *Ding*. He tightened his index finger on the handgun's trigger, anticipating the opening doors. Sucked in another calming breath. No one was inside. Tucked his handgun between his belt and watermelon belly. Stepped inside.

The building's lobby was empty. The security guard had gone home at 10:00 p.m. The condo board didn't believe it necessary to have him stay longer. Their Rosslyn, Virginia, neighborhood was relatively crime-free. The man walked to a wall of mailboxes directly across from the elevator. Ran a finger along the tenants' mailboxes, stopping at the second box on the third column. His neighbor's. He inserted the envelope into it. From his jacket he drew a second envelope, which he dropped in the outgoing mail.

Behind him, the sound of laughter. A couple entering the building through its double glass doors. The man at the mailboxes noticed that the woman was younger. Giggling, holding her male companion's arm. Her loud chatter and wobbly walk suggested she was drunk. A Saturday-night date, perhaps a one-night stand. The condo building was across the Potomac River from the nation's capital, an inexpensive Uber ride from popular Georgetown pickup bars.

The approaching couple appeared harmless, still. The man returned to the elevator and pushed the call button, hoping to board and depart before they reached him. The couple quickened their pace. The old man reached inside his jacket, resting his hand on his pistol. He noticed that she was wearing a gray wool stocking cap and scarf. He wore a red Washington Nationals baseball cap, and the collar of his dark-blue coat was turned up. Difficult to see faces.

The elevator doors opened.

The woman straightened, lunged forward, grabbed the old man's left arm. At the same moment her male accomplice slipped in front of him. A blade before the old man could draw his handgun. Directly into his heart. One thrust. One twist. No time to cry out. Who would hear? The woman steadied him. Pushed the man's body forward. He hit the elevator floor hard, face-first. Its doors shut.

TWO

The loud belching of Brett Garrett's Norton Commando Interpol motorcycle—manufactured in 1975 by the Brits for police use only—reverberated inside the condo building's underground parking garage. The bike was his most prized possession, discovered in a Belgian barn, shipped home, rebuilt. He'd always been good with his hands.

Riding on Virginia's rural blacktops away from the congested DMV—shorthand among those who lived there for the District, Maryland, and Virginia—helped, blocking out all extraneous thoughts. A one-lane road and a speeding motorcycle. A patch of loose gravel; a pothole; a fox darting unexpectedly across the blacktop; topping a hill pushing a hundred miles per hour and discovering a farmer's slow-moving tractor blocking the path—Garrett knew the statistics. Five thousand motorcycle fatalities each year in the United States.

His solitary rides had become much more frequent, daring death, forcing adrenaline into him. He needed the rush. At thirty-six, Garrett knew he had been put to pasture, a bitter irony in a life filled with much irony. The media once had labeled him a national hero. He'd been feted at the White House, praised by the president. But the federal agencies that could benefit most from his talents had no interest in him now.

Initially, he'd blamed his addiction. Opioids for chronic pain from multiple burns. A helicopter crash in Africa. A terrorist's RPG.

It had taken him months to heal, only to confront the fact that he had become addicted to pain pills. He'd started using Suboxone to wean himself off opioids and found it took him longer to kick his addiction to medication than to heal from his burns. Finally he had become drug-free, and a Navy psychiatrist had cleared him of post-traumatic stress disorder. He'd been ready for a new assignment, but no one called. What was it that made him unhirable? he asked himself, although he knew. His last kill.

A car was parked in his reserved condo space. Garrett cursed, and for a moment considered flattening its tires. Controlling his impulses was something he'd been working on. He inspected the car as he rolled past. An unmarked police car. He parked the Norton between two thick concrete pillars. Four more Arlington County squad cars took up visitor spots near the elevator.

Garrett boarded the garage's underground elevator, taking it up into the lobby.

"You live here?" a uniformed officer demanded as soon as Garrett exited the elevator.

"Me and about four hundred others," he answered.

"Let's see some ID."

"Why?"

"Just do it!"

Garrett unslung his backpack and had begun to reach inside for his wallet when the young police officer spotted a handgun.

"Raise your hands!" he yelled, drawing his Glock.

His holler set off a chain reaction among the other half dozen police officers inside the lobby. Each pulled their weapon, all aimed at Garrett.

"Let's just chill," Garrett said in a calm voice, letting his open backpack slip onto the floor while lifting both hands into the air. "I got a permit."

Keeping his pistol pointed at Garrett's chest, the officer kicked the backpack across the marble floor toward a colleague. She reached inside and removed Garrett's Sig Sauer P226 handgun from the top of the bag, where it had been lying in plain sight.

"Why you carrying this?" she asked.

"I've been squirrel hunting." Garrett smirked. "Like I just said, I got a permit."

The young officer was clearly trying to figure out what to do next when a voice behind him called out: "Don't you know who this is? Put down your weapons."

A fifty-something bald man wearing lieutenant stripes stepped toward Garrett and offered his hand. "Sorry, Mr. Garrett. You live here?"

"Afraid so."

His brass nametag read LIEUTENANT MORGAN.

"Recognized you from the television," Morgan said. "You and that FBI agent—that female—what you two did at the Capitol, well, it was incredible. How's she doing?"

"Not sure. Haven't seen her in a while."

"If the president of these United States gave me a Medal of Freedom," Morgan continued, "I'd be wearing that fricking medal around my neck every day and shoving it into everyone's face."

Garrett smiled but didn't respond.

The female officer returned his backpack and Sig Sauer.

"Why the barrage?" Garrett asked.

"One of your residents was murdered. His body was found in the elevator this morning. Stabbed right in the heart. Just once." Morgan made a thrusting motion with his right hand. "Killer knew what he was doing."

"Catch anything on the cameras?" Garrett nodded at one in the ceiling near them.

"The entire system went down last night. Some kind of computer glitch." Morgan glanced at his notepad, where he'd written the dead man's name. "Nasya Radi. You know him?"

Garrett shook his head. "I stay pretty much to my own."

"Which floor is yours?"

"Sixth."

"His too. Maybe you passed him in the hall."

"Maybe. What'd he look like?"

Lieutenant Morgan called over a plainclothes detective.

"This is Detective DeAngelo from homicide," Morgan explained. "Show Nasya Radi's photo to Mr. Garrett."

DeAngelo produced what was clearly a passport picture. "Didn't have a driver's license," the detective said. "Got here in 1979. Lived alone as far as we can tell."

"Probably fled during the revolution," Garrett said.

"Say again?" DeAngelo replied.

"Iranian Revolution. February of '79," Garrett answered. "Islamic radicals drove the shah out. You probably should check with State to see if he was granted political asylum."

"I remember," Lieutenant Morgan said. "American embassy hostages."

"Oh, yeah," DeAngelo said. "Think he was someone important over there?"

"State might know." Garrett studied Radi's passport picture. "Can't say I recognize him from the building, but it's an old photo."

"Here's my card," Morgan said. "Call me if there's anything I can ever do for you."

Detective DeAngelo produced a card too. "In case you remember anything."

Garrett paused. "Think he might have been murdered because he's an Iranian?"

"Could be a hate crime, but I doubt it," DeAngelo said. "We got lots of foreigners living around here. Immigrants. Sometimes the most obvious is what actually happened, and this looks like a robbery to me. His wallet is missing."

"I figure if the Iranians wanted him dead because he fled after the revolution," Morgan added, "they'd've killed him years ago."

"Like I said, a robbery. We've had an uptick in them," DeAngelo said.

"Arlington's gone upscale," Morgan explained. "Lots of highly paid millennials moving in, so naturally they're going to be targeted."

Garrett took another glance at the photo. Radi hardly fell into the millennial category, but he decided to move on without comment. Both elevators had been sealed off by the police, so he took the stairs. When he exited on the sixth floor, another officer approached him.

"You on this floor?" the policeman asked.

"Live right down the hall. Lieutenant Morgan and Detective DeAngelo already talked to me."

"Which one's your condo?"

"Six-fifteen. On the left."

"That's only two doors from the victim. You know him?"

"No, like I said, I already talked to Morgan and DeAngelo."

"If you don't mind me asking, where were you last night?"

Garrett released a sigh. "I was out. Actually I've been gone three days." He stepped past the policeman.

"Hey," the officer said, "we're not done."

"Actually, we are. Like I said, Morgan's already talked to me. Call him."

As he entered his one-bedroom condo, he turned on his cell, which he'd intentionally kept off until now. It immediately rang.

"Where you been?" Thomas Jefferson Kim asked. "I've been trying to call you for days."

"Out communing with nature. Why, you got a job for me?"

"C'mon, Garrett. You know better."

"What I know is, you're supposed to be my best friend. You own your own international security company. And you're telling me there's not a single job opening anywhere in the entire world for me?"

"You know why. You're persona non grata and I can't risk it. Too many government contracts."

"So why are you calling?"

"Lunch."

"Give me a job, then we'll have lunch."

Garrett hung up, stripped, and stepped into the shower. He had three days of roughing it in the Monongahela National Forest in eastern West Virginia to wash off. Three days of solitude. Basic survival. A way to strip yourself mentally and physically. But ghosts recognize no geographical boundaries. Multiple tours in Afghanistan. Cameroon. Water splashed on his unshaven face. Boko Haram. He ran a washcloth over the burn scars on the side of his abdomen. A reminder of the helicopter crash. Those on board had counted on him to save them. Little girls. Hostages being rescued. One face stuck out. Little Abidemi.

He walked naked across the cold white tile out into his condo's kitchen. Checked the fridge. Two beers. Leftover take-out Chinese. He grabbed the beers, tossed the Chinese. In his bedroom, he swallowed an Ambien, nursed one beer, and channel-surfed. For some unknown reason, he'd started watching cable cooking challenges. Considering how empty his cupboards and refrigerator were, it was an odd choice. Irish cuisine. Was there such a thing? Bangers and mash. Finished the second beer. Dozed off.

Garrett's body shook. His eyes popped open. A nightmare, a recurring one. He checked his watch: oh two hundred. He slipped on running shorts and a worn pair of Asics. An early-morning jog helps clear the head. The elevator floor had been scrubbed clean. All the cops were now gone. No sign of a murder less than twenty-four hours ago, except now the condo's security guard, Calvin Russell, was sitting in the lobby, fidgeting with his cell phone.

"Got you working nights now, Russell?" Garrett asked.

"They sure do, Mr. Garrett. From now on, lobby guards twenty-four hours a day. I'm on overtime until they fill the slots. You should apply."

Not that desperate, Garrett thought as he pushed the interior glass door. It wouldn't budge.

"Sorry," Russell called out. "I got to buzz it open. They installed it this afternoon." He pushed a button freeing the door.

Garrett sucked in the chill autumn air. Almost time for the Marine Corps Marathon. Thousands of runners invading the neighborhood. He stretched and noticed a homeless man curled up in the doorway of a bagel shop directly across the street. Lying on cardboard, his belongings piled in a grocery cart, his face hidden under a gray wool blanket. Otherwise the street was empty.

Five miles was a good distance. Time to think. Clear your mind. He pushed himself. He always did. Checked his watch. Six minutes the first mile. He could do better. He returned sweaty. The homeless man was still sleeping.

"How was it out there?" Russell asked.

"Always better when no one is around," Garrett replied.

"Same for this job."

"You see that homeless guy across the street?"

"Started showing up a few days ago. Been getting complaints from tenants about him, but I think the bagel shop owner gives him a bagel and coffee. Like a stray dog. You feed 'em once, and they settle in."

Garrett pushed the elevator button and then hesitated. He'd been distracted by the police when he'd first arrived home and forgotten to collect his mail. He removed two keys from a pouch that he wore while running: one to his condo, the other to his mailbox.

It was stuffed with junk mail, along with bills. Coupons. Nothing unexpected. Wait. A brown envelope. His name written in cursive. No postage. No return address. He opened the letter. It was written in Farsi, which he couldn't read, but he did recognize the signature.

Nasya Radi.

THREE

The residents of the Mayfair district, described by Sotheby's as the epicenter of luxurious London living and an internationally recognized world premier address, were comfortable with excess. But even the heirs of Britain's aristocracy were jarred when Taras Aleksandrovich Zharkov purchased the legendary Fallbrook Manor on Brook Street. A consortium of investors had been in the midst of converting the nineteenth-century mansion into four apartments, each priced at £10 million (roughly US$13 million), when Zharkov surfaced.

As the sole owner of Russoil, the sixth largest oil company in Russia, Zharkov was a billionaire several times over. As with other Russian oligarchs, gossip about his close ties to Kremlin kleptocrats and his alleged connection to organized crime raised eyebrows, but didn't stop anyone from gleefully accepting his money. He'd paid more than £50 million for Fallbrook Manor. His onetime secretary—now his fourth wife—spent another £30 million decorating it, making Zharkov's residence the most expensive in London other than the British royal palaces. The magazine *Haut Monde* published a ten-page spread complete with a flattering profile of its new owners—without any mention of his questionable connections. His home's high ceiling entrance hall was lined with Art Deco mirrors, and the floor was marble, Bianco Perlino and Silver Emperador. The ceiling was covered in fourteen-carat gold. The master suite occupied the entire third floor, with sweeping views toward Claridge's, London's famous five-star hotel, dating back to 1854. The kitchen featured blackened bronze Bulthaup cabinetry and Gaggenau appliances with Taj Mahal marble backsplash and worktops for the four full-time chefs, part of a staff of twenty, not counting Zharkov's private security team, whose exact number was secret, although it was believed they were former Spetsnaz soldiers.

Given the Russian's notoriety, few onlookers thought it odd when a black stretch limousine arrived late one afternoon. What was odd was the fifty-something man who stepped from it. More the sort who would be a driver than passenger in a luxury vehicle. He wore a snug black T-shirt that displayed his ripped biceps inked with the sort of tattoos that sailors bought during drunken shore leaves or convicts applied with contraband tattoo guns. He was mostly bald and had a boxer's broken nose. Commander Boris Petrov, a former Russian submariner, had once been imprisoned for stealing military hardware—but now he was Zharkov's "fixer," and one of his closest confidants.

Zharkov's London assistant escorted Petrov to a massive office on the second floor, protected by cutting-edge antisurveillance devices.

"Welcome, Commander!" Zharkov called out cheerfully from behind an ornate desk. "Come, come, sit." The short and hefty Russian billionaire nodded toward a carved armchair directly across from him. "Your flight to London, it was comfortable?"

"It was all right," Petrov replied without emotion as he glanced around the office. It was his first visit since Zharkov had bought and renovated Fallbrook Manor.

"Only all right? Come now, my friend." Clearly Zharkov expected more appreciation for dispatching one of his finest private jets to collect Petrov. "The women I put on your flight," he continued, "did you not enjoy them? They were former Olympic gymnasts."

Petrov dropped his right leg over his left and rested his clasped walnut-shaped knuckles on his lap. "That explains their flexibility," he replied, breaking into a smirk.

Zharkov guffawed and slapped the desktop. "You must tell me the details."

"Now, that wouldn't be gentlemanly, would it? Sharing such details with a man of your high position."

"A man of my position? My friend, you have known me long enough to realize the only position I care about hearing is which positions you were in with those two gymnasts!" Zharkov announced, laughing even louder.

A knock on the door interrupted them. One of the chefs from the manor's kitchen entered.

"Sir," he said, "the mistress of the house has arranged a proper English tea for your guest and you. She instructed me to present it to you now. May we proceed?"

"Trying to civilize me," Zharkov said. "Yes, yes, bring it in."

Two women carrying silver trays joined them. One poured tea from a monogrammed porcelain pot into matching monogrammed porcelain cups while the other spread out finger sandwiches, scones with jam and cream, and curd tarts.

"Will that be all?" the chef asked.

"Yes, yes, you may go."

As soon as they were alone, Zharkov put aside his teacup.

"Don't bother," he said as he stepped from his desk toward a nearby liquor cabinet, where he withdrew a bottle.

"Iordanov exclusively for me," he boasted. "What Russian wouldn't prefer a good vodka to Earl Grey tea?"

"Certainly not me," Petrov replied.

Zharkov moved to the front of his desk and handed Petrov a crystal glass. He poured a generous portion into it and his own.

Lifting his glass, Zharkov offered a crude, illustrated toast. "May you always have a stiff drink in your hand." He thrust his hips upward as if he were having sex. "Stiff in bed too." He laughed. "And more money than you can possibly spend before you die."

"If this screwball plan of yours actually works, I will have all three."

Both emptied their drinks. Zharkov poured another round and returned to his desk, where he reached for a cucumber sandwich. "We have come a long way from when we first met," he reminisced. "It was fortune that brought us together that day in the gulag."

"And your father's fortune that kept you alive and freed us."

"Yes." Zharkov grunted. "I hired you to protect me from some rather unsavory characters intent on doing me harm, and I quickly saw a way to profit from your skills. Remind me, Petrov, how many fights did you win before we were released?"

"You mean, before your father bribed three judges to erase our crimes? Thirty-seven. Twenty knockouts."

"And when we returned to Moscow and moved over to the boxing game, before I got into the oil business, what was the record of our best pugilist—Yuri something, right?"

"Yuri got himself twenty-one knockouts. One more than me, but mine were bare-knuckle."

"No rules. Broken bones. Gouged eyes. You were good at it."

"Still am."

"I imagine so. Our pompous president asked me several times to arrange a bare-knuckle between you and Yuri for him and his Kremlin comrades. I explained that you worked only for me, but added you could be persuaded for the right price."

"Anything for the right price," Petrov said. He lifted his now-empty glass and looked at Zharkov, who nodded approval. Leaning forward from his chair, Petrov took the vodka bottle from the desk and poured himself another glass.

"It was Yuri who always refused," Zharkov said.

"With good reason. I would have ruined his pretty face." Petrov raised his now-full glass. "A toast to President Vyachesian Leninovich Kalugin, a self-declared martial arts expert." He chuckled. "Even I would have taken a dive if he challenged me."

"Do not mock our illustrious leader," Zharkov replied. "He was the one who secured my spot in Russoil."

"For which you have been paying him handsomely," Petrov said. "And I was the one who helped you persuade the other shareholders to sell their interests."

"For which I have paid you as well."

Zharkov emptied his glass and set it on his desk. "Enough from the past. When will you be ready to depart?"

"No later than three weeks, two if we're lucky. But I have no control over the Iranians."

"The Iranians," Zharkov said. "What Iranians? Each time I have a conversation with them, they play a silly game." In a mocking voice, he continued, "'Why, Mr. Zharkov, Tehran is in full compliance with its promises to the West. Iran is a peace-loving nation. Iran is not an aggressor. We do not have nuclear capabilities.'" Zharkov laughed. "I must listen to this nonsense each time we speak. But, to answer your question, I've been told by the 'sellers' that they are on schedule."

"Good," Petrov said.

Zharkov waved his hand dismissively, as if shooing off a pesky fly. "The Iranians are mongrels. Dogs. If I could have obtained what I required from anyone else, I would have. Sadly, they are the only ones reckless and arrogant enough to help me."

He plucked a second cucumber sandwich from the silver platter and stuffed it into his mouth. While chewing it, he said, "Petrov, eat a sandwich. Do not disappoint my wife."

Petrov removed one from the tray. "Finger sandwiches," he said. "The English are so delicate."

Zharkov tapped the screen on an iPad, summoning his personal assistant, who entered, carrying two metal cases, each the size of an airplane carry-on bag. He nodded toward his assistant to open both.

"I love money," Zharkov said. "I have no use for cryptocurrencies. Money should be held between your fingers. It should be smelled."

Petrov glanced at the stacks of cash lined up in the cases.

"A million American dollars," Zharkov said, "consists of ten thousand $100 bills. Weighing nine kilograms, or twenty pounds. Three million in US dollars would weigh just over twenty-seven kilos, or sixty pounds. Even someone as strong as you would find carrying sixty pounds tiresome."

"Not when it is money."

"True, but why bother with dollars when euros weigh about twelve pounds per million? That reduces the weight of each of these cases to eight-point-six kilograms, or eighteen pounds."

Zharkov looked lovingly at the euros. He enjoyed putting his wealth on display. "This should cover the cost of your crew before departure." Looking up at his personal assistant, he said, "Take the cases to Commander Petrov's car. He has a plane to catch. . . ." He turned back to Petrov. "Unless you would like to spend the night?"

Before Petrov could respond, Zharkov opened a desk drawer and pulled out a Greek fashion magazine whose cover featured a young starlet wearing only a man's white button-down shirt.

"This lovely goddess will be coming for drinks after my wife retires. She believes I am interested in financing a movie for her." Zharkov smiled. "You could have her after I am finished."

Petrov inspected the cover. "A generous offer, but if we want to stay on schedule, I need to return to the Black Sea to prepare for the delivery from your 'sellers.'" He stood and turned to leave.

"Ah, now that you are on the verge of a better life, you have no interest in my hand-me-downs," Zharkov said. "Tell me, what do you know about fine furniture?"

"Furniture?" Petrov paused at the doorway, looking puzzled. "Do I look like a man who knows or cares about furniture?"

"One of the pieces in my office is a fraud and the other a masterpiece. Can you tell me which is which?"

"A guessing game? I will play along. Which furniture?"

"The chair you were sitting in and my desk."

Petrov studied both. "I'm guessing the desk is not a real antique."

Zharkov showed a smug grin. "This desk is original. It is from the Alexander Palace. The favorite palace of Nicholas the Second, our last Russian emperor. During the war, the Nazis commandeered his palace and used it for their high command. They sat behind this very desk, obeying Hitler's orders, just as the czar sat here before the revolution. The Romanovs. Hitler's generals. Think of the history that has been made behind this desk. The power wielded by those who sat at it. Russian curators were mystified when it disappeared from the royal palace. Without a trace." Zharkov smiled. "Now it is my desk, and I sit behind it, and it brings me much pleasure."

"It must have cost you a fortune."

"What joy is there in money if you can't buy what others can never obtain?"

"And the chair?"

"It is a fake even though I trusted the man who sold that chair to me when he insisted it was original." Zharkov paused for a bit of unnecessary drama before adding, "That lie cost him his life."

Now it was Petrov who smiled.

"You think his death humorous?" Zharkov asked.

"You paid a fortune for your desk but the man who sold you the fake paid an even higher price."

Zharkov grunted. "The two of us are cut from the same cloth, Petrov. If anyone attempts to deceive either of us, they will pay a heavy price. Isn't that true?"

"Enjoy your evening," Petrov said.

FOUR

Swollen eyes. A young woman's hands shaking.

General Firouz Kardar glanced at her with contempt. She'd been dragged into an empty office that he'd commandeered inside the underground bunker, and forced to her knees before his highly spit-shined boots.

"Her confession," the captain said, standing next to her. He offered Kardar a paper.

Kardar didn't bother to accept it. Instead, the sixty-five-year-old general kept his eyes focused on the woman. Bruised cheeks. Bloody lips. Dressed in a hijab and manteau. Correctly covered. What tortures had been inflicted underneath her modest dress did not concern him. She smelled of sweat. Urine.

"What is your first name?" he demanded.

"Yasmin," she whispered, casting her eyes down onto the green speckled tile floor.

"Yasmin," he repeated. "You're one of the *monafeqin*," he said, using the disparaging term for Iranians fighting to overthrow their own government—in the Qur'an, people of "two minds" who "say with their mouths what is not in their hearts" and "in their hearts is a disease."

"It's a mistake," she said, not daring to look up at him.

"But you have signed a confession," he replied.

She didn't respond.

"General," the captain said, "we found her outside the compound with this." He handed him a cell phone clad in a bright pink protective cover. A kitty emblem on it.

The woman began to gently sway on her knees. She tried unsuccessfully to shut her swollen eyes. Praying.

General Kardar scrolled through the images. White-topped guard towers. Fortified antiaircraft guns. Photos from outside the chain link fence that encircled the Iranian fuel enrichment plant where they now were standing. A nearly 400,000-foot military compound buried beneath layers of reinforced concrete on the outskirts of Natanz, Iran.

The woman glanced up. Tears in her eyes. "General, you must believe me. I found the phone. It is not mine. I was forced to say it was mine."

Kardar rested his right palm on his sidearm—an American-made M1911 semiauto, .45-caliber. Until 1986, standard issue of US Armed Forces. He'd taken it from a dead Iraqi soldier in 1980 after Saddam Hussein invaded Iran, setting off an eight-year war that ended with both sides claiming victory.

Kardar unholstered his pistol, leaned forward. The woman immediately lowered her face again. He placed the barrel tip against the top of her skull. Pushed it against her scalp. She began trembling again. The two guards on either side of her and the captain stepped away, anticipating blood splatter.

"Are you accusing my men of forcing you to lie?" he asked, taunting her.

She began to quietly sob.

The general chuckled and holstered his weapon.

Yasmin looked up at him. Confused. He reached under her chin with his left hand and gently raised her face. He appeared sympathetic.

"Should I send you to Tehran to face trial?" he asked softly. "Give you an opportunity to defend yourself? Prove your innocence? Renounce your confession?"

She dared to smile, revealing broken front teeth from being tortured. Blood.

In a lightning-fast move, he slashed her throat with a knife that seemed to appear from nowhere. He let go of her chin and she collapsed on the tile, making a gurgling sound under the buzzing neon ceiling lights. She raised her fingers to cover the deep wound. A final look of shock before dying.

Leaning down, Kardar wiped his blade across the dead woman's cloak. "Get rid of this filth," he ordered.

He watched her body being dragged away, leaving a bloody red smear. Satisfied, he turned his attention to another matter. Strolling behind a gunmetal-gray desk, he sat before a computer. Opening a program used to send encrypted messages, he typed quickly.

Final payment under way for ridding us of the traitor Nasya Radi. Bitcoins as you requested being transferred now.

A few seconds later, a reply:

Payment received.

Seconds after that response, the conversation, and all the metadata of its existence, was destroyed.

Kardar summoned the underground facility's director, a thin, scholarly-looking nuclear scientist wearing a white lab coat, and the head of security, an overweight bearded man wearing a drab green military uniform. Both noticed the blood smears on the floor when they entered. Stepped around them.

"How long before it is ready?" General Kardar demanded.

"Ten days," the scientist replied.

"The woman was *monafeqin*," Kardar said to the security chief. "Have you found her accomplices helping her from inside?"

"Everyone has been interrogated," the security chief replied. "She was from outside. We have files about all the workers' families. They would not dare speak about our mission. Dare help her."

"Then why did a *monafeqin* in America named Nasya Radi learn about our plans?"

The security chief stared straight ahead. He began perspiring. He licked his dry lips.

Kardar seemed to be staring through him.

The general was known for his violent temper. Everyone who knew him was aware of it, just as they were aware of his past, especially his childhood. It helped explain the permanent joyless look etched on his bearded face.

The general was conceived in a brutal rape. Abandoned at the hospital hours after his birth. Reared in an orphanage with other discards. Cruelty had marked his earliest years. He'd learned quickly the feel of a lash. While a teen he'd been recruited into SAVAK, the most despised and feared secret police force during the shah of Iran's reign. His skills—beatings, intimidation, mutilations, and murder—had been perfected there. When the shah had been driven from Iran, the Islamic Revolutionary Guard had started executing SAVAK officers. But the pious ayatollahs had quickly realized that a sadist such as Kardar could be useful in identifying and eliminating their enemies. His life had been spared. In an ironic twist, Kardar had embraced the revolutionary guard's fundamentalist interpretation of Shi'ism. By age twenty-three, he'd become a religious zealot, adhering to the strictest religious rules without abandoning his fondness for inflicting pain on his perceived enemies. He'd moved up the ranks to his current position—a general in the Quds Force, Iran's secret military unit, in charge of waging unconventional warfare against its three most hated enemies: the United States, Israel, and Saudi Arabia. It was the Quds Force that had trained the Lebanese Hezbollah, Hamas, Yemeni Houthis, and Shi'a militants. It was the Quds Force that had taught terrorists in Iraq how to make IEDs to kill Americans. It was the Quds Force that had plotted unsuccessfully to assassinate the Saudi Arabian ambassador to the United States, and bomb both the Saudi and Israeli embassies in Washington, DC, back in 2001.

"The Americans and their Zionist whores still have lackeys working in our midst," Kardar declared. "This should not surprise anyone who knows our history."

The security chief continued to stand at attention. Not daring to speak.

Kardar was making a historical reference. Demonstrating his knowledge. In 1953 the United States and United Kingdom toppled Iran's leader through a coup d'état after he'd threatened to national-ize the nation's oil fields. To stabilize their puppet, the United States sent a handful of soldiers to create Iran's secret police force. Among them was US Army major general Herbert Norman Schwarzkopf. He would later be credited with training virtually the entire first generation of SAVAK personnel. (His son later would be the com-mander of all forces during the Gulf War.)

"The warehouse thefts revealed how many traitors still are rooted among us, serving their American and Zionist masters," Kardar con-tinued, his voice rising.

Another reference. This one about the January 2018 burglary of a warehouse where all of Iran's nuclear weapon research had been hid-den from the West. Fifty thousand pages of important documents. A hundred and sixty-three discs, guarded inside thirty-two safes. Every safe broken into. Every record stolen. The thieves—Iranians working for Mossad.

"I do not trust your people," he sneered. "I only trust my Quds Force soldiers. I know they are loyal. Do you know why I am so certain of that?" He did not expect a reply. "Because I execute those who are not."

He stepped forward so that he was now inches from the terrified security chief's face and whispered: "This woman will not be the only one to have her throat slit if these breaches continue. Now get out of my sight."

FIVE

"Have you found them?" Garrett asked.

Thomas Jefferson Kim, the founder and CEO of Intel-Eye-Check, one of the nation's largest private cybersecurity firms, frowned.

"Have some faith, brother. I broke into CERNET. Hacking into forty-six cameras in your neighborhood was easy."

"CERNET?" Garrett replied. "Speak English. And did you say forty-six cameras?"

"China's first internet service, and yes, forty-six cameras. They're everywhere now. Doorbells. Backyards. You need to crawl out from under your rock, man."

"Show them to me."

Garrett stepped behind Kim, who was sitting at his cluttered desk, looking at three computer monitors.

"This is from a rooftop camera outside your condo building," Kim said, staring at the center screen. "Its backup files show the two at-tackers approaching your building."

Garrett examined the grainy images. The woman in a stocking hat and scarf, the man in a baseball cap and turned-up collar.

"I can't see their faces," Garrett complained.

"And you won't. Not on any one of those forty-six cameras."

"How's that possible?"

"They must've done what I did. Identified all forty-six and plot-ted their every step to hide themselves."

Kim pulled up multiple images on the two monitors on either side of the center one. None showed the killers' faces.

"They hacked into your condo's security system too," Kim continued. "Shut it down at just the right moment."

"The cops said it was a computer glitch."

"I don't believe in coincidences."

Kim pulled up a new image on the center screen. "This is from a condo's hallway camera before the murder. Every hallway has one."

Garrett watched Nasya Radi leave his condo. Walk to a door. Try to slip an envelope under it.

"That's my condo," Garrett said.

"I know."

Unable to push the letter under, Radi drew a pistol and walked to the elevator.

"Your neighbors always pack heat when they venture out?" Kim asked.

"Pack heat? What's that from? You need to come out from under your rock."

Kim tapped on his keyboard, and the center screen showed views from cameras located in the lobby. Radi emerged from the elevator. Walked directly to the wall of mailboxes. Removed two envelopes from inside his jacket. The camera became fuzzy, a mass of gray and white dots.

"This is when they shut the cameras down remotely," Kim said. "But there is one camera that recorded the entire murder. A tiny one in an ATM directly across the street from your entrance. You can't see faces."

Kim clicked his wireless mouse, and a video clip appeared. Two fuzzy images of a couple assaulting Radi while he waited in front of the elevator.

"Wait," Garrett said. "Show me that tape of him putting letters into the mailbox."

Kim did.

"There are two letters! He has two letters in his hand," Garrett said. "He sent one to me. What'd he do with the other one?"

"Hard to tell because they cut off the lobby cameras. He didn't have it on him when they found the body. I hacked into the Arlington police department's system and read the detective's internal report. There's no mention of either letter. They don't know about yours."

"And the second one?"

"I'm guessing he either dropped the second one into a mail slot, or the killers found it and took it."

Garrett walked to the windows that made up an entire wall of Kim's spacious but cluttered office. "Since you've been busy hacking everyone else, can you hack into the postal service and find that letter, assuming he mailed it?"

"Actually, it's possible," Kim said. "Every piece of mail in this area gets photographed while it's being processed for delivery. What'd he write to you in that letter?"

Garrett moved from the windows and plopped himself on a chair directly across from him. "I really don't know. Except for his signature, everything in the letter is in Farsi."

"Easy enough. I have software that can translate it."

"Thanks, but I already got someone lined up."

He noticed a framed photograph on Kim's desk, barely visible because of the stacks of papers and reports that not only covered every inch of the desktop but threatened to cascade from it if slightly jarred. The mess reminded Garrett of arcade machines that he'd seen where players deposited quarters, hoping they would strike previously deposited coins in such a way that they would tumble into a hole where they could be claimed. He reached forward and carefully removed the picture.

Kim said, "From Afghanistan."

Garrett snorted. "What? You don't think I recognize the two of us and know where this was taken? I ain't senile."

"That was right before I got hit and you saved my ass."

Garrett put the photo facedown on a jammed manila file folder close to the desk's edge. "You'd've done the same for me."

"I would have tried, but you know me. I was a computer geek sent to win hearts and minds, not a SEAL."

Kim's wife, Rose, interrupted them. "Conference call with Singapore in two minutes," she announced. "Time for Garrett to step outside. I have some questions for him."

Kim chuckled. "You thought the cops were threatening when they interrogated you at gunpoint."

"Let's go," Rose ordered. "This call is important." She led Garrett into Kim's outer office.

"Where you been?" she demanded. "You just disappeared from us."

"Out finding myself."

"You still look lost. In fact, you look like hell. Why haven't you shaved?"

"Beards are in fashion."

"You look like you've just come back from the dead, only you're still in your coffin."

Rose slipped behind her desk. A second executive secretary usually sat adjacent to her, but that worker was at lunch. Garrett fell into a black leather and chrome chair.

"You shouldn't be out looking for yourself," Rose continued. "You should be looking for a woman. Go to an island. Meet a beautiful girl. Get drunk. Relax. Enjoy life."

"Enjoying life and meeting women usually don't mix for me."

Rose rolled her eyes. "Is that supposed to be funny? You have an old-man sense of humor. It's why you're not married. You need to find a woman who is smarter than you, like my husband did. It should be easy for you."

"Got one in mind?" he asked, and immediately regretted it.

"Valerie Mayberry."

"What makes you think she's smarter than me?"

"She's smarter, and she's rich. When was the last time you spoke to her?"

"She was still in rehab. A place in Connecticut."

Rose nodded at a Presidential Medal of Freedom displayed behind glass on the wall directly across from her, hanging above Garrett's head. A photo of Kim posing along with Garrett and President Randle Fitzgerald was next to the award.

Garrett followed her eyes. "What happened to your Picasso?"

"*Le Rêve*—French for 'the dream.' Showing off the medal is better for business."

He nodded.

"It wasn't right," she said, "that Mayberry didn't get her medal at the White House with my husband and you."

"She was still in rehab."

"The president should've waited."

"I'm certain he presented her medal to her later. Probably in a private ceremony."

"It's not the same," Rose said. "I deserved a medal too. I saved you in the hospital when that man came to kill you. Without me, you'd be dead."

"I'll give you mine the next time I stop by."

"You do that. I'll put it next to my husband's. You should thank me."

"Thank you," he said with a smirk.

"Maybe I shouldn't have saved you. When you disappeared in Russia—when they caught you and locked you up there—my husband told me to plan your funeral, remember?"

"You've mentioned that—several times."

"I'd planned the best Korean funeral ever."

"Rose, I'm not Korean."

"Duh. A Korean man would have been married by your age."

"I'm only thirty-six," he said.

"Too old to be single."

"Tell me all the nice things you were planning to say about me at my Korean funeral."

"About you? Nothing. There's no eulogy in Korean funerals. Mourners come and bow at your urn and then turn and speak words of comfort to grieving family members. Your parents are dead. You're an only child, so they would be talking to my husband and me. Comforting us. Three hundred of our friends and customers were invited."

"Would I have even known anyone?"

"Who cares? You'd be dead. Probably only Valerie Mayberry. Assuming she would come."

Kim joined them from his inner office.

"I found the second letter—Radi mailed it moments before he was murdered. It was addressed to the Israeli embassy."

SIX

Because Garrett's Norton Commando motorcycle had been manufactured specifically for motorcycle cops, motorists could still make out the word POLICE in faded letters on the bike's batwing-shaped fairing. Drivers who saw him approaching from behind immediately assumed he was an officer and slowed, making room for him to pass. That reaction never failed to make him grin.

Garrett took the exit ramp from Route 7 onto the Dulles Access Road en route to DC. He glanced to his left and right and was reminded of why Kim had located the IEC headquarters at Tysons Corner. It was home to dozens of beltway bandits, federal contractors headquartered along the sixty-four-mile highway known as the Capital Beltway. Some were IEC rivals, others customers.

Nearly a century earlier this patch of Northern Virginia landscape had been rural. A pair of mom-and-pop stores and a fruit stand owned by William Tyson at the joining of two roads that dated back to the Civil War had been replaced by high-rise condos, towering office buildings, and massive shopping centers. Tysons Corner Mall was billed as the largest covered shopping center ever built when it opened in 1968. Even more exclusive, Tysons Galleria Mall catered to the one-percenters. More than 55,000 shoppers every day came to gawk and buy. Foreigners were known to land at nearby Dulles International Airport, ride in limousines to the malls, and return home that same day with stuffed bags from Cartier, Gucci, Prada, Versace, and Ermenegildo Zegna.

Garrett didn't care about any of this. He was indifferent to much that defined the nation's capital, and yet the idea of returning to his childhood Arkansas never entered his mind. Washington, DC, held a hypnotic grip on him, and on most others who'd abandoned their midwestern roots. Call it Potomac fever. Call it whatever you want. It is difficult to describe until you feel its pull. Events seem more important in the nation's capital. In New York, Wall Street does the talking. Money rules. In Los Angeles it's Hollywood and Silicon Valley. The allure of fame. Striking it rich. Washington, DC, offers a different siren's call. Power draws many to its flame. Anyone could become someone here. With enough hard work, enough ambition—you could be Lincoln rising from a log cabin, Carter coming from a peanut farm. A black boy abandoned by his African father becoming president. Or so everyone believes.

There is another motivation besides fame and the lust for power. Public service. Doing something that matters. Being something more than you can be. Rare but not as rare as many believe. That was what had a hold on Brett Garrett. He had been seduced as a teen by a military jingle: *Be all that you can be.* That coupled with a deeply held belief—some would call it naive—that America was better than any other nation. His country's principles mattered. An example for the world. It needed protection.

Garrett had risked his life in Afghanistan, Russia, and Africa. In doing so, he'd found purpose. Freedom. Democracy. Brotherhood. Devotion. He was a true believer, cut from old-fashioned heartland beliefs. That enabled him to look beyond the frivolous spending, the lust for power, and the chicanery of politics to see—not what was, but what should be.

The government had trained Garrett to kill, and he was good at it. For reasons that he didn't understand, it did not bother him.

Self-rationalization, perhaps. To him, each killing was justified. Valerie Mayberry had viewed it differently, as a character flaw on his part. It was an issue that remained between them.

Garrett stayed in the left lane on the Dulles Access Road heading toward Interstate 66, which would guide him into the District. The chilly autumn air felt good against his cheeks.

A van appeared behind him. White. Ford Transit. Blue lettering on its front: FIX-IT PLUMBING. Maryland plates. Its driver accelerated. He was aiming at Garrett.

Garrett cut into the slower-moving right lane just in time. Instead of shooting by him, the van braked. Slowed. A tinted window lowered. A pistol barrel.

Garrett jerked farther to his right, sending the Norton onto the highway's shoulder while turning its throttle, putting a Toyota Tacoma truck between him and the gunman in the left lane.

Phew! Phew! Phew! The sound of gunfire was muffled inside Garrett's helmet. But he'd heard enough gunshots to identify the sounds. A slug popped through the Tacoma's window, barely missing its driver. That driver panicked. Hit the brakes. Instinctively swerved right, barely missing Garrett, who shot forward to avoid being clipped.

With the Toyota Tacoma now out of his way, the van's driver shifted from the left to the right lane to be closer to Garrett. The Norton's 828 cc engine erupted as the 420-pound bike, with a top speed of 115 mph, rushed forward.

Leaning from the passenger window, the gunman fired again but missed. Garrett was now trapped on the shoulder. A steady line of vehicles kept him from swerving back onto the highway. On his right was a barrier wall.

The van's driver tried to follow Garrett on the shoulder but quickly realized that his vehicle was too wide. He decided to change course, pulling left into that faster-moving lane, but soon found himself frustrated by its gradually slowing traffic.

The van's driver honked at a red Chevy Cruze directly in front of him. It had nowhere to go. Refusing to slow down, the van swung onto the highway's left shoulder but not before clipping the Chevy's rear bumper, hitting it with such force that the compact was shoved into the right lane, where it collided with an older Mercedes-Benz. The lighter-weight Chevy crumpled, and its gas tank ruptured. Within seconds, sparks from the crash had ignited the fuel. Black plumes. Fire engulfing the car. Good Samaritans stopped, abandoning their vehicles to help.

The van and Garrett were now on opposite sides of the highway separated by two lanes, but that didn't keep the van's gunman from continuing to fire across the vehicles between them. Garrett lowered his chest against the Norton's fuel tank.

The chaser and the chased reached the junction where the Dulles Access Road merged onto I-66. *Pop, pop, pop.* It wasn't gunfire. It was the van striking the side mirrors of vehicles on its right. The shoulder had narrowed, and the van was now running a gauntlet between slow-moving cars on the right and a chain link fence on the left. That fence kept motorists from entering the median, home to a Washington Metro subway line.

The gap on both shoulders widened slightly and the van and Garrett sped up. Fifty, sixty, seventy-five miles per hour.

The gunman reached from the passenger side window, grasped the edge of the van's roof rack, and pulled himself up, rolling between two extension ladders tied to the chrome rack. From that higher perch, he could look over the stalled lanes of traffic that separated him from Garrett. He fired.

A slug shattered the edge of the Norton's fairing, causing Garrett to swerve, sending the Norton's back wheel into a side spin. A less experienced rider would have lost control, but Garrett kept his beloved bike upright.

Motorists in their stopped vehicles began telephoning the Fairfax County Police to report that a man clinging to the top of a speeding plumbing truck was shooting across the highway at a motorcycle policeman.

A Fairfax patrol officer a quarter of a mile ahead heard the dispatcher's report. He could see the van racing toward him along the left shoulder. Switching on his blue lights and siren, he pulled his car to the left, blocking the van's path.

Rather than slowing, the van's driver sped up. Ramming speed. Hoping to knock the police cruiser out of the way, just as he'd done to the Chevy Cruze. The police officer jumped clear and drew his weapon. He opened fire.

One of his rounds struck the driver's face. He slumped forward, dead. The van bounced like a pinball, back and forth, off vehicles on one side and the chain link fence on the other as it continued racing toward the squad car, driven by momentum and the dead driver's foot, still pressed on the gas pedal.

The van hit the squad car with tremendous force. A horrific sound. Metal ripping through metal. The van's front wheels climbed the side of the parked police car. It came to rest at a 45-degree angle, its front axle on the police car's flashing roof lights. The collision shot the gunman from the van's roof into the late-afternoon sky as if he were a circus performer being fired from a cannon. He flapped his arms wildly before his body fell, hitting the ground hard atop the subway train tracks in the highway median. His right arm flopped against the third rail. Six hundred and twenty-five volts rocketed through him, shaking his body uncontrollably. An oncoming engineer couldn't stop in time. The train ran over the gunman, dragging his body underneath its cars.

The gunman's gruesome, spectacular death—captured on the camera phones of dozens of onlookers—diverted attention from Garrett, who took the Glebe Road exit off I-66. He drove onto Fairfax Drive, through a yellow traffic light, turned left onto a side street, and entered an underground parking garage.

By the time a police helicopter and emergency vehicles reached the crash site, Garrett was entering Uncle Julio's Mexican. He ordered at the bar and watched a live newscast of the mayhem. The plumber's van had been stolen earlier that day, a breathless local television reporter declared. Neither the driver nor passenger had been identified. Cell phone footage taken by motorists caught the gunman being thrown into the air and hit by the speeding train. Viewers were warned about the gruesomeness of the recordings. Additional cell videos showed a brief clip of a motorcyclist speeding away. The Norton's small license plate couldn't be read.

Garrett ordered a Dos Equis, ate two enchiladas, and lingered at the bar for another hour, nursing a single-malt whiskey, before calling an Uber, leaving his Norton parked underground.

It was late by the time he entered his condo. The adrenaline rush that had flooded into him had dissipated. He felt the low that always came after the high.

Garrett walked into his bedroom, got down on his knees, and reached under his bed. It took only seconds for him to find the pill bottle that he'd duct-taped there.

He tugged it loose from its hiding place and held the brown prescription container in his right palm. Oxy. Was it still potent?

He stared at the bottle. Shook it. Listened to the capsules rattle inside.

Garrett returned to the living room, carrying the pill bottle with him. He flipped on the local news just in time to hear a reporter at the crash scene.

"The driver and passenger have been identified as—"

The men's names didn't matter. It was where the reporter said both were from. Iran.

Why were they trying to murder him? Garrett could think of only one explanation.

Nasya Radi.

SEVEN

The captain of the *Drakon*, Israel's most modern Dolphin 2–class submarine, stared at the sonar screen.

"It's a mistake," he said. "Check again."

"Yes, sir."

Tap, tap.

"It's showing a Soviet Romeo-class diesel-electric submarine. One hundred percent certainty, our computer says."

The captain checked the computer data bank for himself. Discovered that a total of twenty Romeo-class submarines had been built between 1957 and 1961, when they were immediately replaced by nuclear submarines. Egypt was the only remaining Mediterranean country still on record as owning the Russian-manufactured ships. All other boats had been decommissioned, scrapped, or converted into training vessels.

"Speed?" the captain asked.

"Twenty knots submerged."

"The computer says Romeos have a top speed of thirteen."

"Sir, it's doing twenty."

"Then it can't be a Soviet Romeo. What's its course?"

"Aegean Sea."

"Possibly the *Papanikolis*," the captain said. He did a computer comparison.

Papanikolis, Greek navy submarine, length 213 feet, 3 inches, beam 20 feet, 8 inches. Soviet Romeo-class, length 251 feet, 3 inches, beam 22 feet.

"Sir," an aide said, "Haifa reports all of Egypt's Romeos are accounted for and docked in Alexandria. All reportedly inactive and under repair."

"Check again," the captain ordered his sonar operator.

Tap, tap.

"Sir, it's gone."

"What? That's impossible!"

"It's not there any longer."

Later that same day

Julian Levi studied the report for a third time. Big Jules, which is how he was known in intelligence circles, was a thorough man. A necessary trait for the director of the Mossad. A naval report about appearing-and-disappearing submarines would not usually find its way onto his desk. But this was the third sighting by an Israeli vessel of what appeared to be a Cold War relic performing at speeds that exceeded its original capabilities. Every sighting had been in Greek waters near the Turkish straits that led into the Black Sea—home to Russia's Mediterranean fleet and its newest "stealth" submarines.

For much of the Cold War, Soviet submarines had been much noisier than their Western counterparts, making them easier to identify and, if necessary, destroy. In the 1980s the Soviets managed to import technologies from Japan and Norway that they used to build Akula-class attack submarines that equaled US naval vessels in acoustic stealth. The Russians now had a new submarine class—the Borei—that used sound-dampening rubber coating to significantly improve its ability to hide. The West had become alarmed when a Borei-class submarine disappeared in Atlantic waters in 2018, armed with enough nuclear firepower to fire seventy-two nuclear warheads—each ten times more destructive than the bomb dropped on Hiroshima—at targets nearly six thousand miles away.

What puzzled Big Jules was why the Russian navy would undertake retrofitting a Cold War relic with stealth technology when Romeo-class submarines had been obsolete as soon as they were manufactured.

Big Jules swept his right hand across his chin, a habit that he had developed when he had a beard. He had been forced to shave after the doctor spotted melanoma and wanted his skin clear and easy to examine. He turned to Isser Dagan, his second-in-command. "Well, what have we learned?"

Dagan was physically the opposite of his boss—rail-thin, weighing less than a hundred and fifty, a good hundred pounds under Big Jules, whose six-foot-four-inch frame carried the extra weight well.

"This 'ghost submarine'—if it exists at all—does not appear to be part of the Russian fleet based in Sevastopol," said Dagan.

"Covert, an off-the-books operation? What does Ivy Tower say?" Big Jules was referring to the code name of one of the Israelis' best assets, a high-ranking GRU general in the Russian Ministry of Defense in Moscow.

"He confirmed that it's not connected with any military service."

"A covert operation?"

"Anything is possible, but it's unlikely that Ivy Tower would not be aware of it."

Big Jules studied the report about the most recent sighting again, as if it contained some hidden clue to the puzzle. "A submarine has to have somewhere to go," he said. "A port."

Dagan removed a map from a file he had brought with him and offered it.

"What am I supposed to see?" Big Jules asked.

"During the Cold War, the Soviets constructed a top secret submarine base outside Sevastopol," Dagan explained. "It was buried four hundred feet inside Mount Tavros to protect it from a nuclear attack. Seven medium-size submarines were protected by a hundred-and-sixty-five-ton blast door. Of course it became useless with the development of bunker-busting bombs capable of penetrating its natural protection."

"You suspect this is where the Russians are hiding their ghost submarine?"

Dagan peered over his half-glasses. "The last Soviet submarine left the base in 1992, when the Soviet Union disbanded. You will recall that all former Soviet Black Sea ports were surrendered to Ukraine, only to have the Russians reclaim them when they invaded Crimea to prevent the pro-Western Ukraine government from allowing NATO to use them."

"I don't need a history lesson," Big Jules replied impatiently. "What was the fate of this base?"

"According to the locals, it remained abandoned until its neighbors persuaded the Kremlin to open it as a museum glorifying Soviet sea power. They believed it would attract tourists."

"A doomsday Harry Potter World," Big Jules remarked.

"No tourists came, and the base was presumably sealed tight until four months ago, when it was bought by a Turkish salvage company. Trucks began arriving at night. Dozens of construction workers from Azerbaijan."

"What did the Americans say?"

"Nothing. When I asked, neither the CIA nor NATO showed any interest."

"The Turkish salvage company?"

"Paperwork in Moscow shows the government sold the old base to a straw firm in Ankara, along with all of the mountain's contents."

"So it is part of some covert operation."

"I don't believe so. Russian president Kalugin personally signed off on the transaction and is listed in the paperwork. If it were covert, he wouldn't be so blatantly involved."

Big Jules grunted. "If Kalugin signed off on it, it would be to line his own pockets. He's a *mamzer* who surrounds himself with a big crowd, but not a human in sight. He would sell every inch of Russian soil and every Russian child to be ground up for meat if he could pocket a single ruble from it."

"Our people have traced this straw company through sixteen more shells in five countries."

"And who was at the end of this trail?"

"We don't know. It currently ends in China. Whoever bought the base doesn't want to be identified. But we will continue to search."

Again Big Jules swept his massive paw across his chin. "I want you to send someone to this base. Learn if this ghost submarine is operating from it, and if so, who's behind it and this base."

"Chiram Yosef is in the region."

"He's a good man," Big Jules said. "I served with his father in the Paratroopers Brigade."

A knock. Big Jules's personal assistant asked for permission to join them.

"You'll want to read this," he announced. "It's a copy of a letter that our embassy in Washington received by regular postal mail. A letter written by an Iranian physicist who has been murdered."

EIGHT

Saeedi "The Roc" Bashar busied himself while his daughter, Tahira, finished her morning prayers. She still believed. It was her mother's influence. When she rose from her prayer cloth, he looked away from the McMillan TAC-50 sniper rifle that he was working on.

"Did you sleep well last night?" he asked her. "I heard you walking around."

"I had a nightmare," Tahira Bashar quietly answered. She was embarrassed.

"Was it the Iranian?"

"It is of no consequence."

"Then why did it trouble you?" He knew his daughter well enough to know when she was hoping to avoid his questions.

"Are you ready for coffee?" she asked.

"First, tell me about your dream."

"Yes, it was the Iranian."

"Tell me."

"We were at the elevator. You had just stabbed him, but after you turned to leave, he rose up from the floor and grabbed my leg. I screamed, but you didn't hear me. He would not release me. I couldn't get away."

The Roc did not respond. Instead, he turned his attention back to the sniper's rifle. There were no commercial sniper's rifles that could be broken down for easy transport and hidden in a briefcase, despite what was seen in movies. He was customizing the McMillan to fit such a case.

"Time to eat," he said.

Tahira went quietly into the galley kitchen in the two-bedroom Paris flat that she'd rented. She was happy they were in the Montmartre district. She'd read that it had once been home to Pablo Picasso, Georges Braque, and Amedeo Modigliani. She liked to learn the history of the neighborhoods where they lived. It gave her a feeling of connection, even though they rarely stayed anywhere longer than three weeks. Pay rent for a month. Always cash. Leave early without leaving traces. It had been this way ever since the deaths of her brother and mother. Always on the run.

The flat when they first arrived had smelled of stale cigarette smoke, which she'd been unable to wash away. It was a minor annoyance.

Like most other historic Paris buildings, their apartment was in a six-story stone structure constructed between Napoleon's reign and World War I. Her father had insisted it have access to the roof. She had admired its tall ceilings and was sorry both of its fireplaces had been sealed. It was nicer than the apartments they generally rented. From her window, she could look out into the working-class neighborhood that edged the rue Ordener.

She fixed his Arabic coffee, spiced with cardamom and unsweetened, just as he liked it, and returned to the main room, where he was still laboring over the long rifle. Marking where he intended to cut it into pieces. She served his coffee hot. That was how he wanted it. He took a sip. Smiled approvingly. Only after serving him did she return to the kitchen to pour herself a cup.

"Coffee in the morning reminds me of you and Mother," she said, returning to the table. "Mother would wake me to wash for prayers and chores, and later I'd see the two of you outside with coffee and *fattet hummus*."

"Before the Jews murdered her," he said, continuing to work on the rifle.

"It was back when you still prayed," she said.

He made eye contact, and she lowered her eyes. She knew her comment had angered him. There was a time, immediately after the deaths of her mother and brother, when he would have slapped her for being insolent. But time had turned him—or was it her age, and the fighting skills that he had taught her?

She resembled her mother. Slim. Athletic. Strong. The same dark features, high cheekbones, only her hair was cut short, like a boy's. She knew he didn't approve, but he had allowed her some choices. She had just turned twenty. She knew he would have been more comfortable if she had been a boy. But the Jews had killed his son. She didn't need prodding to hate Jews and their American surrogates. All Palestinian children living under the Jews' oppression knew who their oppressors were. Despite her gender, he'd trained her to be a soldier, and she had accepted that fate to please him. Still, preparing to kill someone and actually committing the act were not the same.

As he watched her, the Roc quietly wondered how much longer she would remain a subservient daughter. He'd struggled to balance his control over her with the need to prepare her to survive on her own if he were killed. His biggest fear—if he died—was that she would not continue to fight against their enemies. If that happened, he would have failed as her father. Her nature as a child was kind, and that had been more difficult to redirect. Under other circumstances, he would have encouraged her to study medicine, as he had. But that was before. Now he worried about her unlimited access to the internet, where she could be seduced by corrupt Western teachings. Having her help him kill the Iranian had been the first in a long series of preparatory steps.

He watched her sitting across from him, taking a sip of her coffee. Blowing across the liquid to help cool it. "Tell me again about how you and Mother met," she said.

"What does your dream mean?" he asked. He favored a slightly altered version of the Socratic method, taught to him by his professor father when he was a child living on the West Bank. The caveat. At the end of each of his conversations with her, he would tell her what she should conclude.

"It was just a dream," she said. "It means nothing."

"Then why did it keep you awake? Are you troubled by guilt?"

"The Iranian was a traitor. A lover of Jews," she replied. "He deserved to die."

It was what he'd expected her to say. What she had been taught to say. Yet . . .

"Do you remember when we were a happy family?" he asked.

"Yes, Papa. When you worked at the hospital, saving the lives of our people."

"And what happened? Have you forgotten?"

"How could I ever forget? I was playing with my cousins when the Israeli bombs came."

"You would have been with your brother and mother otherwise. You would have been slaughtered too by the Jews. This you must remember."

"Yes, Papa."

"Remember your brother's face. Remember your mother's face. Remember how they looked when you arrived with your aunt and found me frantically digging through the concrete of what had been our apartment. Our home. It is their faces that you must see in your dreams at night. Not the face of an Iranian traitor who was no different from the Jew who dropped the bombs."

"Yes, Papa."

His voice became emotional. "I held your dead mother in my arms. I see her when I dream. I see your brother. I smooth his hair, and your mother says to me, 'Saeedi, you must be strong. You must stop them. You must avenge my death.' My son, your brother, says to me, 'Papa, why did the Jews kill me? I did nothing to them. Don't let the Jews kill other little boys and girls like me.'"

Tahira's eyes were glistening with tears, and he was glad when he saw them.

"Listen to the pleas of your mother and your brother." He put down his coffee cup. "Now, tell me, my daughter. Will you be ready to do what your mother asked, what your brother demands? Will you do your duty as a soldier? Will you obey the Qur'an and kill the idolaters wherever you find them? Or will you spit on the memories of your mother and your brother?"

NINE

The phone woke Brett Garrett.

"You're in the paper," Thomas Jefferson Kim announced.

Garrett's first thought was the two dead Iranians who'd chased him the day before. He switched on a bedside light. Checked the time: 4:23 a.m. Swung his legs over the edge.

"About yesterday—the car chase?"

"Yesterday? Car chase? No, Africa. The assassination of Andre Gromyko. What'd you do yesterday?"

"Which newspaper?"

"The *Washington Interceptor*. I can't believe you spoke to its reporter."

"I didn't. I never talk to reporters—you know that."

"That's not what the paper says. I'm sending a link."

Garrett moved to his portable computer on a glass-topped coffee table in his living room. All of the condo's furniture was from the previous owner. He rubbed his eyes. Flipped open the laptop. Tapped on the link and found himself looking at his own image—the official White House photo of him posing next to President Fitzgerald and Kim at the White House medal ceremony:

Medal of Freedom Hero: A Cold-Blooded Assassin?

By Investigative Reporter Robert Calhoun

Washington, DC—An investigation by this newspaper has uncovered evidence that Presidential Medal of Freedom awardee Brett Garrett murdered a Russian general in the African Republic of Guinea-Bissau.

Until now, the gruesome killing of General Andre Gromyko, a former adviser to Russian president Vyachesian Kalugin, has remained unsolved.

Garrett skimmed the next several paragraphs, which described Gromyko's stabbing death, stopping when he reached these words:

According to multiple sources, Garrett recently was questioned by the Arlington County Police about another stabbing death, this one involving an Iranian immigrant named Nasya Radi. Garrett and Radi were neighbors in the same Rosslyn condominium complex.

Rogue Operative/Black Ops

A former Navy SEAL, Garrett was court-martialed and imprisoned for disobeying direct orders during a failed CIA "black ops" mission that resulted in the deaths of three American soldiers and three civilians.

"He's unhinged," one source said.

When contacted by the *Washington Interceptor* for comment, Garrett denied he had anything to do with either Gromyko's ghoulish death or the recent unsolved fatal stabbing of his neighbor. "If you print anything, I will hunt you down," he threatened this reporter before slamming down the phone receiver.

Kim was still on the phone. "Did you actually threaten to hunt down a reporter?" he asked. "That's ballsy even for you."

"I never talked to this clown. Never heard of him. And I couldn't have slammed down my phone, because all I have is a cell. It's fake news."

"Fake or not, it's out there now, and people will read it."

"Kim, you can get anyone's number. Find his for me."

"Whoa, brother. Calling him is a bad idea, a very bad idea."

"The man lied about me. Made stuff up."

"Let it slide. No one will remember it tomorrow."

"I will, and so will employers who keep refusing to hire me."

Ten minutes later, Garrett was dialing *Interceptor* reporter Robert Calhoun's personal cell.

"Listen, you bastard," Garrett began, "you never interviewed me, and I never threatened to hunt you down."

"Mr. Garrett," said Calhoun, "let's talk about this like two rational adults. What exactly are you disputing about my story?"

"Are you stupid? I just told you. You never interviewed me. You fabricated a quote. You claimed I threatened you."

Calhoun was quiet for a moment. "Mr. Garrett, I understand why you're bothered, but let me tell you how I see this. You would not have agreed to talk to me, isn't that correct?"

Garrett replied with a profanity.

"I thought so. That's why I did my due diligence. I interviewed people about you, people who knew you, and then I published what you would have said if you had talked to me. You can't deny that what I wrote is accurate, whether or not you said it. And now you are threatening me, aren't you?"

"This is bullshit."

"Mr. Garrett, I sympathize. You'd probably like to kick my ass right now."

Garrett's cell phone shook, indicating he had received a text while talking. He lowered it from his ear. From Kim.

He's tweeting about you! Kim wrote. Get off your phone. He'd forwarded Calhoun's tweet.

On the phone talking to a furious and profane Brett Garrett. Threatening to "kick my ass" for exposing the truth in today's edition about two brutal murders. Read my exposé about a CIA assassin.

When Garrett raised his phone back to his ear, Calhoun was still talking. "These sorts of misunderstandings happen, Mr. Garrett. I feel badly, so let me give you an opportunity to set the record straight. Let's go completely off the record. Just talk like two guys having a beer after work. Now, are you denying that you murdered Andre Gromyko as part of a CIA covert action?"

Another text message from Kim. Hang up! It included a new tweet that Calhoun had just sent.

Garrett refuses to deny he's a CIA hit man. Refuses to deny he committed murder. Confirms my exclusive reporting in today's edition.

"I'm reading your tweets!" Garrett shouted.

"Gromyko's autopsy showed you tortured him with a knife," Calhoun continued without hesitating. "'Slice and dice'—that's the term, isn't it? Was your neighbor a CIA 'slice and dice' operation too? The Iranian scientist?"

Another tweet followed, forwarded by Kim.

B. Garrett refused to deny Gromyko was tortured. Joked—in CIA parlance: "Sliced and diced."

Quickly another:

My newspaper has hired 24-hr protection for me after B. Garrett called my unlisted cell phone. He won't silence me. Free press = Free America. Read my exposé in today's paper.

Garrett ended the call. Kim rang him. "I warned you to leave it alone. He's playing you. Working you. He's got nearly a million followers. He's riding your back to a *Morning Joe* spot. Now listen to me, Garrett. I got a team that specializes in reputation protection, damage control, and rebranding. I'll get them to help you."

"I don't need damage control or rebranding," Garrett said. "I've got nothing to hide."

"Yeah, you do. Readers follow him because they believe him. They aren't going to believe you."

"I don't tweet, and I don't need lawyers to fight my battles."

"That's my point. You got no following. No social network. And the fact that you got a Medal of Freedom makes you a public figure, so you can't sue him for libel. Now he's riled you up. Poked the bear. He's going to keep at it. He can literally write anything he wants, and there's not a damn thing you can do about it." Kim paused. "Besides, you and I both know you'd be insane to ever say a word about Gromyko—even if Calhoun was an honest reporter and wanted to tell the truth."

"Are there any?"

"Garrett, I'm your best friend, and when I read what he'd written, I thought you had talked to him. It sounded like you—getting in his face, threatening to hunt him down. Don't forget, I was in Africa too when you took out Gromyko."

Garrett ended their call.

The prescription bottle of oxy was still where he'd left it the night before. He shook one out. Held it in his open right palm. Stared at it. Every dose could be deadly, but doubly so after you were hooked, stopped, and started again. Receptors. Neurotransmitters. "You'll likely kill yourself if you start taking them again," his doctor had warned.

He slipped the capsule back, closed the bottle.

Within minutes Calvin Russell, the condo's front desk guard, called from the lobby. Two television crews and a *Washington Interceptor* reporter had arrived downstairs.

"I told 'em to get out, so now they're congregated on the sidewalk. I can't do nothing to get rid of them because it's a public sidewalk," Russell explained. "Thought you should know they're waiting to ambush you."

Garrett made a mental note to give Russell more than ten bucks at Christmas as a gift. As he stripped and turned on his shower, he fantasized about confronting Calhoun. Beating him bloody. The hot water felt good. Helped revive him. He needed a plan. He needed to get Nasya Radi's letter translated. To do that, he had to return to the parking garage where he'd left his motorcycle. Before Russell had tipped him off, Garrett had planned on hailing an Uber. Now that would be too noticeable. He'd pose as a jogger. Get a few blocks away and then summon a ride. The reporters wouldn't be expecting that. He slipped on a black pair of long Nike pants, a tight running shirt, and a light jacket. Once he'd added sunglasses and a stocking cap, he was ready. The elevator took him to the condo's underground garage, where he walked up the exit ramp. Opening a door locked from the inside, he peeked out.

A camera crew was positioned at the corner of the condo building, on his right. To his immediate left was a commercial dumpster. No camera crews in that direction.

Garrett heard the grinding sound of the electric motor that lifted the underground garage door. A Cadillac Escalade was coming up the ramp, about to exit the garage. Perfect cover. He waited and then made his move. Using the Cadillac as a shield, he darted to his left, keeping his back to the camera crew, and slipped into the narrow gap between the building's exterior wall and the large green dumpster. By the time the Cadillac had pulled onto the street, Garrett had ducked around the rectangular dumpster's end. Safely out of sight of the camera crew.

"Ahhh!" a man screamed.

Garrett had stepped on a homeless man lying next to the dumpster. He recognized him—the man who usually slept across the street from the condo building, in the bagel shop doorway.

"You okay?" Garrett asked.

The man glared at him.

"I should have been more careful," Garrett apologized.

The man braced his back against the dumpster and pulled a half-eaten bagel from under his dirty blanket. He took a bite, revealing a missing front tooth.

Garrett peeked around the edge of the dumpster. The camera crew was still at the corner, less than twenty yards away.

The homeless man noticed Garrett's running suit. "Who's chasing you?" he asked.

"Just out for a morning run."

"I've seen you before. Look here." The homeless man tossed his bagel aside and lowered the gray blanket wrapped around him, revealing a badly faded T-shirt with an imprint of the US Marines raising the flag on Mount Suribachi during the Battle of Iwo Jima. A participant's shirt from the Marine Corps Marathon.

"You ran it?" Garrett asked, surprised.

"Took me four damn hours, but I did it. Never stopped neither. Hoorah!"

"Oorah," Garrett replied.

"No!" the man snapped. "I was a Navy corpsman. It's 'Hoorah' for us. Lot of people don't know the difference, but I do."

"I'm a Navy vet too. Where'd you serve?" Garrett asked. He wanted to wait for a few more seconds before making a break from his hiding spot.

The man raised the blanket covering his shirt. "You a cop?" he muttered.

"No. Navy SEAL. Tours in Afghanistan. You?"

"Was there before you. Operation Enduring Freedom, December 15, 2001. A year after I ran the marathon. Can't run now."

He lifted the bottom of the blanket, exposing his legs. "IED took my leg. Most people don't know Navy was in-country, but we was."

Garrett hadn't noticed the prosthetic. He guessed the man was in his early fifties, but he could have been younger.

"You ever run it?" the man asked.

"Marine Corps? Three times, but it's getting harder and harder to get in." Garrett dropped to his knees, stuck out his hand. "I'm Brett Garrett."

The man looked at his hand. Turned his head away.

"You a cop? You look like a cop."

"No." Garrett withdrew his hand.

"Jacob," the man said, still looking away. "That's my first name. You don't need to know my last." He mumbled something unintelligible, as if he were speaking to someone besides Garrett.

"I've seen you sleeping outside the bagel shop," Garrett said.

"You spying on me! You a cop!"

"No, no, I just notice you there sometimes when I run."

Jacob stared blankly ahead. "Yeah, I've seen you running in the mornings." More mumbling. "You spare a cigarette?"

"Don't smoke," Garrett said. "Must be tough living on the street."

"It's not illegal!"

"Jacob, I didn't say it was. Just wanted to make conversation."

"That bagel woman gives me coffee before she opens, but I always leave before her regulars arrive. Don't want to scare away business with my unsavory self." A brief laugh turned into a deep cough. Jacob turned his head and spit. Regained his breath. "She's got a brother on the streets, she told me. But he's not like me. He's batshit crazy."

Garrett could smell alcohol emanating from the filthy wool blanket, but Jacob was clean-shaven, his hair neatly combed. Garrett noticed a cut above his right eye.

"Where do you go during the day after you get your bagel?" Garrett asked.

"Why, you a cop?"

"No, just curious."

"Georgetown. A church there. Georgetown Ministries. They let you get your mail. Take a shower. Wash clothes. There's a cupcake shop there. Sit outside. People buy cupcakes for me. They're good. Maple flavored. That's my favorite."

"But not today? You're here."

Jacob grunted. "You a cop? Someone called the cops on me, you know. They came here."

"They weren't after you," Garrett said. "They came because a man in my building was stabbed in the lobby. Not because of you."

"Your friend—the dead man?"

"I didn't really know him."

"You a cop?"

"No."

Garrett rose from his knees and looked around the dumpster's edge. The TV crew was still positioned at the corner. One of them was looking his way. He would see him if he left the dumpster.

"Would you be willing to sell me your blanket?" he asked Jacob.

"I need it. Gets cold out here."

"How about I rent it? You let me wear it, and when I get down to the end of the street and turn up that side street, I'll drop it by the building there on the sidewalk."

Garrett fished a twenty from a zippered pouch around his waist that he was using to carry his cell phone, ID, license, medical card, cash, and the letter from Nasya Radi that needed translating.

"How do I know you won't keep it?" Jacob asked.

"Because we're both vets," Garrett replied. "Hoorah!" He pulled out another twenty and added it to the first.

Jacob snatched both bills. He awkwardly stood on his game leg and removed the blanket. "You leave it at that corner. Don't steal it."

Garrett wrapped the blanket around himself.

"I saw them, you know," Jacob said.

"Who? The police? I told you, they weren't after—"

"No," Jacob said. "The killers. I knowed them. He was wearing a Washington Nationals baseball cap. She had on a stocking hat and scarf. Killing him was a mistake, I'm telling you. They was looking to kill me and got him."

Garrett froze.

"You saw them kill my neighbor in front of the elevator?"

"Yeah, from the bagel shop, but they were looking for me," Jacob repeated. He raised his right index and pointed to the cut above his eye. "She hit me that afternoon, outside Clyde's."

"Clyde's? Clyde's of Georgetown?"

"He shoved me. I took a swing but missed. It was the girl who sucker-punched me. Got me good. Laid me out. Stronger than she looked."

"Wait a minute. You got into a fight with them before they murdered my neighbor?"

"That's right. Mister, I felt really bad when I heard about your friend. Maybe he looked like me. But it was me they were after. All I did was ask them for spare change. I swear it. He took a swing, and then she hit me. No call for any of it. A man's gotta eat."

Before Garrett could ask another question, Jacob lowered his finger to his lips. "Shh! They're listening."

"They weren't after you," Garrett said. "It wasn't your fault."

Jacob took out his cell phone. It was an old flip version. He whispered into it, even though he hadn't dialed a number, and the phone hadn't rung. "Go away. I'm watching for them—the hajis," he said softly.

Garrett recognized the derogatory reference to Muslims, used by combat troops in Afghanistan.

Still clutching his phone, Jacob said, "I killed 'em, but they're coming for me. All them hajis." His facial expression changed. Tears filled his eyes. He snapped shut his phone. "You're a cop. Get out!"

Jacob slumped back down on the pavement. Opened his phone again. Whispered into it.

Garrett tried to think of something he could say. But Jacob had turned his head away.

"I can make some calls," Garrett said. "Get you into a shelter. Maybe a vet program."

"LEAVE ME ALONE!" Jacob hollered.

The television crew. Jacob had screamed loud enough to attract unwanted attention. Garrett stepped from behind the dumpster, pulling the blanket over his head. Covered head to foot, he crossed the street. When he was safely around the corner and out of sight of the reporters, he folded the blanket, placed it on the sidewalk, and used his cell to call Kim.

"I need you to hack into the cameras anywhere near Clyde's in Georgetown. We've been looking in the wrong spot for the killers. Find images of a couple fighting with a homeless man around noon on the same day that Radi was murdered."

"How'd you come up with this?" Kim asked.

"It doesn't matter. If we're lucky, we'll see their faces."

TEN

You don't waltz into FBI headquarters on Pennsylvania Avenue unannounced and skip by the guard's desk unchecked. Especially if you haven't been cleared in advance, have no appointment, and aren't certain the special agent you'd like to see is willing to see you.

Fortunately, Brett Garrett was familiar with Valerie Mayberry's lunch habits. She wasn't a Hard Rock Café grilled burger and french fries fan, even though the restaurant chain operated a café conveniently across from the bureau. Nor would she be tempted by hot dog sidewalk stands or food vending trucks. When Mayberry took her break, Garrett was certain she would walk two blocks east to the Capital Club, an upscale eatery where lunch prices were geared more to corporate expense accounts than to tourists.

Just to be certain, Garrett called the restaurant and said he was supposed to meet Mayberry for lunch but had forgotten the time. The hostess confirmed 1:30 p.m., but added that Mayberry's reservation was for only one guest. Garrett blamed his nonexistent scheduling secretary for the error. Meeting Mayberry in public was important. Less chance of a scene.

He'd deposited his Norton in a nearby parking garage and, seeing that he was early, walked to the US Navy Memorial on Pennsylvania Avenue, where he paused to admire *The Lone Sailor*, a bronze sculpture of a seaman with his duffel bag, standing watch, ready to ship out and fight America's enemies. Garrett felt an odd kinship with the sculpture.

Garrett had always wanted to go into combat. He'd fled his native Arkansas the day after receiving his high school diploma. Ignoring baseball scholarship offers from a half dozen colleges, he'd chosen the US Naval Academy. It had taught him discipline and leadership. Becoming an elite Navy SEAL had shown him how far he could push himself. Combat tours in Afghanistan had hardened him to life's grim realities.

A gaggle of elementary children swooshed by him like water rushing over stones. They giggled and hollered as they ran between the memorial's two fountains, their sneakers pitter-pattering across a map etched in the monument's floor that showed the world's oceans. A granite sea.

Time to go.

He walked through the matching lion statues at the Capital Club's doorway and got two steps inside before being stopped.

"Sir, we have a dress code," the maître d' said.

"Er, okay, you must have a spare jacket?"

The maître d' looked at his running suit.

"I'll take whatever you got in the back," Garrett said.

When the maître d' returned, he was carrying a dirty brown blazer that was clearly too small. Garrett suspected the ill-fitting garb was intended to dissuade him from staying.

"Looks great," he said, taking it. He removed his running jacket, slipped the coat over his T-shirt, and stepped into the bar, anticipating Mayberry's 1:30 p.m. arrival.

She entered smiling, looking healthy—unlike the last time they'd been together. She'd been wheelchair-bound then. She looked good.

Many Washington career women's closets were filled with Hillary Clinton power suits. Some intentionally downplayed their sexuality to be taken seriously. Mayberry was pure haute couture, forbidden as a child by her wealthy parents from owning any off-the-rack items or denim jeans. Today's choice was a black pencil skirt, floral silk blouse, and tailored black jacket. Garrett had no idea who the designer was, only that it would be a pricey label. Old money handed down. Greenwich rich.

He waited until she was being escorted to her table to step up behind her.

"Glad I caught you," he announced. "Sorry I'm a few minutes late."

Slipping around the maître d', he pulled out her chair.

He wasn't certain whether it was his unexpected appearance or his unorthodox dress that surprised her the most. He slid into the seat opposite her before she could ask that he be tossed out. Looking at her, he grinned. She was wearing only the slightest touch of makeup. He'd always believed she favored the actress Keri Russell. Quiet beauty. Inner toughness.

The waiter gave him a hesitant look before citing the chef's lunch-time specials.

"I'll have the salade Niçoise with a light splash of Parmesan vinaigrette," Mayberry said. "And a glass of pinot. Do you have one from Ankida Ridge?" All traces of the slight stutter once inflicted on her by Russian nerve gas had vanished.

"Yes, we stock several Virginia wines."

"I read that its pinot is a surprise hit, especially coming from Virginia."

Garrett hadn't paid attention to the waiter or checked a menu. "I'll just grab a burger," he said, "and rye."

"Which burger, sir?" the waiter asked, not hiding his contempt. "We have the lobster and crab burger, and our short rib, chuck, and brisket burger by Pat LaFrieda, with candied applewood smoked bacon and Vermont cheddar."

"Ah, the second one," Garrett said.

"And do you care what brand of rye?"

"One that's wet."

He glanced at Mayberry and cracked, "Even hamburgers in Washington are named after someone." She didn't laugh.

He took a sip of water. "You look good."

"You look as if you've just come out of a public shelter," she said coldly, "and I don't need you to tell me how I look. I need you to tell me why you are here in such a ridiculous outfit."

"I was out for a morning jog, and I thought it would be nice to come see you."

"How special. It's been nearly two years. Why are you really here?"

"We're friends."

"Friends don't wait that long."

"Valerie, I thought it was best to put some space between us."

"Guinea-Bissau," she replied. "That's what you're referring to, isn't it? When I heard General Gromyko had been assassinated, I knew it was you."

"No comment." But he smiled.

"Twenty-eight surgically placed wounds. None fatal until the last. That's torture."

"Maybe he ran into someone who just wasn't very good with a knife."

The stern look on her face didn't change. "Torture is never justified, even when it comes to someone as despicable as General Gromyko."

"I imagine whoever killed him simply closed his eyes and thought about how he had tried to poison our entire US Senate, and succeeded in poisoning you."

"Don't put his death on me. I wanted justice, not torture."

"If you ask me, what he got was justice."

"I saw the newspaper article about you this morning. I can't believe you actually bragged to a reporter about killing him. And what's this about another stabbing?"

"I never talked to that reporter."

"He sent out tweets."

"I swear it."

"The quotes sounded like you."

A sommelier appeared and poured a small amount of pinot into her glass for her to swirl. She inspected the wine as it ran along the side. She held the glass to her nose. Smelled it before tasting a sample.

"It's fine, but let it breathe," she instructed.

Garrett took a sip of rye without fanfare.

"Gromyko's death explains why you stayed away the first year," she said. "I'll believe your line—that you wanted to protect me. That you were afraid someone might have thought you murdered him for me." She took a sip of her wine. "How do you explain the second year?"

"I've spent it trying to find myself."

"No wonder you were gone a year," she said. "And did you find yourself?"

He shrugged his shoulders.

"Does that mean you're clean now?" she asked.

He took another sip of rye. "No beating around the bush with you, is there? Yeah, that was part of it too. My only nasty habit now is this." He raised his glass.

An awkward pause while their entrées were served. He lifted the burger rather than cutting it with his knife and fork. Took a big bite. Wiped his mouth with a napkin and caught a whiff of the strong perfume worn by a matron who was being seated at the table next to them. She politely nodded at Mayberry and gave him a puzzled stare.

"You happy to be back at work?" Garrett asked Mayberry.

"Small talk? Okay. Happy? At a desk job? They told me it would be temporary, but they're lying. They can't fire a national hero." She looked down at her right hand, which was resting on her lap. He'd noticed that she was only using her left. "I can't qualify anymore."

FBI shooting test for field agents. Sixty rounds, eight shooting spots, both hands gripping a semiauto. Use of support hand required, especially when doing a speedy reload.

"Permanent nerve damage from the gas," she explained. "I can't close the thumb and three fingers on my right—not yet. Thanks for your obvious concern," she added in a sarcastic voice.

"Like I said," he whispered, "Gromyko got what he deserved in Africa."

She put down her fork and reached with her left into her purse. Removed a prescription bottle. Positioned it clumsily against her frozen right fingers, now on the tabletop. Struggled to remove the cap.

"Let me help," Garrett said, starting to reach across the table.

Mayberry jerked back the bottle and glared at him. "I don't need your help! Or your sympathy! I don't need you saving me and settling scores."

After several tries, she managed to pop off the top, turned the bottle sideways, and shook out two capsules. XTAMPZA ER was printed on the label. Generic oxycodone.

She noticed him staring. "Just because you got addicted," she said, "doesn't mean I will. And don't you dare judge me."

He raised his hands. "I'm not!"

She swallowed one of the pills, struggled to put the other back. "Now, what's the actual reason you decided to intrude on my lunch? What do you want, Garrett? Say your piece, and take your burger with you when you go."

Garrett started to claim that he didn't have a motive. That he'd missed her and simply wanted to see her. That was true, but so was her point. He'd come for a reason. He took out his phone and opened an email that Kim had sent him less than a half hour before. Pushed the phone over to her. "These images are from a street security camera outside Clyde's."

Mayberry looked at the photographs. The first showed a couple exiting Clyde's and being confronted by a panhandler. The next showed the homeless beggar being knocked to the sidewalk by the woman. Mayberry studied the woman's face and then the older man with her.

"Oh my God," she whispered. "It can't be him."

"That's his scar. I remember the first time I heard about him, years ago, when he was picking off Israeli soldiers while they were on patrol. Incredible shots by a sniper who always managed to disappear in the West Bank before anyone could catch or kill him."

"That was before he graduated to high-profile political assassinations and got everyone in the West's attention. He also got a hefty price put on his head." Mayberry used her left index finger to expand the image. "I was told the Israelis killed him."

"That's what everyone thought. He's either come back to life or the Israelis screwed up and killed someone else."

"I saw the drone footage. I saw a missile hit the car he was riding in. The Mossad confirmed the Roc was one of its occupants."

"I double-checked. Both bodies in that car were badly burned. The Israelis didn't kill him. That's Saeedi Bashar, aka the Roc. I'd recognize him anywhere."

Mayberry looked at the woman. "Who's she?"

"Kim used IEC's advanced facial-recognition software, and based on bone structure and other similarities, he thinks she's the Roc's daughter."

"You've already dragged Kim into this?" She pushed the phone across the linen tablecloth to Garrett. "If this man is the Roc, and he has a daughter, tell me, why were they in Georgetown?"

"Because they're the ones who murdered my neighbor in the condo lobby. An Iranian named Nasya Radi. I'd like you to read something." He reached into the fanny pack that he was wearing around his waist and removed Radi's folded letter. Placed it on the table, but didn't yet share it with Mayberry. "Right before my neighbor was stabbed to death, he put a letter into my condo mail slot. He'd seen me on television at the White House ceremony."

"The ceremony that was held without me."

"Yes, but that wasn't my fault. Anyway, turns out Radi and I lived on the same floor in our condo building."

"Was he there because of you?"

"That thought has crossed my mind. He bought the condo two months before he was killed, but he never approached me directly. I didn't recognize him when the cops showed me his passport photo."

"I assume that's Radi's letter," she said, finishing her first glass of wine. "What's it say?"

"I need your help with it."

"Of course you do. Otherwise, you'd still be out in the woods trying to find yourself," she sneered.

He ignored the slight. "It's in Farsi."

"You could have gotten Kim to translate it, or simply typed it into a computer. What's the real reason?"

"I need you to get me a meeting with Connor Whittington. I'm persona non grata at the agency, as you might suspect. Have been ever since Gromyko showed up dead, but he'll see you."

The waiter poured her a second glass while they sat silent, looking at each other.

"Why don't you just wear your medal and knock on the agency's door?" Mayberry said mockingly. "Or better yet, show up wearing your ugly brown jacket?"

"Kim did a background investigation," Garrett said evenly. "Radi was a member of the People's Mujahedin Organization of Iran, the MEK. The MEK operates out of Albania now, and is still trying to overthrow Iran's leadership. He was trained in nuclear physics."

"So?"

"So someone killed him." Leaning closer, he whispered, "And two Iranians tried to run me over yesterday because, I guess, they correctly assumed he'd contacted me." He pushed Radi's letter across the table for her to read.

She pinned down the envelope with her right hand and used her left to withdraw the single handwritten page. When she'd finished reading it, she looked up at Garrett.

"What does it say?" he asked.

"Garrett, you're a son of a bitch," she replied. "When do you want to meet with Director Whittington?"

ELEVEN

"They're ruining everything," the small boat's captain grumbled. "Me, my father, my grandfather. All fished this sea. You could see porpoises." He gazed at the sheer cliffs and jagged peaks off the bow. "Now everything is dying. Fish, plants, the whole damn Black Sea."

Chiram Yosef checked his air regulator, only half listening to the captain. Before being recruited by the Mossad, he'd become an experienced diver in the Israeli military.

"It's the damn Americans."

Yosef glanced up. "Americans?"

"Ronald Reagan." The captain, who'd been leaning against the outer wall of the pilot house, stood upright, raised his right arm, and pointed his forefinger as he made a dramatic 360-degree turn. "Russia. Ukraine. Bulgaria. Romania. Turkey. Georgia. All of them use this as a toilet." He flipped the butt of his cigarette into the water. "Who cares?"

"What's that got to do with Reagan?" Yosef asked.

"Him and Gorbachev. When the Soviets were in power, they didn't allow any of this. Gorbachev still has a dacha here. I would piss on any fish he bought from me."

Yosef moved starboard. Spit in his scuba face mask.

"You know," the captain said, "you couldn't have come here in the old days, but you know that. It ain't fish you've come to see."

Yosef hesitated.

The captain nodded toward one of the highest cliffs. "The underwater entrance is there."

"You know?"

"Why else would you dive here? The water's murky. Everything's dead or dying. It's the old submarine base you've come to see."

"I was told it was built to survive a nuclear bomb."

The captain laughed. "If a nuclear bomb was dropped here, would you want to survive?"

Yosef slipped overboard into the bay.

The captain had been right. He could see only a few feet ahead of him. His wrist compass guided him. If he'd known that the captain already understood why he'd hired a boat to bring him here, he would have suggested they sail closer to the underwater entrance. It took him nearly twenty minutes to reach what once was home to the Soviet navy's Fourteenth Submarine Division. He swam for another hundred yards along a man-made canal cut deep inside the mountain before surfacing in what reminded him of a subway tunnel. Removing his face mask, he lit a flare and gagged. The air reeked of the stale garbage floating around him. Graffiti on the curved walls showed that he was not the first to explore. The curious. Looters. Teens looking for a secluded party spot.

Yosef climbed onto the tunnel's walkway. Slipped off his gear. Walked into the mountain's mouth. Seventy-five feet deeper, the flare he was grasping illuminated the top half of a closed blast door, a massive rectangular steel barrier. Grooves gouged into its exterior showed where vandals had tried to break through, but whatever was behind that door remained entombed.

Yosef pulled two miniature cameras from a pouch, checked their batteries, and attached them along the curved wall, pointed at the blast door. Using black spray paint, he attempted to blend them into existing graffiti, camouflaging them.

The cameras had been tested in southern Israel's Timna Valley, where copper ore has been mined since the fifth millennium BC.

They were capable of sending images from underground for as long as their batteries lasted, fifteen days.

He pulled his scuba gear back on and dropped into the channel. When he reached the bay, he found his visibility even more restricted. The sun was setting. At best, he could see perhaps nine inches in front of his face mask. When he extended his arms to pull himself forward, his hands disappeared.

He decided to swim closer to the surface. A spiny dogfish appeared, startling him. Another. He had swum into a school of the world's most common smaller sharks. Despite the fishing captain's grousing, the fish surrounded him. A bump against his thigh. He swam faster, hoping to pass through them.

They seemed to be swimming with him, so he turned upright to allow them to pass by.

A sting. In his right thigh. A jab, followed immediately by another. Needlelike. Not a shark bite. He reached down to swat. A third painful puncture. He decided to swim deeper, but his hands didn't respond. His feet froze.

Yosef felt vomit rising up from his stomach, bursting from his mouth and out into his air regulator as he began to sink.

TWELVE

Taras Aleksandrovich Zharkov wasn't surprised when dignitaries from the Bulgarian Ministry of Economy were waiting at Varna Airport to welcome him. The Russian oligarch had revealed plans to construct a four-hundred-room luxury hotel on the shores of the Black Sea—a convenient excuse for his frequent trips to the region.

During the next three days, Zharkov consulted with architects and paid bribes to governmental officials. Adequate time for his superyacht, the *Red Triumphant*, to reach port. Zharkov ended his visit with a lavish party on the largest private yacht in the world, at six hundred feet. VIPs were ferried aboard via two helicopters. Partygoers danced in the ship's disco hall to the beats of Bulgaria's best-known DJ. Topless models soaked in four hot tubs. An unending supply of Dom Perignon White Gold was poured. Zharkov mingled until dawn.

Twelve hours after his last guest had departed, the *Red Triumphant* sailed across the Black Sea toward the Crimean coast near Sevastopol. It was time for the actual purpose of his trip.

Once anchored, Zharkov ordered the yacht's DeepFlight Dragon personal submarine to be lowered into the water. A man joined him in the two-seater, which the oligarch piloted underwater into Balaklava Bay. Within minutes he'd entered the concrete canal that led to the former Soviet submarine base. Its blast door opened.

The submarine rose to the surface, and Zharkov popped its clear bubble dome. He struggled to pull his chubby frame up the metal ladder onto the concrete dock, and was winded by the time he was standing on it. The mini submarine's second occupant hurried up behind him.

"Welcome," Commander Boris Petrov said, greeting Zharkov and his companion. The Iranian general Firouz Kardar was standing on the dock next to Petrov.

"General," Zharkov said, "wonderful to see you. It seems you made the delivery on schedule."

"I arrived yesterday," Kardar said.

"I put it in the same room where the Soviet nuclear missiles were kept," Petrov said with a sly smile.

Kardar looked past Zharkov at the stranger whom the Russian billionaire had brought with him in his mini submarine.

"Who is this?" Kardar asked.

"An Armenian nuclear scientist," Zharkov said, without bothering to formally introduce him. He turned to the scientist. "Go with Commander Petrov to authenticate my purchase, and do it quickly."

"Follow me," Petrov instructed, leading the man from the dock.

"General," Zharkov said, "there's something beautiful I wish for you to see."

"I need to return to Tehran as soon as possible," said Kardar. "With full payment."

"Yes, yes, but first, come with me." Zharkov led him along a tunnel large enough for a city bus to drive through. It curved sharply, a Cold War precaution to deflect nuclear blast waves, before entering a massive cavern. Zharkov waved his arm toward a Romeo-class Soviet submarine docked there. "This is the *Golden Fish*," he proudly announced.

Kardar eyed the submarine, noting that it bore no identifying numbers or insignias.

"Its name comes from a Russian fairy tale," Zharkov continued. "Do you know it?"

"No." Kardar checked his watch.

"From a Pushkin poem," Zharkov said, still admiring the vessel. "A fisherman catches a golden fish. The fish offers to grant him any wish in return for being set free. The old man asks for nothing, but when he tells his wife, she sends him back again and again to the fish with new and bigger demands. A larger house, more money. Finally, the woman wants to replace the fish as Supreme Ruler of the Sea."

Zharkov looked for a reaction, but Kardar's etched scowl remained unchanged.

"The angry golden fish takes away everything he has awarded the couple. He punishes them for their greed, thrusting them back into poverty. Just as my golden fish will punish the greediest nation on our planet." He smiled smugly.

Zharkov noticed his guest appeared uncomfortable breathing the damp air that smelled of oil and diesel fuels mixed with the odor of specialized rubber paint which workers were applying onto the submarine's skin. Kardar removed a white kerchief from his pocket and pressed it against his mouth.

"You should have seen my golden fish before I rescued it," Zharkov chattered on, ignoring Kardar's uneasiness.

"I assumed it was left by the Soviets when they abandoned this old structure," Kardar said, hoping to hurry the conversation.

"No, no, I found this submarine in a Krasnoye Sormovo salvage yard."

"You sailed it here without being seen?" Kardar asked, surprised.

"No, no. The Atlantic is too carefully watched. I cut it into pieces and transported it on trucks through Russia."

Kardar stared at the nearly two-thousand-ton ship. "How was that possible?"

"With enough money, General, everything is possible." Zharkov laughed. "Would you like to inspect my golden fish?"

"I fight on land. Not in a metal tin made from scrapyard pieces."

"Ah, my friend. You underestimate Commander Petrov's skill

and what he can do with my money. He has taken my golden fish on three test voyages, and each time disappeared from those tracking him. What you see is better than the original ever could have been."

Kardar watched workers scampering to load the submarine with supplies. "You bought an entire mountain base," the Iranian said. "You bought a scrapyard submarine. You are paying Commander Petrov and these men. Now I am delivering an item to you at a cost of a half billion US dollars."

"General," Zharkov said. "Do not spend my money for me, or question my motivation. I do what I do because I will profit handsomely from it. Otherwise, why would I do it? That is enough for you to know. If I take no profit or pleasure from what I do, why do it?"

"You will find a way to profit from this, despite the costs?"

"There is always a way to profit from another man's suffering. Now, enough talk about money. Please join me in Commander Petrov's office, where we can enjoy libations and celebrate."

"As a devout Muslim, I do not drink alcohol. You know this."

"Yes, that is why I will drink your share."

The Russian escorted Kardar down a corridor to a door that opened into a brightly lighted office. Freshly painted light-blue walls. Thick brown carpeting. Built into one wall, a floor-to-ceiling aquarium filled with dozens of exotic fish.

Kardar examined the aquarium while Zharkov went to a liquor cabinet and filled two crystal glasses with bourbon before flopping into a seat covered with alligator hide, one of four matching chairs in the room. "A nice job of interior design," he said as he lifted his first glass. "Impossible to tell that we are inside a mountain."

Kardar tapped on the aquarium's glass face. "As a child, I always wanted a fish tank," he said. "These are tropical fish. Not from around here."

Zharkov shrugged. "I eat fish."

"What will happen to these beautiful specimens when Commander Petrov leaves here?"

"This entire underground base will be burned clean. Scorched by fire, so only the concrete will remain." Zharkov finished his first glass. "I guess you could say the contents of that aquarium will participate in a fish fry." He chuckled at his joke just as the office door swung open.

"You're admiring my aquarium," Commander Petrov said as he entered with the Armenian physicist. "Most don't see my personal favorites."

Petrov strolled next to the general and pointed at the bottom of the huge tank. The general followed Petrov's finger but saw nothing.

"The translucent tubes poking from the floor, like tiny horns," Petrov said. "They are sensors from buried mollusks."

"Commander," Zharkov called out from his chair, where he was sipping his second bourbon, "why don't you get one of your mollusks to show our guests?"

Commander Petrov opened a narrow door that allowed access behind the tank.

Turning to the Armenian, Zharkov asked, "Will the device that General Kardar delivered go boom?"

"Yes, it is a nuclear bomb."

"And its blast ratio? Will it accomplish the requirements that I have given you?"

"Based on the schematics and my examination, it will—theoretically."

"I don't pay for theoretically."

"Then yes, it will produce a nuclear explosion powerful enough to accomplish what you require."

"Detonation?"

"The device has been fitted with a remote-controlled detonator that uses a numerical code."

"Excellent." Zharkov rose from his seat. "Time for your payments." Still holding his drink, he walked toward a computer on a nearby desk, but paused when Commander Petrov reappeared, clutching a six-inch-long shell that he'd plucked from the aquarium. The shell was pearl-white, speckled with brown spots and lines, like a monochrome stained glass window.

"*Conus textile*," Petrov announced.

"I believe," Zharkov said, "my Armenian guest would like a closer look."

"Feel how smooth its shell is," Petrov said, approaching him.

Commander Petrov raised the large mollusk to eye level and began to violently shake it as the scientist bent back his head.

Petrov jammed the snail against the Armenian's neck. A harpoon made from modified tooth matter shot from the mollusk's mouth, piercing the scientist's skin near his jugular.

"Ahhhh!" the Armenian screamed. "What are you doing!"

"When you agitate *Conus textile*, it becomes aggressive," Petrov replied, pulling back the snail. "In a muscle spasm it fires its only weapon, thinking it's under attack, making it one of the most deadly killers in the oceans."

The dumbfounded Armenian grabbed his puncture wound, staring in disbelief at Petrov, who again thrust the mollusk toward him. Its harpoon struck the scientist's hand, which he was holding over the wound on his neck.

Petrov took a step backward with the mollusk.

"We think of snails," Zharkov said, "as being slow, only good when bathed in butter and sautéed. I certainly didn't see them as predators until Commander Petrov enlightened me."

Petrov said, "Like all *Conus textile*, this one's venom is toxic—a nerve agent."

The Armenian scientist tried to speak, but no words came out. His legs went out from under him. When his body hit the floor, it began to shake.

Still clasping the mollusk, Petrov walked to his office door and hollered to three workers. They carried the still alive but paralyzed Armenian away.

"Killed by a snail," Zharkov cheered, clearly amused. He shot Kardar a stern look. "When Commander Petrov told me he had used one of his deadly snails to kill a Mossad agent spying on this base, I was skeptical, so I asked for today's demonstration."

"A Mossad agent came here?" Kardar asked.

"I suspect he came because someone in Iran told them about my base and submarine."

The general's eyes darted between Zharkov and Petrov, who was still holding the deadly snail. Kardar was unarmed, having been asked to surrender his pistol when he'd arrived at the underground base.

Zharkov noticed. "Commander Petrov, it's time to put your killer snail back into its tank. You are making our guest nervous."

Petrov disappeared while Zharkov continued his conversation with the Iranian general. "The *Golden Fish* is not fully ready, and now I have the Jews to deal with. How do you intend to keep them from disrupting my plans?"

"You can't blame me for the actions of the Jews," Kardar snapped.

"But I do." Zharkov emptied his second glass. "You see, my friend, the bomb you have delivered and this base and submarine will be of no use if the Israelis or the West arrive before Commander Petrov is ready. If you wish for full payment to Tehran, I'd like to hear your suggestions."

"You cannot hold back the half billion because of the Jews," Kardar declared. "I have kept my end of our arrangement."

"I can, and I will. But rather than discuss my options, let's discuss yours."

For a moment, neither spoke. Finally Kardar said, "I know of a way to distract the Jews. But it will cost you."

"I'm listening."

"I will hire a man to kill the head Jew—Julian Levi."

Zharkov turned his attention to Petrov, who had just rejoined them. "Commander," the Russian billionaire said, "our Iranian friend has just suggested I hire someone to kill the head Jew in the Mossad as a distraction. What do you think?"

"Killing Big Jules will not be easy," Petrov said, in a cautionary voice. "He rarely leaves Israel and is always heavily protected."

Zharkov turned his eyes back on Kardar, waiting for the Iranian to respond.

"It doesn't matter if he is killed," the general said, "it only matters that an attempt is made. That should buy sufficient time to finish here without interruption from the Mossad."

"That could work," Petrov said. "If you can find someone willing to commit suicide by attempting this murder in Tel Aviv."

"The Jews are not the only ones with spies," said Kardar. "The head Jew will be traveling to Italy in secret in four days to attend a family wedding."

"That would make it easier. Is four days enough time to arrange it?"

Kardar glanced at Zharkov. "With enough of your money, everything is possible—am I correct?"

"This assassin cannot know about me. Or about Commander Petrov, or the *Golden Fish*. If he is captured—"

"He will not tell anyone," Kardar said, cutting him short. "Whether he manages to kill the head Jew or fails, I will have him killed afterward. It is the best way to ensure secrecy. I will make all the arrangements."

"How much will this assassin cost me?"

"Not as much as you might believe."

"And why is that?"

"Because he is a Palestinian who hates the Jews more than any man I know."

THIRTEEN

Big Jules Levi had just arrived at a private dinner party in a Tel Aviv penthouse hosted by one of Israel's many billionaires when he received word that Mossad operative Chiram Yosef was dead. It was ten o'clock. The head of the Mossad spoke briefly to his wealthy host and his wife before excusing himself and returning to his office, where his deputy director, Isser Dagan, was waiting despite the late hour.

"What happened to Yosef?" Big Jules asked as he removed his dinner jacket and loosened the black bow tie from around his thick neck.

"A fisherman found his body floating in Balaklava Bay. We had not heard from him for forty-eight hours, so we already were on alert."

"The cause of his death?"

"When the locals discovered he was an Israeli, the Russian government took control. Their representative has told us it was a freak accident. Yosef was poisoned while scuba diving."

"An accidental poisoning? While swimming? Do the Russians expect us to believe such a story? What poison was used—ricin? Novichok?"

"The toxicology report identifies the poison as cone snail venom."

"Venom from a snail? A snail was used to murder him?"

"The Russians are theorizing that Yosef either stepped on or brushed against a mollusk while swimming. Apparently this type of accident has happened before in the Black Sea. Although the number of mollusk poisonings is rare, a boy died last year roughly in the same location. The Russians insist it was accidental, and they are expressing outrage about his presence so close to the Russian naval base at Sevastopol. They have filed a formal protest against us, accusing Yosef of being a spy."

"Have you been able to communicate with Ivy Tower in Moscow?"

"Fortunately, he sent us word without prompting when he learned about Yosef's death. He said it was not the Russians who murdered Yosef, if in fact he was murdered. Our people also confirmed that mollusks can produce venom that has over eight hundred different toxic elements."

"Any evidence of a hypodermic injection?"

"The photos that we received show bite marks on his leg. No other bruises or signs of force being used against him."

"This was not some freak accident caused by a snail," Big Jules declared. "Nasya Radi was murdered after mailing us a letter, and now Yosef turns up dead when we send him to investigate this closed base. Where is Gelleh Peretz?"

"I told her to report here as soon as I learned about Yosef's death," Dagan replied. "She is waiting in her office. I will call her."

Five minutes later, a slender woman with long brown hair fixed in a bun joined them, wearing spiked black heels, snug denim jeans, and a white long-sleeve bodysuit shirt that favored her curves.

"I apologize, Mr. Director, for my casual dress," she said. "I came directly from a club where I was with friends when the deputy director called. I'm sorry about Yosef. He was a good soldier, and a better friend."

"To all of us," Dagan interjected.

"We suspect he was murdered," Big Jules said. "I need you to go to the Crimean Peninsula to investigate. Deputy Director Dagan can fill you in."

"Sir," Peretz said, "I'm scheduled to leave tomorrow for Lake Como. Your niece's wedding."

"I'd forgotten."

"We have several others who can oversee your security detail there," Dagan volunteered, "especially since most of the preliminary work already has been done."

Before Peretz could answer, Big Jules said, "No. I need you with me at the wedding. My sister is familiar with you."

"She knows me as Esther," Peretz said, using her code name.

"I am not going to risk upsetting my sister and my niece on her wedding day by having a stranger, someone unfamiliar with their home, take charge. She considers 'Esther' more as a guest than as someone in charge of my personal security."

"Who, then, shall we send to Balaklava Bay?" Dagan asked.

"Let's begin by going through the official channels that are expected to obtain the body and medical reports," Big Jules replied. "This will avoid suspicion." He nodded at "Esther," and said, "After my niece's wedding, you will leave for the Crimea to complete Yosef's original mission. Deputy Director Dagan will brief you, and you will report directly to him."

"What about the Americans?" Dagan asked.

"The new CIA director is a timid man, a deal maker," Big Jules said. "We will wait until we know more before sharing any information."

FOURTEEN

"Dedicato par aevum."

"Latin? From you?" Valerie Mayberry said.

"It means 'Dedicated to service.'"

"I know what it means. I'm the one who speaks five languages."

"Kudos to your Ivy League upbringing," Garrett replied sarcastically. He nodded toward a granite marker to their left. They had stopped at a traffic light on Route 123 at the CIA's main entrance in Langley. "Those words are inscribed there."

It was dusk, and the lights positioned around the monument came on as he spoke, as if on cue, spotlighting the marker.

"I remember," she said.

"Two dead. Three wounded. All shot by a Pakistani who'd bought a fake passport in Karachi. Came here and got a delivery job. That's how he knew when people would be coming to work in the morning and get stuck at this signal."

"Walked from car to car, shooting," she said, "but only males, because it was against his religion to kill women."

"You know what really pisses me off, Mayberry? There's another memorial about these murders, only it's in Pakistan and named after him. An entire mosque dedicated to a 'martyr.' It—"

The sound of Valerie's Jaguar F-Type's exhaust pipes drowned out his sentence as the signal turned green and she spun into the agency's driveway, stopping a few hundred feet in at an intercom where she identified both of them. Once cleared, she pulled forward to another barricade, then through a maze of concrete barriers meant to prevent anyone from crashing through with explosives. Up a slight rise, she found a visitor spot to park. They entered the old building, where they submitted to yet another credential check before being escorted to a boardroom next to Director Connor Whittington's upstairs office.

"Have you met him?" Garrett asked as they settled on either side of a highly polished conference table.

"Only once. He came to the bureau. He was polite but formal, somewhat cold toward me. I wasn't surprised. I mean, he was appointed to clean up the mess that his predecessor left behind—a mess that involved us. Did you notice the photos in the hallway of former agency directors?"

"Yeah, one picture was missing."

"Serves him right. Director Harris was a bastard, liar, and manipulator."

"And you think Whittington isn't a bastard, liar, or manipulator?"

"Dial back the cynicism, Garrett. We're here to ask for his help."

An aide appeared. "The director is running a few minutes late, but he will be with you shortly. Can I offer you coffee, tea?"

"That would be nice," Mayberry replied.

"Not unless you have scotch," Garrett said.

They sat quietly for several moments, Mayberry sipping coffee, Garrett tapping his foot on the plush carpet, until Director Whittington appeared. Garrett had only seen him on the news—a tall, broad-shouldered, sixtyish former Texas senator. An outdoorsman who prided himself on making deals.

"I'll give you ten minutes," Whittington said. "I'm due at the White House." No pleasantries. No apology for making them wait.

Whittington sat at the head of the conference table, with Garrett to his left and Mayberry on his right. Before either of them could speak, he looked at Mayberry. "Your director asked me to take this meeting because he said you have information I should hear.

Otherwise I would not have met with either of you." He looked Garrett up and down, adding, "Especially you, especially after reading that article where you bragged about killing General Gromyko and acknowledged being a CIA hit man."

Garrett opened his mouth to respond, but Mayberry cut in. "Thank you, sir. We'll be brief, and it is important. We brought you photos." She nodded to Garrett, who opened a manila envelope and spilled several on the table.

"What am I looking at?" Whittington asked.

"Pictures of Saeedi 'The Roc' Bashar and, we believe, his daughter, in Georgetown outside Clyde's," Garrett replied.

"Impossible," Whittington sniffed, lifting a pair of reading glasses from a lariat around his neck. He glanced at the pictures and then put them aside.

"I'll admit the photos bear a slight resemblance," he said, "but the Roc was killed during a drone attack. A kill confirmed by the Mossad."

"The two bodies in that car were burned beyond recognition," Garrett said.

Whittington begrudgingly took a second look at the photos. "I was on the Senate intelligence committee when the Mossad took him out. We knew about his death because it was one of our drones that got him. He was a cold-blooded Palestinian killer. An assassin, although I forget why they called him the Roc."

"A nom de plume from Persian mythology," Mayberry volunteered. "The Roc is a powerful bird of prey that swooped down and terrorized its targets."

"I don't care what the Mossad told you," Garrett said. "That's him, and he's back."

"Based on what? Your keen eye?" Whittington scoffed. "Haven't you ever heard that everyone in the world has a doppelgänger?"

"Actually, sir," Mayberry said softly, "facial recognition software verified it."

"Whose facial recognition software? The bureau's?"

"No, sir," she said. "Thomas Jefferson Kim, at IEC. His firm has a number of government contracts—some with the agency, as I'm sure you are aware. So you know he's reliable."

"Having a government contract only means you have a government contract," Whittington snipped. "You'll have to do better than this if you want me to second-guess the Mossad. Now, if this is all you had to show me—"

"We have more than this," Garrett said, producing another photo. "The Saudis arrested Bashar in Riyadh after one of the royal family members was fatally shot by a sniper. This was back when he was first crafting his image as the Roc. We believe it was his first important kill."

Whittington looked at the photo of a young man with a badly bruised and bloody face. "The Saudis slashed his face with a knife while he was being interrogated at al-Ha'ir Prison," Garrett continued. "You can see a cut that runs from his right ear to his neck. If you compare this photo of him, taken by the Saudis, to the one of the man exiting Clyde's in Georgetown, you'll see it's the exact same scar. It's him. The only prisoner who ever escaped alive from al-Ha'ir."

Director Whittington pushed the photo back toward Garrett and checked his watch. "Like I said, I'm due at the White House, and nothing you have shown me has changed my mind. The Roc is dead."

"Director," Mayberry said, "you might recall that about a year ago an assassin mortally wounded Jabir Abboud, a presidential candidate in Egypt, who was friendly with the West. This was long after the Mossad had reported that the Roc had died in that burning car."

"A single shot killed Abboud, and it was fired from three thousand, six hundred and thirty meters," Garrett said. "The longest recent recorded sniper kill was about a football field shorter than that shot. Which would make it a record if we gave records to assassins."

"What's your point?" Whittington asked.

"Only the Roc could have pulled off a shot like that."

"He's rumored to be one of the finest marksmen in the world," Mayberry said.

"Rumors are not facts."

"Here's a fact," Garrett said, raising his voice. "After Jabir Abboud was murdered, Egyptian authorities found photos of a man—with a scar that matches the Roc's—in its customs computer data bank. He'd used a false passport to enter Egypt. Saeedi Bashar, the Roc—whatever the hell you want to call him—is alive and killing again."

"Most recently," Mayberry said, "Garrett's neighbor, an Iranian nuclear physicist, in Arlington."

"Okay, let's assume he is alive, and the Mossad misidentified the two men killed by our drone. Why would the Roc show up here to kill this Iranian?" Whittington asked.

Garrett removed the letter that Nasya Radi had put into his mailbox, along with a translation that Mayberry had prepared.

"My neighbor fled Tehran after the shah was tossed out," Garrett said. "He was a member of the MEK. He put this letter in my mailbox moments before he was stabbed to death by the Roc."

Whittington raised his reading glasses, skimmed the translation, and looked up from the letter. "This self-exiled MEK devotee writes you a letter that says Iran is planning to launch a submarine attack against one of our major cities and explode a nuclear bomb that it has made. Is that the gist of this letter?"

"Yes, sir," Mayberry said.

"Did either of you stop to consider this is not the first time the People's Mujahedin has accused Iran of building a nuclear bomb? In fact, I've lost count of how many times the MEK has claimed that Iran's manufactured a nuclear weapon, and not one claim has been verified. Zero. Nada. The MEK likes to get right-wing political groups in our country excited so they will send it money."

"With all due respect, Director," Mayberry said, "the MEK hasn't always been wrong. Its members have told the West the location of several secret nuclear facilities in Iran."

"And let me remind you, Agent Mayberry," Director Whittington replied, "that the MEK has been called a terrorist organization by several of our allies. In addition, international inspectors have repeatedly verified that Iran does not have the resources to build a nuclear bomb, and there is no rational reason for them to build one, because they have been made aware of the consequences. Sure, they may spin up their centrifuges and rattle their sabers, but there is no verifiable evidence that Iran can actually build a bomb. And if you think I'm going to go run to the president and tell him that a terrorist has risen from the dead and Iran is about to attack us with a nuclear bomb on a submarine, you are badly mistaken."

"But sir—," Mayberry started.

"Hold on, Agent Mayberry," Whittington said. "Did you show the photos and letter to the FBI director?"

"Not the letter, but the photos, yes. That's why he agreed to call you about meeting us."

"Agent Mayberry, if the FBI director believed any of this, why would he have sent you two over to me? The bureau could pursue this on its own." Without giving her a moment to reply, Whittington said, "I'll tell you why, Agent Mayberry. Because he doesn't want the bureau getting involved, but at the same time he's covering his ass. Do I need to remind you of the entire WMD debacle that led to the war in Iraq? It was the result of bogus claims by so-called intelligence sources. Your director is passing the buck, and I deeply resent it."

"Sir," Mayberry said, "in his letter, Radi states that the nuclear bomb is being built inside an underground fuel enrichment plant at Natanz. He lists details about what materials the Iranians are using to construct it."

"Information anyone who searches long enough on the internet can obtain. We've known for a long time about the Natanz fuel enrichment plant, and you just told me that Radi was a nuclear physicist.

Just because someone can describe how to make a nuclear bomb doesn't mean they got one made."

"What about his warning?" Garrett asked. "Using a submarine to attack us."

"That should have been your first tip that his letter is nonsense," Whittington sneered. "Do you know how many submarines Iran has?" He raised his right hand. Separated his fingers. "Five. Count 'em. Five submarines capable of launching a nuclear bomb. The rest are all miniature submarines used for harbor attacks, not transatlantic voyages. The idea of a submarine attack by Iran is completely ludicrous. Just more MEK saber-rattling. I can't believe either of you would fall for it."

"Maybe they have a submarine we don't know about," Garrett said.

Whittington glared at him. "Along with NATO, we keep constant track of Iran's navy. We can destroy every vessel in their fleet in a matter of minutes. Even if a submarine made it to the Mediterranean, we would intercept and destroy it long before it crossed the ocean and reached our shores."

He checked his watch. "Leave me copies of the photos and letter, and I'll make certain they get the attention they deserve," he said dismissively.

"Which means you and your people will do diddly-squat," Garrett said.

"Which means I'm not going to get excited just because you're seeing ghosts and believing a load of crap written in some letter."

"A letter whose writer was murdered," Garrett shot back. "Maybe we are talking to the wrong intelligence service. Radi sent a letter to the Israeli embassy. I'm guessing it was identical to mine."

"You want to take your dog and pony show over to the Mossad? Be my guest. They'll laugh you off their embassy grounds."

"Director Whittington," Mayberry said in a calm voice, but Whittington was still focused on Garrett.

"Tell me, Mr. Garrett," he said, "when you came in to see me, what exactly did you expect me to do?"

"I'd like you to authorize me to hunt down the Roc and find out who paid him to murder my neighbor. I'd like you to authorize me to investigate Radi's letter."

A look of sheer disbelief swept across Whittington's face. "You really are delusional, aren't you?" he said. "Did you seriously believe that after listening to you, I was going to green-light you to go vigilante? Send you off on a one-man mission to stop an Iranian nuclear attack?"

"Last time the agency sent us after terrorists, Mayberry and I stopped an attack on the United States Senate," Garrett replied.

Whittington shook his head and looked at Mayberry. "Was this your plan too? Go chasing after the Roc and investigating this dead man's charges?"

Mayberry flashed an irritated glance at Garrett. "I didn't realize that's what Mr. Garrett was expecting. I thought we were simply alerting you to the Roc's reappearance and Mr. Radi's warning, so you could take appropriate action."

"Well, well," Whittington replied with a smug look, "I guess Mr. Garrett was not as honest with you as he should have been." He stood. "I shouldn't have to remind you that the director before me is currently in a federal prison for lying to Congress and conducting a black ops mission without our president's knowledge." Staring at Garrett, he added, "Nor should I have to explain that one reason I gave up my Senate seat and became director was to put an end to this agency's cowboy, off-the-books antics—by you and others, but especially by you."

Whittington's assistant, who had joined them, said, "There's an escort outside the conference room, waiting to take you to the lobby."

Ten minutes later, Mayberry slammed the car door of her parked Jaguar shut and pushed its ignition.

"I should never have let you talk me into this," she said bitterly. She fumbled with her purse, extracted her pill bottle, and swallowed a pill.

"How bad is it?" he asked. "The pain?"

"A hell of a lot more, now thanks to you. I'll be lucky to still have a job after Whittington complains to the bureau."

She drove through the barriers toward the exit without speaking.

When they reached the highway, Garrett's cell phone rang. Mayberry could only listen to Garrett's end of the conversation. "Okay. Yes. Great work. Who else knows? Let's keep it that way. I knew I could count on you.

"That was Kim," Garrett explained when he ended the call. "The Roc and his daughter just cleared passport control at Leonardo da Vinci–Fiumicino Airport. They're traveling under assumed names. The Italians don't have a clue who they are."

"What? How'd Kim find them?"

"He put the Roc's face into his worldwide system. One of his companies has the airport security contract in Rome. Facial recognition monitoring."

"I don't think Whittington or the bureau will go after him," Mayberry said. "I guess we should tell the Arlington police, since they are investigating your neighbor's murder."

"You're kidding, right? Don't you see it? This is our chance to get the Roc."

"Our chance? Catching him is not our responsibility. Didn't Director Whittington make that clear enough for you?"

"C'mon, Valerie. Do you really believe a bunch of local cops are capable of finding and arresting the Roc—in Rome? Or investigating, if Iran has developed a nuclear bomb and wants to keep it secret?"

"The best we can do, then, is have Kim talk to my bosses at the bureau. Assuming the director will listen."

"No, you can't do that. You can't drag Kim into this. I'm certain there's some regulation or privacy law or something about him using his company to watch the goings and comings at an Italian airport without first getting all the proper clearances and paperwork filled out."

Mayberry turned her Jaguar onto a side street in McLean and parked next to the curb but kept the engine running. "What do you want from me?" she demanded. She raised her crippled right hand and shook it at his face. "You should have never contacted me."

"You can't close your fingers," he replied. "So what?" He stared at her face, illuminated by a streetlight. "Hey, I don't speak Latin. Everyone has their faults."

"Oh my God, is that the best comparison you got? My crippled hand, and you only speak English."

"Well, a few words of Latin," he said, smiling. "That hand doesn't define you, or at least the old you. You're still an FBI agent."

"Is this all a joke to you?" she said. "My pain isn't a joke. And neither is my career."

"Valerie," he said softly, "I can't do this without you. You carry a badge. That opens doors. You're rich. You can afford to fly us to Rome and wherever the Roc runs."

"So that's why you need me. My money. You've gone unicorn on me, Garrett," she whispered. "Living in a fantasy world."

"If the bureau authorized you to go after the Roc, you'd go. If Whittington sent me after the Roc, I'd go. So what's the problem if we go on our own?"

"The bureau didn't, and won't. The agency didn't, and won't. That's the problem."

"We can do this without them." His voice softened. "Listen, we both could use this right now. Ask yourself: Do you really want to file reports in the bureau's basement for the rest of your life?"

"I'm not in the basement."

"You once said you became an FBI agent because you wanted to stop wolves from eating rabbits. The Roc is an alpha wolf. He's going to continue eating until someone takes him out. And if that nuclear bomb threat is real, millions of rabbits could die."

Mayberry swallowed a deep breath. Slowly released it. She was staring straight ahead through the windshield. It started to rain. The

Jag's automatic sensors turned on the car's wipers. She could hear the engine throbbing. She glanced to her left as a car drove past them. The rain started coming down harder.

"I'll drop you at Tysons," she said. "It's on my way home, and you can take the Metro back to your place."

Neither spoke until they reached the subway station's kiss-and-ride drop-off.

"I'm going to Rome," he declared. "With or without you."

"Get out, Garrett."

She watched him walk toward the station in the rain. Honked. Pulled up next to him and lowered her passenger window.

"I'll order us tickets," she said. "Get your passport and meet me at Dulles."

"It would be quicker if you drove me home, rather than me taking the Metro."

She left him standing in the rain.

PART II

We should forgive our enemies,
but not before they are hanged.

—*Heinrich Heine*

FIFTEEN

"It is only you?" Signora Alessandra Rossi asked as she unlocked the door to her one-bedroom apartment on the fifth floor of the centuries-old building.

"Yes," Tahira Bashar replied, looking inside. "I am traveling alone."

An antique double bed, a mahogany armoire, two wooden chairs, and a hot plate resting on a small table. Bright white walls. It was more a bedroom than an apartment.

"The shared toilet is down the hall," Signora Rossi explained. "Yes, my room is small, but the view alone is worth what I charge."

Tahira walked to an oval window facing Lake Como. Because the apartment had been constructed in what used to be an attic, the window was waist high. She bent slightly and gazed through it across Lake Como to the opposite shoreline.

"I will need it for a week," Tahira said.

The stooped older woman frowned, shook her head. "Two weeks would be better. You can't see everything in Bellagio in a single week, and two weeks makes life much easier for me. Did I say that you can walk to the basilica of San Giacomo from here?"

"Two weeks, then," Tahira replied.

"You mentioned on the telephone you would be paying in euros," Signora Rossi said. "It's best to not always go through AirBnB. My son handles AirBnB for me but I prefer meeting in person and cash payments. I am curious—how did you find my phone number?"

"The internet."

"I have no use for it," Signora Rossi answered, waving her bony fingers. "Filled with filth. Pornography."

"And phone numbers," Tahira cheerfully responded. She hadn't seen her own grandparents in years. After the deaths of her mother and brother, her father had severed all contact with relatives. But she imagined her grandmother was much like her Italian hostess. "Where will you be staying while I am here?" she asked the old woman.

"With my son at his apartment in Varenna. It's not far. He never married, so there is room. It's such a disappointment not having grandchildren. You young people care too much about work and making money and not enough about living life. Family. It is all that matters. Tell me, why is a young woman like you traveling alone? You are so pretty."

"Like you said, we work too hard. I need a vacation, and I always wanted to see Lake Como."

"George Clooney, that is why all you young girls come here. You hope to see the American movie star. What chance does my son have, when all the women come to see a famous actor? It's a mother's burden."

"I'm not here to see an American movie star."

"I attend mass each morning. I pray that my son will meet a nice Catholic girl. Give me grandchildren. Tell me, are you a believer in our Lord Jesus Christ?"

Tahira noticed a crucifix hanging above the headboard. It was the only decoration in the flat.

Signora Rossi didn't wait for a reply. "Our basilica is in Piazza della Chiesa, on the hillside. I can tell you the best times to attend mass before it becomes crowded with tourists. You are Catholic, aren't you?"

"I'm not a religious person." That was easier, she decided, than to admit she was a Muslim and possibly prompt suspicion.

The woman crossed herself. "Everyone is a child of God. I'll pray for you. It is never too late. Too many young people are lost. Greed, pornography." She opened the armoire and removed a worn black satchel that she placed on the floor. "Let me open the window for fresh air, sometimes it sticks," she said, shuffling toward it.

The room smelled musty.

The window pushed outward and was hinged at its top. The signora propped it open with a metal rod, much like the one that holds the hood of a car open.

"Much better," Signora Rossi said, taking in a deep breath. "I will need two weeks' rent now, and a deposit of a hundred euros that I will return after I check my room for damages." She dropped her voice into a whisper. "Some who stay here are filthy pigs. And you will not be bringing men to my bed, will you?"

"No!"

"Good, I thought you were a good girl. I can tell, you know, by looking."

Tahira counted out the euros, which Signora Rossi folded and inserted into an embroidered pouch. She deposited it into the pocket of the white apron that she wore over her black ankle-length dress and flesh-colored leggings.

"You did not say where you are from," Signora Rossi said. "Let me guess. Your skin is light brown."

Tahira interrupted, wanting to control the answer. "I'm from Portugal, a good Catholic country."

Rossi nodded approvingly. "And yet you are not Catholic. I will pray for you." She walked to where she kept her worn Bible and placed it in her satchel. "I always keep this with me, but I can leave it for you, if you wish."

"Thank you," Tahira said, "but you should keep it with you."

The woman started for the door.

"May I help you with your bag?" Tahira asked. "I'm going downstairs to fetch my luggage from my car."

"Did you park nearby, in a public spot? There's no parking in front of the building."

"Yes, it is not far." Tahira picked up the woman's satchel.

"Such a thoughtful young woman. You aren't married, are you?"

"No."

"A pity, such a pretty girl like you. Don't go through your life alone. You need a husband. Otherwise you will grow lonely. Although children can be a disappointment. You spend your best years raising them, and then they forget you and only come by when it is convenient. It is how life is. We can't complain, only accept what God gives us."

As they moved into the hallway, Signora Rossi offered Tahira the room key. "Enjoy my Villa Cielo Blu, even though it is only one room!"

Tahira carried the woman's bag onto the elevator at the end of the hall. "My son will be picking me up in his car," the old woman continued. "I warned you the police do not allow cars to park outside, but he tells them I am handicapped. He drives a red German car with only two seats and barely enough room for my bag. It is not for me. But he pays me no attention." She waved her hand to her side and frowned. "My son. He needs to meet a nice girl like you."

Tahira left the woman and her bag on a bench outside the apartment building, facing the lake. It was a clear morning, no rain forecast nor any strong breezes. Tahira walked up the hillside between the city's Romanesque buildings until she reached a public parking area where her father was waiting in a rented van. He saw her approaching, stepped from the driver's seat, and met her at the van's rear doors.

"You took longer than I expected," the Roc said.

"The old woman was lonely. Asked me questions."

"About what?"

"If I were Catholic, and why wasn't I married. She has a son she wanted me to meet."

He looked at his watch. "The wedding will begin at five o'clock, after *riposo*."

"Do the *polizia di stato* also nap in the afternoons?" she asked. A joke that he ignored.

"The view," he said. "Will it work?"

"Better than what was shown in the photos."

He removed a hard-shell suitcase and a backpack from the cargo area. "I'll help you set up in the apartment, and we'll review the plan."

Tahira frowned. "Not again, Papa. We went over it in Paris every night. I know it."

"Tahira," he said sternly. "The Israelis are serious people. They will kill you if they suspect. They will kill me. Now do as you are told."

He handed her the backpack and picked up the heavy suitcase.

"Take me to the apartment," he said.

"Papa, I left the old woman sitting out front by the entrance. She will see us together."

"Find the back entrance. I will be waiting there for you to let me inside."

He glanced around, noted that the street was empty, and reached into the front of his tan cargo pants, withdrawing a Glock 26 Gen4 subcompact ten-round pistol, one of the most popular concealed-carry handguns. She took it from his palm and slipped it into the front pocket of her gray utility jacket.

She shouldered the backpack and started back to the apartment. He waited before following with the heavier suitcase. Signora Rossi was still sitting outside.

"My son is late," she complained. "He cares nothing for his poor mother."

It took Tahira only minutes to find the ground-floor back entrance, where the Roc was waiting. They rode up the elevator. Once inside the flat, he began assembling the McMillan TAC-50 from the suitcase. Next was a motorized stainless-steel boot affixed to a tripod. He slid the old woman's table toward the open window, positioning it about two feet from it—far enough inside so it would be impossible to see from the street below, and improbable for someone on the other side of Lake Como to spot through binoculars. He placed the short tripod on the table and checked to make certain there was no wobble. Satisfied, he took a moment to admire the autonomous weapon that he had prepared in Paris.

Without bothering to speak, he withdrew a portable computer with a joystick from the backpack and synchronized the computer with the motor and rifle. A slight twist of the joystick, and the rifle barrel moved. The computer screen showed a series of gauges as well as the view from the rifle's Vortex PST Gen II 5–25x50 scope.

"Tell me the plan," he said.

"The head Jew will be attending his niece's outdoor wedding at the villa directly across from this apartment. Distance: three kilometers. The air is thinner here because Lake Como is at the base of the Alps. There will be less drag. The bullet will fly faster, with a flat trajectory."

"Elevation, temperature, windage," he said. "The computer program that I installed will help you calculate, but it will be you sighting in the head Jew. Now, if it begins raining?"

"Papa, look outside. The sky is clear. It will not rain."

"And if it does?"

"Every bride who plans an outside wedding has a contingency," she said. "If I don't see the head Jew, I am to fire into the chalet's windows. Cause panic."

"Good." He removed a recent eight-by-ten-inch photograph of Big Jules and placed it in her hands.

"Papa, I know what he looks like."

"At this distance, you must aim at the biggest body mass. This is not the television, where you aim at the head."

"Yes, Papa, you've told me many times, but even in France when I practiced, I only hit the target once out of every ten shots, and you are giving me only one opportunity."

"A professional needs only one bullet," he said, slipping a BMG—Browning Machine Gun—round into the single-shot rifle's chamber. "If you are worried about firing a second one, you will not concentrate on the first. Firing only once reduces the chance of you being seen, and having you stay in the apartment to reload only puts you at greater risk."

He looked into her eyes. "Tahira, I have taught you how to shoot. You can kill him, but only if you want to."

"Yes, Papa."

"As long as you cause panic, the Mossad will follow protocol, and I will deal with him."

"But if I miss, I will be putting you in danger."

"Then don't miss." He stared into her eyes, looking for signs of doubt. "The first time you kill another human being is the most difficult," he said. "But the Jews are not human beings. They are dogs. Now do as I told you. If you hesitate, think of your mother and your brother. This Jew was responsible for the bombs that killed them and would have killed you and me."

Someone knocked on the flat's door. A key was inserted into the lock. Signora Rossi's voice: "Buon pomeriggio, signorina! My son is downstairs, and I thought—"

The elderly woman opened the door and froze. Looking at the Roc. Looking at the rifle at the window. Trying to understand what her eyes were seeing.

The Roc reached her in two steps. He slipped behind her before she could scream, covering her mouth with one hand and drawing his knife with the other. He jammed the blade downward in a little gap between the first vertebra and the base of the skull, cutting her spinal cord. She collapsed on the floor. The Roc grabbed a pillow from the bed and held it over her face, but she was already dead.

"Help me," he ordered his daughter. She shut the door while he pulled the top blanket from the bed and placed it on the floor.

Together, they rolled the old woman onto it. He wrapped the material around her, and they slid her out of the way.

"Her son?" he said.

Tahira moved to the window but was unable to see directly down onto the building's front entrance because of a decorative ledge. She checked the hallway. No one was in sight.

A car horn honked outside.

"The son," the Roc said.

Tahira drew the Glock that he'd given her earlier. Cocked it and hurriedly attached a suppressor from the backpack.

From outside, they heard the *hee-haw* whoop of an Italian police siren. Tahira stuck her head out the window as far as possible to listen. An argument. A police officer ordering the son to move his car from the no-parking zone in front of the apartment building.

Again, a car horn honking. Longer bursts. It was the son. Impatient. Signaling his mother to come down.

"Papa, what should we do? The police? Should we run?"

"No." The son would find his mother dead. Find the sniper's rifle. There wouldn't be time to dismantle it. The police would inform the Mossad. There would be a massive hunt for them. He suspected Signora Rossi had bragged to her son about the beautiful young woman who'd rented the flat. Possibly described Tahira. No. There might never be a better opportunity to kill the head Jew.

They heard the whining noise of the old elevator climbing to the fifth floor, of its door opening and footsteps coming down the hallway. The Roc pointed to a spot directly in front of the door for her to stand. She would be the first thing the son saw when the door opened. Would he come alone or with the police? Tahira held the Glock behind her while her father slipped against the wall by the doorway, clutching his knife. The door would swing inward, which meant it would open between whoever was entering, with the Roc behind it. He looked at Tahira. She was breathing rapidly. Perspiration was beading on her face. Some ran into her eyes, and she began blinking. The Roc tugged down a hand towel hanging on the back of the door and tossed it to her. It smelled like the old lady when she wiped her face. She dropped it on the floor and watched the old black doorknob turn. The flat's door swung open directly in front of her.

"Mama?" the son called out.

He took a step toward Tahira and then spotted the rifle.

"What the—"

The Roc slammed the door closed behind him and lunged forward with his knife drawn. But Signora Rossi's son was not an elderly grandmother. He sensed the attack and instinctively turned with his arms raised in a defensive position. His left arm blocked the knife, and he grabbed the collar of the Roc's shirt with his right hand.

The Roc fell into him, knocking the younger man backward onto the floor, near Tahira's feet. She fell to her knees and pointed the Glock directly at his face. He reacted with a stunned look, frozen. In that mini-second, the Roc swept his knife downward, plunged it into the man's chest, and began jamming it in and out.

"The pillow!" the Roc exclaimed.

Tahira grabbed it and pushed it onto the son's face to mute his cries. After several seconds, Signora Rossi's son stopped moving.

Tahira tried to stand, but she felt weak. She vomited.

Hee-haw, hee-haw. It was the police siren outside. As Tahira used the discarded towel on the floor to wipe her mouth, the Roc reached into the dead man's front pant pocket but found nothing. He checked the dead man's other pocket and removed a key fob. Porsche insignia.

"She said he drove a sports car," Tahira said, her face bright red and glistening with sweat.

The Roc handed her the keys. "You must go outside," he said. She stood and swept her hand through her short hair. She could still taste the vomit in her mouth as she stepped into the hallway.

Tahira emerged from the building, intent on making a scene.

"This man is an idiot!" she hollered in Italian. "Everyone knows there is no parking here, but he always does this. I will move his car!"

"Who are you?" a police officer standing next to the squad car asked.

"I live in the apartment next to Signora Rossi. She's always trying to arrange for her son to meet me. She got so worked up now, she fainted. He's with her. He gave me his keys." She dangled them in front of the two officers and lowered her voice. "I believe she is faking it. Being dramatic to make her son pay attention to her."

Both officers were running their eyes across Tahira's body.

"I'll move it," she said, unlocking the Cayman S model with its electronic fob. The officer nearest her hurried to open the sports car's door for her, smiling as she slipped behind its wheel.

"Italian mothers," he said to her. "They're all the same, you know. But usually they choose someone ugly. This man is an idiot if he ignores you."

She smiled suggestively and pulled away slowly, checking the mirror. They fell in behind her in their squad car. When she reached a side street, she lowered the Porsche's window and waved at them as they continued driving forward while she turned onto the street to her right.

"Grazie!" she called.

Within minutes she had parked the Porsche on the street at the entrance of the same public lot where the Roc had left the rented van. She left the keys on the floorboard, out of sight.

When she returned to the apartment, the Roc was gone. He had pushed the son's body next to his mother's and covered it with another blanket.

Tahira placed the portable computer in her backpack, stepped into the hallway, locked the apartment door, and went into the toilet at the end of the hallway. She washed her face and cupped water in her hands to rinse her mouth. She looked into a mirror above the sink and felt guilty. Signora Rossi was not a Jew. Not the enemy. Neither was her son. Nor were they like the Iranian traitor who had cooperated with the Americans and Jews.

When Tahira reached the street, she sucked in a deep cleansing breath and steadied herself. She called her father on a disposable phone.

"Are you intending to fix dinner tonight?" he asked when he answered.

"Yes, Papa," she replied. "I will."

It was code.

SIXTEEN

The Bellagio taxi driver talked continuously from the moment the Roc entered his cab.

"You can rent my taxi for the entire day," the driver offered as he drove them outside the city limits around the edge of Lake Como on a narrow, picturesque road. "There is much to see, and I am familiar with all of the best locations. Restaurants, historical sites, where the rich live, and the nightlife too." He glanced in the rearview mirror at the Roc in the back seat. "What do you say, my friend? Would you like me to turn off the meter and charge you a flat daily fee?"

"I am meeting a friend who has a car."

"Do I know this friend of yours? There are not so many of us who live here that we are strangers. What is his name?"

"He doesn't live here," the Roc replied. "Like me, he's a tourist, but he is driving here to meet me."

"Then you should consider hiring me to drive, so you don't get lost and both of you can enjoy the beautiful sights." He raised his hand and waved toward the scenery outside. "There is nothing here more beautiful than our lake, except for our women." He touched his fingers to his lips and threw a kiss. "*Bella donna!* Did I tell you I know the best nightclubs? You will not get a better price."

The blacktop snaked down the hillside to the water's edge.

"Pull over here," the Roc said.

"What? Sir, there is nothing here. This can't be where you are meeting your friend."

"I wish to walk for a while. I will telephone my friend, and he will meet me here."

"But walking on the road is not safe. There are no stores. No bars, not even a bench to sit on if you become tired."

"This is where I wish to stop," the Roc said firmly.

The driver shrugged and stopped his cab on the roadway, since there was no verge for him to pull over on. He turned his head. "I hope your friend arrives soon," he said. "If not, call me." He handed a business card from the front seat.

"Grazie."

The Roc watched the cab do a U-turn. He waved as the driver lowered his window while passing him. "Remember to call me. I will give you the best price." When the taxi was out of sight, he walked a half mile farther along the road before slipping into the woods. He moved silently through the trees for another half mile, using the compass on his watch to guide him.

He and Tahira had hidden items under leaves and dead branches earlier after finding an ideal location courtesy of Google satellite images. He found the unmolested stash. First he took out a camouflaged ghillie suit and tins of black and green face grease. He draped the heavy suit over his muscular frame, applied the makeup, and holstered two Beretta 92 semiautomatic pistols—model M9A1, popular with US Marines fighting in Afghanistan—where he could reach them through slits. Another walk through the woods brought him to his hiding spot, on a slight rise above a single-lane road that broke from the highway. It was the only road in and out to the lakeside villa where Big Jules would be attending his niece's wedding. He crawled to the base of a chestnut tree, keenly aware of men in black suits armed with automatic rifles walking on the road below him. Lying prone, he quietly smoothed leaves over his suit, making him impossible to detect. In fact, he blended into the scenery so efficiently that a parade of ants soon began marching inches from his face up across his right shoulder, carrying insect larvae back to their nest.

Now there was nothing to do but wait. And think. About Tahira. And wonder. Would she pull the trigger? Would she aim to kill? He tried to push all doubt from his thoughts.

After his wife and son were murdered, he had considered asking relatives to take custody of Tahira. At the time, he had found himself hating the sight of her. He'd deeply loved his wife. Been proud of their firstborn son. He'd also loved his daughter, but she had become a painful reminder of how much he had lost. There was another reason why he'd considered abandoning her. His heart could not take another loss. Better to cut all ties. Care about no one. But in the end, he'd chosen otherwise.

His hatred of the Jews had become more all-consuming with each passing day. His legacy had become ensuring that Tahira shared his hatred. It had been difficult at first; her youthful innocence naturally made her soft and kind. She was too much like her mother. Over time, he had broken her down, remade her more like him. The world was a cruel place. They could only trust each other. Their only purpose in living was to avenge the deaths of their slaughtered family. It had gotten more difficult as she aged. This is why he had taken her to America to kill the Iranian traitor. This is why he had brought her to Lake Como. She was at a tipping point. She had to choose now.

The Roc had once waited for thirty-six hours without moving from a sniper's lair. He was a patient man. Only this time he was not armed with a rifle. Instead, it was a remote switch.

He thought again about his daughter. He had always assumed he would leave her an orphan. He had prepared her for that day, making her memorize the numbers of his bank accounts and how to retrieve his Bitcoin savings. He had no will, no legal document bearing his given name. He led the life of a ghost. She would have enough to live a comfortable life, whether she chose to follow his training or disgrace him by no longer seeking vengeance. It was difficult for him to visualize Tahira as an obedient wife to any man. What he had never considered was that she, rather than him, might be captured or killed.

A branch breaking. Someone was moving through the woods.

Another sound. A voice. Speaking in Hebrew.

The Roc had learned the language of his enemy, along with other commonly spoken tongues. He and Tahira had practiced together, speaking only French for one month, only English another, moving next to Russian. They had become fluent. The man speaking was reporting that everything was okay. A Jew security guard checking the forest before the wedding started.

From his position, the Roc could not see the intruder, but he knew from the loudness of his voice that he was coming closer. Too close. Slowly moving his hand, the Roc grasped the knife inside his camouflage suit.

The security guard reached the tree where the Roc was hiding and stopped, less than a foot away from his face. The odor of cigarette smoke. The guard was taking a break, completely unaware that an assassin was hidden under the leaves and brush within inches of his shoes. He dropped the cigarette butt on the ground. With the toe of his shoe, he smashed its glowing tip.

The Roc heard the sound of an approaching motorcade, but he dared not react as the vehicles hurried by on the road below him.

SEVENTEEN

4:55 p.m.

Julian "Big Jules" Levi arrived after the other wedding guests had been screened and seated on the terrace outside Villa Como, a five-story neoclassical mansion built between 1808 and 1810 by a protégé of Napoleon Bonaparte. The villa was *pied-dans-l'eau*, "feet in the water," its massive marble patio extending out from the shore over the lake.

The bride's father and villa's owner, Eitan Cohen, was waiting to embrace his famous brother-in-law.

"Shalom, my dear brother!" Big Jules happily exclaimed as he stepped from the Audi 8 armored car that had been flown in specifically for him.

Cohen beamed. "Adinah will be so excited when she sees you. I've been wanting to tell someone, but I haven't said a word, not a word—isn't that right?" He glanced at a thirtyish woman standing nearby whom he knew only as Esther. She was dressed in a tailored black tuxedo.

"Yes," Esther said, "you have been the perfect host. As always."

"And now the day, and you are here," Cohen chirped.

"How could I miss my favorite niece's wedding?" Big Jules asked. "God would never forgive me."

"God? It would be my wife—your sister—who would never forgive you!" Cohen replied, smiling.

Esther fell in behind Big Jules as Cohen led them through the ground floor of the villa out onto the terrace, where a hundred invitees were waiting. A chuppah decorated with Juliet roses intermixed with white orchids had been built on the patio's edge over the lake, taking advantage of a magnificent view. The light fragrance of lilac and sweet vanilla lingered in the afternoon air. A string quartet was playing. Cohen signaled the wedding coordinator to begin.

5:10 p.m.

Tahira Bashar was sitting at a sidewalk café less than a block from Signora Rossi's apartment with her back to the eatery's stone and glass facade. She had an unobstructed view of Villa Como across the lake.

"Another cappuccino?" a waiter asked, approaching.

"Yes, please."

Her laptop screen was masked by a privacy filter that allowed only the user directly in front to see images. Being outside enabled her to make last-minute adjustments for windage if needed.

She watched the waiter leave, weaving through a dozen other tables before entering the café. He was handsome, although at least ten years older than her. She had never been with a man, and for a moment she imagined what the waiter would be like as a lover. Her eyes swept across the others around her. Tourists. She could tell by their conversations. English. French. Korean. She could identify the Americans by their slang, weight, loudness, and clothing. Her eyes settled on a young couple. The girl in khaki shorts, wool sweater, and hiking boots. Him in denim jeans, running shoes. Virginia Tech maroon hoodie. Backpacks next to their chairs. Tahira assumed they were in love, and wondered again what it would be like to have a boyfriend.

The waiter put a fresh cup on her table.

"You're playing—what game?" he asked, looking at the joystick attached to her computer.

"What? Oh, *Grand Theft Auto*."

"Have you tried *Fortnite*?"

"Killing zombies—is that what you do for entertainment?"

He smiled, revealing slightly crooked teeth. "Is stealing cars and running over pedestrians your thing?"

He left to serve a nearby customer, and she checked her computer screen. The magnified rifle scope showed a large figure being escorted between two ushers to a front-row seat. She increased the magnification to positively identify her prey but only confirmed that it was the head Jew after he'd already been seated.

Or had she unconsciously delayed taking a shot? Knowing that she would need him to be standing before firing, because then he would be a bigger target.

5:20 p.m.

"Look for blue lines," Thomas Jefferson Kim said through the satellite phone being relayed over the car's internal speaker. "Blue lines in Bellagio identify that the lot is for public parking. You should be approaching one with a stone retaining wall and sign that has an arrow pointing to Giardini di Villa Melzi."

"I see it," Brett Garrett answered as they slowed their rental Fiat 500 Abarth. He'd chosen the subcompact to blend in with other travelers.

"I don't see the Roc's white van," Mayberry said.

"It's there," Kim replied. "Parked near that yellow toilette building that should be on your left as you enter the lot."

"Glad to know you're watching over us," Mayberry replied, glancing through the Fiat's dirty passenger window into the sky. Somewhere above them was one of Kim's IEC satellites.

Kim had tracked the Roc and Tahira from Rome to Bellagio via the white rental van's GPS—a surprising mistake on the assassin's part. Obviously, he had assumed their false passports would be enough to cover their tracks from prying eyes.

"I see it," Garrett announced as he entered the public parking lot and slipped into an empty space a few rows from the van.

"It doesn't look like anyone's inside," Mayberry said.

Garrett reached behind the driver's seat and pulled his Sig Sauer P226 pistol from a backpack.

"My Glock?" she said.

He looked at her crippled right hand.

"Give me my damn gun."

He pulled it out of the same backpack. She held it in her left. "If we have to use these," she said, "we'll be the ones arrested. We don't have any authority here, and the Roc and his daughter haven't been charged with any crimes in the States."

"If you're getting cold feet, stay in the car."

He opened the driver's door and stepped out, intending to check out the van. She fumbled with her right hand to open the passenger door.

"Don't shoot me by accident," he said.

"It won't be by accident."

5:21 p.m.

The rabbi finished singing. The groom wrapped a champagne glass in a white linen cloth. Placed it on the marble patio floor.

Across Lake Como, Tahira watched from the café. She had studied YouTube videos of Jewish weddings to familiarize herself with the ceremonies. The traditional breaking of the glass. Once he stepped on it, the guests would rise from their chairs and cheer: *Mazel tov!*

Big Jules was sitting on the same row as his sister—the bride's mother—and the bride's father. She thought his nickname appropriate, and recalled her father's lecture. The more body mass, the better the chances of hitting him. Still, Big Jules was sandwiched in by relatives.

"Shall I bring a check, signorina?" Tahira had not seen the waiter approaching her table.

"Yes," she replied, not bothering to look at him.

"Are you killing many?" he asked.

"What?"

"Pedestrians. Your video game."

"Go away," she snapped.

A slight wisp of air grazed her cheek. Enough windage to ruin her shot? No, she decided. She would not recalibrate.

On Villa Como's patio, the groom dropped his foot onto the glass.

"Mazel tov! Mazel tov!" The wedding guests erupted from their seats. Big Jules stood too.

It was now or never. She hesitated and then thought of her dead mother and brother.

Tahira fired.

The McMillan TAC-50 sniper rifle in Signora Rossi's apartment responded. Its single .50-caliber round took less than ten seconds to cross the lake, traveling at 792 mph, faster than a commercial Boeing 747 jet. The half-inch-diameter slug created a small shock wave, but no one at the wedding heard the sound until after the 800-grain bullet struck. It hit the bride's oldest brother, standing next to Big Jules. Passed through him. Deflected by his shattered bones, it exited his chest and hit the string quartet's cellist, seated some twenty feet away, bursting through her instrument and knocking her from her chair. Both were dead.

Tahira watched the confusion and panic on the screen. Big Jules dropped to his knees next to his dead nephew. Four Mossad security guards swarmed around him, holding portable black bullet-resistant shields to protect him. Frantic guests ran toward the villa's open patio doors. Under the chuppah, the bride, groom, and rabbi stood stunned, not yet entirely certain what had happened.

The last person on the patio whom Tahira saw before snapping the computer shut was a woman dressed in a tuxedo, staring through binoculars at the Bellagio shoreline.

Tahira deposited the computer into her backpack and fished out a twenty-euro note. She used a bottle of virgin olive oil to pin it on the table. More than enough to pay the cost of her cappuccinos and amend for her rudeness.

She walked onto the street, tormenting herself with the knowledge that she'd let her father down. Now it was up to him to kill Big Jules.

5:40 p.m.

Three vehicles sped up the winding, half-mile private road that connected Villa Como to the highway.

The Roc watched them approach from near the base of the chestnut tree, grasping a remote controller.

Big Jules's armored Audi 8 was between two SUVs. As the vehicles neared him, the Roc pressed the remote, launching a drone from the hillside. It was armed with two kilograms of C-4 plastic explosive.

Big Jules's security team reacted, the front SUV swerving sideways to protect the Audi. The drone slammed into the SUV, exploding with such force that it knocked the heavy vehicle from the roadway, blocking the Audi 8's path. Big Jules's driver shifted the Audi into reverse as a Mossad security guard leaped from the second SUV. Its driver also reversed, pulling off the road so the Audi 8 could get by it in reverse.

A second drone appeared from the hillside. The Mossad agent, now standing on the road, shouldered what appeared to be a rifle but instead had a toothy blade that resembled a hedge trimmer attached to its stock. He squeezed its trigger, blasting signals on all radio frequencies at the drone, effectively cutting off the Roc's remote controller. The second drone fell harmlessly onto the road.

The Roc had expected this. As the Audi started back the narrow road toward Villa Como, he pressed a switch connected to a wire to avoid radio frequency jamming. Buried in the ground, the wire extended two hundred and fifty yards from his hiding spot to a stack of discarded tree branches. Hidden in them: an RPG-32 Russian-designed grenade launcher, powerful enough to stop an Abrams tank. The RPG fired, and its grenade blasted into the Audi's midsection, causing a deafening explosion. The German sedan was instantly engulfed in flames, an inferno that killed everyone inside it.

EIGHTEEN

"Look!" Mayberry exclaimed. "Isn't that her?"

Garrett studied the woman walking casually toward the parking lot.

Mayberry tucked her handgun into her waistband and raised her iPhone, feeding a live image to Thomas Jefferson Kim back at IEC headquarters.

"It's her," Kim declared. "A hundred percent facial recognition match with the image taken outside Clyde's of Georgetown."

Garrett and Mayberry slowly started walking to intercept Tahira before she could enter the white rental van and escape. Garrett was holding his Sig Sauer pressed against his thigh outside his denim jeans, hoping to hide it.

Tahira saw them. Two strangers. Spotted the pistol. She started to run, but instead of entering the parking lot and trying to reach the white van, she hurried to the red Porsche Cayman S sports car parked closer to her on the street, where she'd abandoned it. Scooping its keys from the driver's floor, she sped onto Lungo Lario Manzoni, a narrow street that ran parallel to Lake Como's shores.

Garrett and Mayberry dashed back to the Fiat.

"Can you track her?" Mayberry asked Kim.

"Red Porsche?" Kim asked. "Got her. She's heading into the historic city."

"She'll have to slow down," Garrett said. "Way too many people."

But Tahira didn't. She honked at pedestrians, causing them to leap clear. There were shops on her right side, Lake Como on her left. She could only continue straight.

"She'll have to turn right opposite the ferry terminal," Kim said from his satellite vantage point. "The street turns one-way after that, and she'll be driving headfirst into oncoming traffic."

"If she turns on that street," Garrett replied, "we'll never keep up with her."

The Fiat Abarth could keep up with the Porsche on the narrow, crowded shoreline road, but on a thoroughfare, it would be no match for the German car's 350-horsepower engine.

As Tahira neared the right turn onto the larger road out of Bellagio, a semitruck pulled in front of her. She checked her rearview mirror. The Fiat was gaining, the truck turtle slow. Tahira accelerated, shooting around the truck, missing the right turn, and driving directly into oncoming traffic.

A motorcycle rider swerved, barely missing the speeding Porsche. A car behind him jerked sideways, careening from the road into a row of decorative concrete barriers protecting a sidewalk café.

"She's crazy!" Mayberry said as Tahira continued driving toward Bellagio's famed Hotel Metropole in the heart of the old village. Initially the grand hotel had been confined to the shoreline, but with time it had extended backward into the city, necessitating the construction of a narrow tunnel, only wide enough for a single car, that passed under its second floor into the Piazza Giuseppe Mazzini.

Tahira pounded on the Porsche's horn, clearing the tunnel of bicyclists and pedestrians, as she jammed on the car's brakes, bringing it to a sudden stop directly under the historic hotel. The Porsche was now blocking the opening. Flinging open the driver's door, she stepped clear while raising her Glock 26 pistol.

She fired at the Fiat chasing her.

Garrett and Mayberry had no room to turn. Knee-high concrete barriers lined both curbs along the street to prevent vehicles from striking pedestrians on the cluttered sidewalks.

Garrett downshifted, pushed hard on the car's gas pedal, and activated the Fiat's electronic parking brake while turning its wheels. Most Abarths are front-wheel drive, but Garrett had specifically rented one that had been converted to rear-wheel drive, something done in Italy for car enthusiasts who want to drift at rallies. The Fiat's rear wheels locked, and the car spun. A hundred and eighty degrees.

Three rounds punched into the rear of the Fiat, shattering its tiny window and engine compartment, barely missing Garrett and Mayberry.

Garrett flung himself from the driver's seat onto the asphalt, twisting midair so he landed on his right shoulder, a move that enabled him to fire his Sig Sauer at Tahira.

She was gone, disappeared into the piazza behind her.

"C'mon!" Garrett hollered, standing.

"Wait!" Mayberry cried. "She doesn't have her backpack!"

"What?" Garrett asked, pausing.

"Her backpack!" Mayberry screamed.

Garrett turned his eyes away from Mayberry and looked at the Porsche just as it exploded. A fireball shot from under the hotel, knocking both of them off their feet.

On his back, Garrett mentally performed an inventory of possible injuries. His face was singed. He moved his toes, raised his arms, forced himself into a sitting position. Mayberry was on her back some ten feet away from him. Not moving. He crawled toward her. Noticed she was bleeding from her ears and nose.

"Valerie! Valerie!"

He glanced around him.

The C-4 in Tahira's backpack had cut a jagged black gash into the second floor of the five-story hotel. Flames were shooting from the structure. Metal fragments and broken glass had been propelled much like shotgun pellets from the exploding Porsche. Only its twisted and charred frame remained.

All around them were the dead and wounded. A bicyclist near the passageway had been tossed through the air onto a sidewalk café's chairs and tables. His broken body now sprawled facedown on the sidewalk, his clothing and skin scorched from burns. Flying debris had killed at least four more, wounded a dozen. Everywhere around Garrett people were screaming for help. Moans came from the injured.

Garrett heard police sirens. Ambulances. Emergency personnel approaching. On his knees, he looked down at the still-unconscious Mayberry. He noticed blood on his left sleeve. A pencil-thick piece of jagged metal was protruding from his biceps. Still in shock, he had not noticed it before.

"Don't move!" a voice ordered.

He looked away from Mayberry. Two Italian police officers, guns aimed at him, barking orders that he only half heard.

Garrett suddenly realized he was still holding his Sig Sauer. He released it onto the blacktop. One of the officers rushed him, pulled back his arms, handcuffing his wrists, forcing him to stand.

He looked down at Mayberry and shouted, "Help her!"

NINETEEN

Russian oligarch Taras Zharkov locked the double doors to his master bedroom suite and strolled to the centermost bookcase on a wall of floor-to-ceiling shelves. He was careful not to spill the after-dinner liqueur that he was holding as he removed a copy of *Eugene Onegin* from the fourth shelf.

Zharkov had not read this lesser-known novel by Russian poet Alexander Pushkin, although he had read many of the hundreds of books displayed in his library. Setting his drink on a side table, he removed a leather-bound copy of *Father and Sons* by Russian novelist Ivan Turgenev from the third shelf. He tucked each book in the other's spot on the shelves.

As soon as the switch was made, he heard the sound of a motor and stepped back as a section of the wooden bookcase moved forward and sideways, revealing a 650-pound reinforced-steel door. The biometric lock was coded to read Zharkov's left eye and right-hand thumbprint. It also opened outward, allowing Zharkov to enter an eight-hundred-square-foot safe room whose walls, ceiling, and floor had been constructed with ballistic-resistant materials that could not be penetrated by bullets and could withstand temperatures of up to a thousand degrees.

Zharkov slipped into a high-backed chair modeled for his hefty frame. The wall-size monitor before him—capable of showing as many as sixteen different images simultaneously, or a single one—

came to life, automatically sensing his presence. With a swipe of his finger on a handheld control pad, Iranian general Kardar's face appeared on the massive monitor.

"General," he said, "have you been successful?"

"The Jew is dead," Kardar reported. "Killed today, leaving his niece's wedding."

Zharkov looked for his tumbler to offer a toast but realized he had left the liqueur outside his hidden chamber.

"Commander Petrov," the oligarch said, "should be under way in the *Golden Fish* within the next forty-eight to seventy-two hours. I will share the good news that the Mossad will be too busy burying its leader to disturb him."

Zharkov waited for Kardar to react, but the sullen general remained stone-faced.

"As you are aware, General," Zharkov continued, "you have completed the first half of your obligation by making the delivery to my underground base. Now for the second round. Have you found someone willing to detonate the bomb?"

"Not only did I find a jihadist willing to attack the Americans," Kardar replied, "he will take credit for killing the Jew."

"A bonus!" a delighted Zharkov replied.

"He is a Palestinian named Fathi Aziz."

Zharkov typed Fathi Aziz's name into his control pad. An internet profile appeared on the monitor alongside General Kardar's larger image.

Fathi Aziz: head of Jihad Brigade, a Palestinian Islamist terrorist organization formed in 1981 whose objective is the destruction of the State of Israel and establishment of a sovereign Islamic Palestinian state. Jihad Brigade is labeled as a terrorist group by the US and its allies. Primary funding from Iran and Syria. Active in West Bank and Gaza Strip.

Strongholds include cities of Hebron and Jenin. Operations: suicide bombings, attacks on Israeli civilians, firing rockets into Israel. Much in common with Hamas, with both fighting against the existence of the state of Israel.

Zharkov asked, "You have explained everything to him privately?"

"I have told him what he needs to know."

"And me? Did you mention my name?"

"No. All Aziz was told is that his brothers and sisters in the fight against the Zionists have chosen him to serve as Allah's messenger. It will be his reward to kill millions of infidels. He knows Iran cannot be associated with such an attack."

"You trust him?"

"Trust has nothing to do with choosing Aziz. I am a general who understands what motivates men. In his case, Aziz is a zealot. Martyrdom is his most powerful motivation. Are you familiar with any scriptures found in the Holy Qur'an?"

"Absolutely none. Mine is a Leninist view of religions. I seek my salvation between the legs of young women and a chilled Killian."

"The Prophet said, 'Nobody who enters Paradise will ever like to return to this world even if he were offered everything, except the martyr who will desire to return to this world and be killed ten times for the sake of the great honor that has been bestowed upon him.' Aziz cannot be tempted with worldly pleasures. He has only one desire—to be a martyr for Allah, blessed be his name. When the time is right, he will do what he is told and detonate the bomb."

"Wonderful for him—and for us."

"The agreement we have," Kardar continued, "calls for the payment of a finder's fee now that I have recruited Aziz."

"Yes, yes, two million in US dollars. I'll need you to come to London as my guest to receive it and engage in further discussions about the attack."

"I expect payment now," Kardar said.

"We should wait until Commander Petrov is under way for your visit," Zharkov said, ignoring him. "I will send one of my private jets."

"My money," Kardar said, raising his voice.

"My friend, think for a moment. I can transfer the funds immediately into your bank in Tehran, but what would happen if word leaked out to the Grand Ayatollah? How would you explain such a large transfer? Would your religious leaders not be suspect? Better for me to pay you in cash and in person here."

Kardar was not a man who tolerated having others tell him what he could and couldn't do, but he realized the Russian was correct. "Have you chosen the six-digit code needed to detonate the bomb?" he asked, changing the subject. "I will require it for Aziz."

"When you come to London, we will discuss the code. Wait for me to make the arrangements."

TWENTY

Valerie Mayberry heard a voice. She did not recognize it. Slowly it became clearer as she regained consciousness. An angry voice spewing from a television.

"*Brothers and sisters,*" the voice declared, "*the Jihad Brigade has delivered justice to the Zionist invader Julian Levi—a destroyer of our houses, committer of sacrilegious acts against our holy places, assaulter of children and women, and murderer of our people.*"

She opened her eyes. Blinked. A television mounted on the wall. It showed a man identified at the bottom of the screen as a Palestinian terrorist named Fathi Aziz. He was sitting cross-legged with the Holy Qur'an on his right, an AK-47 assault rifle on his left, and the black jihadist flag bearing the Shahada hanging behind him—by now the standard background for proclamations by terrorists.

"*Thanks be to Allah. All praise be to Allah and prayers and peace be upon the Prophet and his family and his companions and those who follow him. Our victory in killing this Jew is another revelation of the truth in our actions against the international Zionist agent—America—the sellers of Palestine—England and France—and the Jew invaders. We recognize no borders, no barbed wire or checkpoints, which the disbelieving aggressor has imposed, and no maps which the apostate tyrant has drawn.*"

Aziz's voice became louder.

"*By my hand and my people, by the fire of pain I endure as a warrior,*"

*I will remain a warrior, I will die as a warrior—until my people are free
and rid of the cancerous tumor of Zionism forced upon our people. Great
Satan and your Zionist usurpers, hear my words. I will soon deliver a
flood over your cities from beneath your oceans, and the wrath of Allah will
destroy you."*

Mayberry shifted her eyes away from the television to the rest of
the room. Heavy lace curtains. Pale yellow walls. A bedroom. She
could see framed photos on a desk. Images of a young girl and her
parents. Mayberry tried to raise her crippled right hand. Couldn't.
Same with her left. Still groggy. She didn't understand until she
looked down at her sides. Her hands were bound to the bed with
scarves. Silk. Her feet too.

"You're awake," a man said as he entered the bedroom, followed
by a woman. He produced a penlight. Placed his right fingers around
her eyes, forcing them open as he examined her pupils. He checked
her pulse. Felt her forehead.

"Vitals normal," he announced.

"Who are you?" Mayberry asked. "Where am I?"

He exited without answering, closing the door behind him.

For a moment, Mayberry wondered if she were dreaming.

"Valerie Mayberry," the woman said, "you're a United States of
America FBI agent."

The woman was wearing a drab olive jumpsuit—a military uniform, but one without any identifying marks. She spoke English
without a hint of an accent.

"Do I know you?" Mayberry asked. "What's your name?"

"Esther."

"Please untie me. I've not done anything wrong, and I need my
pain medication. There's a prescription bottle—"

"Yes," Esther said, holding up Mayberry's xtampza er. "It was in
the satchel in the Fiat that you and the other American were driving."

"His name is Garrett. Brett Garrett. Where is he? Is he okay?"

She looked at the pain medication. "Please untie me and give me two of my pills."

Esther lowered the prescription bottle out of sight. She dragged a chair closer to the bed so she was at Mayberry's eye level.

"First, you need to answer my questions," Esther said. "Then I will untie you and give your medicine."

"Who are you? Garrett, is he alive? Tell me! Listen, I'm in a lot of pain. Can you at least free my hands and feet? I'm an American citizen. I have rights."

"Answers first."

"Who are you? Italian police? Am I under arrest?"

"Answers by you—not me. Who was the woman you were chasing in the red Porsche that exploded?"

"I demand to speak to someone from the US Embassy. I'm not saying anything until you tell me who you are and whether Garrett is alive. I'm not saying another word until I get my pain pills."

Esther raised the prescription bottle high enough for Mayberry to see. She opened the bottle and removed a single half yellow, half white eighteen-milligram capsule, holding it between her thumb and index finger. "How much pain are you in? Would this help?" she taunted.

Mayberry felt a wave of nausea.

Esther continued, "Why did the FBI send you here to Bellagio?"

"No one sent us. We're on holiday." Mayberry tugged on the restraints.

"Tell me the name of the woman who you were chasing."

Mayberry's head felt as if it would burst. Her entire body ached, especially her already crippled hand, which was in chronic pain. "I demand to speak to someone from the US Embassy."

Esther carefully placed the pain pill back into the prescription bottle and snapped shut its lid. She stood and left the room.

Mayberry glanced at the television. It was showing scenes from the explosion on the streets of Bellagio. The image changed to a photo of Julian Levi, identified as head of the Mossad. Pictures of wedding guests.

Mayberry blacked out.

The last time Brett Garrett saw Valerie Mayberry, she had been unconscious on the pavement. He had been handcuffed and put in a police car, fully expecting to be driven to an Italian police station for interrogation. Before the patrol car could leave the scene, a woman wearing a black tuxedo had appeared with two men. She'd checked Mayberry for a pulse and then spoken to the police officers. The police had surrendered Garrett, and a hood had been placed over his head. When it was removed, he was in a windowless room, hands and feet duct-taped to a heavy metal chair. No toilet, no bed. A single bare bulb dangling from the ceiling. Enough cord to hang himself. That suggested he was not inside a jail or prison cell. From the stone walls and musty air, he suspected it was some sort of basement.

A man entered the room. Refusing to speak to Garrett or answer questions, he removed the metal fragment that had been stuck in his arm when the Porsche exploded, bandaged the wound, and left.

For an hour Garrett waited, unable to move. The woman he'd last seen dressed in a tuxedo on the street entered, only now she was wearing a drab olive military uniform.

"The American who was with me," Garrett said. "Her name is Valerie Mayberry. Is she okay? Did you get her to a doctor?"

"Who is this woman to you?"

"We're traveling together. Is she conscious? Where is she?"

"An FBI agent and former CIA soldier on a holiday together," the woman said. "Chasing a sports car that explodes. Both armed with pistols. You expect me to believe you are merely on holiday?"

"I don't care what you believe. Is Valerie all right? Is she in a hospital?"

"She's asking for her medication."

The woman produced Mayberry's prescription bottle. "Tell me, Mr. Garrett, what is the name of the woman you were pursuing? Tell me, and I will give your friend her pain pills."

"You're supposed to be on our side," he said. "You're Mossad. Last time I checked, we're allies."

Her face showed surprise, given she wasn't wearing any identification.

"It's your belt," he said. "Israel Army Tzahal IDF field uniform. Standard issue."

"The woman you were chasing," she said. "I need her name."

"You tell me your name, I'll tell you hers."

"The woman in the Porsche participated in an attempted assassination. Tell me her name."

"Who was she trying to kill?"

"You don't know?"

"If I did, I wouldn't bother asking, would I?"

"The director of the Mossad."

"Big Jules? Julian Levi?"

"Do you know him?"

"Everyone in intelligence knows about him. He's a legend. Is he okay?"

"By intelligence, you mean you are still employed by the CIA."

"No. The agency doesn't have any use for my special talents."

"What is the name of the woman who you were chasing?"

"You give Mayberry her pain pills and free me, and I'll tell you everything I know."

The door behind her opened.

"Esther," Julian Levi said, entering with two security guards. "Let's undo Mr. Garrett's restraints."

Esther brandished a knife, cut free his legs and wrists. She handed Mayberry's prescription bottle to one of the men standing nearby, who left the room.

"The Roc and his daughter obviously failed to assassinate you,"

Garrett said, rubbing his wrists where the tape had torn loose surface skin. "That's good for both of our countries."

"The Roc?" Big Jules replied. "You're mistaken. We killed him with an American drone."

"No, I'm not mistaken. He's not dead, despite what your people reported. I've seen him and his daughter."

"Are you absolutely certain of this?" Big Jules asked.

"A hundred percent. Backed by facial recognition software and a visual ID."

"Assuming you are correct," Esther interjected, "if you knew the Roc intended to assassinate Director Levi, why didn't you warn us?"

"If I'd known, I'd have told anyone who would've listened. Mayberry and I followed him to Italy because the two of them murdered an Iranian who happened to be my next-door neighbor in the States."

"Nasya Radi," Big Jules said. "The letter writer."

"That's right," Garrett replied. "Radi left a letter for me on the night he was murdered, and sent another letter to your embassy in Washington."

"How do you know that?" Esther asked.

"Our post office takes photos of letters before they're delivered."

"Your friend, Thomas Jefferson Kim, no doubt traced it," Big Jules said. "Did he also identify the Roc and his daughter?"

"Let's just say the two of them were positively ID'd on security video while leaving a Georgetown restaurant."

"Tell me, Mr. Garrett, what did this exiled nuclear physicist write in the letter that he sent to you before he was murdered?"

"I imagine he wrote the same thing he sent in his letter to your embassy. The Iranians have manufactured a nuclear bomb. They intend to attack the US with it by using a submarine."

"And what did you do with the letter that he wrote you?"

"Mayberry and I shared it and our concerns with Director Whittington, but he blew us off. Now, I'd like to see Mayberry."

"Esther," Big Jules said, "have Ms. Mayberry join us."

She left, and Garrett said, "The Roc doesn't fail very often. You're damn lucky."

"Thank you for telling us he is still alive," Big Jules said. "I will investigate how we made such a mistake, and once I confirm what you are saying is accurate, I will notify Whittington and correct our error. I've already spoken to him today."

"He doesn't believe Mayberry and me, but he'll listen to you."

"Sometimes he does, but not as often as you might think. Whittington is a suspicious man when it comes to my country. Now, when it comes to the Roc's attempt to kill me, I owe my escape to Esther. Let's go somewhere more comfortable than this basement storage room."

Big Jules led him upstairs into the expansive Villa Como. "This was supposed to be a magical day," he said as they walked. "My niece's wedding in the home of my sister and her husband. Now it is a day of pain and suffering. Of mourning. Pain that I brought into this happy home. The oldest son murdered by a sniper's bullet intended for me. Five of my men killed during an ambush intended for me. A decoy, naturally, arranged by Esther."

"The Roc thinks you're dead?"

"The entire world does, I suppose. Minutes ago, a Palestinian terrorist claimed responsibility on the internet for murdering me."

"Seems like a lot of folks who are supposed to be dead—like you and the Roc—are still walking around."

Big Jules sat on a lavender sofa in a room on the villa's main floor. There were no windows for outsiders to see in. He gestured for Garrett to take a seat on an overstuffed chair next to him. He'd just sat down when Esther arrived with Mayberry.

Garrett stood. "You're okay!"

"Now that I finally got my pain medication." She flashed a hateful look at Esther.

"A concussion, some minor cuts, soreness," Esther said in an unsympathetic voice. "Nothing life-threatening."

"Please, Agent Mayberry, join us." Big Jules motioned for

Mayberry to sit near Garrett. She did while Esther slipped next to the director on the sofa. His two bodyguards remained at the room's entrance.

"Tell them what we know," Big Jules instructed.

"A sniper's rifle was found in an apartment across Lake Como in Bellagio," Esther explained. "Fired remotely. An older woman and her son were in the apartment too, both dead. The rifle shot missed our director, causing panic. A second assassin was hiding along the only road in and out of Villa Como. He used drones and an RPG to attack a decoy."

"Most likely, Tahira Bashar had fired at you moments before we spotted her coming up the street to the public parking lot," Mayberry said.

"The Porsche she was driving belonged to the dead man in the apartment," Esther said.

"I'm guessing from your questions that you didn't catch Tahira after the Porsche exploded," Garrett said. "And since you didn't know the Roc was alive, he got away too."

"Several people saw a woman fleeing on a bicycle."

"A bicycle! And neither you nor the Italians caught her?" Mayberry said. "Riding on a bicycle."

"If we had known about her before you chased her through Bellagio," Esther replied, "we could have caught her without innocent people being killed by a car explosion."

Big Jules cleared his throat, and everyone fell silent. "I've talked to Director Whittington about you both," he said. "To confirm your identities and ask why you were sent here. He told me that neither of you are working on behalf of the US government, and quite frankly, he was angry that you were involved in a deadly car chase and explosion."

"Like we explained," Garrett said, looking at Mayberry for backup, "we're on vacation."

Big Jules chuckled. "Would you be surprised if I told you Whittington urged me to turn you over to the Italian authorities for prosecution?"

"On what charges?" Mayberry asked.

"This is Italy," Big Jules replied. "They don't need charges."

"Is that what you plan to do—turn us over to the Italians?" Garrett asked.

"I said, Director Whittington suggested I turn *you* over, Mr. Garrett. Not Agent Mayberry. He recommended that she be sent home on the first available flight."

"We aren't especially close, the director and me," Garrett said.

"We also discussed Radi's letter and the threat of a submarine attack with a nuclear bomb."

"Let me guess," Garrett said. "Whittington isn't buying the whole submarine attack scenario."

Mayberry said, "You have sources in Iran. What have they told you?"

"We've always known the Iranians were constructing a nuclear bomb, despite the West's doubts."

"Then why doesn't Whittington believe it?" Mayberry asked.

"Your director looks at Iran and thinks, 'If I were an Iranian leader, would I develop a nuclear weapon?' He analyzes the situation logically, weighing the pros and cons and concluding that it would not be worth the price the Iranians would pay in sanctions or, worse, in a lopsided military confrontation. Whittington doesn't understand that the Iranians are not rational when it comes to Israel."

Big Jules paused for a moment and spoke to one of his security guards. "I'd like some water, and I'm certain Mr. Garrett and Ms. Mayberry are thirsty."

Returning his attention to the Americans, he said, "Your director also doesn't believe Iran has a submarine capable of sailing to your borders. He believes we are exaggerating the threat." He looked at Esther and nodded.

Esther said, "In the Black Sea there is an old Soviet submarine base burrowed into a mountain. One of our operatives was sent there to investigate after we heard rumors of activity at this base. A few days ago, our man was found floating in the sea, supposedly dead from a freak scuba-diving accident. Three naval officials also have reported sighting an old Soviet submarine in the area."

Big Jules said, "I was sending Esther to investigate our man's death and these reports immediately after my niece's wedding, but her schedule is now being changed. I'm sending someone else there."

He removed a slip of paper from his pocket. "Fathi Aziz is claiming credit for my death. When I listened to his rant, I scribbled down his words: 'I will soon deliver a flood over your cities from beneath your oceans, and the wrath of Allah will destroy you.'"

"Could be a submarine attack," Garrett said.

"Do you intend to continue hunting the Roc?" Big Jules asked.

"Absolutely," Garrett replied. "I've got to think the killing of my neighbor, the attempt to kill me, the assassination attempt on you, and all of this talk about a nuclear bomb and submarine are related."

"I agree," Big Jules said. "They are pieces of the same puzzle."

"The Roc and his daughter are our best leads, besides that submarine base," Garrett said.

Big Jules looked at Mayberry and said, "What about you?"

"Maybe we should let you, the Italian authorities, and Interpol do your jobs," she said.

Garrett shook his head. "No offense, Director Levi, but until we got involved, you thought the Roc was dead."

Big Jules ran his tongue across his dry lips. "Ah," he said, "our water has arrived." A housekeeper entered with a tray of glasses and a pitcher. The Mossad director took a long drink while she was serving the others. "Mr. Garrett," he said, putting down his glass, "might I suggest you help us find the Roc and his daughter." He nodded toward Esther. "Esther has agreed to take charge of hunting him down."

"You would be serving strictly as an adviser," Esther said.

Garrett looked at Esther. "You want my advice: catch him, interrogate him, and kill him—and his daughter too." He turned and looked at Mayberry. "I'm in," he said. "What about you?"

TWENTY-ONE

Tahira Bashar had not been harmed by the explosion in Bellagio because she had taken refuge inside a Deutsche Bank office in the Piazza Giuseppe Mazzini. The bank's security camera showed her entering the lobby seconds before she detonated the C-4 inside the Porsche that she'd abandoned less than ten yards away. The bank's fortified glass security door had shielded her and its customers. She'd joined the others in rushing outside. Scooping up a bicycle whose rider was lying dead on the sidewalk, Tahira had pedaled from the piazza onto Via Giuseppe Garibaldi, a street leading out from the city's historic center.

When Tahira reached the Parcheggio Valassina parking lot, she traded the bicycle for a Volkswagen T-Cross.

After the attack on Big Jules, Tahira was supposed to pick up her father in their rented white van. But two strangers had intercepted her before she could reach the van, forcing her to improvise. She was reluctant to drive to the agreed-upon rendezvous point, fearing that she might lead those pursuing her to her father. Nor could she telephone him on her disposable phone. In her rush to escape, she'd left it and her billfold inside the Porsche. She was on her own.

The Roc had told her that if they were separated, she should return to Paris as quickly as possible and wait, but only for forty-eight hours before moving on. They'd already rented a flat in Athens. She sensed her father was still alive. The thought of being alone frightened her.

The shortest route to France was northwest through Switzerland. It was part of the Schengen zone, so there would ordinarily be no passport checks at the Italian, Swiss, and French borders. But because of the shooting and explosion, security at those borders would be tightened, and she had no passport, and no money to bribe her way through.

An hour-and-a-half drive south brought her to Milan, where she ditched the Volkswagen; enough time had lapsed that it might have been reported stolen. As she walked through the city, she tossed the Glock 26 pistol that she still was carrying into a *navigli*, one of the river channels designed by Leonardo da Vinci to divert water from the river Po through Milan. She paused to count the few euros stuffed into her pockets, discovering that she had enough to buy a train ticket to Claviere, a ski resort on the French border. She could walk through the woods and mountains there to the French town of Montgenèvre.

It was a good plan, and at 10:00 p.m. she arrived at the Claviere rail station. It was too dark and too late for her to cross the border through the forest, so she looked for a place to rest. A red neon sign within eyesight of the station glowed: HOSTEL. An older man was smoking a cigarette outside its entrance, leaning against the building's brick wall. He watched her walk past him into the dimly lighted lobby. The room's yellow tile was dirty and needed mopping. The odor of human sweat seemed trapped in the drab walls. She tapped a silver bell at the lobby's unmanned counter.

No one responded. She dinged it again.

Tahira heard the door from the street opening behind her. The man from outside dropped the remains of his cigarette on the floor, smashing it under his black right shoe as he approached her. She noticed he was slightly dragging his left foot.

"You need a room," he said in a bored voice, stepping behind the counter. She couldn't tell if it was a question or statement.

"How much for one night?"

He studied her while she did the same to him. Gray beard needing a trim. In his mid-sixties. Long, oily black hair pulled into a man bun. A cream-colored button-down shirt with a banded collar. He looked like an Arab.

"Thirty-six euros—that's forty US—per night, and I'll need to see your passport to register you."

He coughed the cough of a three-pack-a-day smoker while Tahira pulled out what euros and coins she had left—a pair of five euro notes and less than a euro in change.

"Not enough," he said, watching her.

She stuffed the bills back into her pocket and turned to leave. She'd sleep on a bench at the rail station. But when she was midway across the lobby, he called to her. "It's late, and we have empty beds. I'll take what you have."

She returned and paid him what cash she had. She watched him put the euros in a drawer with other cash.

"Passport?" he said.

She didn't respond.

"I didn't think so," he said. "No luggage either."

"I'll leave, but I want my money back."

"No," he said. "You can sleep in the first room up the stairs. Bathroom in the hall."

She could feel his eyes as she walked toward the staircase.

"Have you eaten?" he called out. "I'd like company."

"I'm not hungry," she said, although she was.

"You should not decline my invitation. If I called the police, there could be trouble. Come sit. I'll get food."

He waved toward a table with four chairs in the lobby's corner before disappearing, and for a moment she considered grabbing the money in the counter drawer and running. But that would've guaranteed a call to the police, so she sat. He returned carrying a tray with a bottle of water, bread, cheese, and hummus.

"You have a name?" he asked, sitting.

"Sarah," she lied as she sat across from him.

"Mine is Farrokh. And it is my real name."

He poured the water into two glasses and gave her a knife to cut the loaf and cheese. "Just passing through?"

"On holiday. Meeting friends tomorrow to ski."

"Without luggage," he noted, skeptically.

"They're bringing it."

"You're what? Maybe twenty. Traveling alone. Without a change of clothes. Do you know sex traffickers look for refugees trying to cross the border into France? They kidnap them. Rape them. Take them to Warsaw to work in sex clubs."

"I can take care of myself," she said.

He lit a cigarette. Let it dangle from his lips. She began eating the bread and cheese while he watched without talking.

"I think I'll go to my room now," she said when she finished. "Thank you for the food and water."

"You've not tried the hummus." He waved his half-spent cigarette in the air. "What's the rush? You have nowhere to go this late. Eat more."

He watched her rip a piece of bread loose and dip it in the hummus.

"I had a daughter who would have been your age," he said. "You remind me of her. More guts than common sense."

"You *had* a daughter?"

"In Zarabad. That is where she and her mother are buried. Have you heard of my village?"

"North of Tehran."

"Yes!" he said approvingly. "Zarabad means 'Built by the Gods.' It is surrounded by cherry orchards, rice fields, and walnut trees, and is very beautiful. But today it has a big cemetery. Do you know why?"

She shook her head.

"The eight-year war with neighboring Iraq. My village lost the most, I think, young and old men."

"Your limp?" she asked, and immediately regretted calling attention to his fault.

"Yes. I fought." He showed no reaction.

"Your daughter and wife? Were they killed during the war?" Despite her better instincts, Tahira couldn't help but feel a kinship with the man. He too had lost his family.

"No. They weren't soldiers. They died from Crimean-Congo hemorrhagic fever. Have you heard of it?"

"No. What is it?"

He stuffed the butt of his cigarette against his plate, using it as an ashtray.

"The doctors called it the most widespread disease of humans in the world. It comes from infected ticks or diseased animal blood and tissues. At least, that's what the American scientists have told the world."

He sounded skeptical.

"You don't believe the Americans?"

"No," he scoffed. "The Americans created this disease. A way to kill us without being blamed. If you look at where the disease is spreading the fastest, it is in Muslim countries."

"I'm sorry that your daughter and wife died," she said. "I'm very tired. I should go to bed."

"You don't believe me? You think me crazy, a crazy old man. During the war with Iraq, Saddam Hussein used nerve gas and mustard gas to kill more than seven thousand Iranian soldiers. Who was his ally? The United States. I will cheer when that nation is destroyed. I hate Americans, including those who come here to sleep."

She pushed back her chair, which caused a squeaking noise on the worn tiles.

"Wait!" he said, more an order than request. He moved behind the counter and returned with an item wrapped in a blue cloth, which he placed between them on the table.

"For you."

She hesitated.

"Take it!"

She reached forward and unwrapped the cloth.

"A nine-millimeter," he said, "but I suspect you know that, don't you? *Sarah*?"

"Why are you showing me this pistol?"

"It's Iranian. Called the Thunderbolt."

He lit another cigarette. Took a long drag and blew the smoke through his cracked lips toward her.

She wrapped the cloth around the handgun and slid it back to him.

"I have no need for a gun."

"Don't be foolish."

He was about to say more, but he began coughing. Violently until he caught his breath.

"I saw the news," he said. "Earlier today people tried to kill the director of the Mossad during a wedding ceremony in Lake Como. One of them was a young woman who escaped in a red sports car. When they trapped her, she detonated a bomb."

"Then she must be dead," Tahira said.

He took another puff. "No. They have bank security camera footage of her, which is being shown on television and on the internet. They are searching for her now." Their eyes met. "The bank photo looks very much like you."

She grabbed the pistol. Dropped its clip from its grip. Checked to see if it had bullets. Reinserted it and pulled back the slide, putting a round into the chamber. She did it quickly and pointed the pistol at him.

He took another long drag without flinching. Unafraid.

"If you hope to scare me, you will not," he said. "After the war, after my family was killed, I became Quds Force despite my leg. Intelligence. Interrogation. Do you know what members of Quds Force live for? One purpose: to die for Iran."

Still holding the pistol, she said, "You didn't die, though, did you?"

"A long story not worth telling." He smashed out his second cigarette in the plate next to the first butt.

"What do you want?" she asked him.

"On the news, they said there were two assassins," he said. "A woman fired at the Jew from an apartment in Bellagio where two people were found dead. Another ambushed the Jew while he was leaving the wedding. That means you have a partner. Will that person be joining you here tonight?"

"I already told you that I'm traveling alone. On holiday. Meeting friends tomorrow to ski."

"Yes, that is what you said. If I wanted to turn you in, I would've called the police and collected a reward. If I wanted to harm you, I would not have given you my gun, would I? I told you that I hate the Americans and the Jews. I intend to help you escape." He lit a third cigarette.

She placed the gun back on the table. "Why do you have an Iranian handgun?" she asked.

"Protection from robbers," he replied.

She let her eyes stray, glancing at the bleak lobby. "Robbers? Here in this hostel, when there are fancy ski resorts in town?"

"I have friends in Tehran," he said. "On television, the Jihad Brigade has taken credit for the attack on the head Jew. Are you a jihadist?"

"I know nothing about this group."

"Israelis never forget. They will hunt you down and kill you, your family and your friends."

"I have no family or friends," she said.

"The news said C-4 was used, drones, sniper equipment, RPGs. You were familiar with my pistol. Checked the clip before cocking it to see if it was loaded. Yet you claim you are not a jihadist. Who trained you? Hamas?"

She did not reply. She was becoming unnerved by his questions.

"Like you," he continued, "I wanted the Mossad director dead. I want Israel removed from the face of the earth. The Israelis would be eaten alive if not for the Americans. So I will help you escape. A car will be here at four in the morning. Two men will take you across the border to wherever you wish in France. They know ways to avoid the authorities. You will not make it on your own if you try to cross through the woods, even with my pistol. The sex traffickers will catch you."

"Why should I trust you, or these two men?"

He shrugged. "Don't trust them. Shoot them. It matters not to me. But you would be wise to accept my help."

"I thought these two were your friends."

"Not friends. They work for me."

"Are they sex traffickers?"

"A woman without credentials and money should not be asking so many questions."

"A woman without credentials and money should be asking many questions," she replied.

He chuckled slightly. "Yes, they are sex traffickers, which is why you can trust them to cross the border without being stopped by the police. But I will make sure they do not molest you. And you will have my pistol."

"Why are you helping me?"

"I already have told you. Americans killed my wife and daughter. They are no different from the Zionists."

He placed both of his palms on the tabletop. Leaned on them to push himself up. "I am old. If you choose not to accept my help, do not come down at four. Either way, now that I have given you my pistol, I must insist you return the kitchen knife that you dropped into your lap after first cutting my bread. Before you began tearing pieces from the loaf."

He held out his hand.

She reached down and retrieved it. She'd not realized that he'd seen her stealing it.

"Good night," she said, taking the pistol with her as she walked up the stairs to her room. "I will return at four for the ride."

He waited fifteen minutes to see if she would return to the lobby to sneak away. When she didn't, he slipped a cell phone from his front pant pocket. The first call was to the two sex traffickers who worked for him.

"Drive her to France. Just be certain I know exactly where she goes."

The second call was to a number in Tehran.

TWENTY-TWO

"I want Garrett arrested the moment he steps on US soil," Connor Whittington declared.

"That might not be possible," Peter Carter, his deputy, replied. "It's a gray area."

"There's got to be some statute against him being a vigilante."

"I checked this morning, and there are currently more than a hundred Americans overseas fighting against ISIS, al-Qaeda, and the Taliban as volunteers. Because the Roc is a known terrorist, Garrett legally falls into that same protected group."

"What are you talking about?" Whittington snapped. "Who in the hell are these people?"

"Mostly ex-military, but some are idealistic young men who've turned their video game joysticks in for the real thing."

"What you're telling me is that any American citizen can buy an airplane ticket and . . . do what? Pick up a gun and fight for a foreign military force?"

"It depends on several factors, but overall, yes," Carter said. "During the Spanish Civil War in the 1930s, our government encouraged Americans to go fight fascists overseas. There was a group of Americans known as the Abraham Lincoln Brigade."

"But Garrett isn't fighting with a brigade. He's a damn vigilante."

"Volunteering to kill terrorists, whether on a battlefield in Syria or chasing one across Europe—as I said, our legal department says it's a gray area and is advising against going after him with any sort of criminal charges," Carter said.

"I don't care what legal says. We need to get the Justice Department to charge him—and fire her."

"Sir," Carter said, "you might want to consider the political downside in going after them. Like them or not, Garrett and Mayberry received presidential medals for stopping a terrorist attack in the US Senate. Their pictures were on magazine covers. They were called American heroes."

"Heroes, ha," Whittington said contemptuously. "Julian Levi called and told me the Mossad made an error. He now is convinced the Roc is very much alive and was responsible for the attempt on his life. That news is just encouraging Garrett and Mayberry. If we don't stop them now, they'll just keep going after the Roc."

"Again, trying to stop them could come back to hurt us politically," Carter said. "The American public loves the idea of the lone vigilante seeking justice. The cowboy who is as ruthless as the land baron who is terrorizing the cowardly townspeople. It's in our DNA. Besides, there may be other ways to force them home without trying to prosecute them and facing public backlash. If that's what you want to do."

"Such as?"

"Thomas Jefferson Kim has been helping them. Our agency has multimillion-dollar contracts with Kim and his company—IEC. Contracts he wouldn't want to lose." Carter continued, "Valerie Mayberry is on leave from the bureau. It has regulations against its agents going rogue. Like you suggested, the bureau could terminate her."

"Kim and Mayberry aren't the ones whom I want to stop. Garrett's the real problem."

"I know Garrett," Carter said. "He's bullheaded. He's not going to stop. Here's a thought. Why not put him on the payroll? Welcome him back. He happens to be very effective as a field operative, and he has a large number of friends working here."

"Including you?" Whittington said in a scornful tone. "It will never happen while I'm director."

"It would be one way for you to better control him."

"Let's deal with the immediate," Whittington said. "I'm briefing the Gang of Eight this morning about the attack on Julian Levi. I'm not comfortable with them asking me about Garrett and Mayberry, and why I didn't respond when they told me about the Roc and Nasya Radi's murder and letter. That's a can of worms."

"Garrett and Mayberry haven't been identified in any foreign press accounts. Yes, you know about them because Director Levi called and told you. He later confirmed that the Roc is alive. But there's a very good chance no one on the Hill knows any of this. Not yet."

Whittington nodded approvingly. "Garrett and Mayberry really aren't my responsibility, are they? Even if word leaks out that I met with them. All I have to say is we're investigating."

An hour after meeting with Carter, Whittington was riding east on Constitution Avenue to the US Capitol, Romanesque federal buildings on his left and Smithsonian Institution museums along the Mall on his right. Although he considered himself tough and independent, he couldn't help but feel alone. CIA employees had correctly seen him as an outsider, someone who had never worked as an intelligence analyst, never handled a human asset, never served in a foreign station or overseen a covert mission. Who was he to clean up their agency? From the start, obstructionists and saboteurs had undercut him. In his darkest moments, he even wondered about his deputy, Peter Carter. During their morning meeting, Carter had suggested rehiring Garrett. Said that Garrett had friends in the agency.

Whittington had expected strong congressional support. After all, he'd served in both the House and Senate before taking the directorship. His fellow members of Congress had liked him. That changed the moment he joined Fitzgerald's administration. Former colleagues turned on him. They didn't trust the CIA, and with good reason. Two commissions—one appointed to investigate why the agency hadn't known about the 9/11 attacks, and a second investigating the false weapons of mass destruction claims in Iraq—had laid a foundation of Capitol Hill skepticism, distrust, and hostility. And then there was the bitter politics—the Republican-versus-Democrat bickering and backstabbing that puts party loyalty before country.

Federal law required the president to keep intelligence committees in both chambers "fully and currently informed." The White House could limit sensitive operations to the Gang of Eight—which comprised the Republican and Democrat leaders in the US Senate and House of Representatives, plus the chairs and ranking members of the Senate Select Committee on Intelligence and its counterpart, the House Permanent Select Committee on Intelligence. But there was no guarantee that classified information would not be leaked to the media. Even presidents couldn't be trusted. Jimmy Carter's team had told the world about advanced stealth technology that made US fighter aircraft nearly invisible simply to prop up falling voter polling numbers. In a city where partisanship triumphed over patriotism, Whittington had come to believe, as CIA director, an adage dating back to Benjamin Franklin: "Three can keep a secret if two of them are dead."

He arrived at the Capitol knowing that a target was on his back, despite the handshakes and smiles.

"Director Whittington, we appreciate you appearing before us this morning," Harriet Katz, the Senate majority leader, announced when Whittington entered the secure windowless basement chamber with burgundy carpet, fluorescent ceiling lights, and walls designed to prevent electronic eavesdropping.

Although he had not been sworn in, Whittington was directed to a witness chair facing the Gang of Eight, who were sitting in elevated seats like courtroom judges. As he twisted in the chair, trying to get comfortable, Whittington suspected that the chair had been intentionally designed to make him fidget. It was wide, armless, and appeared to be well-cushioned, but when he sat, he could feel two lateral support bars jutting into his tailbone. The arch of the chair's back forced him to stick his chest out and hips back to gain any sort of lumbar support. Within minutes, he was hurting, but he had no other choice.

"First," Whittington began, "let me confirm that Julian Levi, while the target of an assassination, was not injured while attending a wedding in Lake Como. There are two suspects, and both remain at large."

He briefly recounted details of the attack. "Thankfully Director Levi was smuggled out of the villa in a wedding caterer's truck and rushed to the airport. He is safely on his way back to Tel Aviv."

"Let's begin with the obvious," Senator Katz said. "Who tried to kill him?"

"Fathi Aziz, a Palestinian terrorist who leads the Jihad Brigade, has taken credit for the attempt. I have spoken to Director Levi, and he has identified the actual perpetrators as an assassin by the name of Saeedi Bashar and his daughter, Tahira Bashar."

"Saeedi Bashar," the veteran senator repeated. "Why does that name sound so familiar? I remember now. He was known as the Roc. I thought we helped the Mossad terminate him with one of our drones."

"You are correct, Senator. We assisted the Israeli government in a drone attack that destroyed a vehicle that the Mossad believed Bashar was riding in. Director Levi now says his agency was mistaken, and the Roc is alive."

"Some of us were not on this committee when that event happened," Representative Ginger Shaklee, the House majority leader, said. "It would be beneficial, Mr. Director, if you would share with us more about this Palestinian assassin."

Whittington opened a folder that he'd brought. "Saeedi Bashar was born in Gaza City in Palestine. His parents returned there after graduating in the 1960s from colleges here in the States. His father, Bijan Bashar, fought in the Six-Day War against Israel in 1967, was wounded, and lost both of his legs. He later became a philosophy professor at the Islamic University of Gaza. His wife taught English in a local school for girls."

Whittington glanced up from her file. Everyone appeared to be listening intently.

"Saeedi Bashar graduated from the Tehran University of Medical Scientists. While a student, he met his wife, Sana, a nursing student. They married and settled in Jabalia in northern Gaza, where he worked at the al-Awda Hospital as an emergency room surgeon."

"A surgeon?" Shaklee interrupted. "This suspected killer was once a surgeon?"

"A very good one, actually," responded Wittington. "Then Jabalia was hit by numerous Israeli air strikes in retaliation for Palestinian rocket attacks. To the best of our knowledge, before these air strikes, Bashar was not politically active. But his wife and his only son were killed when a bomb exploded in their apartment building."

"You mentioned a daughter—Tahira," Shaklee said.

"That's right. His other child. Apparently she was at a relative's during the air strike and was not injured. It appears that after those strikes, Bashar joined Hamas, where he underwent his military training. Although he initially worked as a doctor for Hamas, he began gaining notoriety as a highly skilled marksman. The Mossad lists him as being responsible for the sniper deaths of a dozen Israelis in Hamas border attacks. He was arrested after he was sent to Riyadh to assassinate a royal Saudi family member, but he escaped from prison. He next appeared in a series of videos uploaded on the internet, although his face was blurred out. The videos showed him shooting at Israeli soldiers on patrol in Gaza. In one, he fatally shot three men. The Mossad targeted him after linking him to at least fifteen Israeli fatalities, including one of the army's major generals, in a daring attack."

"'Daring'?" Shaklee asked.

"Yes, he somehow managed to slip through Israeli security and enter the general's well-guarded home. Apparently, the Mossad still doesn't know how he penetrated its security. He tortured the general by surgically removing patches of his skin before puncturing his heart. It was a horrific death."

"Is he still part of Hamas?"

"Before the drone attack, the Israelis reported that he had left Hamas and was operating on his own. A gun for hire, of sorts, as long as the target is someone from the West, primarily Israelis."

"What about his daughter?" Katz asked. "I don't remember any mention of her before."

"We only became aware of her in the last few days. We don't know much, but we assume he has trained her to help him."

Several long minutes later, Whittington's time in the torture chair ended. He was pleased with his performance. No one had mentioned Garrett or Mayberry. There'd been no questions about the murder of Nasya Radi in Arlington, and Whittington had intentionally avoided any mention of it and them.

He was outside the Capitol, about to enter the government car waiting for him, when someone yelled his name.

"Director Whittington! Time for a question?" *Washington Interceptor* investigative reporter Robert Calhoun was hurrying toward him.

The two security officers protecting Whittington immediately stepped between the director and the approaching reporter.

"Brett Garrett and Valerie Mayberry," Calhoun shouted. "Did you send them to Lake Como? Are they working for the agency or the bureau?"

Whittington slipped into the waiting limousine's back seat without answering. Once inside, he cursed.

TWENTY-THREE

4:38 a.m.

The motion detector emitted a quiet beep, waking the Roc in his rented Paris apartment. He'd hidden its monitor in an air vent next to the staircase. He checked the miniature camera that he'd positioned in the hallway. Tahira was approaching the flat's door.

Although he didn't see anyone with her, he still reached for his Heckler & Koch VP70 handgun—a 1970s-era pistol that could fire three continuous rounds with a single trigger pull. Excellent for close-range combat, in case she was being followed.

A full moon cast slivers of light around the edges of the heavy blankets that he'd draped over all the windows. He reached the door before she did and detached a trip wire connected to a US military claymore directional mine.

She rapped on the door. Two times. Then three more. Their signal. He turned the lock.

"Papa," Tahira whispered as she entered the dark room, shutting the door behind her.

"I'm here," he said, switching on a lone bulb. She moved toward him, smiling, bowing her head. He grasped her shoulders with his hands, but they did not embrace. It was as affectionate as he ever had been with her.

"Tell me everything," he said, leading her to the room's table and chairs.

She described being chased by the two strangers, the Porsche explosion, her train ride to Claviere, the hostel clerk who'd arranged for two sex traffickers to bring her undetected into France.

"What was the name of this hostel clerk?" he asked.

"Farrokh. He did not tell me a last name, but he said he was from the Iranian town of Zarabad, where his wife and daughter are buried. He said they were killed by a disease created by the Americans, and he gave me this for my protection."

She showed him a pistol.

"This is Iranian made," he said, "and new. It is polymeric, issued to Islamic Revolutionary Guard intelligence officers."

"He told me he was former Quds Force."

For several moments, the Roc remained silent, pondering what she had just told him.

"The men who brought you to Paris, these sex traffickers, how did they treat you?"

"They never spoke to me. I had them drop me at the Champs-Élysées because I didn't want them to bring me here."

"In the dark, it is easy to be followed," he said. "By someone trained. By former Quds Force."

"I made certain no one followed me."

"We need to leave now," he said.

"Papa, please, I've not slept and I'm hungry."

She did look exhausted. "Two hours," he said. "No more. I'll gather our things and wake you."

5:38 a.m.

"Remember you're here only to observe," Esther whispered.

"We understand," Valerie Mayberry said.

Esther looked at Garrett.

"Yeah, sure," he said, "only as advisers. But tell me, how do you know the Roc and his daughter are hiding here?"

"We have sources."

"Yeah, I'm sure you do, but before you kick in the door of a Paris apartment where a professional killer is hiding, you might want to be a hundred percent certain your sources are telling the truth."

"This address came directly from Director Levi."

"Where'd he get it from?"

"The person who gave it to him."

Garrett, Mayberry, Esther, and four Mossad operatives were moving quietly along the rue Simart, a diagonal street that intersected with the rue Ordener. All eyes were on a corner apartment on the top floor of a building at the intersection of the rue Ordener and the Square de Clignancourt. They crossed the rue Ordener and entered the square, which consisted of parkland surrounded by apartments and businesses.

"RAID? GIGN?" Garrett asked, using the acronyms of France's elite counterterrorism units.

"RAID," Esther replied.

"The gendarmes would have been a better choice than the local police," he said. "I've dealt with both before."

"You're an adviser," she scolded.

"Yes," he retorted, "and I'm advising."

An eighteen-foot-long black van was parked under trees across the square from the targeted apartment. The RAID commander greeted them when they entered but didn't offer his name. His face was hidden behind a black ski mask, which was customary for RAID—*Recherche, Assistance, Intervention, Dissuasion*—operations.

"Each exit is covered, especially on the roof," he said. "Now that you are here, we can proceed."

A map spread out on a table offered a bird's-eye view of the area. Monitors on the wall were linked to body cameras worn by the first squad of eight RAID commandos responsible for capturing the Roc and Tahira.

Each of the newcomers was given an earpiece.

"Allons-y!" they heard the RAID commander say. On the monitors, they watched the squad cross the park and enter the 1860s-era building. Despite modernization, the structure's bones remained largely unchanged. A French bank occupied the street level with apartments on the five floors above it. A single staircase led to them. No elevator. The suspects' apartment was on the sixth floor. When the commandos reached that floor, they paused on the top stair and the squad's leader used a miniature camera at the tip of a flexible extension to peer around the corner into the hallway. The Roc and Tahira were in a unit at the corridor's farthest end on the commandos' right. The RAID team would have to pass by four apartments on each side of the hallway before reaching it. To the left of the staircase were eight apartments, four on each side and a ninth on the end: a mirror image. Using hand signals, four of the commandos stepped into the empty hallway. Two looked left, two right, protecting each other's backs. One commando on each side crouched low. The other stood directly behind him, ready to fire over his shoulder. All four were armed with Beretta M12 submachine guns.

The hallway was now secure, so the commandos on the staircase pressed forward. The lead officer was clutching a sixty-pound blast shield capable of stopping rounds from a Kalashnikov-style assault rifle. Those behind him each held the shoulder of the officer in front of him, doing their best to stay behind the shield. In centipede fashion, they moved quickly down the hallway, arriving at the end unit's door without being challenged.

"They are now ready to breach the door," the RAID commander inside the control center told Esther, Garrett, and Mayberry, all of whom were transfixed on the body-cam images that could be seen clearly on the monitors. All of the commandos except one now squeezed together behind the blast shield. The one who wasn't protected was carrying a tactical battering ram, used to smash through locked doors.

In a well-practiced move, the officer swung back the battering ram and slammed it hard against the apartment door, busting the door from its frame. When it flew backward, it hit the trip wire attached to the claymore. More than seven hundred steel balls exploded into the hallway. The velocity of the deadly projectiles knocked the RAID officer clutching the blast shield off his feet, sending him backward into his fellow team members. Although the commandos were wearing body armor and protective helmets with clear face shields, and were hiding behind the blast shield, the steel pellets ripped into their exposed arms, legs, and necks. All of them collapsed on the hallway floor, either dead or seriously wounded.

The blast was so powerful that even the four officers midway down the corridor, whose job was to keep the hallway clear, were pelted by the flying steel balls.

The claymore at the apartment entrance was not the only booby trap. Identical claymore mines had been placed facing each of the flat's four windows, meant to kill anyone rappelling from the rooftop. Linked to the one at the front doorway, they all exploded, breaking the morning silence and peppering the parked cars below with projectiles and broken glass. Some steel balls flew across the park, striking the command-post van.

Inside it, the RAID commander ripped off his headphones, grabbed a submachine gun, and ran out the doorway across the park to the apartment building. Flames licked from the flat where the Roc and Tahira were believed to be hiding.

Esther removed her headset.

"You coming?" she called, moving toward the van's exit.

Mayberry was right behind her, but Garrett hadn't moved away from the monitors.

"Garrett?" Esther yelled.

"Advisers, remember?" he calmly replied.

They left him alone in the van.

Garrett moved from the body-cam screens to the neighborhood map on the table. The apartment building was connected to its neighbors, creating a giant horseshoe when seen from above.

Garrett returned his attention to what was happening inside the building when the monitors showed the RAID commander with his backup team entering the sixth-floor hallway. Several began dragging the dead and wounded back to the staircase. The commander, backed by three of his commandos, entered the apartment. The sprinkler system had doused most of the flames, creating clouds of gray smoke. They checked the main room.

"Clair! Clair!"

Next was the larger bedroom, where they froze, surprised by what they found. Garrett watched through the body cams. A hole big enough for a man to drop through had been cut into the floor, allowing access to the apartment directly below.

Garrett exited the van and ran across the park away from the apartment building to an opening that led onto the rue Joseph Dijon. By the time he reached that narrow street, he'd drawn his Sig Sauer. To his right was the boulevard Ornano intersection and a couple walking about twenty yards ahead of him, not paying attention to the sirens and speeding emergency vehicles rushing to the apartment building.

He chased after the couple but by the time he reached boulevard Ornano, they were descending into the underground Simplon Metro station. He continued the chase and hurried down its steps but stopped when he reached the bottom of the stairs. A convex mirror mounted on the ceiling showed him what was waiting around the corner: the Roc, armed with his Heckler & Koch VP70 handgun.

Garrett took a deep breath. Steadied himself. He would drop low and fire as soon as he turned the corner. But when he checked the mirror, the Roc had retreated.

Garrett hustled around the corner.

The 1908 underground station was similar to those found in New York City, only cleaner—white ceramic tiles illuminated by buzzing fluorescent ceiling lights, billboard ads posted on the curved walls of the half-moon-shaped chambers. There were two levels, a mezzanine and, underneath it, boarding platforms. Double tracks ran through the station's center. Northbound passengers descended the staircase on the left side of the mezzanine. Southbound customers crossed over a bridge to descend the right-side stairway. Still holding his Sig Sauer, Garrett dashed onto the center of the mezzanine bridge so he could see both platforms.

It was a few minutes after 6:00 a.m. Paris trains had been running for a half hour, and morning commuters were congregated on both sides beneath him. From his mezzanine perch, he scanned the passengers, searching unsuccessfully for the Roc and Tahira.

A horn sounded, warning those waiting on the left platform that a northbound train was arriving at the station.

Anxious, Garrett did another eye sweep. There he was. The Roc had embedded himself in a gaggle of teenage girls dressed in yellow-and-green school uniforms—unknowing human shields on the northbound platform.

Garrett held his pistol close to his leg, making it harder for those hurrying around him to see, as he walked toward the staircase. He kept his eyes on the Roc, who'd noticed him too.

The Roc showed no immediate sense of alarm. If he were clutching a pistol, Garrett thought, surely one of the teenagers milling around him would have screamed. But none was paying attention to the Palestinian assassin.

Commuters pushed against Garrett as they descended the stairs onto the platform, reaching it at the same moment that the arriving northbound train came to a stop. The Roc was now thirty yards away from him, but both men were mobbed by passengers.

The Roc entered a railcar seven down from where Garrett was standing.

Garrett began pushing through the throng of commuters, but he couldn't reach the seventh car before its doors closed. He hesitated, turned slightly, and realized his mistake. Tahira was standing twenty feet behind him. The Roc had been luring him out onto the platform, away from the mezzanine bridge, under which she had been hiding.

She now had a clear shot. He spun to face her, raising his pistol, as the subway train started to move, leaving them alone on the platform.

Tahira was aiming the Iranian-made Thunderbolt pistol. She had the drop on him. He would be her first face-to-face kill. It had always been her father who pulled the trigger, wielded his knife, or set off booby traps. Now she would be responsible for taking another life.

Their eyes met. She hesitated. Garrett had no idea why.

His round tore into her left biceps, shattering the bone. Tahira screamed, but still she didn't discharge the pistol.

His second shot punctured her heart.

Garrett ran to her. No blood was gushing from her chest wound—her heart was no longer pumping. He dropped to his knee. She was dead.

Garrett had never fatally wounded a young woman before. He looked at her tender young face. She was a terrorist. Her gender and age shouldn't have mattered. Yet they did.

Garrett glanced at the subway train's final car as it disappeared up the track.

PART III

If you prick us, do we not bleed? If you tickle us, do we not laugh? If you poison us, do we not die? And if you wrong us, shall we not revenge?

—*William Shakespeare,* The Merchant of Venice, *act 3, scene 1*

TWENTY-FOUR

Commander Boris Petrov piloted the *Golden Fish* into an inlet off the northern African coast—a safe hiding place before attempting to sail unnoticed from the Mediterranean Sea into the Atlantic Ocean.

The assassination attempt on Big Jules Levi and round-the-clock shifts had enabled Petrov to depart from the Cold War submarine base in Balaklava Bay four hours before a Mossad team arrived to investigate suspicious activities there. Nothing remained inside the mountain hideaway except scorched concrete.

The title of commander was self-given, although Petrov had served on submarines in the Russian navy before his career was cut short. Two Russian military police investigators had identified him as the leader of a ring selling stolen military supplies on the black market. Petrov had been jailed in the Black Dolphin prison in Orenburg, home to Russia's "worst of the worst." It was there that he had encountered a cowering Taras Aleksandrovich Zharkov, whose rich father made him easy prey. Petrov had become Zharkov's personal bodyguard for a hefty fee, and after they were released he was the muscle behind Zharkov's business enterprises.

Fighting came naturally to Petrov, who'd been born and reared in West Biryulyovo, an impoverished, crime-ridden Moscow neighborhood boxed in on two sides by rail lines and the third by the Moscow Ring, the major highway that encircled the city. There were no Metro stops in West Biryulyovo; city officials hoped to keep its ninety thousand residents contained. Gangs ruled. Petrov had a long arrest record by his fifteenth birthday. A local tribunal had given him a choice: either join the military or be sent to an adult prison. Enlistee Petrov had been assigned submarine duty because few others wanted it.

With the enthusiasm of a weekend mechanic turning a rusty Lada into a hot rod, Petrov had used Zharkov's unlimited budget to retro-mod the *Golden Fish*. Gone were the submarine's original diesel engines. The Cold War relic's twin propellers had become a single screw. Batteries that rarely could hold a full charge had been replaced with giant lithium-ion ones. Petrov had paid special attention to the old hull. Romeo-class submarines had been based on Nazi Germany designs. Their hulls could take a submarine to three hundred meters before being crushed by pressure. Engineers had redesigned the *Golden Fish* hull, adding another hundred meters to its crush depth.

Petrov had recruited two other experienced submariners who'd served with him. Neither could live comfortably on their paltry military pensions. Dimitri Kozlov was his second-in-command; Yuri Suslov, the submarine's sonar operator. The remainder of the crew were young and inexperienced. As long as they did as told, Petrov didn't care.

He'd taken the *Golden Fish* on three earlier trips to test it and his novice crew. Oxygen levels in submarines are kept low to minimize risk of fires, resulting in crew members who tire easily and often become irritable. Despite Petrov's improved designs, the recirculated air smelled of diesel gas, cooking, hydraulic fluid, human sweat, cigarette smoke, and sewage. There was no need for torpedoes, so that space had been expanded for Petrov and his two officers. All others "hot racked"—climbing into a bunk after a six-hour shift while their replacement was crawling out.

The submarine's fore contained one and a half decks. The upper housed living accommodations and a galley. Beneath, the lower level was home to batteries and fuel tanks. The aft was a single deck that contained the diesels and propulsion machinery. The boat's conning tower rose slightly back from the submarine's midsection. Directly under it was the control room, with its periscopes, radar, and communication gear.

On each of the *Golden Fish*'s test voyages, Petrov had pushed the submarine to twenty knots submerged. His cutting-edge sonar identified other ships, including the Israeli submarine *Drakon*, long before they spotted him. When they did, he'd taken advantage of the submarine's Russian "black hole" technology. It was what had enabled him to slip unnoticed through the closely watched straits connecting the Black Sea to the Mediterranean.

There had been one problem during the test runs. Keeping the diesel engines running for hours had caused the engine room temperatures to soar past a hundred degrees, and that heat had quickly spread throughout the sub. As they dove to three hundred feet, water droplets began dripping from the walls, and the *Golden Fish*'s compressed metal skin made a groaning sound. The fear of water bursting in, making the submarine into a submerged coffin, had caused a crew member to panic, becoming unhinged.

Petrov had ordered the terrified crew member brought to him, and beaten him unconscious with his bare hands.

"On my boat, every man must do his duty," he'd declared. "One weak man will bring us all death."

Now lingering near the lip of the Strait of Gibraltar, Petrov was about to face another challenge. NATO and US forces closely monitored traffic through the Strait, searching especially for Russian submarines.

Petrov had studied the two traditional methods for tracking submarines. The first was visual. A submarine normally had to dive to three to four hundred feet, where the sunlight dissipated, to avoid being spotted from aircraft.

The second tracking method was acoustical. The *Golden Fish* would have to evade not only sonar but also echo sounding and IFF (identification friend or foe) technology as it passed through the Strait's narrowest section, a 7.7-nautical-mile-wide strip between Spain and Morocco.

It was nearly dusk when Petrov's sonar operator identified the HMS *Aware*, a nuclear-powered Royal Navy submarine approaching the Strait, bound for the Atlantic.

"Its speed?" Petrov asked.

"Twenty-five knots," Yuri Suslov replied.

Petrov navigated the *Golden Fish* from its hiding spot in the inlet and chose a course aimed at the British submarine's midsection. Petrov's intent was to pass directly beneath it.

"Now we'll see how invisible we are," he declared.

Second-in-Command Dimitri Kozlov ordered silent running. Electric power was quieter than nuclear. All but essential crew were restricted to their bunks, toilet doors and their lids taped to avoid slamming, the galley sealed tight.

As they approached the Brits, Petrov used hand signals to issue commands. The HMS *Aware* was two hundred fifty meters from the surface. Petrov dropped the *Golden Fish* to its limit, four hundred meters.

The sensors on the British submarine should have been sounding an alarm as the *Golden Fish* neared. His face drenched in sweat, Petrov stayed on course. Afraid to move, speak, sneeze, or cough, his crew stood frozen like department store mannequins.

They were now near enough to hear the sound of the Rolls-Royce nuclear reactor as the 318-foot-long HMS *Aware* continued west into the nine-mile strait.

The *Golden Fish* continued northward.

It happened. The rogue submarine sailed underneath the midsection of the HMS *Aware* undetected. Nothing. No reaction. No alarms.

Petrov resisted his urge to celebrate. Instead, he turned the *Golden Fish* away from the Strait. He returned later that same day, and seventy-five minutes after entering the Strait, the *Golden Fish* emerged with its nuclear bomb in the Atlantic Ocean, on a course for the United States.

TWENTY-FIVE

"Your first time inside our headquarters?" Connor Whittington asked.

"No, but I've never gotten farther than the lobby," Robert Calhoun replied. "But I assume you already know that from your records."

"What brought you to our lobby?"

"The Memorial Wall. A story about it. One of the best-read pieces I've written. Got more than a million hits, and thousands of shares too. What are there now? A hundred and ten stars on the wall?"

"Sadly, we've just added more than a dozen," Whittington replied.

"Oh yeah, one of them was an employee who killed herself, and people got upset about putting her on a wall with those who'd died heroes."

A waiter entered the CIA director's private dining room and offered menus from white-gloved fingers.

"Most days I eat a sandwich at my desk," Whittington said, "but I wanted to carve out time to meet with you. Thank you for agreeing to do this completely off the record."

"I won't tell anyone what you're ordering for lunch," Calhoun joked.

Whittington didn't find the comment especially clever, but he smiled just the same. "Have you eaten in the Senate dining room?" he asked. "On most Thursdays it serves meals from individual states. Last week, it was Iowa, and they sold out of chicken potpies."

"So that's what they eat in Iowa?"

"I had to choose the less popular glazed bacon and scallop salad with shiitake mushrooms and plum tomatoes."

"And what did the senator you met there have?"

"I'd rather not say," Whittington said. "But I will tell you the bacon was from an Iowa hog, and the scallops were not."

Calhoun was enjoying this tête-à-tête. The trick to getting information was befriending sources, getting them to relax. Calhoun liked to share a few personal stories, often embarrassing. That way, his sources let their guards down and forgot that he might skewer them on the next day's front page. "Are you a cat or dog person?" he asked.

"I didn't invite you here to discuss pets." Director Whittington was not a novice when it came to reporters. If anyone was going to manipulate this relationship, it would be him. He'd ordered a backgrounder. Robert Calhoun: Born in Topeka. Father a local judge. Mother a homemaker. Graduated from the William Allen White School of Journalism. Kansas University. First job at White's famous newspaper—the *Emporia Gazette*—before the website POUNCE— more *National Enquirer* than hard news—lured him to Washington. Switched to *Washington Interceptor* two years ago. Paper had a far-left slant. Thirty-three. Divorced. Workaholic.

The director ordered a Cobb salad. He was watching his weight, trying to combat endless meetings and little time for exercise. Calhoun ordered grilled beef medallions with shiitake sauce atop a bed of creamy polenta.

"I don't believe as director that I've invited a reporter to lunch," Whittington said. "When I was on Capitol Hill, I dealt with lots of you, but not here. What's the *Washington Interceptor*'s circulation now, around six hundred thousand?" He'd checked before meeting him.

"That's our print run. Twice that many online. We're producing podcasts now, and I constantly tweet."

"You ambushed me when I was leaving the Hill the other day," Whittington said. "That's a specialty of yours, isn't it?"

"The people have a right to know. It's my job to get answers for them."

"I assumed you simply wanted to sell newspapers. Get your name on the front page. You've published some real trash." Whittington was purposely insulting Calhoun, curious when he would buckle.

"I guess we all rationalize what we do at times, don't we? Spying on others, recruiting traitors, undermining foreign regimes, lying. Yet in the lobby—what's the quote? 'And ye shall know the truth and the truth shall make you free.'"

Whittington spread a linen napkin across his lap. "You asked if I sent Brett Garrett and Valerie Mayberry to Italy. You planning on writing about them?"

"Still digging. We don't really have much of a foreign staff anymore. No one based in Italy, so I've been working the phones and doing interviews by email. I got the Bellagio cops to confirm that two Americans were involved in a high-speed chase and handed over to the Mossad after that failed attempt to kill Julian Levi."

"What makes you believe those two Americans were Garrett and Mayberry?"

"I know they met with you recently here at the agency."

Whittington hid his irritation. He had a leak. "You were pretending you already knew, hoping I would confirm Garrett and Mayberry were involved."

Calhoun took a sip of the Diet Coke he'd ordered. The ice clinked against the side of the glass. Whittington recalled a time in Washington when having a cocktail at lunch was expected. Not now. "Mr. Calhoun," he said, "who told you that Garrett and Mayberry met with me?"

The reporter had a ready reply. "Sir, if I revealed my sources to you, then you'd know I couldn't be trusted to keep our lunch conversation a secret."

Their white-gloved server arrived with entrées served on china plates emblazoned with the CIA seal. He refilled Whittington's iced tea and Calhoun's soda. They waited until he'd gone to continue their conversation.

"How trustworthy are you really, Mr. Calhoun? You promised our talk today would be off the record, but based on my experiences on the Hill, that can mean different things to different reporters."

"You're right. Sometimes politicians get confused. Off the record means I won't use anything you tell me, but if you tell me something I already know, or I might hear later from a different source, then I'm free to use it, I just won't attribute it to you."

"This later source," Whittington said, "now will he or she be real or imagined? You see, Mr. Calhoun, I know a bit about how you reporters operate. I tell you something today, and later I get a call from you, saying someone else told you the same information. But you can't say who told you because it's a confidential source. When in fact you're lying and simply looking for a way to put in print what I told you."

"That's not how I operate," Calhoun said. "I must say you have a rather dim view of reporters."

"I have a realistic one, born from experience in this city. I can't stop you from publishing what I tell you under the pretense you've heard it from someone else. But if you want to have a long-term relationship with me, you will not play games."

"Why'd you invite me here if you don't trust me?"

"There are few people I trust," Whittington said. "I read your story about Brett Garrett and how he was suspected of murdering Andre Gromyko in Guinea-Bissau. You also implied he might have been involved in the killing of an Iranian who lived in a condo on the same floor as him."

"Actually, my story didn't say they lived on the same floor," Calhoun said. "Obviously you know about Nasya Radi's death."

"I'd like to forge a relationship with you, Mr. Calhoun," Director Whittington said. "On two conditions."

Calhoun, who'd been busy cutting his beef tenderloin, put down his knife and fork. "What sort of conditions?"

"You can never reveal publicly that I am a source. Ever. You want me to be your Deep Throat, you need to make certain my name remains secret. Even if I die before you. No one can ever know we talked."

Calhoun nodded.

"It will take more than a nod. Let me be perfectly clear. If you ever reveal I provided information, I will not only deny it, I will do everything I can to ruin you personally and professionally."

"What's the other condition?"

"I'll help you focus your stories."

"You want to edit me."

"Don't act as if that never happens. You and I both know your sources all have a reason for talking to you. All I am asking is that you write your story using my information the way I intended. In return, you get a backdoor channel. With my help, you'll be the next Bob Woodward and win a Watergate Pulitzer."

"Not to split hairs, but Bob Woodward never won a Pulitzer for Watergate. The newspaper got it." Calhoun picked up his utensils. Tasted a cut medallion. Gave the illusion that he was weighing his decision. Posturing. "I'd want to have twenty-four-hour access and your private cell."

"I can agree to that."

Calhoun pushed his plate aside. "Did you send Garrett and Mayberry to Italy?"

"I'll get around to them, but first let me explain how they are part of a bigger problem. Are you familiar with HUMINT?"

"Human intelligence—spy-versus-spy stuff."

"That's right. I intend to move this agency away from depending on HUMINT, with a bigger emphasis on technological intelligence gathering and artificial intelligence analytics. We can intercept cellular calls almost anywhere in the world. Our satellites are capable of showing us every square inch on this planet. I can tell you how many hairs on his head Russian president Kalugin lost last week. Technology is the future of modern intelligence, Mr. Calhoun. Imagine our ability to anticipate our enemies' next moves by using predictive analytics."

"Sounds intriguing."

"Yes, it is. Unfortunately, the White House, Congress, and the public are enamored with *Tinker, Tailor, Soldier, Spy*. George Smiley. John le Carré. That's old thinking. Human intelligence is often wrong and can't be trusted. It's biased. To be blunt, our country doesn't need the Brett Garretts and Valerie Mayberrys of the world running around trying to catch terrorists. Not with our superior technology."

"So it was Garrett and Mayberry in Italy, right?"

"The most effective way for me to shift this agency away from HUMINT is by showing the public how dangerous these James Bond antics are. Which brings me to Brett Garrett. You've already raised questions about his possible role in two murders."

"You want me to write a story critical of Garrett and Mayberry?"

"A story? Do you remember President Gerald Ford?"

"I have read about him and I know he pardoned Richard Nixon and was a klutz."

"Klutz. Why do you know that?"

"I remember something about him falling down the steps of Air Force One. Hitting a spectator in the head when he was playing golf. Jokes about how he'd played football without his helmet."

"Exactly. Chevy Chase mimicking him on *Saturday Night Live* so much in Washington everyone said Ford's vice president was just a banana peel away from succeeding him as president. That image didn't come from one story. It came from a barrage of unfavorable press. I want you to use Garrett to destroy the entire James Bond mythology."

"Why do I feel this might be more personal than about agency priorities?" Calhoun asked.

"Does that matter? You want access. I'll give it, but I want you to be relentless and ruthless in investigating and exposing Garrett's every flaw, his every failed move—Mayberry too, if she sticks with him. I want you to destroy his reputation."

"Mind if I take a few notes?" Calhoun reached for a notebook inside his jacket pocket.

"That won't be necessary. You won't have a problem remembering what I tell you."

TWENTY-SIX

The Roc saw his daughter collapse on the subway's northbound platform, shot twice. When the northbound train reached the next stop, he crossed over the tracks and caught a car back to the Simplon station, arriving about fifteen minutes later.

The northbound platform was swarming with police and EMTs. Most were clustered around Tahira's body, which had been covered. His daughter was dead. He didn't see the man who'd fatally shot her.

It was pointless for him to get off the subway. He continued riding south and eventually found his way to the French town of Chartres, about sixty miles southwest of Paris, where he checked into a mom-and-pop hotel called Le Parvis, near the famous cathedral of Notre-Dame de Chartres. Once in his room, he released his anguish, biting into a towel to muffle his screams.

He'd known this was possible, but somehow he'd never believed it would happen. He did not blame himself. He blamed the man who had pulled the trigger and ended his daughter's life. If there had been any mistake on his part, it was tenderness. He should have insisted they flee Paris the moment she returned to their flat. Instead, he'd let her eat and sleep. As the hatred boiling inside him intensified, so did his hunger for revenge. The French RAID unit had known exactly where he and Tahira had been hiding. How? He'd been sure to hide his tracks when he left Lake Como. Someone had followed his daughter.

He tried to sleep, but couldn't. He arose while the morning was still dark and stood half naked in front of his room's bathroom mirror. Before checking into the hotel, he had stopped to buy a gym bag and fill it with clothing, toiletries, a digital voice recorder, and other needed items. Among them was a sharp pair of scissors, which he used to cut his hair and beard before going over his skin with a razor. His bare flesh glistened under the water he splashed over himself to remove any leftover bits. Next, he shaved off his eyebrows before again checking his reflection, turning slightly so he could better see the jagged scar that ran from his ear to his neck. A forever reminder of his torture by the Saudis. His disguise was in plain sight. Bald and missing his eyebrows, he resembled a cancer patient undergoing chemo. His scar subtly reinforced the impression of an ill patient. The image staring back at him from the mirror looked nothing like the guest who had checked into the hotel. Still, he left through a window to avoid passing its front desk clerk.

He would retrace his daughter's steps after she fled Bellagio. It was a six-and-a-half-hour train ride from Chartres to the Italian Oulx train depot, with a connection to the Claviere ski resort. Exhaustion set in midway during his trip, and he slept for three hours before the sun woke him, magnified through the railcar's window so that it burned his freshly shaved cheeks.

For a moment he'd forgotten Tahira's death, and he looked at the empty seat next to him, fully expecting her to be there. Now fully awake, his sorrow and bitterness again surfaced. He tugged on a vest over his long-sleeve shirt, successfully hiding his Heckler & Koch VP70 handgun. It was the only weapon he'd grabbed when fleeing their Paris flat. His thoughts returned to those final desperate moments. The motion detector hidden in the staircase had alerted him that the RAID team was coming for them. He'd awoken Tahira and led her to an escape hole that he'd created in the apartment's floor. He'd purposely flooded the unit below on the day he returned from Italy, causing its occupants to flee temporarily, giving him time to create an escape route. The morning of the RAID assault, neither Tahira nor he had panicked. It wasn't until he'd spotted a stranger following them near the subway that he had become concerned.

His thoughts were interrupted by a middle-aged woman in a business suit who claimed the empty aisle seat next to him. He usually preferred the aisle—better maneuverability—but sitting next to the window helped shield him from the prying eyes of passengers walking up and down the passageway.

His seatmate began reading a copy of the *International Herald Tribune*. He could see the front-page headline: SIX PARIS POLICE OFFICERS DIE TRYING TO CAPTURE FATHER-DAUGHTER TERRORISTS. A photo of him from when the Saudis had imprisoned and beaten him was displayed next to the article. A second photo showed Tahira's body at the subway station, taken by someone with a camera phone, before first responders had arrived.

"Voulez-vous lire mon journal?" the woman asked.

"Vous êtes trop gentille," he replied.

She handed him the newspaper's first section. He scanned the first several paragraphs before turning to an inside page to finish. Next to the main story was a sidebar and two additional photos. This sidebar was from the *Washington Interceptor*, written by a reporter named Robert Calhoun.

AMERICANS GO HOME:
Former American Heroes in Deadly Encounters Anger Police

Washington, D.C.—The *Interceptor* has learned that two Presidential Medal of Freedom recipients interfered with law enforcement officers in Italy and France who were pursuing a team of vicious murderers—Saeedi Bashar and Tahira Bashar, both Palestinian terrorists. Because of the American duo's recklessness, innocent civilians have been killed.

Former Navy SEAL Brett Garrett and FBI agent Valerie
Mayberry were not authorized by the US government to pursue
the father-and-daughter killers.

"They are acting as vigilantes, and foreign law enforcement
agencies are furious and want them gone," one highly placed
government source told me.

Based on confidential sources, I've been able to track Garrett
and Mayberry and document their frightening antics.

Days ago, they engaged in a high-speed car chase through
crowded streets in Bellagio, Italy, in an attempt to capture
Tahira Bashar. She and her father had attempted to assassinate
Julian "Big Jules" Levi, director of Israel's Mossad, while he was
attending his niece's Lake Como wedding.

The reckless Americans' unauthorized pursuit ended when
Tahira Bashar bolted from her vehicle in the heart of the historic
city and detonated C-4, a powerful explosive. More than a dozen
bystanders were killed, and nineteen suffered major wounds.
Most were tourists, many enjoying the day at sidewalk cafés. The
explosion caused significant damage to the Bellagio's historic
Hotel Metropole.

Italian law enforcement officials were in the process of sealing
off major roads to prevent the would-be assassins' escape,
but Garrett and Mayberry took it upon themselves to chase
Tahira Bashar, an incredibly dangerous move that resulted in
unnecessary deaths and resulted in Tahira Bashar successfully
escaping.

Blood on Their Hands

"If these two Americans would have gotten out of our way and
let us do our jobs," one incensed police official told me, "we
would have caught the terrorists without deaths and injuries to
tourists and residents. Blood is on their hands!"

Rather than complying with Italian officials' multiple requests for them to return to the United States, Garrett and Mayberry appeared in Paris two days later when one of France's highly trained antiterrorist squads was about to surprise the Bashars while they were asleep in a Paris flat.

Unbeknownst to French officials, the Bashars were tipped off. They escaped after detonating booby traps that killed six French police officers and critically wounded two others.

When asked if Garrett and Mayberry were directly or indirectly responsible for alerting the terrorists, a highly placed French source said, "The assassins knew our team was coming to arrest them—that's all I will say."

Refused to Help Wounded Officers

Garrett refused to assist French RAID commandos rescuing their fallen comrades outside the booby-trapped apartment. By chance, he spotted the Bashars fleeing the area, but instead of alerting French authorities, he chased both of them into an underground subway station mobbed with morning rush-hour commuters. Garrett caused a panic when he began firing through the crowds. Fortunately, no one except Tahira Bashar was fatally wounded. Her father escaped.

"This American should have told us," a French police officer complained. "His Wild West actions put French lives in grave danger, including innocent schoolchildren. We are trained to do our missions with minimum civilian casualties—something Garrett ignored."

Said another highly placed French source, "These two glory seekers are no longer welcome here. They need to go back to the United States and stop getting in our way before others are killed because of them."

The State Department issued a statement that said neither Garrett nor Mayberry is acting on behalf of the US government. An FBI source said Mayberry was on vacation. In an unusual move, CIA director Connor Whittington issued a statement that said Garrett was not employed by the CIA or any other intelligence agency.

A top CIA aide, speaking off the record, commented: "Brett Garrett is violent, dangerous, and out of control. He should give back his presidential medal. He no longer deserves to be called an American hero."

The Roc finished the article and lowered the newspaper. He had a name and photo: Brett Garrett. The man who killed Tahira.

The French businesswoman sitting beside him gathered her belongings as the train neared a station. He offered the newspaper back to her.

"Non, non," she said, waving it away as she stepped into the aisle.

"Je vous remercie," he replied.

After she had gone, he tore out the photos of Garrett and Mayberry and put them into his gym bag.

It was midafternoon when he reached Claviere. As he stepped from the train, the thought occurred to him that Tahira had come to this same station four days earlier from Bellagio. The hostel was easy to spot, but he didn't go directly there. He would wait until nightfall.

When it was dark, he entered the hostel's lobby and thought again of Tahira as he walked across its dirty tile floor, approaching a night clerk behind a counter. The older man was smoking a cigarette and reading *Oggi*, one of Italy's most popular newsmagazines.

"Are you Farrokh?" the Roc asked.

The man looked up suspiciously from the magazine at the stranger before him. Hard men recognize other hard men. It's a survival skill learned on mean streets and in jails and prisons—an ability to sense whether the man you are facing is a coward hiding behind bluster or a genuine threat. When a hard man senses danger, rote memories kick in. One foot falls back for leverage. One shoulder drops. Ready to lunge. Ready to throw the first punch.

The Roc spotted the clerk's tells.

"Farrokh is not here," the clerk replied. He opened a drawer under the counter on the pretense of putting his magazine away. It was where he usually kept his pistol. In that moment, he realized he'd given his handgun to the young woman who was fleeing the police. He owned a second gun, but it was in his bedroom nightstand.

"Maybe you can tell me where he has gone," the Roc said. "Does he live close?"

The clerk shrugged. "I don't know, and unfortunately we're out of rooms for the night."

"You look Iranian. Perhaps from Zarabad."

"No, I'm from Jordan. The resorts around here are probably sold out too. You'd do better to catch the return train to Oulx. It leaves in less than an hour."

"You have no idea where Farrokh might be?"

"None. You see, I only recently started working here, and I do not know him well."

The Roc noticed the ashtray on the counter, stuffed with butts.

"How about a cigarette?" he asked. "I'm out."

"Yes, of course," the clerk said. "But I have smoked my pack and need to get a fresh one in my bedroom. Wait, and I will bring you one."

The clerk turned. Began to walk away. Dragging his left foot.

Tahira had said Farrokh limped. A war injury. The Iraq/Iran war. Quds Force.

The clerk opened a door behind him, the door to his bedroom, a former storage closet with no windows. He half shut the door and went directly to the nightstand where he kept his pistol. But before he reached it, a knife blade pressed against his neck.

"Farrokh," the Roc whispered.

"What do you want?" Farrokh asked.

The Roc had his left arm wrapped around Farrokh's chest, his blade pressed against Farrokh's carotid artery. He pulled Farrokh tighter, his chest pushing against Farrokh's back. Too close for Farrokh to break away without having his neck slashed.

"Unhook your belt," the Roc ordered.

Farrokh unbuckled it, slid it from the loops.

"Your hands. Behind your back."

In a swift motion, the Roc looped the belt around Farrokh's wrists, locked it in place, and pushed Farrokh onto his knees. Still pressing his blade against Farrokh's neck, he retrieved the miniature digital recorder that he'd purchased to record their conversation.

"How did the French know where my daughter and I were in Paris?"

"I don't know."

The Roc sliced Farrokh's neck, but only enough to draw a trickle of blood, red intermingling with Farrokh's sweat.

"You had two sex traffickers bring my daughter to Paris. They followed her and told you our address." He dug his knife deeper into Farrokh's neck, inflicting more pain, drawing more blood.

"I didn't tell the French. I hate Jews, just like you. I was trying to help your daughter."

"Who did you tell?"

"Tehran," Farrokh whispered. "A nephew in Quds Force. I thought the Iranians would want to help you."

"His name?"

"The call was transferred to a general."

"Which one?"

"Kardar."

"What did you tell him? Be exact if you want to live."

"I said you were in a flat on the rue Ordener."

"You didn't really believe General Kardar would help us. You called Tehran because you wanted a reward. You sold us for money."

"He said he'd pay me, but he said he'd help you both escape from Paris. You must believe me. I gave your daughter a pistol."

Both heard the hostel door opening. The ding of the counter

bell. The Roc checked the monitor next to the bed. A lobby camera showed a deliveryman waiting with a package.

"Do not move or speak," he ordered.

He grabbed the second handgun from the nightstand. Tucked it into his waistband next to his own pistol. Looked again at the monitor.

"Do you know this deliveryman?"

"No."

"You expecting a package?"

"No."

"Your guests?"

"We don't accept packages for them."

The deliveryman tapped the bell again. Called out: "Ciao! Bonjour! Hello!"

"I'm coming," the Roc answered in English. He again put his knife under Farrokh's chin, and for a moment Farrokh believed his throat would be slit.

"Where's the key to this bedroom?"

"The nightstand."

The Roc took the key, put away his knife, and stepped calmly from the bedroom, shutting its door behind him. Because it was a former storeroom, it could be bolted from outside. Using the key, he locked Farrokh inside.

"Package for Farrokh Zimar," the deliveryman said.

"He just stepped out," the Roc said.

The deliveryman seemed confused. "I was told he was working here tonight."

"He's having dinner nearby. But I'll accept this for him."

The Roc picked up the shoebox-size package on the counter between them. Felt its heft.

"I'm not certain I can leave it," the deliveryman said. "It's a personal package."

"Aren't all packages personal?"

The Roc looked at his wristwatch. "He'll be back in twenty minutes. You can wait in the lobby if you would like." He nodded toward the worn furniture.

The deliveryman reached for the package, but the Roc pulled it back. "Farrokh would be furious with me if I didn't hold this for him. You can come back in twenty minutes for his signature—if you need it."

The deliveryman let out a sigh. "You will keep it here at the front desk and give it only to him?"

The Roc bent, placed the package on the floor. "It will be safe right here for when he returns."

The deliveryman turned and walked toward the door.

The Roc saw his loafers. Ferragamo.

As soon as he exited, the Roc dimmed the lobby lights and walked to the hostel's front windows. The deliveryman was walking south toward a black Mercedes E-Class. He opened the sedan's back door, illuminating its interior. Two men were in the front seat, watching the hostel.

The Roc found the hostel's alleyway exit. Five minutes later he was approaching the Mercedes from behind on the deserted street. He drew both handguns from his waistband. Ten feet away, he began to run forward, raising both.

The Mercedes' windows were open because its passengers were smoking cigarettes. An irony. Iran, the biggest cigarette manufacturer in the Middle East, yet the aroma the Roc recognized was Marlboro's international brand.

No one in the luxury car noticed him until he reached it. The Roc fired Farrokh's nine-millimeter at the deliveryman in the back seat, simultaneously firing his H & K VP70 pistol with his other hand at the front-seat occupants. Emptied both clips. More than twenty rounds. Enough to kill all three.

The Roc opened the front passenger door, checked the dead man closest him for identification. A diplomatic Iranian passport. In his wallet a military ID.

A remote detonator was resting on the console between the driver and passenger. The Roc tossed Farrokh's pistol on the floorboard and took the device with him.

As he walked to the train station, he pressed the remote's trigger.

The deliveryman's package inside the hostel exploded, blowing out the hostel's front windows and shooting a giant fireball out into the street. The entire building was in flames. Within moments, the Roc could hear the approaching sirens. Police. Fire. By the time the first responders arrived, he was boarding the final train to Oulx.

There was only one logical explanation. His daughter had unknowingly led her sex trafficker escorts to the Paris flat. Farrokh had called General Kardar, seeking a reward for the location, and Kardar had notified either the French authorities or the Mossad. Now the general was tying up loose ends. Covering his tracks. Getting rid of witnesses. As the Roc rode in silence, he decided that there were two men responsible for Tahira's death. General Kardar, and the American named Brett Garrett. He would find and kill them both.

TWENTY-SEVEN

The *Golden Fish* burst through the ocean's surface into the night-time darkness twenty-two miles west of the Azores archipelago, midway between North America and Europe. The Atlantic waters were calm as Commander Petrov stood on the submarine's conning tower, lighting a smoke. Except for the glow from the cigarette tip, Petrov was enveloped in darkness, on a black sea invisible in a starless night. A spray of water wetted his cheeks. The salt burned his dry lips. Petrov preferred the sea's vacant vastness. Prison had cured him of the need for social connection. He relaxed long enough to finish his cigarette before tossing its filter into the ocean and going below for his scheduled call with Zharkov.

"We should arrive at the rendezvous point in thirty-six hours," Petrov reported. "Is the cargo ship on schedule?"

"Yes," Zharkov replied. "It will meet you."

"The next time we talk will be after I position the *Golden Fish* at its final resting point." Petrov disconnected and ordered Dimitri Kozlov, his second-in-command, to dive back into the vast ocean's depths.

At that same moment in London, Zharkov exited the safe room hidden behind bookshelves in his master bedroom and proceeded through his mansion to where the Iranian general Kardar was waiting.

"Ah, General. I apologize for this unavoidable delay."

"I need to return to Tehran tonight."

"And you will, but first a celebration. My wife has arranged a special dinner for us. Then we'll finalize our business."

"This trip comes at an inconvenient time," Kardar complained.

"My friend, even I do not risk insulting my wife."

Zharkov led him through the mansion's expansive main dining hall, capable of seating sixteen guests, to a more intimate side chamber. It took Kardar a moment for his eyes to adjust to the brightness of the all-white room. Five thousand shimmering fiber-optic cables dropped from a white ceiling along the room's shiny white walls. The polished white marble table was arranged with white Hermès china and Puiforcat silverware. Glasses were Saint-Louis crystal.

Zharkov motioned toward a seat. Kardar adjusted his pistol as he sat in the cushioned chair. A few minutes later, Britt Bjorge-Zharkov entered, wearing a Carolina Herrera tie-sleeve, sparkle-embroidered trench gown in robin's-egg blue. She was two decades younger than her husband, a former Norwegian model turned secretary turned billionaire's wife. Blond shoulder-length hair. Lithe movements. Fluent in four languages.

Zharkov stood to pull back her chair. Kardar reluctantly rose.

"When my husband told me of your visit, I asked our chefs what would be an appropriate dish for a gentleman of your military authority," Bjorge-Zharkov said in her soft voice. "They provided me with a list of Iranian delicacies to choose from, and since I had no idea which you might prefer, I told them to prepare everything."

She laughed and tapped the screen on her always-present iPad, summoning a chef and three servers.

"For your enjoyment tonight," the chef said, "we have beef, chicken, and lamb liver kebabs. Smoked fish, falafel, and noodles. We will begin with hot and sour shrimp, and for dessert, we have caviar, rosewater-scented ice cream, and grilled lamb's testicles."

"Bring me a vodka," Zharkov snorted. "If my wife forces me to eat grilled lamb's testicles, I'll need several."

"Will the Oval Swarovski Crystal be your choice tonight, sir?" one of the servers asked.

"An excellent suggestion. Our guest doesn't drink, so water for him."

"With or without gas?" the server asked Kardar.

"With."

"Bring me a carafe of d'Auvenay Chevalier," Bjorge-Zharkov said.

For the next forty minutes the three exchanged pleasantries, until Bjorge-Zharkov announced it was time for her to leave. "I never ask my husband anything about his business affairs."

"This meal was wonderful," Kardar said, rising from his chair, "but not as pleasant as sharing time with you. May I compliment you on your beauty."

"You are displaying your Middle Eastern charm," she replied, smiling.

Zharkov watched from his chair without comment, slightly amused. He knew that Kardar was a vicious sadist, with a penchant for torturing poor young girls, whose corpses he dumped on Tehran's backstreets. He took no offense at the general's flirting with his wife, quietly finding it humorous that she had no clue about the depravity of the man whom she had so graciously entertained.

When they were alone, Kardar said, "My plane is waiting to return me to Tehran. I came for my finder's fee and for the detonation code to share with Fathi Aziz, not to socialize."

"Send your plane home," Zharkov replied. "One of my pilots can get you to Tehran in my fastest jet. Nothing is more important than what I'm about to show you."

With his ever-present drink in one hand, Zharkov led his guest to the mansion's second-floor office, where the Russian walked to a boardroom table and spread out a large map of the North Atlantic Ocean.

"In addition to my excellence in math and consuming large

quantities of vodka," the oligarch boasted, "I'm accomplished in geography and topography. Are you familiar with the Sargasso Sea?"

"You will recall I am not a sailor," Kardar said.

"This sea is the most unique body of water in the world because it is a sea inside an ocean, with no land boundaries."

He pointed at the map with his right index finger. "On its west is the Gulf Stream, flowing along the American coast. The North Atlantic Current runs along its north side, the Canary Current provides its eastern border, and the North Equatorial Current is its southern border. A sea surrounded by ocean currents."

Kardar checked his watch.

"Am I boring you?" Zharkov asked.

Kardar lowered his wrist.

"All four currents hold this sea within its boundaries," Zharkov continued. "Unfortunately, the sea's surface is covered with miles of plastic bottles and refuse, as well as a thick brown seaweed of the genus *Sargassum*."

He pressed his finger down on the map. "Crossing this will be difficult for Commander Petrov because even though its surface is covered with debris, the ocean here is a deep blue and exceptionally clear, making the *Golden Fish* easy to spot if it ventures near the surface."

Zharkov paused, expecting a question, but Kardar said nothing.

"Once the *Golden Fish* passes through the Sargasso Sea, Petrov will guide his ship to this location." He unrolled a second map that showed the Virginia and North Carolina coastlines. "This is where the *Golden Fish* will forever change history with its nuclear bomb."

For the first time, Kardar appeared interested. "You will not attack Washington? Baltimore? New York?"

Zharkov broke into a smug smile. "General, what do you know about tsunamis?"

Kardar didn't like being cast in the role of a student. He didn't respond.

"A tsunami caused by the great Sumatra-Andaman earthquake of 2004 killed nearly three hundred thousand, and even though it began in the Indian Ocean, it impacted waves as far north as Nova Scotia and as far south as Peru."

"Tsunamis are caused by faults in tectonic plates," Kardar said. "Not by nuclear bombs."

"General," Zharkov replied approvingly, "I'm impressed. You do know something about seismology. They are caused by collisions—faults in tectonic plates. Sadly, America's eastern coastline has not been vulnerable because there is a lack of subduction zones—where the tectonic plates meet—off its coast."

Zharkov paused, savoring his reveal and sipping his drink, before continuing.

"During the Cold War, the leaders of the Kremlin asked our best Soviet scientists to find a location where a nuclear bomb aboard a submarine could be exploded near America to cause a tsunami. The KGB believed that the Kremlin could explain the explosion away as a nuclear accident to avoid retaliation, and since our technology was so far behind that of the Americans, that would have been a believable excuse."

"If it was so brilliant a plan, why wasn't it done?"

"Because our scientists weren't certain it would work. Risk versus reward, my friend. Even scientists today are skeptical. If you look on the internet, you will find a computer simulation that postulates what would unfold if the world's biggest bomb—the Tsar Bomba, with a yield of fifty-eight megatons of TNT—exploded at the bottom of the Marianas Trench, the deepest cavity in the earth's crust."

Zharkov looked at Kardar through bloodshot eyes and suddenly exclaimed: "Boom!" He laughed. "Nothing would happen. No cities would be flooded. The earth would not be blown from its axis. No massive deaths marking the end of mankind. Water pressure at nearly eleven thousand meters below the surface would contain the nuclear blast, overpower it, and by the time it reached the surface, it would barely cause a ripple."

"You have spent more than a billion dollars for what? A Cold War plan that is unproved?"

"Tectonic plates crashing together is not the only phenomenon that causes a tsunami. The largest tsunami ever, in terms of wave height, happened off Alaska when a magnitude seven-point-eight earthquake caused an underwater landslide. A chunk of earth six hundred feet wide and fifty feet tall broke away from an underwater cliff, sending three million cubic yards of dirt crashing down—much like an avalanche, only submerged. That rockslide caused twenty-foot-high waves to crash into Alaska, traveling as far inland as five hundred meters."

He pointed to the Virginia coast. "About seventy-five miles east from the shore here, the ocean floor drops from two hundred meters to eight hundred meters. This is where the American coastline really ends. It is the continental shelf."

Pausing only long enough to take another sip of vodka, he said in an excited and slightly slurred voice, "Most people are ignorant. They do not understand that sixteen thousand years ago, ocean waters were much lower than today. This explains the land bridge that once linked North America and Asia but now is the Bering Strait."

Kardar was growing tired of this lecture. "What about my payment and the code?"

"Do not hurry me!" Zharkov snapped. "What I am describing is brilliance that should be savored. My plan will change the world. Now, before the ocean levels began to rise, strong rivers and melting ice cut canyons and channels into the continental shelf. In Africa, the Congo Canyon extends from the Congo River's mouth nearly five hundred miles, and is almost four thousand feet deep. An underwater Grand Canyon."

Zharkov stared down at his maps. "Why does my geography lesson matter? Why should it concern you? German U-boat commanders understood the value of what I have told you. They would hover a few feet above the ocean bottom along the continental shelf, hiding in the uneven underwater topography, then rise to fire on unsuspecting American ships. They sank forty-five ships in six months."

Kardar was becoming more frustrated. "What is your point?"

"My point is," Zharkov said, exasperated, "that a deep canyon runs through the American continental shelf—a canyon deep enough and wide enough for the *Golden Fish* to slip into. Petrov can sail unnoticed—just like those German U-boats—making his way close to the Virginia shoreline." He touched his finger onto the map. "Right here is a hole six hundred meters deep that was created centuries ago. This is where he will pilot the *Golden Fish*. This is where its nuclear bomb will explode. This is where a massive landslide will create a mega-tsunami unlike anything the world has seen."

Zharkov slid his finger from where the submarine would be exploded toward the shore. "Directly in its path is Norfolk, home to the world's biggest naval base. The Americans' Atlantic Fleet. It will be hit before anyone can sound an alarm. Aircraft carriers will be knocked over as if they were bathtub toys." He continued sliding his finger from Norfolk up the Chesapeake Bay to the Potomac River, finally stopping on Washington, DC.

"My computer simulations," he boasted, "show the entire city will be flooded. Washington will become a modern-day Atlantis. Millions will die. Monuments will be toppled. The White House drowned. Waves from my mega-tsunami will hit the entire coast from Boston to Charleston." He ran his finger up and down the shore.

"Such a long distance—it seems improbable," Kardar said.

"Mathematical calculations don't lie, but even if the waves only destroy the Atlantic Fleet and flood Washington, my goal will be accomplished." Zharkov stepped away from the table and pointed toward two valises near his desk. "Your finder's fee," he said. "Take it."

Kardar stepped quickly to the cases, which he opened.

"Two million in US dollars, as you requested," Zharkov said.

"And what of the six-digit code needed to detonate the bomb? I will need to tell Aziz."

Zharkov grunted. "Tell him any six numbers. I have no intention of providing the real ones to him and letting him decide when to detonate my bomb. All that matters is that he believes the digits are real, so that when you tell him to use them, I can explode the bomb with him receiving all the blame."

Zharkov walked in unsteady steps to his desk and slumped in the chair behind it. From a drawer, he removed a fresh bottle of vodka. He waved his hand at the Iranian general, dismissing him.

Kardar picked up the two heavy valises and walked downstairs. Two of his security guards were waiting in the foyer. They opened umbrellas; it was raining hard outside. There, two additional guards were waiting, also holding open umbrellas. The umbrella entourage shielded him as he entered his limousine, steps away.

Unknown to Kardar and his men, directly across from Zharkov's mansion, a lone man was lying prone on a rooftop. Because of the umbrellas, the Roc did not have a clear shot. His eyes shifted to Zharkov's mansion. A light appeared on its third floor.

TWENTY-EIGHT

"Why did Robert Calhoun write that awful story about us?" Mayberry asked. "I'm not certain I'll have a job when I get home."

"None of it was true," Garrett said.

"Don't be naive, Garrett. Truth doesn't matter in Washington. It's all about perceptions, and my bosses at the bureau frown on that sort of publicity." She reached into her purse. Removed her prescription bottle. Swallowed two capsules without water.

"Those aren't going to help," he said.

"Don't be that guy, Garrett. There's nothing worse than someone in recovery who believes he knows all the answers because of what he's been through. Not everyone gets addicted. People take pain pills in the hospital and go home and never take them again."

"You're not in the hospital, are you?"

"Your burns healed! My hand won't! You need to back off!"

The woman in front of them turned, having overheard their exchange. Garrett returned her stare with a menacing glare. She took a step forward in the Charles de Gaulle airport's passenger screening line. Fifteen passengers ahead of them, waiting to be cleared for their departure gates.

"I don't want you to go," he said. "We're a team. Join me and the Israelis in hunting down the Roc."

"Excusez-moi."

A woman's loud voice, coming from behind them. Someone

cutting through the line. Garrett glanced back. It was Esther, with two men.

"Please come with me," Esther said to Garrett.

He looked at Mayberry. "Let's go. Just hear her out."

"I came for you," Esther said. "Let her go back to Washington. We don't need her."

"Yes, we do," Garrett said, slightly raising his voice. He rested his palms on Mayberry's shoulders. "I'm better with you."

Mayberry nodded. They followed Esther out of the terminal to a Mercedes-Benz Metris cargo van. Its driver pulled away from the airport.

Big Jules Levi spoke to them through a television monitor in the van's cargo area. "I need you both to accompany Esther to London."

"What's in London?" Garrett asked.

"Not what, who. A Russian oligarch named Taras Aleksandrovich Zharkov."

Esther joined the conversation. "Late yesterday our analytics team identified a company owned by Zharkov as the owner of the submarine base in Balaklava Bay. It took some digging. Twenty-two shell companies spread over four continents."

"It appears Zharkov is involved in all of this somehow," Big Jules said.

"Let's assume Radi's warning about a nuclear attack by a submarine is accurate," Garrett said. "Why would this Russian get involved?"

"Panic selling on the worldwide stock exchanges," Mayberry said. "Millions can be made when there's chaos. The New York Stock Exchange remained closed for six days after the nine-eleven attacks. When it reopened, it set what then was a record for the biggest loss in exchange history. More than a trillion dollars."

"Your privileged upbringing serves you well," Big Jules said.

"We'll never get by his lawyers to question him," Mayberry said. "Something I learned from my 'privileged' background."

"Esther will not be going through his lawyers," Big Jules countered.

The Mercedes cargo van parked outside the majestic stone facade of the Gare du Nord, a grand railway station built between 1861 and 1865. Life-size statues of figures representing major European cities lined its curved peak.

"The Eurostar can get us to London in two hours and sixteen minutes," Esther explained. "I have a hotel suite where we can wait until it gets dark."

"I'm not sure I'm comfortable with this," Mayberry said.

"Our driver can take you back to the airport," Esther offered.

"Why do you need us?" Garrett asked.

"Director Whittington remains skeptical," Big Jules said. "He thinks we're just trying to stir up trouble with Iran."

Garrett grunted. "If he doesn't believe the Mossad, why would he listen to us? He's not a big fan."

"I read the newspaper story about you," Big Jules replied. "What you are underestimating is your influence beyond Whittington. At the White House with the president. He did give you both presidential medals. If we get the evidence, you can go directly to him in support of what our prime minister certainly will be sharing with him. That should be more than enough."

"I need a moment to speak privately to Brett," Mayberry said, dropping her voice to a whisper. "We can't be part of interrogating a Russian oligarch in London."

Garrett spoke to Big Jules and Esther. "What exactly are you expecting us to do in London?"

"That's between you and Esther," Big Jules said. He signed off.

"You can help me or wait at the hotel," Esther said. "If you have no stomach for this."

"Stomach for what?" Mayberry asked.

"We can't risk not helping," Garrett said. "Not if an attack is under way. Besides, we're already in this so deep, what do we have to lose?"

"You, nothing. Me, everything."

"We need to catch the train," Esther said, opening the cargo door and stepping outside.

Garrett hurried after her. Mayberry remained seated, but only for a moment. She let out a sigh and joined them as they dashed into the station.

"The Eurostar terminal for London is on the first floor," Esther said.

"We don't have tickets or bags," Mayberry said.

"Your bags will be delivered to London."

"That's good," Garrett said. Hoping to add levity to their conversation, he added, "I'd hate to be in London without a change of underwear."

"I don't bother with underwear," Esther teased.

The old-style compartments on European trains shown in movies don't exist on modern Eurostar railcars. Two seats on one side of an aisle. A third single seat on the other. Hoping to take a nap, Garrett chose the single seat, causing Esther and Mayberry to sit together across the aisle. While other passengers were filing past them, Esther lowered her voice and said, "We're working together now, so tell me, what is your relationship with him?"

She nodded at Garrett, whose head was tipped back, his eyes closed, seemingly unaware of their conversation.

"What do you mean?" Mayberry asked.

"I find him handsome. That's rare in the opportunities we have. I thought you might know if he's open to an approach."

"I certainly wouldn't know."

"Then it may be me who will be possibly sharing that information with you in the future." Esther laughed.

"You barely know him," Mayberry said.

"I have no choice but to work quickly. Every week a new country, new people. Live every moment, because it could be your last. It has been a long time since I could worry about love and romance."

"Sounds like a rationalization for not caring about people."

"Do you not rationalize your lack of emotional attachments? I can tell you have known real loss. I read about your late husband. A freelance reporter killed covering the war."

"I have attachments. I just don't flaunt them." Mayberry felt her face flush. "That's a price I am willing to pay. I will always prefer having my heart broken to meaningless anything."

Esther looked at Garrett. "It won't be meaningless to me if he responds."

Esther had rented the Grand Piano suite at Claridge's in London—nearly two thousand square feet, decorated by Diane von Furstenberg. A marble fireplace, two bedrooms, with an additional bedroom attached through an adjoining door, and a grand piano. A whiff of freshly cut white orchids, not in one vase but ten, placed strategically throughout the rooms.

"I chose this suite for its view, not its luxuries," Esther said, pushing an electronic pad that opened floor-to-ceiling window screens. "Zharkov's Fallbrook Manor is there." She pointed toward his mansion, a few blocks away. "His office is on the second floor, and his master bedroom—large enough for Zharkov and his wife to have separate sleeping chambers—occupies the entire third floor. There's a safe room hidden behind bookcases in his bedroom. I'll have to get to him before he reaches it and notifies his security guards."

She called Garrett to the windows. Handed him binoculars. "Two security guards stationed outside the entrance," he noted.

"And a few more inside." Esther glanced at Mayberry, who'd taken a seat on a beige couch.

"What's a few?" Garrett asked, lowering the binoculars.

"A dozen. Spetsnaz soldiers."

"Spetsnaz? You've got to be suicidal if you think you can break in and do a number on Zharkov."

"There must be alarms too," Mayberry said. "Security cameras."

"This is why I will simply walk through the front door," Esther announced. "Hopefully with Mr. Garrett at my side."

"I thought we were observers?" Mayberry said.

"To make this work, I require his help." Esther affectionally touched Garrett's arm.

"Doing what?"

"The oldest trick. I will offer Zharkov sex. His wife is a former fashion model, a beautiful woman, but like all men of his type, he constantly seeks attention, excitement. He feels entitled. A glutton who needs his ego stroked."

"Sounds like you're going to do more than stroke his ego," Garrett said.

"The promise of sex will get me alone with him," Esther explained. "Zharkov belongs to an exclusive London men's club where he mingles with other rich men, mostly Russians. One of them will call and offer me as a gift."

"A gift," Garrett repeated.

"Yes, as I admitted, not an imaginative approach, but one he will not resist. And because I will be a gift from a friend, he will not be suspicious."

"Is Big Jules pimping you out?" Mayberry asked.

"He has arranged for my photo to be sent to Zharkov's security team, and he has given me a convincing legend. A reputable high-priced London call girl."

"Reputable? Is there such a thing among prostitutes?" Mayberry sneered.

"If you'd rather take my place tonight, I'm certain Big Jules can arrange it. Or perhaps we could go together—two for the price of one."

"No, thank you!"

"How do I fit in?" Garrett asked.

"Women like this always travel with a bodyguard."

Esther walked toward one of the suite's expansive bedrooms.

"I need to change clothes for tonight." She looked at Garrett and added, "Big Jules has sent over several dresses. Perhaps you will give me a man's point of view in choosing one."

"Before you go whore up," Mayberry said, "how about answering some questions? You've read dossiers about us—you mentioned my husband's death—but we know absolutely nothing—"

Esther cut her short. "Yes. Valerie Mayberry, the black sheep of a wealthy New England family. Wanted to be a doctor. A psychiatrist, which in my opinion is the basement floor for doctors. Instead, you joined the FBI's counterintelligence branch. Married to Noah Williams, a journalist killed on assignment in Afghanistan. Your right hand is crippled because you were poisoned during an attack at the US Capitol, and based on what I've observed, you are addicted to opioids for your chronic pain."

Esther turned to Garrett. "High school athlete. Fastball pitcher. Dad a coach—and an alcoholic. Your father crashed his car with your mother as a passenger, killing them both. You left Arkansas for the US Naval Academy. Became a SEAL. Got rejected by a fiancée. Served in Afghanistan, where you met your best friend, Thomas Jefferson Kim. Saved his life during a deadly firefight. Kim left to become a multimillionaire cybersecurity expert. You went to work for the CIA. Your career—"

"We know our own backgrounds," Garrett said.

"I was raised in Ofra, a settlement on the West Bank. When I was sixteen, I became sick with spinal meningitis. The doctors told my parents that I would be dead in twenty-four hours. They told me the same." Esther looked directly at Mayberry. "When you believe you only have hours to live, there is no time to worry about the next day. Every breath tastes sweeter, every rose blooms brighter."

"You clearly recovered," Mayberry said.

"Yes. It is not a cliché when I say I live in the moment, and always without regrets. I am not the only Israeli who believes this. My final year in school, I kept score. Palestinians killed forty-two Israelis and two visiting tourists in twelve months."

"How many Palestinians did Israeli forces kill?" Mayberry asked.

"Our side killed two hundred and forty-two Palestinians, and every one of those Palestinians deserved to die. My mother was murdered by a suicide bomber while picking out fruit in a neighborhood market."

"I'm sorry," Garrett said. "Is that why you joined the Mossad?"

"Our military first, and later the Mossad. As you probably have guessed, I am not married. I have no children and no serious boyfriend." She looked directly at Garrett. "But—how do you Americans put it?—I enjoy friends with benefits."

"Have you ever worked with the CIA?" Mayberry asked.

"Yes, it's no longer classified. I was sent to assist one of your army majors. Her name is Brooke Grant. Our mission was to track and kill a specific terrorist. Unlike me, she had an adopted child. A terrorist caught Grant by surprise. Luckily, she escaped from her farmhouse in Virginia mere seconds before he blew it up. I killed the terrorist, but not before he stabbed me."

Without embarrassment, she began unbuttoning her blouse, exposing her breasts and a jagged red scar across her abdomen.

"It took me a year to recover physically. You see, the two of you are not the only ones who have been burned and crippled." She buttoned her blouse and again directed her comments at Mayberry. "You don't know me, and you can't understand my life, so don't you dare judge me. From the moment of my birth on the West Bank, someone has been trying to kill me. You do not understand what that is like. In America, you can wake up and go outside without being afraid. You can see a stranger on a street without feeling fear. You can go to bed without thinking you might be killed in your sleep. It is not only on the West Bank. It is true for Jews everywhere. Auschwitz-Birkenau taught us that. How did your grandparents die? Do I need to explain how mine did?"

"I'm going to get some rest," Mayberry said, entering the suite's second bedroom. She shut her door and locked it.

Esther stepped into the other bedroom, glancing back at Garrett. She left the door slightly ajar.

Garrett waited a moment, considering what had just transpired. How each of them had been shaped by the situation in which they were born. Their parents and the events of their childhoods. It seemed clear to him that no one gets through life without being scarred. He did not judge either woman. He opened a beer at the bar. Walked over to the window, and looked again at Fallbrook Manor.

TWENTY-NINE

CIA Director Connor Whittington was, as the native Texan was fond of saying, "covering his butt."

"Mr. President," Whittington said, "every day we receive tips about possible terrorist attacks—everything from radical Islamic terrorists plotting to murder gamblers in Las Vegas casinos to bombing attacks at Mount Rushmore. What separates this tip from the others is that Director Levi called me personally about it."

Whittington had included a copy of Nasya Radi's warning letter and an edited transcript of his telephone calls with Big Jules in the presidential packet delivered earlier.

President Randle Fitzgerald leaned forward and placed his elbows on the Theodore Roosevelt desk that he'd chosen for his tenure in the Oval Office. He clasped his fingers together and peered over his hands at Whittington, sitting before him. "I've never met the Mossad director," he said. "What I do know is that the Mossad has a hell of a lot more sources inside Iran than we do."

"That's true, but I must admit I'm a bit suspicious of Israel's motivation," Whittington said. "Israel is always accusing Iran of not abiding by any international nuclear agreements. They've cried wolf before. Nonbiased international inspectors have assured us that Iran is not developing nuclear weapons, and there is no satellite or other technical evidence to contradict that. Based on our predictive analytical models, we do not believe Iran will have nuclear capabilities for several years, and in fact we further believe that developing a nuclear bomb is not a high priority. The Israelis are constantly raising the threat for their own political reasons without tangible evidence, and Iran uses that fear for leverage."

"What about this old Soviet submarine base in Balaklava Bay and this rogue submarine that the Israelis say they spotted?"

"Mr. President, if there was such a rogue submarine, who does it belong to? The Israelis couldn't satisfactorily answer that when we last spoke."

Randle unclasped his hands, raised his elbows from his desk, and leaned back in his chair. He rubbed the gray stubble on his chin. He had no public appearances planned today, so he'd skipped shaving, gaining himself a few extra minutes in his exhausting daily schedule. He was sixty-nine, but felt much older. When he looked into the mirror before showering, he'd wondered who owned the worn face staring back at him. Once he'd been handsome. Now, drooping jowls, bags under his eyes. In his youth, an NFL quarterback. Nimble. Ripped abs. Now he carried the male version of a muffin-top waist. Too many days sitting at his desk. Too much stress. He felt confident that his mind was just as sharp as when he'd called plays in the huddle. Yes, he was that old. A different era, before offensive coordinators made the call. His mind wasn't what was failing him. A Washington reporter had compared his watery blue eyes to the color of a calm mountain lake on a chilly winter morning, and his temper to that of an angry charging bull wounded with banderillas. He'd loved that description—except for the watery eyes. He no longer loved being president. A year left before his second term ended and he could retire. Those seeking to replace him already had begun criticizing his tenure, and it was like being plucked to death by geese. They listed his every slipup, every perceived failure and fault. They were running against him, not for what they could do better. He did not want to finish his presidency being accused of ignoring a warning about another pending 9/11 attack.

"Director Whittington," the president said, "I know this seems implausible, but I'm not going to get caught with my pants down. I expect you to stay on top of this, as if it is a genuine attack."

"Yes, sir, I'm planning to," Whittington said. "Is there anything else?"

"There is." The president reached into a desk drawer and removed a copy of the *Washington Interceptor*. It was rare for him to have an actual newspaper; as president, he received an edited version of the top news each day, specially prepared for him.

"Someone leaked information about Garrett and Mayberry to this reporter," he said. "The article says you felt compelled to issue a statement saying they are not working for the agency. I've been around Washington long enough to see a smear job, and I don't like it. I gave those two our country's highest civilian medal, and stories like this—about them running around Europe, causing havoc—make them and me look bad."

"I had little choice but to distance the agency from their actions in Italy and France," Whittington said. "I'm sure the reporter was just reporting information that he'd gleaned from sources. And may I point out, the article is critical of them, not you."

"Whittington, I've already got a slew of heel biters telling voters how I've screwed up as president and how much better they'll do this job. They're looking at my every word, my every decision, hoping to exploit my record and me for their own personal political advancement. Don't delude yourself. An attack on Garrett and Mayberry is a backdoor attack on me."

He tossed the paper into a nearby trashcan. "Besides, I happen to like those two."

"Sir—" Whittington said.

The president raised his hands to cut him off. "You need to find out if someone in your agency is leaking information to this reporter. If so, you need to cut their balls off."

At the same time that Whittington and President Fitzgerald were meeting in the White House, the Italian container ship *Bella Sofia* was entering the Sargasso Sea. It was one of the last Panamax cargo ships, with a maximum capacity of 5,000 TEUs—twenty-foot-equivalent cargo containers. More modern ultra-large bulk carriers could transport 14,000 TEUs, which explained why this was the *Bella Sofia*'s final voyage. Everything about the 965-foot-long and 106-foot-wide ship was old, including its rattling diesel engines and rusty propellers.

The loud sounds emanating from the *Bella Sofia* could be heard inside the *Golden Fish* as the submarine rose toward it from the depths, approaching its stern like a jaguar about to bite into the hind legs of its prey.

When the submarine was less than two hundred meters from the surface, Petrov ordered Kozlov to level it and increase speed. The churning noises from the *Bella Sofia*'s screws became almost deafening as the *Golden Fish* passed directly underneath those blades. When it was aligned under the cargo ship's belly, Petrov gave a command to keep the submarine steady.

He was copying a Nazi U-boat trick. Active sonar used to identify submarines worked on the same principle as a bat's radar. Sound waves were sent out, and when they struck an object, they bounced back. If a submarine traveled at the same speed and on the same course as another vessel, it was difficult for trackers to discern between the two. In addition to active sonar, the *Golden Fish* had to elude detection by passive sonar and hydrophones spread across the ocean floor. Even when the *Golden Fish*'s engines were shut down and its crew silent, it still made noises—machinery used to circulate air, for instance—that could be picked up by hydrophones. A moving boat also disturbed water, and the sound of moving water created an imprint—sound waves—that could be detected. The United States coastline was protected by thousands of such listening devices permanently installed on the sea's bottom. This is why the Nazis' old trick was Petrov's best evasion technique. If the *Golden Fish* stuck close to the cargo ship's underbelly, it was hard to detect the disturbed water and noise it created.

The *Bella Sofia*'s captain knew a submarine was running beneath his ship. The cargo vessel was owned by one of Zharkov's companies, so the captain ensured that his boat and the submarine remained married.

The two ships had traveled midway across the Sargasso Sea when a US Navy P-3 Orion, an antisubmarine tracker, appeared overhead. A crew member on board the plane tossed out a long cylinder. A red parachute slowed its descent.

In the control room of the cargo ship, the captain watched the sonobuoy strike the water. Its listening microphones immediately began returning readings to the aircraft from a predetermined depth. There was nothing the *Bella Sofia*'s captain could do to thwart the submarine-hunting device.

He warned Petrov, traveling below him, with a coded transmission, and the two of them waited anxiously, unsure how to react if detected.

The P-3 Orion crew flew four long circles around the container ship, checking the water, before turning south and disappearing.

Relief.

While traveling under the cargo ship proved effective camouflage, the nonstop churning of the surface ship's screws quickly became nerve-racking. Sleep was nearly impossible. Tempers grew short. A fistfight broke out in the engine room. Bleary-eyed men covered with sweat, sweltering in the heat from the diesel engines, plugged their ears with wax, but nothing shut out the churning noise completely. Nonstop sounds were not the only self-inflicted torture. Mentally, there was fear. Dread. What if they collided with the ship above them? Petrov, Kozlov, and Suslov were the only ones on board who were armed. The crew had watched Petrov beat one of their fellow sailors unconscious after he panicked. There was no talk of mutiny. Given the harsh conditions and plugged ears, there was little talk at all, and when there was, it was about how each man intended to spend the $1 million in cash promised upon completion of their voyage.

When the submarine had finally crossed the sea and was nearing the US coast, Petrov gave Kozlov the order to increase speed and dive. The agonizing drumbeat of engines and turbulence dissipated as the two vessels parted, the *Bella Sofia* continuing toward Norfolk's busy port, and the *Golden Fish* entering the silence below.

Petrov used his charts to find the canyon that had been carved over time into the continental shelf. Like all cuts in the earth made by rivers, the canyon's opening was widest at its mouth—the farthest point from the shore—and grew narrower as the *Golden Fish* moved through it, as well as shallower. The ocean at the canyon's opening was five thousand feet deep, but fifty miles from the Virginia coast, its depth was less than eight hundred feet.

Petrov had read accounts of deadly underwater collisions, the most recent a US Navy submarine that had struck an underwater mountain in the Pacific Ocean southeast of Guam. The captain had been using an outdated chart that failed to identify the mountain. The impact had punched holes in the nuclear submarine's forward ballast tanks, through which ocean water rushed in. The submarine's propulsion system momentarily lost power. The boat's bow dropped as the craft began drifting downward into the deep. The collision sent crew members bouncing like Ping-Pong balls against steel surfaces, knocking sailors to the floor, bloody and unconscious. The crew was saved only when an enlisted man hit the "chicken switches," blowing high-pressure air through the ballast tanks, forcing the submarine to rise to the surface.

That mishap had occurred in charted waters. There was no guide to direct the *Golden Fish* safely through the canyon. No prior accounts written by seafarers foolish enough to enter a crack in the shelf. Petrov had added sensors and underwater cameras to the *Golden Fish*'s outer hull, as well as lights. His eyes darting between the multiple screens positioned before him, he tried not to overreact when a beep signaled the submarine was only a few feet from the canyon's jagged, narrowing sides.

The submarine's hull was not the only worry. Even the bottom of the canyon was threatening. Time and currents had created what appeared to be giant needles jutting upward.

An original Romeo-class submarine had a range of nine thousand miles at nine knots. Petrov had run his boat faster, and despite the replacement engines' improved fuel efficiency, the *Golden Fish* was now low on fuel. Switching to electric helped conserve what was left, but those batteries also were losing power.

Petrov's face shone with perspiration. His black clothing was drenched with sweat. Yet he showed no fear as he maneuvered the *Golden Fish* like a blind man walking down a narrow hallway with razors sticking from its walls.

At last his tenacity was rewarded. The submarine's bow entered a deep hole in the continental shelf, caused by thousands of years of erosion in the softer, underwater rock. Tides and water churning along its walls had created ledges that jutted outward along its circular sides. Petrov guided the *Golden Fish* above a ledge 270 feet below the ocean's surface. The crew became silent as the engines stopped and the submarine floated down, all hands praying the ledge would be strong enough to hold its tonnage.

A jarring stop.

It had settled on the exact spot Zharkov had chosen. Petrov released an exhausted sigh.

"We have made it," he announced through the submarine's speakers. "Congratulations, men."

Cheers. Backslaps. One crew member began to sing. Others joined him. The fifty-man crew had been told that once the submarine was grounded, each man would be issued a bright orange submarine escape immersion equipment (SEIE) suit. The whole-body suit would protect them from hypothermia as they rose to the top, where a boat would be waiting. During training in the Black Sea, each crew member had done a practice run inside an SEIE suit, so they believed themselves well prepared.

"Now you have nothing to do but relax," Petrov said, "and plan how you will spend your fortune. The ship will be waiting for us in six hours. Until then, we party!"

The cook opened cases of liquor. Served cakes and pies.

Petrov, Kozlov, and Suslov spent a half hour with the crew before quietly excusing themselves. They slipped quickly through the submarine, first releasing a steel cable from it, with a float attached. It contained a series of telephonic relays necessary for deep underwater communication with one of Zharkov's global satellites. The test was a call to the Russian billionaire.

"We've arrived," Commander Petrov announced when Zharkov answered from his London safe room.

"Boris, I knew you could do this!"

Now confident that a satellite signal could reach the grounded submarine and the detonator attached to the Iranian nuclear bomb, Petrov and his two trusted colleagues continued from their quarters to where the escape suits were located.

"The engines?" Petrov asked when they arrived.

Kozlov nodded.

He turned to Suslov. "Communications?"

"From now on, only signals from above relayed below. No messages from here."

"It's time to go," Petrov said.

Suslov was the first to exit the submarine in his SEIE suit, followed by Kozlov, and finally Petrov. They followed the steel communication cable upward. Petrov had no idea, nor did he care, when his crew would realize the submarine's engines had been made inoperable and the SEIE suits left for them rendered useless. There would be no million-dollar payoffs—only a horrifying, suffocating death, trapped in a grounded submerged submarine.

As they approached the ocean's surface, Petrov grasped Kozlov's right leg and pulled himself up his body until he reached his comrade's midsection. Unsure what Petrov was doing, Kozlov didn't resist.

Petrov pressed a Russian SPP-1 underwater pistol against his second-in-command and fired a four-and-a-half-inch steel dart from one of the gun's four barrels. A second trigger pull, and Kozlov's limp body sank below him as his punctured suit filled with water, sending out an array of air bubbles.

That left only Suslov. The sonar operator had no clue about Kozlov's fate; his inflated suit prevented him from bending to look downward. But when he saw the bubbles rising past him, he sensed something was amiss.

Petrov grabbed his ankle. Panicked, Suslov kicked his leg free.

They were less than forty feet from the surface now. Suslov released his grip on the steel cable, and Petrov fired. His dart ripped into Suslov's suit and tore through the flesh of his left side. The sonar operator now understood he was being stalked by his friend. Petrov had only one dart left, and he needed to fire it before Suslov was out of range. He released his grip on the cable and shot the final dart. Like Kozlov before him, Suslov drifted down, his dead eyes peering through his face mask at his killer.

As Petrov broke through the surface, his suit expanded even further into a one-person life raft, a doughnut with Petrov riding in its center hole. A wave slammed against him, and he discovered that he'd risen into an angry ocean in the predawn darkness. Blinding rain pelted him, and the sea tossed him back and forth. Zharkov had promised him that a fishing boat would be waiting to take him to shore. But even though his suit was sending a homing beacon and a brilliant white light was flashing upward from his shoulder, Petrov could not see any rescue craft.

His first thought was that the boat had been delayed by the storm. But with each passing moment, he began to fear that no boat had been arranged. Petrov was no stranger to betrayal. He had double-crossed his crew, the men who'd helped him cross the Atlantic. He had murdered the two Russian friends he'd recruited from retirement. And yet he had foolishly trusted the Russian oligarch and his promise of wealth.

Ten-foot waves restricted his vision. He had no control over his movements in the bulky suit, but from the stars, he knew the storm was sweeping him farther out into the Atlantic.

Morning came with an exhausted Petrov welcoming calmer seas. He drifted, burning under the sun, for several more hours before he saw a boat approaching. Perhaps Zharkov had not betrayed him. Perhaps the fishing boat had not been able to rescue him as planned because of the raging storm. Perhaps Petrov finally would be rich and not have to work as anyone's bodyguard and enforcer. Perhaps he'd fulfill his dream, to buy a superyacht and sail the world.

Not until the approaching boat's engines slowed could he read the lettering on its bow.

US COAST GUARD.

THIRTY

"You obviously didn't need my advice," Garrett said, eyeballing Esther as she emerged from her bedroom. She'd selected a bloodred, skin-hugging maxi dress with a plunging V front and an even lower V back, held together with skinny straps. A front slit along her thigh revealed tanned, smooth skin. Ruching accented her backside. She'd undone her no-nonsense bun, allowing her lush brown hair to cascade onto her shoulders. Her makeup highlighted her cheekbones and full lips. There were no undergarments, only the outline of firm breasts shaped like champagne glasses under the fabric.

She returned his compliment. "You wear a black tie well."

"Your people delivered it. Got my size right, even the shoes."

"I'm good at judging a man's size," she said in a flirtatious voice.

Mayberry emerged from the second bedroom. "You certainly look the part," she said to Esther.

"I'll take that as a compliment."

"It wasn't meant to be."

Mayberry looked at Garrett, sitting in an overstuffed chaise next to the grand piano. "A bit overdressed, aren't you, for a pimp?"

He smiled. "Apparently this is what pimps wear in London."

Garrett could smell Esther's perfume as she approached him. Chanel. "Here, put this on," she said, dangling a wristwatch before him.

"I already have one." He lifted his wrist.

"Yours is a sports watch. This is a Rolex, and this Rolex is linked to this." She raised her left wrist, showing off a thin gold bracelet with a solitaire diamond embedded in it.

He removed his watch and wrapped the Rolex around his wrist. Esther pressed a finger against her bracelet's lone diamond.

Garrett yelped. "The watch shocked me."

"A signal if I need help."

"Maybe you should give him a dog collar too," Mayberry said.

"What's your problem?" Esther asked, not hiding the rising anger in her voice.

"My problem is you. Both of you. I never should've agreed to this. I'm an FBI agent, not someone who flaunts the law. Someone who plays tricks. I should have caught that flight home in Paris."

"I'll gladly call you a cab," Esther said.

"Valerie," Garrett said, "the last time you put your rule book aside, we stopped terrorists who were attacking the Capitol."

"You don't have to remind me of that." She glanced down at her crippled right hand. "It doesn't mean we're justified in doing any of this. Think about it, Garrett. We don't have any proof this Russian is involved in a plot against the United States."

"Which is why Esther needs to question him," Garrett replied, "and we need to help her."

"She doesn't need our help. You're chasing this because you need to chase it. You need the rush. Otherwise, you don't matter anymore."

A hurt look swept across his face.

Esther folded her arms across her chest. "Since we're being so insightful, why don't you tell the truth. This is personal between the two of us, isn't it? You and me. You're jealous because of what I told you on the train."

"What'd you say?" Garrett asked.

Mayberry's face reddened. "That's so insulting. We're not schoolgirls! I'm packing my bag." She walked back into the second bedroom.

"I'll go talk to her," Garrett said.

"Why bother? We don't need her."

"We do need her." He nodded at the binoculars by the window. "We need her to watch Fallbrook Manor and notify Big Jules if this falls apart."

"I'm leaving in ten minutes from downstairs," Esther said. "I'll do this without you if you don't show up."

Garrett waited until Esther was gone before he rapped on Mayberry's bedroom door. When she didn't answer, he tried the knob. It turned, so he let himself in.

A visibly angry Mayberry was closing up her suitcase.

"We need you to stay," Garrett said. "I'd like you to stay. Just ignore her."

She turned to face him. "That's the best you got? Just ignore her?"

"Valerie, I wasn't asleep. I heard your conversation on the train, and I'm not interested in her." He stepped forward, gently placed his palms on her shoulders. Impulsively, he moved his head to kiss her.

Mayberry turned her face.

He loosened his hands, but as he was pulling away, she leaned forward and kissed him.

"I'm going downstairs," he said, unsure of how to respond. "I'd really appreciate it if you'd watch us with the binoculars."

Esther was waiting when Garrett entered the lobby. "She'll watch our backs," he said, "but she's leaving first thing in the morning. You need to back off her. She's my partner, and a good friend."

Esther entered the waiting Mercedes-Maybach. "I'm leaving. Are you coming?"

As they neared Fallbrook Manor, Garrett asked, "You carrying? Because I don't know where you could be hiding it in that dress."

Esther opened her Louis Vuitton clutch purse and withdrew a gold ladies' decorative pin, five inches long, with a black rose affixed to its top. She pulled off the rose, revealing a razor-sharp point. She attached the pin to her dress.

"Tiny, but terribly persuasive when stuck in the right spot."

Esther's cell phone rang. "Big Jules says they're expecting us. How do I look?"

She shifted slightly in the rear seat so he could see her, and in doing so caused the V-neck to gap open.

"Breathtaking."

Two Russian security guards met them at the curb and escorted them into the mansion, where they were joined by four goons in the foyer.

"He's expecting her," Zharkov's chief of security said, eyeing Garrett. "Not you. You can wait outside in the car."

"We're a pair. Where she goes, I go."

"A pair? You a whore too?" He laughed, and the other guards joined him.

"It's company policy," Esther said. "He has to be on the premises for my protection. Otherwise, I can't stay."

"Our company policy is, he stays in the car."

"Then we'll be leaving, and you can explain to your employer why you sent us away." She started to turn but was blocked by the goons. "Get out of my way!"

"A beautiful woman with brass balls!" a voice called out. Zharkov descended from the mansion's grand staircase.

"Sir, we haven't checked them for concealed weapons," the security chief warned.

"She doesn't appear to be concealing much," Zharkov replied, but he stopped on the second step up from the foyer floor. "Go ahead."

The guard closest to Garrett frisked him, removing his pistol. "I'll expect that back," Garrett said.

The guard reached into the slit on Esther's dress, ran his hand up her inner thigh, and groped her before lowering his hand down the opposite thigh, as Zharkov watched from the stairs. Next the guard ran his hands over her chest. He noticed the lapel pin and started to reach for it.

"Wouldn't it be easier if I simply stripped naked?" Esther asked Zharkov. "Or is that something you would prefer me to do privately, for only you?"

Zharkov stepped forward. With his beefy right hand, he lifted her chin and kissed her lips while swinging his left paw around her, pulling her close and clenching her buttocks. His guards smirked.

"Have you ever had a Russian make love to you?" he asked, continuing to press her pelvis against his. He smelled of sweat and vodka.

"Make love?" she said. "That's not what I plan to do to you tonight."

He guffawed and leaned in to kiss her again.

"Ah!" he exclaimed, suddenly pulling back.

Garrett assumed Esther had bitten his lip, but it was the black rose on her pin that had poked him. He reached for it. She blocked his hand, but he knocked hers away and removed the pin, tossing it on the floor.

"A family heirloom," she said, starting to bend down to retrieve it.

He stopped her, keeping her upright. "My men will give it back when we're done." Speaking to his security chief, Zharkov said, "Bring her up in an hour. I have a series of telephone calls to make." He looked at Garrett. "Who's he?"

"Her bodyguard."

Zharkov returned to the staircase. "He waits in the kitchen."

Esther bent down to retrieve her lapel pin, but the security guard next to her was quicker. He handed it to the security chief. "Mr. Zharkov said you'll get it back after he is finished with you."

She walked into the parlor. Garrett started to follow.

"Not you. You go to the kitchen."

"After she goes upstairs with him," Garrett said. "I'm not leaving her with all of you alone."

No one stopped him. An English grandfather clock sounded the time. Ten gongs: ten o'clock. Its pendulum counted out seconds on its hand-painted dial. No one spoke. Except for the tick-tock of the clock, there was silence for a nerve-racking hour. Finally the security chief appeared. "Follow me." He looked at Garrett. "You go to the kitchen."

"You should give back her pin," Garrett said. "Like she said, it's a family heirloom."

The security guard in charge picked it from his pocket. "We'll see how much she values it after Mr. Zharkov finishes with her."

Esther started for the grand staircase.

"No," the security chief said, "we use the elevator."

When its doors shut, she said, "I'll take my pin now."

He held it up between them but when she reached for it, he made a fist around it, stopping her from taking it.

"Tell me, how much do you charge for seconds?" he taunted.

"You can't afford me."

He sucker-punched her. She gasped for breath as the elevator doors opened into a third-floor anteroom with a domed ceiling painted with a mural of cherubs and walls of flocked black-and-silver wallpaper.

"To the right," he said, still holding her pin. "We don't need you wandering into Mrs. Zharkov's private quarters." He led her toward the double doors at the end of the hall and rapped on the left one. No answer. He spoke softly into his headset.

"Mr. Zharkov, we're in the hallway."

Esther's mind was racing. Without her pin, she would have to improvise.

No response.

The security chief turned the left doorknob and gently pushed the heavy walnut door inward.

"Mr. Zharkov," he said in a quiet voice.

Whoosh. Whoosh. Two slugs smacked into his chest, muffled by a suppressor. He toppled backward, falling onto the polished marble floor, his crisp white shirt turning red.

Esther dropped to her knees behind the closed right door, using it as a shield. She waited for a moment, readying herself to lunge upward and attack if the shooter came into the hallway. Nothing. No sounds indicating movement. She leaned forward and tugged open the dead man's jacket, exposing a Russian MP-443 Grach semiautomatic pistol in a shoulder holster. She drew it and quickly retreated behind the closed right door.

For an entire minute she did not move; instead she listened for the slightest sound. It was obvious that Mrs. Zharkov down the hallway and the guards on the ground level had not heard the gunshots. She lowered her shoulder and dove forward through the doorway into the bedroom, her left hand extended, ready to fire the commandeered pistol.

Nothing. No reaction. She let her eyes adjust to the dimly lighted room, searching for an attacker. A breeze behind a curtain near the bed. An open window. She felt restricted in her clinging dress, so she pulled it up around her waist as she duckwalked deeper into the room, to where light was shining from an opening between the bookcases. Zharkov's safe room. She rose slowly, letting her dress fall back into place, the pistol still extended before her. The room's steel door was open.

Inside, she saw Zharkov sitting in his customized chair, bound with plastic zip ties. His chin was resting on his chest. His shirt had been torn open, exposing a series of cuts. Esther recognized the technique. Cause maximum pain without causing shock, unconsciousness, or death. A final deep puncture wound into the heart.

She suspected Zharkov had been surprised, thinking he was well protected in his well-guarded home—enough so that he'd left open the safe-room door. She'd heard him earlier tell his guards that he'd had telephone calls to make. She quickly looked for papers, but there was only an iPad control attached to the chair, and it was locked with a pass code. She didn't have more time.

Backing out slowly, she exited the bedroom into the hallway and reinserted the pistol into the dead man's holster. She pressed the diamond center of her bracelet.

"Help! Help! Please help me!" she screamed.

The guards assembled on the first floor could not hear her, but Garrett shot up from his seat in the kitchen at the same time Mrs. Zharkov hit the panic button on the alarm in her quarters.

"You stay here," one of the guards watching Garrett declared, but he hurried after them. They reached the third floor, where a hysterical Esther was perched on her haunches in the hallway, wailing next to the dead security chief's body.

"Someone shot him!" she shrieked. "When he opened the bedroom door, someone shot him!" She rose to her feet and ran to Garrett.

The first guard reached for her arm to stop her, but she brushed by him, continuing to scream. "Someone's in that bedroom! Someone started shooting when he opened the door!"

She thrust herself into Garrett's arms. The guards drew their pistols, now completely focused on Zharkov's bedroom and the possible intruder lurking there.

"Let's go," she whispered to Garrett, nudging him toward the stairs. They found a lone guard in the foyer with his pistol drawn.

"They need you upstairs!" Garrett exclaimed, jabbing a finger up the staircase.

The guard looked at a shaking Esther clutching Garrett's arm. He said something in Russian and pointed his pistol at Garrett, who realized the guard didn't understand English.

"Upstairs! Now! They want you!" Esther hollered in Russian.

The Russian lowered his gun, assuming the guards had allowed Esther and Garrett to flee, and darted past them up the stairway. Now alone in the foyer, Esther ended her theatrical performance and reached for the front door.

"Wait," Garrett said. "Follow me. There'll be guards out front." He led her down the hallway into the kitchen and out an unguarded rear exit. Both broke into a run toward the hotel.

Mayberry was watching Fallbrook Manor through the binoculars when Garrett and Esther burst into the Grand Piano suite. "What happened?" she asked. "I just saw Zharkov's security guards putting Zharkov's wife into a car in front of the mansion."

"She must be heading to the airport—one of his private jets," Esther replied.

"Without Zharkov? Where's her husband?" Mayberry asked.

"Dead!" Garrett said.

"Did you kill him?"

"No. Someone got to him before us," Esther said.

"They're getting the hell out of London," Garrett said. "They won't want Scotland Yard poking around."

"They're loading something into the car," Mayberry said, still peering through the binoculars.

"The bodies," Esther guessed.

"Bodies? More than one?" Mayberry asked.

"Zharkov and a bodyguard," Esther replied.

"That makes sense," Mayberry said, lowering the glasses. "With his fortune at stake, they won't want anyone to know Zharkov is dead. What now?"

"I thought you were leaving in the morning?" Esther replied.

Mayberry glanced at Garrett. "We're partners. Garrett and I."

None of them spoke for several minutes as each pondered what to do next. Garrett walked to the bar to fetch a beer. Esther let out a loud sigh. Mayberry sat near the piano.

"Big Jules isn't going to be happy," Esther said. "We have to find a way to get back inside his mansion."

"Esther's right," Garrett said. "If there's any evidence of Zharkov being involved in a submarine attack, we still need to document it."

"My lapel pin," Esther said. "I'll go back for it. If everyone is fleeing tonight, they'll leave a skeleton crew behind."

"What hooker returns to a house after a double homicide and asks for her gold pin?" Mayberry asked.

"I don't hear you offering a better idea."

"I happen to have one," Mayberry said. "The only reason a prosti-tute and her bodyguard would risk returning would be if they thought they could squeeze some money out of it."

"Blackmail?" Garrett said.

"Yes," Mayberry replied. "Ask for money to keep silent."

"They'd simply kill the hooker and bodyguard," Esther said.

"Not if they showed up with an attorney from a large London law firm accompanying them," Mayberry said. "Here's my thinking. I pose as an attorney. Esther, call Big Jules and tell him we need . . . a nondisclosure contract, and some sort of documentation that makes it appear I'm from a major London legal firm. We'll also need some-one from the Mossad to act as the firm's bodyguard, sent to protect me. Harder to kill four of us, especially if they believe we have an established law firm behind us."

Esther looked at Mayberry. "I thought you didn't want to get involved in tricks."

"This could work. I'll claim the firm has depositions locked in a safe about what you both saw. Then I'll promise that you two will leave town permanently. The only risk would be if they do a back-ground check on my legal credentials."

"I underestimated you," Esther said. "It's crazy enough to actu-ally work. I'll call Big Jules."

They took turns monitoring Fallbrook Manor through the binoc-ulars but saw nothing unusual once the motorcade transporting the recently widowed Zharkov and her husband's body had departed for the airfield. Exhaustion overrode adrenaline. Then they took turns sleeping.

Big Jules's call came at 9:00 a.m. "Everything is arranged for two p.m. Be convincing."

Room service appeared with lunch that Mayberry had ordered, but no one touched it. Shortly before two o'clock, Esther changed into black slacks and a black vest over a white shirt with the top three buttons undone, in keeping with her call-girl image.

Garrett was wearing denim jeans and an untucked polo shirt large enough to conceal the handgun that the Mossad had supplied, since Zharkov's security team had confiscated his Sig Sauer.

Mayberry was dressed in a tight black skirt, cream silk blouse, and matching black blazer. "These will do," she said as she examined the legal documents arranged by Big Jules. She tucked the paperwork into a briefcase. "Is everyone ready?"

A limo driven by a Mossad officer took them to Fallbrook Manor, where the same Russian-speaking guard who'd let them leave the night before was standing watch outside the front door. He looked confused by their arrival.

In fluent Russian, Mayberry introduced herself and handed him a business card bearing the name of a top London firm. He took it inside, leaving them on the sidewalk. Five minutes later, he reappeared and held the door open. Mayberry entered first.

"My name is Nikita," a fiftyish-looking man standing in the foyer said in English, extending his hand. Mayberry put down her briefcase and shook his hand with her left, noting his manicured fingernails and Savile Row three-piece tailored suit.

"I'm here in my role as a solicitor," Mayberry announced. "Are you more comfortable speaking in Russian or English?"

"English is fine. I'm in charge of this estate when Mr. Zharkov and his wife are away. How can I assist you?"

"My clients and I wish to resolve a rather delicate legal matter." She introduced Esther and Garrett using the same fake names that they'd used the evening before.

"A legal matter? Of what sort?"

"We're here to negotiate a nondisclosure agreement."

"Forgive me, but . . . I'm not certain I understand what you are suggesting."

"Then let me make this clear," Mayberry said in a sharp tone. "If you are not interested in negotiating with us, our next stop will be Scotland Yard."

The polite smile on Nikita's face vanished.

"Just to be clear," Mayberry continued, "my firm has hired a bodyguard to accompany us here and is fully aware of our arrival." She nodded toward the Mossad officer without introducing him. "In addition, my firm has video depositions from both of our clients, attesting in detail what they observed last night."

"Mr. Zharkov is a highly respected international businessman who—"

"Who is dead," Esther cut in. "Him and that other guy. The security chief."

He glared at her. "I need to consult Moscow. Let's move into the parlor, shall we?"

He led them into the same room off the foyer where Esther and Garrett had been taken the night before. Same grandfather clock. Same tick-tocking. Mayberry and Esther sat on a sofa near the fireplace. Garrett and the bodyguard stood at each end of the couch. Three other large Russian security guards appeared, standing between them and the front door.

No one spoke. Twenty minutes later, Nikita surfaced. "I've arranged a conference call between you and our lawyers."

"Do you have a fax machine?" Mayberry asked.

"The only fax line is in Mr. Zharkov's private office," Nikita replied. "If you have legal materials, it would be best to send them electronically or by courier."

She lifted her briefcase. "It's in everyone's best interest to finalize this agreement now. A fax is the most secure method to exchange these documents. We're not interested in leaving an electronic trail. Nor are my clients interested in quibbling. When we leave this house, they intend to disappear."

"The lawyers are waiting. You will discuss this with them."

"Nikita," Mayberry replied firmly, "I'm not going anywhere with you without my two clients and our bodyguard. Now, where is that fax?"

"Wait here," Nikita said, again disappearing upstairs. Two more Russian goons joined the others blocking the door. Garrett rested his hand on his hip, closer to the pistol in the waistband behind his back.

Nikita reappeared. "Please come with me. We will use the fax in Mr. Zharkov's office." In Russian, he instructed the guards to remain downstairs, except for the one who'd met them outside on the steps and knew them from last night.

Up the stairs to the second floor, they entered Zharkov's private office. Nikita motioned Mayberry to sit in front of the oligarch's highly prized Nicholas II desk, where a telephone speaker had been placed. Nikita sat behind it while the Russian security guard stood at the door. Garrett, Esther, and their Mossad security guard positioned themselves along a back wall.

A voice speaking Russian could be heard over the speaker, followed by two others, one male, the other female. All claimed to be lawyers. Mayberry introduced herself in Russian.

While they were talking, Garrett began to pace back and forth, looking vigilant. While he was acting like an amped-up hired goon, he was actually looking around the office for anything that could link Zharkov to a planned submarine attack. His eyes settled on two maps displayed on the office's conference-room table. One contained a highly detailed topography of the outer continental shelf off Virginia and North Carolina; the other, the entire North Atlantic Ocean.

As Mayberry handed legal papers from her briefcase to Nikita to fax to Moscow, Garrett walked back toward Esther and caught her attention. He subtly motioned to the table across the room.

"Why is this taking so long?" Esther complained in a loud voice.

"They need to read the contracts," Mayberry replied.

Esther groaned and retrieved a gold-plated makeup compact case from her purse. She raised it to her face and applied rouge as she began to walk toward the maps. The Russian guard noticed and started toward her. "The sunlight is better by the window," she explained, nodding at windows near the table. The bodyguard returned to the door.

Garrett checked the time on the Rolex that he was still wearing. They'd been inside long enough for Moscow to conduct a background check on Mayberry's nonexistent solicitor credentials.

"We need to get the hell out of here," he declared, interrupting Mayberry and the Russian lawyers. "As long as we get our money, we'll keep our mouths shut."

Mayberry picked up her briefcase. "Your lawyers have the required papers, and my clients are clearly uncomfortable remaining here. Quite frankly, so am I. We'll return to my office. My card has a fax number on it for signatures."

One of the Russian attorneys objected over the speaker, but Mayberry had already started toward the door.

"Wait!" Nikita declared, standing from behind Zharkov's desk.

The Russian guard stood ready to stop them from leaving.

"You forgot this," Nikita said. He lifted up the gold lapel pin with the black rose. "I believe it was a family heirloom."

Esther walked to the desk. Took the pin from him.

Five minutes later, they were riding in the limo toward Claridge's. Garrett beamed. "We did it!"

"I misjudged you," Esther said to Mayberry. "You were brilliant!" She removed the gold compact case from her purse and opened it. "I managed to get video of the entire office."

"The maps?" Garrett asked.

"Yes. I'll send it to Tel Aviv. This not only takes video, it senses heat and moisture."

"Meaning?" Garrett said.

"If anyone had their fingers on those maps recently, we'll be able to detect their prints—and, more importantly, the spots they were touching."

Garrett had opened his mouth to speak when a bullet punched through the car's windshield, killing their Mossad driver.

PART IV

I will send rain on the earth forty days and forty nights;
and I will blot out from the face of the land every living
thing that I have made.

—*Genesis 7:4*

THIRTY-ONE

Fathi Aziz rose shortly after 3:00 a.m., dressed in pungent, unwashed work clothes, and pulled the hood of a grimy gray sweatshirt over his head.

A dented, tired GMC Savana van was idling outside, with five construction workers as passengers. Aziz entered and the van began the trip to Checkpoint 300, one of thirteen major crossings where Palestinians with Israeli work permits are allowed to pass through a concrete border wall. Although Israel abandoned the Gaza Strip in 2005, a land, sea, and air blockade continued to contain the 2.6 million Arabs living on the West Bank.

Aziz usually crossed into Israel through a maze of secret tunnels and drainage pipes. But those routes were too risky this morning because of clashes between young Palestinians, throwing rocks and burning tires, and young Israeli soldiers, firing tear gas, rubber-coated bullets, and live ammunition. Patrols had been stepped up.

More than three thousand workers passed through Checkpoint 300 each day, some of the seventy thousand Palestinians allowed to work legally in Israel. Despite those numbers, it would have been difficult for Aziz to slip through unnoticed. Each worker had to press their thumbs on a fingerprint scanner mated to their photo and work permit. Yesterday, Aziz had received word that the scanners at Checkpoint 300 had stopped working. A breach, but only if they hadn't been repaired overnight.

No one inside the van spoke, and everyone but the driver and Aziz nodded off as they traveled north on Highway 60, a de facto memorial to violence. Past the sleepy Palestinian town of Saer, where thirty-five Israelis had been murdered; past Kiryat Arba, a Jewish settlement, whose lights could be seen across the border wall, re-membered as the home of American-born physician Baruch Gold-stein, who killed twenty-nine Muslim worshippers with a machine gun at the Cave of the Patriarchs.

At the age of forty-five, Aziz had never known life in a free home-land. In 1967 Israeli soldiers had captured Jerusalem and crushed Arab forces in a mere six days. Despite a flurry of on-again, off-again negotiations, Israelis still held the Palestinian homeland as a de facto prison. As a child, Aziz had been taught to hate Jews. When barely a teen, he'd thrown a Molotov cocktail against the side of an Israeli Wolf armored vehicle. In most such attacks, the war machine would have continued unfazed, but not this time. Aziz would later declare that Allah had divinely directed the flames through the Wolf's pro-tective barriers, causing Israeli soldiers, on fire, to flee into a barrage of stones, bottles, and death.

The commuter van finally arrived at the Israeli checkpoint, where its occupants hurried into chutes that guided them like cattle through a series of slowly narrowing concrete passageways, forcing them into a single line.

"Are they checking fingerprints?" Aziz asked the Palestinian waiting in front of him. He passed that query up the line. Moments later, a response. No, the thumbprint machines remained broken.

Aziz felt relief and fought an urge to vomit as he moved at a snail's pace along the line, surrounded by the smell of sweat, urine, and filth. Rising temperatures. Men pushing against men. As he slogged forward, Aziz used his body to block younger Palestinians trying to shove ahead in line, taking care not to fall lest he be trampled— all under the watchful eyes of Israeli security cameras. After more than an hour, he could see the metal turnstile that opened into the "aquarium," an oblong room where Israeli soldiers sat behind bullet-resistant glass, comparing the photo on each worker's permit to his face, and—on most days—to his scanned thumbprints.

It was too late now for Aziz to turn back. The mob pressing behind him wouldn't allow him to retreat.

He entered the turnstile and waited for it to be unlocked so he could continue into the aquarium sally port. *Click*. He tested the stile and pushed it around.

The Israelis operated three windows, much like those used by bank tellers. Aziz and two others moved forward. He recognized the Palestinian who approached the first window, a Jihad Brigade brother traveling with him. The worker at the second was a stranger. Aziz moved to the third window, where he raised a forged work permit that contained his photo and counterfeited official stamps.

Fearful that the guard had seen the YouTube video of him threatening the Great Satan, Aziz lowered his eyes and tried to become another faceless Palestinian.

"Where are you working today?" the guard asked.

Aziz recited the name of a street and his Israeli employer's name.

The soldier glanced at Aziz and returned his papers.

"Step back."

Now all three were waiting to exit. Instead, a side door flung open, and five soldiers burst in.

"On your knees!" a guard yelled.

Aziz felt time slowing. A normal reaction, as every extraneous thought yielded to a singular focus.

"Hands behind your heads."

Aziz obeyed. Eyes forward.

"One of you has fake papers," the head guard announced.

Aziz waited. Anticipating what would come next. Handcuffs. Interrogation.

The guard stopped in front of the stranger kneeling between Aziz and his fellow jihadist. Pointed his pistol at the man's head.

"My brother's papers," the stranger declared. "He's sick. Our family needs the money."

Two Israelis grabbed his arms, forced him to stand. Frisked him for weapons.

"My children need to eat," the Palestinian protested.

Plastic cuffs secured his wrists. He was hustled through the same door the guards had used to enter the sally port.

"You two go." The exit door opened.

Aziz hurried from the checkpoint to where buses and cars were waiting to transport workers to their jobs. He and his fellow jihadist rode in different vehicles away from the border wall. Ten minutes later, they reconnected on a side street. Became passengers in a sedan waiting to drive them north.

By the time Aziz and the jihadist crossed the Jordan River, it was midafternoon. Three hours later they boarded a private Iranian aircraft at the Damascus airport for the flight to Tehran. A car waiting there took Aziz and his comrade to a nondescript building on the city's outskirts.

They waited there for an hour in a room furnished with three metal folding chairs and a table. Nothing else.

Like members of Hamas, Aziz and his fellow Jihad Brigade fighters were Sunni Muslims. Their Iranian hosts were Shi'ite Muslims. But their mutual hatred of the United States trumped their religious dispute about who was the legitimate successor to the Prophet Muhammad.

"As-salamu alaikum," General Kardar said when he finally joined them. He marched directly to the table and began removing papers from an accordion folder that his chief aide, who was accompanying him, had brought to the meeting. "The scientific schematics you will need to spark fear in the Americans," he said. Next on the table, he displayed photographs of a nuclear bomb. "For you to upload to the internet."

Aziz said, "The Mossad Jew in Italy wasn't killed, even though you told me he had been assassinated."

"I was misinformed," Kardar said. "What does it matter? You fear it will make your threat less believable? Was there not an attempt to kill him? Did you not claim credit for it? Were you not a hero to our Arab brothers despite his survival?"

"The Jews outsmarted you and embarrassed me."

General Kardar stiffened. "Do not look backward. Give the Americans six days."

"Six days? That is too much time. You risk having them find the bomb, or me."

"They will not."

"When will you tell me the code needed to detonate it?"

"On the seventh day."

"You do not trust me with it now?"

"On the seventh day, when it is time to explode the bomb."

"The money for our cause?"

"Small bundles—Jordanian dinars, Israeli shekels, Egyptian pounds, and US currency. Are you ready to be filmed?"

"And the weapons we requested?"

"Yes, rockets smuggled into Gaza City."

Aziz followed him into a separate room, where a prayer cloth had been spread on the floor. The same props: a Black Standard jihadist flag, the prerequisite AK-47, and the Holy Qur'an. Four Quds Force soldiers with their faces hidden behind masks were waiting to pose behind him. A fifth officer operated a camera.

"Here's your script." He offered Aziz a single sheet of paper.

Aziz didn't bother to take it. "Allah will speak through me."

"You must say these exact words, just like before."

Aziz read the single sentence out loud. "'From the ocean, the Great Satan's destruction will come.'" He shook his head disapprovingly. "These words are too similar to what you instructed me to say after you told me the Zionist had been assassinated. Do you not remember? 'I will soon deliver a flood over your cities from beneath your oceans, and the wrath of Allah will destroy you.' You are telling our enemies too much. Do you want them to know your plan? They will use these words to find the bomb before I can explode it."

"Allah, blessed be his holy name, is using me as his instrument," Kardar said, blatantly appealing to Aziz's religious fervor. "We must trust him. You must trust him. Say exactly what is written."

THIRTY-TWO

Now driverless, the armored Maybach S600 sedan that Mayberry, Esther, and Garrett were riding in swerved into oncoming traffic and ran headfirst into a Mini Cooper. A double-decker bus smashed into its rear, shoving the small sedan underneath the Maybach. The luxury car rolled over onto its right side and came to a stop on the sidewalk at the entrance of a local pub.

The fatal gunshot that had killed their driver had come from the left side of the busy street. This meant that the Maybach's undercarriage was now blocking the shooter's vantage point, temporarily shielding its passengers.

Seat belts and airbags had protected all three from serious injury. Sitting on the left in the front seat of the right-hand-drive car, Esther was the first to free her belt. She immediately dropped onto the dead driver, twisted, and reached up for the handle of the passenger door above her head.

"No!" Garrett hollered from the back seat. "You'll get shot if you climb out!"

"The moonroof," Mayberry said.

Esther pushed the dash button that opened the Maybach's roof. Mayberry, who was nearest the opening, crawled through it at the same moment the limousine was hit by another round. The Maybach's armor was thick enough to protect those seated inside, but the shooter was not firing directly at them. He was firing armor-piercing slugs into the car's reinforced gas tank. Esther was out next, rising to her feet on the sidewalk with a handgun that she'd retrieved from the car's glove compartment. A third shot punched through the gas tank, causing fuel to spew.

Garrett crawled through the moonroof and joined the women. "The pub!" he said. Its entrance was less than four yards from the Maybach. Patrons inside had initially gone outside to investigate, but retreated after hearing gunshots, leaving its door open.

"You first," Esther yelled at Mayberry, who bolted across the sidewalk.

"You next," Garrett told Esther. She dashed to safety without drawing fire.

Garrett started to follow, but as soon as his head appeared, the sniper fired. The round nicked the car, which deflected it, but Garrett was forced to return to safety behind the Maybach. He was penned in. He readied himself for another dash.

The sniper quickly changed rounds. Shooting a bullet into a gasoline tank does not cause an explosion or fire. But now the sniper fired a tracer round, which ignited in the air.

Garrett burst toward the doorway at the same moment the tracer round struck the leaking fuel, creating a massive fireball. Because the Maybach's undercarriage faced the street, most of the flames shot away from Garrett. Even so, the explosion knocked him face-first across the pub's floor. Black smoke billowed upward from the burning wreckage.

Mayberry hurried to him while Esther slipped to the pub's doorway, hoping to spot the shooter.

"You burned bad?" Mayberry asked.

"Is there a way to be burned good?" he replied, pushing himself up on his feet. "I'm okay."

"The sniper was trying to kill you, Garrett, not us," Esther said, joining them. "I think he's gone."

"The Russians?" Mayberry asked.

"Doesn't make sense," Garrett replied. "Why not just kill us in Zharkov's mansion? No need to ambush us and get the police involved."

Esther was already on her cell phone when a City of London constable ran into the pub.

"Anyone injured?" he called.

A pub patron darted past him out onto the street, causing the policeman to curse. "Stay put! This is a crime scene."

Paramedics arrived amid the loud blare of sirens and immediately began treating those cut by flying glass and debris. More constables entered.

Garrett whispered, "Where's a back door?"

"No, don't run," Esther said. "I called my embassy."

Six men in black uniforms and protective vests arrived, and their squad leader marched directly to the threesome.

"You're the ones from the Maybach, aren't you?" he asked. "Malcolm Evans, with London Counter Terrorism Command. Let's have your names." One of his men stepped forward ready to write on a notepad with his pen.

"Diplomatic immunity," Esther said. "I'm Israeli, and they're with me."

"A diplomat, huh?" Evans replied skeptically, eyeballing her skintight black slacks, unbuttoned blouse, and thick makeup. She'd forgotten that she was still dressed like a prostitute.

"Call this number at the Israeli embassy," she said, offering the digits.

"Show me your diplomatic passport," Evans ordered.

"It's at Claridge's," Garrett volunteered.

"The shots came from a rooftop across the street," Mayberry said. "I'm an FBI agent from the States."

"On business, are you? You FBI too?" he asked Garrett.

"No, all of us are on vacation."

"Let me understand this, mate. An Israeli diplomat, a Yank FBI agent, and another Yank bloke just happen to be on a holiday when they're attacked on one of our busiest streets?"

One of his men whispered into his ear.

"It seems there was another one of you," Evans said. "The poor chap behind the wheel outside."

"The gunman was firing armor-piercing rounds," Mayberry said.

"Bloody hell," Evans replied, "aren't you a real Sherlock Holmes?"

"I insist you call my embassy," Esther said.

One of Evans's men slipped behind them and saw the handguns that Esther and Garrett had tucked behind their backs.

He raised his Heckler & Koch G36C rifle and hollered, "They've got pistols!"

Evans took an immediate step back.

"Everyone needs to stay calm," Garrett said, lifting his arms.

Evans's men disarmed them.

"You still expect me to believe you was just on a holiday?" Evans asked. Over his shoulder, Garrett noticed another figure approaching them, with two large men. Clearly his bodyguards.

"Emory Wilson from the Home Office," the newcomer announced. One of the bodyguards flashed credentials. "You and your men may step down now."

Without waiting for Evans to respond, Wilson said, "You must be the Israeli, and the two of you the Americans. Please be good enough to follow me."

"Wait!" Evans stammered.

"No," Wilson said, "there will be no waiting. This is now a Home Office matter. Don't make me call your better."

Evans stepped out of the way, letting them pass.

Two Jaguar sedans were outside. Within moments, they'd reached 2 Marsham Street, headquarters of the Home Office, a rectangular modern structure protected by metal shutters, concrete sidewalk barriers, and security cameras. Architectural color came from a horizontal stained glass overhang with red, blue, green, and yellow squares. Garrett thought it the most hideous government building he'd ever seen.

Wilson led them into a spacious conference room and motioned for them to sit around a table there. Before he could speak, Esther declared, "I expect you to honor my diplomatic immunity. I demand you release me immediately."

"Yes, I've been told you are a cultural attaché," he said, not hiding the skepticism in his tone. "I'm certain someone from your embassy will be joining us shortly." Turning to Garrett and Mayberry, he said, "I've read about you chaps in a not-so-complimentary American newspaper article, and also had a chat with the French about what happened in Paris. For a couple reportedly being on a holiday, you've gotten yourselves into quite a few sticky wickets. A high-speed chase in Italy. A shooting in Paris. Tangling with an international terrorist named Saeedi Bashar whose daughter was fatally shot by Mr. Garrett in the Paris underground. Tell me, is this how you spend all of your holidays?"

One of Wilson's assistants entered with a packet.

"As I'm certain you are aware," Wilson continued, "London has one of the most comprehensive surveillance camera systems in the world. As many as a half million cameras in our city." He removed several photos and showed them. "Let's begin with today's attack. This man was spotted entering the building where the shots came from, and also leaving it after the shooting. Do you recognize him?"

Garrett and Mayberry scanned the images. Esther refused, staring straight ahead. Although the man in the pictures was wearing dark glasses and a hat, a jagged scar was visible on his neck.

"Well?" Wilson asked.

Neither one of them answered.

"Do you recognize this bloke?" Wilson asked, sliding several more photos across the table. They showed Iranian general Kardar entering and leaving Zharkov's mansion two nights earlier.

Again, no response.

"I take it from your silence," Wilson said, "you have no idea what business an Iranian general was conducting with Mr. Zharkov so late at night?"

Garrett shrugged. "You'll need to ask them."

Wilson pulled additional pictures from the file and tossed them on the table: Esther, Garrett, Mayberry, and their Mossad driver visiting Zharkov's mansion earlier in the day, before they were attacked by a sniper.

"What was the purpose of your visit this morning?"

"We didn't see Zharkov," Mayberry volunteered.

"Yes, I am aware," Wilson said. "We checked with his staff this morning and were told that Mr. Zharkov left London last night. Which invites the question, why did you go there this morning, if not to see him?"

Silence.

Wilson produced a final batch of photos. These showed Esther and Garrett coming and going from the mansion on the night she posed as a prostitute.

"These images are especially intriguing," Wilson said. "Taken by a camera across the street. They show you arriving, and later, a number of individuals leaving, presumably Zharkov and his wife. What's missing are photos of you exiting the mansion. How do you explain this?"

Mayberry glanced at Garrett, who remained stone-faced.

"I've been patient with you," Wilson said, intentionally becoming more harsh in his inflection. "Now I must insist. If you continue to not cooperate, I must warn you that the Home Office has considerable discretion when it comes to holding foreigners on suspected terrorism charges. Much like your government, we can make suspects disappear for long periods." He paused to let his threat sink in. "Now what business did you have with Taras Zharkov?"

A knock on the conference-room door interrupted them, and a man and woman entered. The woman walked directly to Wilson, bent down, and whispered in his ear. He responded by gathering the photographs from the table, standing, and leaving the room.

The woman said, "The Home Secretary and Her Majesty must insist that the three of you depart from England within the next twenty-four hours." She turned and left, leaving the man alone with them.

"I'm from the Israeli embassy," he said. "Director Levi sent me. I have cars waiting outside."

"Where are you taking us?" Garrett asked.

"To our embassy. We've arranged for your luggage to be delivered there. I'd strongly suggest you accept our invitation, in case the Brits change their mind."

THIRTY-THREE

"I'm not certain spending the night here is safe," Mayberry said as their motorcade approached the Israeli embassy and chancery near Kensington Palace Gardens.

Even though it was after 10:00 p.m., protestors were waving placards.

STOP THE MASSACRE! STAND UP FOR GAZA! FREE PALESTINE!

From inside the SUV, they could hear a bullhorn.

"I see British people from the left, from the right, from across the board demonstrating here," the speaker proclaimed. "Because this is not a fight between left and right, it's a fight between right and wrong."

Applause. Chants of "Free Gaza!" "Free Palestine!"

"Britain is a United States stooge, and the United States is an Israeli pawn. We demand a two-state solution. Without it, there can be no peace."

An Israeli flag was set on fire, its flames illuminating the angry faces clustered around it.

"This protest is nothing," Esther said, "compared to Nakba."

"Nak-what-a?" Garrett asked.

"Nakba commemorates the day when the state of Israel was officially recognized and thousands of Palestinians were displaced," Mayberry explained.

"Yes. On Nakba, they turn out in the thousands outside our gates."

The Israeli drivers flipped on blue lights and strobes in the convoy's grillwork. London bobbies on horseback forced an opening through the taunting crowd.

A security gate—one of two—opened, allowing the three vehicles to enter the fenced grounds. Garrett looked through the window at the red-brick mansion built between 1860 and 1862 for author William Makepeace Thackeray, now provided with blast-proof windows, reinforced walls, and electronic surveillance defenses.

"Your rooms will be modest—former servant quarters—but adequate for the night," Esther said. She escorted them through a side door guarded by two embassy security officers. "The London police returned my handgun," she said. "Sorry, Garrett, but it appears that they kept the one you were using."

They followed her up a narrow staircase to the mansion's top floor. "This will be for you," she told Garrett, opening a door that he had to duck to pass through. Inside was a twin bed, chair, dresser, and sink, but no closet or windows.

Esther moved directly across the hall. "This will be yours," she told Mayberry. Equally Spartan.

"There are bells above the beds," Esther said, pointing into Mayberry's room at a silver bell with a cord attached. "The bells were used to summon servants."

"And who, exactly, will be summoning me if mine rings?" Garrett asked.

"There's a shared toilet at the end of the hall," Esther replied, ignoring his question.

"What? No chamber pots? How about something to eat? Possibly a shower?"

"You can take a shower in the basement men's locker room. I'll have the kitchen staff send something up."

Garrett nodded toward the security guard stationed in front of the staircase, the only exit from the top floor.

"We can't have foreigners wandering around our embassy," Esther said, "even if they're friends."

"Does your ambassador live here?" Mayberry asked.

"He has a private residence in St John's Wood in northwest London. We're the only ones spending the night."

"Which room is yours?" Garrett asked.

"Not on this floor. The security officer will know how to reach me. Be ready at five. Director Levi has asked us to fly to Tel Aviv to meet with him. Given your tenuous status with the Brits and your own people, it would be best if you agreed."

"I'm going to grab a shower," Garrett said after Esther left them. "You want to talk about all this when I get back? Hopefully over food."

"My hand is killing me. I'm taking my pain pills and getting some rest."

"Valerie," he said softly. "I think we need to talk. Not just about the Roc, but what happened between us in the hotel."

He watched her face turning red. "It was a mistake," she said. "There's nothing more to say."

He started to respond, but stopped himself. Turning, he began walking toward the security guard stationed at the staircase.

"Knock on my door," she called after him. "If I'm up to it, I'll join you for a bite."

An escort took Garrett to the basement, where he stripped, spent fifteen minutes alone in the sauna, and lingered another ten in a hot shower before wrapping himself in a white terry-cloth bathrobe that he found next to a stack of towels. His ribs hurt from when he had been thrown across the pub floor. Opening the robe, he checked his torso in a waist-high mirror. Scars from the helicopter crash he'd endured in Africa covered most of his right side. When he twisted, he could see the light-red burns on his left, caused by the Maybach explosion. He closed the robe.

His escort was waiting outside the lockers to guide him upstairs.

Garrett went to tap on Mayberry's door, but paused when he heard voices inside.

"Valerie?" he asked. "Mayberry, you okay?"

The door opened a crack. Esther looked out. "She's busy right now." Through the narrow opening, he caught a glimpse of Mayberry in a robe sitting on the edge of her bed with a stranger.

"What's going—"

"It's okay," Mayberry called. "He can come in."

Esther opened the door wide enough for Garrett to get a good look at the stranger. An older Asian man wearing a white lab coat, closing a case next to the bed.

"Mr. Wen Ho Lee is the best acupuncturist in London," Esther explained. "He treats a lot of us, mostly for chronic back pain."

"I feel more relaxed," Mayberry said. "But that could just be exhaustion."

"You must wait twenty-four hours," the acupuncturist announced. "Your back and hand will be much, much better."

A kitchen worker appeared in the hallway, carrying a tray with covered dishes.

"Where should I put this?" he asked.

"Not in here," Mayberry said. "I need to get dressed."

"Across the hall in my room," Garrett volunteered, opening his door.

"I told them to send up three plates," Esther said. She walked into his room and showed the worker where to put the tray. "I warned the kitchen you were Americans."

Esther removed the covers, revealing two hamburgers with fries. "Obviously, these are for you and Mayberry."

She uncovered the third. "For me, shawarma."

"What the heck is that?"

"Slow-cooked turkey with hummus, tahini, salad, pickles, and cabbage served on *laffa*—what you probably call pita bread. For dessert, vanilla ice cream and *knafeh*."

Garrett picked up a box drink on the tray. He couldn't read the Hebrew label.

"*Shoko b'sakit*, which translates as 'chocolate milk in a bag,'" she said, sitting on the bed's edge.

He dragged a chair opposite her and took a bite of his burger. "Why'd you do it? Arrange an acupuncturist for Valerie."

"Try some of this." She tore off a piece of *laffa*, covered it with shawarma, and held it up to his mouth. He bit into it, but half fell on the floor. She laughed.

"The acupuncturist?" he said, wiping his mouth.

"You Americans love pills. A pill for a headache. A pill if you are sad. A pill if you are happy. Pills, pills, pills. The Chinese have been practicing holistic medicine for centuries."

"I'm not talking about that. Why did you help her? You're not friends."

"Perhaps we are becoming friends."

"No emotional attachments, remember?"

"You were listening to our conversation on the train. Pretending to be asleep." She took another quick bite and then stood to leave. "The ice cream and sweets are all yours, but if you're smart, you will share them with her."

THIRTY-FOUR

"Why does God stand by the Palestinian people?" Fathi Aziz asked in a freshly uploaded video. *"Why does God stand by the brothers of the Jihad Brigade? Because we welcome martyrdom, this is why he stands by us."* Subtitles ran across the bottom of the screen. He spoke in a confident and calm voice. *"Remember in the battle for the Khaybar, the Prophet handed the Flag to the one who had earned the right to bear it. This man won victory not by military strength but because he believed. He did not fear death, and those who try to frighten us with death merely hand us badges of honor."*

The CIA analyst in Langley responsible for monitoring and analyzing Aziz's statement was only half paying attention when a coworker entered with coffee.

"This one saying anything new?" the coworker asked.

"Just a bunch of SJB," the analyst replied. "Standard jihadist bullshit."

"Heed my words," Aziz continued. *"You followers of Satan and infidels. God sent the prophet Noah to warn his people. Even his own wife and son laughed at him. They disregarded his warnings. God sent the deluge and drowned them and the people."*

"Sounds like he's taking a page from a Southern Baptist televangelist," the coworker quipped.

The camera closed in on Aziz's face. His eyes narrowed. *"God has given me the Flag from Khaybar."* His voice changed, becoming more intense. More deliberate. *"God has given me a nuclear bomb to destroy Sodom and Gomorrah. He will honor the martyrs who toppled their towers. From the ocean, the Great Satan's destruction will come."*

Aziz hesitated. Raised a forefinger and pointed directly into the camera lens.

"You have six days, America, before death will visit your shores."

Schematics of a nuclear bomb appeared on the screen, and still photos of what appeared to be a finished bomb with the obligatory words "Death to America!" painted on its silver exterior.

Aziz reappeared. *"Here are our demands. Your Zionist puppets must leave the West Bank, East Jerusalem, the Gaza Strip, the Golan Heights, and the Sinai Peninsula. All Jewish settlements must be abandoned. The West must recognize Palestine as a sovereign state and end all financial and military support for the Jews. In six days, this must be done if you wish to escape nuclear annihilation."*

A black-and-white video appeared. The Nevada desert. A bright light and mushroom cloud. Footage uploaded from the famous 1964 "Daisy" attack ad of a nuclear bomb test that so terrified Americans that they voted against Republican presidential hopeful Barry Goldwater.

Such a blatant threat about a nuclear attack was not SJB.

The analyst grabbed his desk phone. He needed to warn his superiors about the video so they could decide whether or not to remove it. His call and their decision would come too late. Within minutes, social media was spreading Aziz's threat. The *New York Times*, the *Washington Post*, and other major newspapers posted news bulletins on their sites. Facebook began spreading stories about an imminent nuclear attack.

President Fitzgerald summoned Director Whittington to the John F. Kennedy Conference Room, better known as the White House Situation Room, in the West Wing.

"Talk to me," President Fitzgerald said impatiently. "Does this psychopath have a nuclear bomb?"

"According to our technical analysis, we believe there is a less than four percent chance that he does. We have reviewed all phone traffic in the region and found none between Aziz and his people that would suggest they have obtained such a device. A computer inventory of known weaponry has found that all known nuclear devices are fully accounted for, and as you are aware, we keep in close contact with our allies about possibly lost or stolen bombs. Even Russia has assured us that none is missing.

"Mr. President," Whittington continued in a reassuring voice, "Aziz is the same jihadist who announced that his Jihad Brigade had successfully assassinated Director Levi in Italy at his niece's wedding, and we know Levi is alive and well. Consequently, we have a high degree of confidence that his threat is simply bluster."

"Someone did try to kill Julian Levi," the president said.

"Yes, sir, but we question whether Aziz and his organization had anything to do with that attempt. We've expended considerable time and resources investigating Aziz, and he is known as a bragger. Logic dictates that he would have known that Levi was still alive if he'd sent someone to kill him and that assassin failed."

"You're telling me this video is a huge hoax."

"We are continuing to thoroughly investigate it, but yes, at this point I do. The Jihad Brigade has less than two hundred known devotees—and all live inside Palestine, around which, as you know, Israel keeps a tight noose. None of the major terrorist organizations—Hamas, even ISIS—is known to be affiliated with it, and Aziz's religious teachings are so extreme that even the most radical clerics reject him. A psychological profile has established that Aziz has narcissistic personality disorder and ultra-grandiosity, both of which are evident in his new message."

Whittington paused. "Mr. President, you might feel more at ease if we go through our analysis of his threat frame by frame."

Aziz's video appeared on a large wall monitor. Whittington played a snippet.

"In this part Aziz mentions the Khaybar Flag, a clear sign of his delusional thinking. It's a reference to the year 628, when Muhammad attacked a Jewish stronghold in the Khaybar Oasis. The Jews there were better trained and better outfitted. Although the Jews were vastly outnumbered, they were able to defeat their attackers. According to the story, Muhammad announced that God would choose a new military leader and guarantee him victory. Muhammad's greatest soldiers lined up, thinking they would be selected to carry the Khaybar Flag, but God directed Muhammad to give it to an unknown soldier named Ali. He had no military training, but he defeated the Jews because he loved God, obeyed God, and was eager to die for God."

Whittington looked from the monitor at the president.

"Mr. President, is there a better example of his narcissism and delusions of grandeur? Aziz is declaring himself God's chosen one and implying through the Khaybar Flag story that all other terrorist groups have failed at defeating us. He's promoting the idea that he alone can defeat God's enemies. And there were other religious references."

President Fitzgerald said, "Sodom and Gomorrah. Noah."

"Again, using religion to puff himself up. Sodom and Gomorrah were destroyed by fire and brimstone. The 'deluge,' as he called it, refers to Noah's flood. Both reinforce the belief that God has chosen him to bring about the destruction of the infidels. He mentioned the 'martyrs who toppled their towers'—an obvious reference to nine-eleven and the Twin Towers—suggesting that he will follow their lead. He adds that his attack against us will come 'from the ocean' or rise from the sea."

"I could discount all of this as the rantings of a religious zealot," the president said, "except for one troubling fact."

"Yes, sir, what is that?"

"Radi's letter. Radi warned us that the Iranians had manufactured a nuclear bomb, and planned to attack us with it, carried in a submarine. To my ears, that sounds exactly what Aziz is now threatening to do."

"Sir, the Jihad Brigade has no wealth nor benefactors. Its members are young, impoverished Palestinians."

"Have you considered that the Iranians might have simply given Aziz a nuclear bomb?"

"Let's assume they actually have made a nuclear bomb, even though there is no credible evidence supporting this. The Iranians are Shi'a, or Shi'ite Muslims. The Jihad Brigade and Aziz are Sunni. Our analysts doubt that Iran would trust Sunni Muslims with a nuclear bomb. In addition, our predictive analytics show that if the Iranians had successfully developed a bomb, their first target would be Israel."

Whittington wasn't done. "We also have to ask ourselves, where would a largely insignificant, fledgling Palestinian cell with no funds obtain a submarine from a foreign military and find a crew? Even the Iranians don't have a submarine capable of making a transatlantic voyage—especially without being detected."

"You said in our last briefing that the Israelis had reported seeing a rogue submarine in the Mediterranean."

"Yes, an old Soviet submarine from the Cold War. But even if that submarine exists, our navy has not reported any such submarine approaching or entering our waters."

The president rocked back in his seat, thought for a moment. "Aziz uploaded schematics. Showed a photo of an actual bomb."

"Yes, sir," Whittington said, fast-forwarding the video to the schematics. "The Israelis have confirmed that these are Iranian plans, but they could have come from any source on the internet. There also is a problem with the bomb in his video. It is the type made to be dropped out of an airplane, not shot through a torpedo tube or launched from a submarine."

"What if he is using something other than a submarine?"

"Bringing it through one of our ports on a cargo ship?" Whittington suggested.

"Exactly. I have been trying to get Congress to fund better border security, and it is refusing."

"Assuming Aziz somehow obtained a bomb, it would be a valid concern. As you know, Mr. President, we have something like twelve million shipping containers entering our ports every year, and Congress's refusal to back your plans does put us in jeopardy. But only if Aziz has secured a nuclear weapon. And that is a big if."

"He's given us a six-day deadline," Fitzgerald said. "If all of this is bluster, why would he put a firm deadline on it?"

"Because he's completely delusional. He wants to spark fear and cause panic. It's quite possible he has simply convinced himself that God will provide him with a bomb in six days. Once the deadline passes, there's a good chance he will announce that Allah told him not to use the bomb. Who understands the words of a madman? Sir, you appointed me to take charge of the CIA because you needed someone there with a steady hand and calm head. We'll keep investigating his threat, but based on our data and analysis, we believe Aziz is a grandiose loudmouth, not a serious player."

"Just to be safe," Fitzgerald said, "I don't want anything larger than a minnow getting near our coasts without us knowing about it. And get back on the phone and talk to the Israelis."

The president started to stand but paused midway up from his chair. "Where are Garrett and Mayberry? They're the ones who told us about Radi's letter."

"They're still in Europe, chasing after the Palestinian who they believe is responsible for Radi's murder. I received a call from the British Home Office about the two of them being involved in an incident in London."

"An incident?"

"They were unharmed, but a car they were riding in was attacked by a sniper."

"Is any of that linked to Aziz?"

"Sir, in my opinion, they are on a wild-goose chase."

Ten minutes later, as Whittington was leaving the White House, his private cell phone rang. The caller ID showed the number as that of Robert Calhoun at the *Washington Interceptor*.

Whittington ignored it.

THIRTY-FIVE

Neither Garrett nor Mayberry had been to the pristine Mediterranean coastal city of Tel Aviv on the outskirts of an ancient Arab city called Jaffa that, over time, had been overwhelmed by two aliyahs—waves of Zionist immigrants.

As the private jet circled, both gazed down on Tel Aviv's White City, more than four thousand sleek, blindingly white buildings designed in the 1930s by German Jewish Bauhaus architects fleeing Nazi persecution.

"The world calls Tel Aviv an international party city," Esther commented. "I call it a jewel in the hand of God."

Sparkling beneath the aircraft's wings was a crystalline blue sea and flawless white beach leading to a metropolitan area dotted by sand-colored ancient homes mixed with skyscrapers of steel and glass.

An SUV emerged from a private aircraft hangar to meet them, and when they sat in its back seat, Esther produced two hoods.

"Put these over your heads," she said.

"You're joking," Mayberry replied.

"We do not advertise our headquarters like your highway signs directing motorists to Langley."

Despite the SUV's air-conditioning, Garrett and Mayberry quickly began perspiring under the heavy masks. Mayberry shut her eyes rather than stare into the black fabric. She tried to ignore the nerve pain in her hand, which was slightly better after the acupuncture treatment but still throbbing. Neither bothered speaking, afraid their breath would be contained in the hoods, making the heat against their faces worse.

After a half hour, the SUV slowed. They could hear a metal door opening and shutting behind them.

"You can remove the masks now," Esther said.

Garrett wiped his forehead. Mayberry brushed her damp hair in place. The SUV continued down the ramps of a multistory underground parking garage until it reached its bottom level. Esther directed them through a steel door guarded by two soldiers who checked her ID. The hallway they entered was empty, and completely silent. Neon lights. Commercial-grade gray floor tiles. Gray-painted walls. After several turns, the glass walls of an executive office suite appeared in front of them, an oasis of color in the otherwise dull grayness of the hallway with its plush light-blue carpeting, red leather chairs, and green ferns. The white-and-blue Flag of Zion hung on a pole near a large emblem of Israel—a menorah between two olive branches—on the wall.

A male receptionist seated in the outer office buzzed them through the thick glass and nodded at Esther as he raised his desk phone, motioning for them to take seats. Seconds later, he announced, "You can go inside now. The director will join you soon."

The adjoining conference room was decorated with more light-blue carpeting, light-gray walls, and an oblong mahogany table with twelve black vinyl swivel chairs. On a side table coffee, water, and pastries were set out with china cups and plates bearing the Mossad's official seal—a menorah with a verse from Proverbs: WHERE THERE IS NO WISE DIRECTION, A NATION FALLS; BUT IN THE MULTITUDE OF COUNSELORS THERE IS SAFETY.

Garrett had just taken a bite of rugelach, filled with apricot, when Big Jules joined them. The director's navy tie hung loose. He wore no suit jacket, and his pressed white shirt was badly wrinkled, the sleeves rolled up. His white hair was matted, and there was white stubble on his chin. It looked like he had worked all night without changing his clothing.

"Tell me about London," Big Jules demanded. "How did someone get to Zharkov?"

"It was the Roc, sir," Esther said. "We know he was in London."

"A camera caught him coming in and out of a building the sniper used to fire at us," Mayberry volunteered. "Too many cameras along that busy street for him to avoid. He was trying to disguise his appearance, but it was him. You could see his scar."

"How about outside Zharkov's mansion? Photos?"

"No," said Esther, "but who else could have pulled this off? We know he's done it before."

"What are you talking about?" Garrett asked.

Esther glanced at Big Jules, waiting to see if he would explain.

"One of our own," Big Jules said. "A major general was killed in his house despite alarms and a top security team. We never knew how the Roc got inside, but it was the Roc. It's one of the justifications we used to convince the Americans to go after him with a drone strike."

Big Jules stood. He moved to a whiteboard and used a marker to write three names: Zharkov, Kardar, and the Roc. He preferred using a board he could erase. No electronic footprint. "Tell me about Zharkov's body," he said to Esther.

"Zharkov was in his safe room. His arms and legs were—"

"Bound to a chair," Big Jules said. "I already know this from your verbal report during your flight here. Tell me about the cuts to Zharkov's chest. How many were there?"

"Six. All rectangular. About one centimeter wide and two centimeters long. And a final fatal puncture wound to his heart."

"What you described is identical to how our major general was tortured and murdered. Now, I need you to look at some old photos."

Big Jules nodded to a nearby aide, who distributed them. They showed a twentysomething soldier whose hands were strung above his head by a rope attached to a ceiling beam. His olive-drab Israeli military shirt had been ripped open, exposing a blood-smeared chest. Rectangular pieces of skin had been cut away, discarded on the floor.

"This young man was captured when the Roc was still associated with Hamas. Do the cuts resemble what you saw in London?"

Esther stared at the man's face. He was a fellow soldier. Someone who mattered. She wanted to remember him. She examined the wounds on his chest.

"Yes, these are identical to the cuts I observed on Zharkov."

"You're absolutely positive?"

"Yes," she said, raising her eyes from the gruesome photos.

"Putting his surgical skills to work inflicting pain," Garrett said. "If you know that's how the Roc murdered the general and that soldier, then he was definitely the one who murdered Zharkov."

Big Jules drew a line on the whiteboard, linking the Roc with Zharkov. "There's our first solid connection." He let his marker stay pressed under Zharkov's name. "Our people have learned that Zharkov purchased a Romeo-class submarine from a Russian scrapyard."

"That explains the submarine our navy kept seeing," Esther said.

"The only item left is the bomb," Garrett added. "The Brits showed us photos of General Kardar visiting Zharkov's mansion the night before he was murdered."

Big Jules traced a line from Zharkov to General Kardar on the whiteboard.

"Not yet a smoking gun," Mayberry volunteered, "but proof that the general and Zharkov had a relationship."

"The only line missing on your diagram now is one linking General Kardar to the Roc," Garrett noted, "and that seems like an easy connection. The Roc killed my neighbor, and two other Iranians tried to kill me. I'd bet my last penny that General Kardar sent them."

Big Jules drew a line tying Kardar to the Roc. All three men were now joined in a triangle.

"That must be why the Roc was in London," Mayberry said, looking at the diagram. "Kardar sent for him to kill Zharkov, and while he was doing that, he spotted Esther and Garrett and decided to stick around the next day to attack us."

"Attack you," Esther said to Garrett. "You're the one who fatally shot his daughter."

Big Jules drew a large question mark on the whiteboard. "Why would General Kardar want Zharkov eliminated?"

"He must not have needed him anymore," Garrett replied. "He'd already gotten Zharkov to buy a submarine and a bomb. He was probably tying up loose ends, getting ready to take full control of the attack."

"He'd only take that risk if the submarine and bomb were in position, or about to be," Mayberry said.

"While you were flying here from London," Big Jules said, "Fathi Aziz, the same jihadist who claimed credit for killing me, posted a new threat against the United States. If his demands are not met in six days, he'll detonate a nuclear bomb."

"Six days? It must be near our shores. What demands?" Mayberry asked.

Big Jules didn't answer. Instead, he waved to his aide, who gave each of them close-up photos of the nuclear bomb that Aziz had shown in his video.

"Could be an empty shell," Garrett said, examining the images.

"The schematics Aziz uploaded came directly from Iranian plans," Big Jules said. "Another bit of circumstantial evidence."

Esther pointed her finger at one of the close-ups. "This shows a detonation switch attached to the bomb. It can be exploded remotely by satellite."

"That's the answer," Garrett said. "General Kardar's motive. He called the Roc to London to kill Zharkov so the only person who knew the remote detonation code would be him."

"The general meets Zharkov and learns the code," Mayberry said. "The next night he sends the Roc to kill Zharkov. General Kardar no longer has to worry about him, and is free to pass the code to Aziz.

It all fits together." She paused before saying in a sad voice, "It seems so much more real, now that we know."

Big Jules continued to stare at the whiteboard. He shook his head. Rubbed his chin. Of them, he was the only one whose gut was telling him there was a critical flaw in their detective work. Something wasn't right. But Big Jules wasn't certain what it was. Not yet.

He moved from the whiteboard to sit at the table with them. "A team has been working all night on the images Esther recorded in Zharkov's office. The map showed multiple fingerprints, all of them on a spot off the Virginia coastline, near the mouth of the Chesapeake Bay. That is where the attack will happen. I will call Director Whittington and brief him. But it would be helpful if you also spoke to him. I have arranged a flight to take both of you back to Washington."

"What about Esther?" Garrett asked.

"She will find Fathi Aziz and keep him from detonating the bomb. We'll deal with General Kardar later."

"What about the Roc?" Mayberry asked. "He's still out there."

Esther looked at Garrett. "He's hunting you."

They were interrupted by one of Big Jules's assistants, who whispered in his ear. "I have an important caller waiting," he announced.

Esther led Garrett and Mayberry from the conference room to a waiting SUV in the garage.

"Good luck finding Aziz," Mayberry said.

"The Mossad's arms are long. We have found Nazis and Olympic terrorists. I will find him." Esther turned to Garrett. "Leich l'shalom."

"I don't have any idea what she just said," Garrett said after Esther left.

"'Go toward peace,'" Mayberry replied. "At least, that's what I think she said. Hopefully it wasn't 'Leich b'shalom,' which means 'Go *in* peace.'"

"'Go toward peace' or 'Go in peace.' What's the difference?"

"'Leich b'shalom' is what you say at a funeral to someone who's dead."

THIRTY-SIX

Big Jules Levi went directly from his meeting with Garrett, May-berry, and Esther into his private office, where Deputy Director Isser Dagan was waiting.

"Everything is prepared for the call," Dagan said.

Big Jules sat and picked up the receiver. "I'm here."

"The last time I called," a voice said, "I told you where Saeedi Bashar and his daughter were hiding in Paris. I did you a favor."

"Yes, General Kardar, and I deeply appreciated it. Unfortunately, Bashar escaped."

"The French are inept. It is their nature. The reason I helped you was to show that my government was not involved in the attempt to murder you at your niece's wedding."

Big Jules noticed Dagan shaking his head as he listened through headphones to their conversation; a clear sign his deputy thought Kardar was lying.

"Do you know where the Roc is currently hiding?" Big Jules asked.

"No. I knew about the Paris flat only because an Iranian expat living in Italy befriended Bashar's daughter, and now she and the expat both are dead."

For a moment, Big Jules considered confronting Kardar about his trip to London. Interrogating him about his meeting with Zhar-kov. Demanding to know if he had sent the Roc to murder Zhar-kov. Accusing him of selling an Iranian-made bomb to Zharkov. But he decided against it. The evidence was still too speculative, at this stage. Kardar was not the type to blurt out a confession or honestly acknowledge his role. Better to remain silent and play along. Kardar had requested this telephone call for a reason, and before Big Jules showed his cards, he wanted to know what Kardar was after.

"You sent word that today's call was most urgent," Big Jules said.

"I need a favor. The CIA director—Connor Whittington—I want to meet privately with him. My government does not wish to use diplomatic channels or ask our Arab brothers to serve as intermediaries. Will you arrange this?"

"The Americans will not agree to a meeting unless they know the subjects to be discussed."

"We are being falsely accused because of Fathi Aziz and his threat. Already members of the US Congress are accusing us of supplying the Jihad Brigade with a nuclear bomb, which is false."

"If you are not involved, then you have nothing to fear."

"Director Levi, I am not naive. Tehran is well aware of how the Americans accused Saddam of having WMDs when he had none. There are many in Washington who want to attack us, even though we are a peaceful people."

"The schematics of the nuclear bomb Aziz showed in his internet video are from Iranian plans," Big Jules said, tweaking him.

"Drawings do not make a bomb. We did not give them to him."

Again, Big Jules watched Dagan shake his head.

"Iran does not have the capability to build a nuclear bomb, despite what you might believe," Kardar continued. "Western inspectors have found no credible evidence. You and the Americans would attack us if we built a nuclear weapon, and the result would be a third world war. We have strong allies in China and Russia. You know where China gets its oil. No one wants a third world war. Now are you willing to arrange a meeting?"

"I will contact the Americans for you, but in return, tell me where Aziz is hiding."

"How would I know this?"

"Now you think I am the naive one."

"I will await our next call about Whittington," Kardar said. "For all of our countries." The line went dead.

Big Jules looked at Dagan. "Your thoughts?"

"Where is there truth in the mouth of a liar?"

Big Jules sat quietly for several moments, thinking. An odd smile appeared on his lips.

"What is it?" Dagan asked.

"I believe I understand General Kardar's game. It is like a puzzle that confounds you until you solve it, and then you wonder how you missed such an obvious solution."

Dagan didn't interrupt.

"Let me tell you a story," Big Jules said. "My brother, Ari, whom you have met, worked in Ktzi'ot Prison, where strong men always preyed on weak ones. One day a prisoner shoved a weaker prisoner down a flight of stairs. Threatened to kill him unless he paid him protection money. The terrified prisoner ran to the guards and reported the incident. The two of them were put into solitary confinement and punished."

Big Jules paused, savoring his story. Dagan knew better than to hurry him.

"There was another prisoner," Big Jules continued. "Another predator who extorted weaker men. He did not push his targets down stairs; he befriended them. One day the weaker prisoner was badly beaten. When his stronger friend appeared, the beaten inmate said, 'If only you had been there, they would never have attacked me.' The stronger prisoner agreed, 'It's true, and you are my friend, but I cannot protect you without putting myself in danger.' The weaker man said, 'I will pay you.'"

Big Jules looked at Dagan.

"I understand," Dagan said. "The stronger prisoner had arranged the beating of his weaker friend."

"Yes, that is exactly what happened. But what could the weaker man do but pay—even if he suspected his friend had betrayed him? I suspect General Kardar intends to offer the Americans his help. He will offer to betray Aziz, as proof that Iran played no role in any of this, but he will ask the Americans for a price—to resolve a problem that he created."

"Will the Americans take his bait?"

"Do they have a choice? 'In a wilderness of mirrors. What will the spider do.'" It was a line from the poem "Gerontion," by T. S. Eliot.

THIRTY-SEVEN

"The Great Satan and the Zionists refuse to submit to the will of Allah, blessed be his holy name," an angry Fathi Aziz declared in a new internet video. *"Two days have passed, and Palestine has not been returned to its people. The prophet Moses called down ten plagues on the Egyptians, the last that every firstborn son in Egypt would be slaughtered. Do you Americans and Zionists believe you are better than those disobedient Egyptians? Allah will punish you with blood."*

Less than an hour after Aziz's diatribe, a young man resting on the steps of the Metropolitan Museum of Art in New York City, the largest art museum in the country, looked up from the Holy Qur'an he was reading. He had been waiting outside the third-most-visited site in Manhattan for two hours. Occasionally he would watch the men, women, and children climbing and descending the steps of the grand Beaux Arts museum. He did not speak to them but returned to his scriptures. It wasn't until he noticed a school bus approaching along Fifth Avenue that he closed his book and placed it next to him while he slipped the heavy backpack that he had brought over his shoulders. The bus parked directly in front of the Met, and when its door swung open, a swarm of students from the only conservative Jewish school in the city began exiting onto the sidewalk.

The young man rose from the stoop and waited until all fifty of the bus riders had gathered on the sidewalk, with two of their teachers riding herd. When they obediently fell into line two abreast and started up the steps, the man walked toward them.

"Hey!" he heard someone call behind him. "Your book?"

He turned his head slightly and saw the Qur'an that he'd left on the steps now being waved in the air by an older man. He looked back at the sixth-grade class of fresh-faced, energetic boys and girls. They were close enough.

"Allahu akbar!"

He squeezed the trigger. His backpack exploded instantly, killing him and those closest to him, including the man clutching the Qur'an. Forty dead, as well as twenty-six Jewish students. More than a hundred outside the Met wounded. When the police searched the room he had rented in Paterson, New Jersey—known as "Little Palestine" because it was home to the largest Palestinian community in America—they discovered he had illegally crossed into the United States over the Canadian border, having flown there from Jordan. He was a member of the Jihad Brigade.

President Fitzgerald was fuming when CIA Director Whittington arrived at the Oval Office.

"Dead Jewish children on the steps of the Met!" the president declared. "We've got to find and kill Aziz. This attack has given credibility to his nuclear threat. People are afraid. Panicked. Didn't you see the protestors marching outside? I've got members of Congress calling for us to pressure Israel into pulling out of Palestine, or at least make a statement saying they're considering it."

"I just spoke to Director Levi," Whittington said. "He called to tell me that General Firouz Kardar, who oversees the Iranian Quds Force, has asked for a face-to-face. He believes this general may have information about Aziz's whereabouts."

"The Iranians are offering to help us stop Aziz?" Fitzgerald said, clearly surprised.

"Levi warned it could be some type of trick. He also told me his people now have proof there is a submarine."

"What? You told me there was no way Aziz could get his hands on one."

"Director Levi said a Russian oligarch in London may have purchased one for Aziz. A scrapped Soviet Romeo-class submarine that was reconditioned in the Black Sea."

"An oligarch? Who the hell is he? Why's he helping Aziz?"

"His name is Taras Zharkov, and Director Levi believes Zharkov was hoping to earn huge profits by crashing our economy."

"Are you telling me the Kremlin is involved in this?"

"No, sir. Director Levi doesn't believe so. Only Zharkov."

"Where is this son of a bitch? Has he been arrested?"

"Zharkov was murdered three days ago in London, although his death hasn't been made public."

"Did the Mossad kill him?"

"Director Levi suspects General Kardar ordered the killing. There are photos of him meeting with the Russian the night before he was murdered."

"The same general who wants to meet with you now?"

"It shouldn't be any surprise, Mr. President, that the Israelis are claiming the Iranians are up to their necks in all of this. That's been Director Levi's position from the start. Ever since we became aware of Nasya Radi's letter warning us."

"A letter you didn't take seriously. Tell me something. Why is the director of the Mossad on top of this, and you and your people aren't?" Fitzgerald didn't wait for an answer. "I should fire you. Up until you walked into my office five minutes ago, you were assuring me this entire submarine/nuclear bomb threat was improbable. That this Aziz crackpot was a delusional, penniless religious zealot."

"With all due respect, Mr. President, we still don't know how much of this is conjecture. We haven't been able to confirm any of it, and we certainly can't accuse Tehran without irrefutable proof. A wild accusation could cripple any attempts to constructively negotiate with the Iranians in the future, and weaken support from our allies. This still could be a hoax."

"A hoax? For God's sake, man, Aziz posted a photo of a nuclear bomb on the internet, along with schematics explaining how it was made. The Mossad has told you a dead Russian in London secured a submarine for Aziz, and that crazy bastard has blown up a school bus load of Jewish children because he doesn't believe we're taking him seriously!"

"Sir, we have been doing our due diligence, using every technical advantage that we have to confirm this, and there are still many unanswered questions. You hired me to rein in the agency—to be skeptical, a calm voice of reason. And that is what I am trying to be. Having said that, I will submit my resignation today, if that is what you want."

"What I want is for you to forget about your predictive analytics and deal with this general face-to-face before it's too late and I have the blood of thousands of dead Americans on my hands. Where does this Iranian general want to meet you?"

"A private residence in Azerbaijan. Someone he apparently trusts."

"Is Levi going to be there?"

"The Mossad wasn't invited, but I'm certain Levi will have his people watching."

Fitzgerald stood up, still visibly angry. "When you meet with this Iranian, you tell him that if we find even the slightest bit of evidence that Iran manufactured a nuclear bomb and sold it to this Russian or Aziz or anyone else, we will hold Tehran responsible. I'm meeting with my national security team today, and we are proceeding as if this threat is a hundred percent legitimate. You need to get on board and do the same. Is that clear?"

"Yes, Mr. President. If I may, we haven't been sitting on our hands. We have been coordinating our efforts with the Pentagon. The Navy has made a grid. Every mile of water off our eastern shoreline is being searched section by section, and all ports have been ordered to check every cargo container. Basically, we're shutting them down until after the six-day deadline passes. Nothing is going to get through."

"Nothing better."

"There's something else I need to tell you, Mr. President, based on my conversation with Director Levi. He said one of his Mossad officers, along with Valerie Mayberry and Brett Garrett, managed to enter Zharkov's London mansion and look at maps in his office."

"You said they were in London chasing a suspected murderer. What the hell do they have to do with any of this?"

"We'll know soon enough, sir. They're on a flight from Tel Aviv back to Dulles. I have a team waiting to pick them up."

THIRTY-EIGHT

The concrete border wall entombing the West Bank was as high as any found at a maximum-security penitentiary. Esther studied the faces of the Palestinian laborers as they emerged from Checkpoint 300 in the early-morning darkness and boarded buses for Bethlehem work sites. The Mossad officer next to her in the Range Rover's front passenger seat lit a cigarette and blew out a smoke ring.

"Roll down your window," she complained. "I'm not dying from your secondhand smoke."

He blew another perfectly shaped ring into the already cloudy windshield and reluctantly lowered his side window. Esther could feel the hot morning air coming inside.

"You should get out to smoke," she said.

He took another long drag and flicked his cigarette out onto the rutted pavement. "You owe me," he said.

"You owe me for saving you from lung cancer."

He chuckled. "A Palestinian bullet will kill me first."

The two officers in the SUV's rear seat laughed. "You two sound like you're married," one said.

"Him?" Esther said. "A goat would be a better husband."

"But a goat couldn't give you this." He grabbed his crotch.

Esther ignored the insult. "The one in the Nike baseball hat—that's Omar Seif."

All four hurried toward a bus that Palestinian workers were

boarding. Omar Seif was waiting to board, third in line. He saw them, and the Palestinians on either side of him stepped away.

Two Mossad agents grabbed Seif's arms, spun him around, and pushed his face against the side of the bus, expertly binding his wrists with plastic cuffs while a third officer frisked him after knocking a plastic bag that contained his lunch onto the pavement. Esther tugged a black hood over Seif's head. No one offered an explanation. They led him to the Range Rover and pushed him into its rear seat. Esther looked back as they were leaving. The line had reformed. What had happened was a common occurrence. A worker scooped up Seif's lunch for himself while the line of workers continued boarding.

Seif was forced into a chair in an interrogation room a few miles away. Esther removed his hood. He turned to the left, then right, inspecting his surroundings. Nothing except a chair facing his.

Esther sat down across from him. "Your name is Omar Seif."

He nodded.

"Speak when you are asked a question!"

"Yes," he mumbled.

"You are twenty-four years old. Your parents are Leyal and Yousef. You have three brothers and two sisters, is this correct?"

"Yes."

His hands were still bound behind his back, forcing him to lean forward uncomfortably. His right leg bounced up and down.

"You are a cement laborer at the new Arabian Nights hotel construction site."

"Yes."

"You are a member of the Jihad Brigade?"

A surprised look washed over his hollow face. "No! No! That's wrong! I'm not a radical."

"You're lying!" Esther motioned to one of her colleagues, who immediately left the room. When he returned, he was pushing a stainless-steel cart. He positioned it near Seif so the prisoner would recognize what was on its tray: surgical instruments and a cloth stained with blood.

Esther picked up a scalpel. Leaned close to his face.

"You are a member of the Jihad Brigade," she said slowly, making it a definitive statement.

"No, someone has lied to you."

She placed the tip of the blade in front of his left eyeball.

"Do you know what happens to Palestinian terrorists? We blind them before they are imprisoned and executed."

Rapid breathing. His entire body trembled, his eyes locked on the scalpel.

Esther pushed the blade closer to his eyeball.

"I believe you," she said. "You do not belong to the Jihad Brigade, but your cousin Khalid does, and that makes you as guilty as him. You know he's a member, don't you?"

Seif seemed paralyzed.

"Don't you!" she yelled.

"Yes, he is, but not me."

Esther lowered the scalpel. Placed it on the tray. Seif dropped his head, stared at the concrete floor.

"This is your cousin Khalid," she said, holding up a photo for him to see.

He examined it. Two Arab men. An outdoor market in Gaza.

"Who is with Khalid? If you lie, I will blind you."

He raised his chin. Stared at her face.

"Ibrahim," he mumbled.

"Yes, Ibrahim Antar," she said. "I was testing you. Answer my questions, and you will be released. We will arrange for you to get a full day of pay. We'll give you a new lunch."

She smiled at him and then, in a lightning-fast move, dropped the photo and snatched up the scalpel. "Lie, and I will cut out both your eyes. Do not test me."

He nodded.

She waved her hand, and a colleague came forward with a new photograph to show him.

"Have you ever seen Khalid or Ibrahim speaking to this man?"

He averted his eyes.

Esther grabbed his throat and shoved him back, squeezing his cuffed hands against the chair, tightening her fingers around his trachea. "Do you know this man?"

He gasped for air, so she released her grip to allow him to answer.

"Fathi Aziz, the man with the bomb. I recognize him from television. His face is everywhere."

"Where is Aziz?"

"I don't know."

"Where does the Jihad Brigade meet in Gaza City?"

He lowered his head again and began sobbing loudly.

Esther shot from her chair, clutched the sides of his chair with her hands, and jammed her right knee into his groin, causing him to scream in pain.

"Where do Khalid and Ibrahim meet?"

"In Shuja'iyya—in a house with a green Hamas flag painted by its door."

She waved to a colleague who produced a satellite-image map of Gaza City, including the Shuja'iyya neighborhood, one of the largest in the city, with up to a hundred thousand residents, and a Hamas stronghold.

"Show me the house."

Two other Mossad agents pulled Seif up from the chair and cut his plastic cuffs, but remained next to him. He rubbed the red marks left by the restraints and examined the map.

"Show me," she demanded.

He extended his index finger and pointed toward a house near the Shuja'iyya Primary School for Girls, a location the Israelis wouldn't attack with missiles for fear of killing children.

"Seif," Esther said, "if you have lied, you will be taken to prison as a terrorist and executed."

"It is where they meet."

A hood was slipped over his head as he was taken away. Once he was gone, Esther said, "He pointed to the same house as the other two."

It was as difficult for an Israeli to enter Gaza as it was for a Palestinian to leave it. By land, visitors had to pass through the border wall and its military checkpoints. Israeli gunboats patrolled the sea. The Gaza airport was useless, having been repeatedly bombed by Israeli jets. Much of Palestine was a refugee camp; two-thirds of Gaza's inhabitants were displaced persons who'd fled or been driven there when Israel became a Jewish state.

The main route into Gaza was at its southern tip, where it shared a border with Egypt. Both countries were suspicious of individuals entering and leaving through the Rafah crossing there. The same was true of travelers in the north at the Erez crossing on the Israel border.

Israelis entering Gaza had to be cleared by the Israeli army before passing through the border wall into a strip of no-man's-land, a desolate, heavily mined stretch about a half mile wide. Beyond it was a Hamas checkpoint where all incoming traffic and travelers were stopped and checked. Israelis were not welcomed.

The last time a Mossad team entered Gaza on a clandestine mission, it had been stopped at a Hamas checkpoint, and an Israeli and three Palestinians had been killed. Hamas's armed wing, the Izzedine al-Qassam Brigades, fired a dozen rockets into Israeli territory in retaliation, hitting a bus and wounding a teenager. The Hamas rocket attacks caused Israeli fighter jets to bomb "known terror targets" in Gaza.

If Esther and her team were captured in Gaza, they would be held as hostages or executed as spies.

Shortly after 1:00 a.m., Esther and four Mossad operatives

dropped into a tunnel that, ironically, had been dug under the border wall by Palestinians smuggling goods. On the Palestinian side, they made their way on foot to a badly beaten Ford van with a paid informant behind its wheel. The four males with Esther were disguised as women in traditional black kaftans, their heads covered with hijabs.

They rode in silence. When they entered Gaza City, Esther saw firsthand the impact of her nation's stranglehold on the besieged city. Third-world conditions. Open sewage in the deeply rutted streets. Webs of wires strung between buildings, providing infrequent electricity. In the quiet, interrupted only by a stray dog barking, they passed rows of bombed houses, rebar jutting upward from concrete chunks like long, thin fingers. Portraits of jihadist martyrs and FREE PALESTINE graffiti covered walls pockmarked by bullets. Amid the ruins, makeshift shelters and an occasional white-painted house with bars on windows and doors. Only the minarets rising above the city's concrete blandness appeared untouched, their red-and-gold spires intact for muezzins to call the faithful to daily prayer.

"We must not be caught by the night patrols," their driver said in a soft voice, switching off the van's headlights.

"You will arouse suspicion," Esther replied.

"No one wants to be visible at night."

There were no working streetlamps, only the stars and lights from inside houses. Esther used her night-vision goggles to make certain their driver was true to his claim that he knew the Gaza City streets so well, he could drive them in pitch blackness.

She glanced up at the sky. Hamas had no aircraft, but Israeli Defense Forces were monitoring their mission from a drone high enough above the city to avoid those beneath from hearing it. The Shuja'iyya neighborhood was a maze of streets, some big enough for vehicles and others only for foot traffic. Esther was depending on aerial surveillance to help guide them through the spaghetti jumble. As they neared their target, a voice in her earpiece warned her that two Palestinian men had been spotted by the drone, loitering outside the suspected Jihad Brigade hideout. She whispered to their driver to pull over.

He parked behind an unhitched donkey cart. Ten minutes passed, fifteen, twenty, as everyone in the Ford checked the street and rooftops for snipers, knowing they were easy targets.

"They're leaving," the voice in Esther's ear said.

She checked her watch. Shortly after 2:00 a.m. At this hour, there would be no explanation for women walking unaccompanied on the streets, especially ones with men's physiques. On Esther's command, the men removed their hijabs, replacing them with tactical helmets equipped with night-vision goggles and cameras. They'd already cut slits in their kaftans, large enough for them to conceal weapons underneath the flowing dresses. Esther and two others were armed with Sig Sauer P229 pistols fitted with noise suppressors and loaded with .22-caliber long rifle bullets, deadly at close range but quiet, sounding much like a car door shutting when fired. The other two carried Israeli-made IWI X95 compact assault rifles that weighed less than seven pounds but could fire 850 rounds per minute. They too had noise suppressors, but in this war-seasoned neighborhood, residents would recognize the sounds for what they were.

Esther guided the driver forward until the van was a quarter mile away from their target. They unloaded, three on one side of the narrow street, two on the opposite, all checking the rooftops. A footpath brought them to the back of the jihadists' house. Two Mossad operatives positioned themselves behind the two-story dwelling as Esther and the other two continued to the front.

Esther was the first to duck into the dark alcove entrance. Pieces of lumber had been covered with corrugated sheet metal that had once been part of a roof to serve as a front door. There was no handle, no lock, not even a rope securing it.

Palestinian informants had watched the house during the day, and reported two men inside it: Khalid Basara and Ibrahim Antar.

Esther slipped her gloved fingers behind the metal door and

gently pulled it outward. It squeaked, and she froze. After a few moments, she tugged it open, exposing a flight of stairs that led to the second floor. That level now served as the house's roof, its original roof having been destroyed. Esther used her night vision to inspect the ground-floor room.

"I'm reading two hot spots," a voice in Esther's earpiece announced.

The advanced infrared imaging on the drone monitoring had found heat readings on the ground and second floors, although there was no guarantee the images were human. Hamas had taught its soldiers that hard rubber tires have nearly the same heat signature as humans. On emissivity scales, people register ninety-seven; hard rubber tires register ninety-four.

"Could be tires they burn during protests," the voice in Esther's ear said. "Use the smoke to hide behind. But I doubt it."

"We didn't come for tires," Esther whispered.

The main room that Esther was now entering served as a kitchen and meeting area. Plates on the floor still held food. A heavy cloth served as a room divider, separating the main room from what Esther suspected was a sleeping area. It was where the sensors had glowed hot.

Esther and the other Mossad operative armed with a pistol moved to the curtain, while the third, with an assault rifle, remained at the bottom of the stairs. He could stop anyone coming down or inside the house from the street.

This is where their training was crucial. Esther would be the first through, dropping to her knees so her partner could shoot above her. She would be responsible for the left half of the room, he the right half. She listened. Heard nothing. Took a cleansing breath and waited to feel her companion's hand on her shoulder, signaling he was in position. He touched her, and in a sweeping move, Esther pushed the blanket to the side.

A man sleeping on a mattress, partially covered by a blanket on the floor. She recognized his bearded face. Khalid Basara—Seif's cousin. His eyes popped open, and he jerked upward, reaching for an assault rifle next to him. Esther fired twice. His body slumped sideways. Keeping her pistol aimed at him, she nudged his feet with her shoe. No reaction. She holstered her handgun and focused on a laptop computer and papers also on the floor. Her colleague backed out to support the third Mossad operative at the base of the staircase.

Esther inserted the laptop into a satchel that she'd brought with her. She next inspected the stack of papers, taking every scrap. She was about to retreat when something moved under the covers. Esther reached through the slit in her dress and grasped the Sig Sauer handgun holstered there.

A naked woman sat upright next to Basara's corpse, so petite that Esther hadn't noticed her before under the blanket. The woman reached for Basara's weapon.

Esther was too quick for her. Two shots into the girl's chest. She fell backward. Esther stepped into the main room just as one of her Mossad colleagues was coming toward her as backup after hearing the muffled pistol shots.

Esther shook her head, indicating that there was no need for him to enter the bedroom. Suppressors and the quietness of .22-caliber rounds appeared to have kept the gunshot noises contained inside the house's walls. There was no noticeable reaction on the street in the hostile neighborhood.

"Girl in there with Basara," Esther whispered. "Antara must be upstairs."

She motioned for the assault-rifle-carrying Mossad operative to remain at the bottom of the staircase as she and her fellow pistol-carrying colleague started up it.

As they did, Esther glanced upward through what had been a roof at the black sky. Esther and her colleague entered the first room, with her ducking low and him high. Trash. Debris. Nothing else. They approached the second. "Getting a hot reading," the voice of the drone operator told her.

It wasn't tires. A man was sleeping on a blanket spread on the floor. Antar. They needed him alive. Esther slipped quietly toward him. Even muffled, gunshots fired in a room without a roof would be heard.

With her colleague aiming his pistol at Antar, Esther holstered her gun and slipped a syringe from under her dress. With her right thumb, she flipped off its plastic tip, then raised her hand and jammed the needle into Antar's neck while covering his mouth with her left. Neuromuscular blocking agents, commonly used during surgeries to prevent patients from moving, swept into his bloodstream, causing near-instant paralysis. The Israeli chemists' compound was so strong that two out of ten times, it killed rather than sedated. Antar's eyes froze half open. His body shook, then went limp. The smell of his bladder and colon voiding caused Esther to nearly gag.

She taped Antar's mouth and, together with her partner, dragged his stiff body to the staircase, where the third Mossad agent helped cart him downstairs. The two operatives from behind the house joined them. Each of the four men grabbed one of Ibrahim's limbs and lifted him while Esther checked the street. No one in sight. They moved outside and quick-stepped to the waiting van.

An hour later they emerged with Antar from a Palestinian tunnel on the Israeli side, where a medical team was waiting with a stretcher and ambulance. Now she had to get Antar to cooperate.

THIRTY-NINE

"The map I saw in Zharkov's office showed the Virginia coastline," Brett Garrett explained as he examined an East Coast shoreline map displayed on a table in Director Whittington's office. He and Mayberry had been brought to Langley directly from the airport. "There were multiple fingerprints found in this area." He touched the water off the shore in a direct line from Norfolk.

Director Whittington didn't immediately react.

"I suspect," Garrett continued, "this is where Zharkov's Romeo-class submarine armed with its nuclear bomb will be heading."

"Tell me," Whittington said, "how many maps did you see on Zharkov's desk?"

"They weren't on his desk," Garrett replied. "They were on a conference-room table in his private office."

"How many?"

"A map of the Virginia and North Carolina coastlines had been placed over a larger map that showed the Atlantic Ocean."

"This stack of maps—"

"Only two," Garrett said, correcting him.

"The two maps were out in the open for anyone to see."

"Yes," Garrett said. "What's your point?"

"That Zharkov and his people either wanted you to see them, or those maps didn't have anything to do with the threatened attack.

Zharkov owns the largest yacht in the world. He could have been planning a pleasure cruise."

Mayberry joined the conversation. "Zharkov wouldn't think he'd need to hide them. It wasn't easy to get inside his guarded office."

"And yet you did," Whittington said. "Tell me, are either of you aware of SOSUS?"

"I'm not," Mayberry said.

"It's our nation's sound surveillance system—hydrophones installed at key locations on the ocean's floor. It's been around for decades. We used underwater listening posts to track Soviet submarines during the Cold War. Since then we've updated it with IUSS, the Integrated Undersea Surveillance System. It's part of our superior technology, a warning system unmatched by any other nation's. It's darn near foolproof. If a whale farts, we know it. It's that failsafe. Because our Atlantic Fleet is based in Norfolk, the entire seafloor, from the mouth of the Chesapeake Bay extending several hundred miles out into the Atlantic Ocean, is blanketed with hydrophones and sensors. Unless Zharkov's submarine dug a tunnel, it can't get anywhere near where you are saying it is headed."

Whittington walked toward his office door, where an aide was holding a suitcase for him. "The president is convinced this threat by Aziz is real."

"Him and everyone else in America!" Garrett said.

Whittington frowned. "Based on our analysis of Aziz's video threats and a computer model that we developed, based on thousands of possible attack scenarios, the highest probability for a submarine attack is the New York area, and that is where I am recommending we focus. I'll pass along your report, but from now on, you need to leave this up to the experts. Now, I need to catch a flight. An escort will show you out."

An agency-provided driver was waiting outside.

"Leave it up to the experts. If we dragged Fathi Aziz into Whittington's office and tossed him at his feet, he'd find a way to criticize us," Mayberry said. "All he ever talks about is his stupid computer models and superior technology."

Garrett grinned.

"I don't find this funny," she said.

"I'm supposed to be the hothead. You're the one who respects authority," he replied. "We need to contact Big Jules. Find out if Esther needs our help."

"No! Listen, Garrett, the entire Israeli intelligence service and their army are helping her. I'm going home. After I get cleaned up, I'm pouring myself a glass of wine and booking a flight west. I've always wanted to see, I don't know, Nebraska."

"Nebraska. We're being threatened with a nuclear bomb attack, and you want to go to Des Moines?"

"Des Moines is in Iowa."

"I know you, Valerie—you're not the type to run away."

"Garrett, weren't you listening? Whittington doesn't want our help. No one does."

Their CIA driver arrived outside the Midtown, Reston's most exclusive high-rise condo building, where Mayberry lived.

"I'll call you after I speak to Big Jules," Garrett said.

"Don't," she said. "Remember? Nebraska."

She turned to leave, but he reached out and touched her left hand, stopping her.

"I think we need to talk about what happened in London between us."

"This again? Why? Garrett, it was a high-stress situation. What happened isn't a big deal. We both said it was a mistake."

"Was it?" he asked.

She stepped from the car.

Traffic slowed leaving Reston, and an hour passed before Garrett reached his Arlington condo. Through the front windshield, he saw Calvin Russell, his building's security guard, hollering at the homeless veteran whose blanket Garrett had "rented."

"What's going on, Russell?" he asked.

"Bunch of your fellow condo owners don't like him hanging around all the time. I'm supposed to shoo him away, but he's been refusing to stay gone."

"He's mentally ill."

"Yeah, he is, but that ain't my problem now, is it, Mr. Garrett? I didn't go to medical school."

"You a vet?"

"Vietnam. Tet."

"He's a vet too. Operation Enduring Freedom."

"Didn't know that and don't much care. I got a job to do."

"We should call someone."

"Already did. Arlington social services. They asked if he was dangerous. I said no, but he's a nuisance, and they told me there ain't no crime being a nuisance. Told me they didn't have time to mess with him unless he's dangerous. Said I needed to call them back after he attacked someone. Stupid, ain't it? Then they'll just take him to jail, and a couple of weeks later, he'll be back madder than he was."

Garrett watched the homeless vet pushing his grocery cart down the street.

"Welcome home," Russell said.

"You've made changes," Garrett replied as they entered the lobby.

"Yeah, since that Iranian got himself stabbed," Russell said, "they installed all sorts of additional monitors behind my new desk here. Can see every floor in the building, back door and entrance too. Now they expect me to sit here and report any time someone visits—even write down what they look like."

Garrett was only half listening. He rode the elevator upstairs. Sixth floor. Waved to Russell via the camera monitoring the hallway. His cell phone rang as he approached his front door.

"Welcome back stranger," Thomas Jefferson Kim said. "Been reading about you. Exploding cars in Bellagio. Shootouts with terrorists in Paris. My life is so boring compared to yours."

"Face it, Kim, you're boring."

"Is Mayberry okay?"

"Yes, thanks for asking about me."

"You answered the phone, didn't you? Besides, Mayberry called and said I needed to keep track of you. She told me the Roc tried to kill you in London. I'm still trying to find him for you, but he's off the grid."

Garrett fished his condo key out of his pant pocket.

"There's another reason I'm calling," Kim said. "I can't get anyone to pay attention, but I think it's important."

Garrett inserted the key into his door's bolt lock.

"The Coast Guard picked up a Russian floating in the Atlantic, trying to enter the US illegally," Kim said. "They assumed he jumped off a cargo ship near Norfolk."

"Did you say Norfolk?"

"Yes, but here's what got me curious. The Coast Guard report said he was wearing an SEIE suit. The type submariners use to escape during emergencies. And get this, a few days later, two other men in SEIE suits washed up on shore. Both were believed to be Russians and both had been fatally shot by someone using an underwater pistol. The authorities have the one who's still alive locked up in a regional jail until they can sort this out."

Garrett withdrew his key from the bolt lock without opening his condo door.

"I need to call Mayberry," he told Kim as he hurried toward the elevator.

It took several rings for her to answer.

"The Coast Guard picked up a Russian wearing a submarine survivor suit near Norfolk. How soon can you be ready?"

"For what? I just got out of the shower."

"We need to interrogate this Russian. He didn't just float across the Atlantic. We're a team, remember? Besides, you're the only person I know who speaks fluent Russian. I'm coming your way. We'll take your car, and no arguments."

He darted across the lobby and out of the building to hail an Uber to go meet her.

From behind his security desk, Russell mumbled, "Didn't stay long enough to change clothes." The security guard had started to return to the crossword puzzle he was doing when he noticed movement on the sixth floor. A man coming out of Garrett's condo.

"What the heck?" Russell said to himself. "Must've snuck by me when I was out chasing away that homeless pest."

Russell walked outside to see if he could flag down Garrett, but he was gone. Returning to his lobby monitors, he checked for the man on the sixth-floor hallway. It was empty. He searched the other cameras and found footage of the stranger, first entering the building through the back door and then leaving the same way while Russell was outside, trying to flag down Garrett.

"Damn it," Russell cursed. He pulled out his logbook and wrote: "Unknown visitor seen entering and leaving Brett Garrett's condo. Description . . . large scar from his ear to his neck." He noted the time and returned to his crossword puzzle.

FORTY

Director Whittington landed in Baku two hours before his private rendezvous with General Kardar—enough time to change clothes and take a final glance at the background file the agency had prepared. He would meet Kardar inside the walled compound of an oil-rich billionaire, an ornate villa on the edge of the Caspian Sea outside the Azerbaijan capital. Accompanying Whittington was a security detail, his personal assistant, and an interpreter, although he'd been told Kardar spoke fluent English. If the general said something to those with him in Farsi, he wanted to know what was being said.

At the agreed-upon time, Whittington descended a marble staircase and made his way toward a first-floor ballroom. He checked the time: sixty hours remained before Aziz's deadline. As he neared the doorway, his personal assistant hurried toward him.

"Kardar isn't inside," Rodrigo Montoya reported.

Whittington went back upstairs to his guest suite. From his days in Congress, he was familiar with posturing. A half hour later the mansion's chief of staff, who was serving as their host, informed him that the general was now ready to begin.

"We'll be down shortly," Whittington answered.

Whittington watched the clock, waited fifteen minutes, and then descended the staircase. He arrived in the ballroom only to discover that Kardar still wasn't there. This time he waited.

Kardar entered fifteen minutes later, without offering an explanation for his tardiness. He took a seat across from Whittington at an ornate Indian Turkish table with mother-of-pearl inlays while the house's chief of staff explained that coffee and finger foods had been placed on a nearby table.

Despite his irritation, Whittington decided to begin their conversation on a friendly note. He prided himself on being a skilled deal maker and found that flattery often worked better than criticism. "My country appreciates your invitation," he said. "As you are surely aware, the terrorist Aziz has taken credit for an assassination attempt on Mossad director Julian Levi and the suicide bombing outside the Metropolitan Museum in Manhattan. We are taking his threat about a nuclear attack against my country seriously, and welcome your help in preventing it."

The general impatiently tapped an index finger on the highly polished table surface and motioned to one of his aides by raising his hand. He whispered something. The aide fetched him a black coffee from a silver urn on the side table.

Whittington motioned to Montoya to fetch him a cup of coffee and slice of baklava.

"The Islamic Republic of Iran has sent me as a humanitarian gesture," Kardar said. "We are a peace-loving people. It is America's support of the illegal Zionist state and its theft of Palestinian lands that has brought you to the edge of a nuclear attack."

"My government appreciates Iran's willingness to assist."

"Your country's aggression against the Arab world and the contempt your president shows toward Palestine and the Islamic Republic of Iran makes it problematic for us to help you."

For the next fifteen minutes Kardar spewed anti-American rhetoric in a clearly well-rehearsed speech.

Whittington listened without comment. When Kardar had finished, he said, "I believe we should take a short break." It was a calculated move. He wanted to show his displeasure at being lectured.

"If you do not admit your country's guilt," Kardar said, his voice rising, "I shall return to Tehran."

"With all due respect, General," Whittington calmly replied, now standing from his chair, "I did not come here to debate American foreign policy." He left the ballroom.

Once upstairs, he told Montoya, "Tell our host that we'll be ready to return to the table in fifteen minutes."

Montoya left with the message but returned moments later, going immediately to the suite's floor-to-ceiling windows. "The general is leaving," he commented, peering down at the estate's driveway.

Whittington hurried over in time to see Kardar entering a Mercedes-Benz. He watched it pull away.

"What now?" Montoya asked.

"The general requested this meeting," Whittington said. "He's bluffing—trying to intimidate. Inform our host we are leaving as well, and have our vehicles brought around."

"Shouldn't we wait at least a few hours?"

"If General Kardar is serious, he needs to get back here. If not, then this was a ruse to make us believe Iran was willing to assist. Either way, we don't have time to waste playing games."

Their host was stationed at the mansion's front doorway when they came downstairs. Whittington thanked him. As their three-vehicle motorcade proceeded away from the house along the palm-treed driveway, he quietly began to second-guess himself. His anxiety grew as they sped away from the gated compound toward Baku Heydar Aliyev International Airport.

Whittington asked Montoya to check his cell phone for possible texts from Kardar's entourage. Nothing. By the time they reached the airport's VIP departure area, Whittington was drenched in sweat. His security detail formed a protective shield as he started toward the terminal.

Montoya's cell phone rang. Whittington stopped midstride.

"General Kardar is here," the villa's chief of staff said. "He's returned from taking a lunch break and is waiting in the ballroom."

Montoya hit mute. "Kardar wants to meet. Claims he left for lunch."

Whittington nodded yes and hurried back into the waiting limousine.

In the ballroom, Kardar was the first to speak.

"The Islamic Republic of Iran has considered your request for help, and has decided against it."

Whittington stared at him, puzzled. But before he could speak, Kardar went on, "However, my government does not wish for the Arab world to suffer additional aggression and interference, and for that reason alone, our Supreme Leader is willing to consult with Aziz."

"Our country would be grateful, but would prefer he not only be stopped from detonating a nuclear bomb but, in addition, be held accountable for his criminal acts," Whittington said. "Are you willing to tell us where Aziz is hiding, or detain him for extradition?"

"The Islamic Republic of Iran will not," Kardar said, slightly raising his voice. "We do not philosophically oppose Fathi Aziz's jihad against your country. However, the Supreme Leader does oppose the use of all nuclear weapons. Nuclear weapons are an affront to the teachings of the Prophet Muhammad, blessed be his name, and the loving nature of Islam. This is why the Supreme Leader is willing to advise Aziz not to use a nuclear weapon."

"Based on what Aziz has put on display in his messages, there is reason to suspect the nuclear bomb that he reportedly controls was made in Iran. We also have heard reports about you meeting with a Russian oligarch in London who may be involved in this. Taras Zharkov."

Kardar slammed his open palms on the table and pushed himself up from his chair. "These are Israeli lies! We have no means to manufacture a nuclear bomb, and I have no relationship with this Russian."

Whittington replied in an appeasing voice, "Let us continue our dialogue, General, about Aziz and your Supreme Leader. I only wanted to warn you of the obvious. When this crisis is over, the United States and its allies will investigate the source of this weapon and how Aziz obtained it, and will take the appropriate action to punish anyone or any countries involved."

Kardar scowled. "I come here to offer you help, and you accuse me personally and threaten my country."

He turned to leave—once again.

"General Kardar, please," Whittington said. "There is no time to waste here. What will it take for the United States to receive the assistance of your Supreme Leader in ending this crisis?"

Kardar slowly returned to his seat. "If the United States wishes for the Supreme Leader to use his influence to prevent a nuclear attack, the United States must end its immoral economic, trade, scientific, and military sanctions against the Islamic Republic of Iran, including financial restrictions that unjustly prevent our people from participating in international banking. It must unfreeze our country's billions' worth of bank deposits, gold, and other properties being held abroad. It must stop levying fines on third-party nations that engage in business with Iran, and it must end its boycott on selling aircraft and repair parts. More than seventeen planes have crashed, killing nearly two thousand Iranians, because of America's cruel and unwise aggression against us. Finally, the United States must re-sign the international Joint Comprehensive Plan of Action that had been negotiated in good faith. If you want our hand in helping you, you must take your hands off our throats. This is nonnegotiable."

"Let's be reasonable," Whittington replied. "I'm certain some sanctions can be lifted, but—"

"All conditions must be met."

"General Kardar, I do not have authority to do what you have asked, but I will speak to the president. If the United States complies, can you guarantee Aziz will not carry out his nuclear threat?"

"Your country should have sent someone with authority to sign an agreement." Kardar left the ballroom.

Whittington's return flight would take thirteen hours. Time was running out before the deadline. On his way to the airport, he called and briefed the president. Montoya joined him as they took seats on the aircraft.

"Think the president will agree to those demands?" Montoya asked.

"What choice does he have? He is convinced this threat is real. He'll have to play ball if the Navy can't find this rogue submarine."

"We don't negotiate with terrorists or their surrogates."

"Except when we do. Remember Oliver North?"

"That didn't end well."

An hour after Whittington's flight from Baku departed, General Kardar also boarded his plane at the Azerbaijan airport for the return trip to Tehran. Unlike Whittington, the general felt celebratory. As he settled in, awaiting takeoff, Kardar allowed himself to gloat. He had outsmarted all of them, and not only the Americans. He shut his eyes and thought back to the beginning, when Iran's president had quietly informed his inner circle that their country had manufactured a nuclear bomb. His revelation had been greeted with cheers, but that revelry had quickly turned into a heated discussion about what to do with the bomb. Israel and its allies would immediately react if word leaked out. They would launch a preemptive strike. It had been Kardar who'd offered a solution—an ambitious plot that others in Iran's top echelon had called impossible and foolish . . . at first.

The president had given Kardar permission to proceed. The first step had been using Iran's connections inside the Russian SVR, the successor to the KGB, to approach Taras Zharkov. Kardar had learned about the KGB's mothballed scheme—to cause a tsunami that would kill and wreak havoc—years earlier, and had correctly suspected that Zharkov would be intrigued by it. That he'd try to profit from it. Kardar had thoroughly studied his target. Zharkov was a money-hungry, inebriated glutton arrogant enough to risk an attack. He'd approached Zharkov with an offer to sell him Iran's nuclear bomb.

The next step had been recruiting Fathi Aziz to take the blame. That too had been risky, but Kardar had orchestrated it perfectly. Brought all the pieces together. There had only been a few glitches. Weren't there always? He had been photographed outside Zharkov's mansion in London, but that could be easily explained. If pressed, he would claim the Russian wished to meet with him about providing supplies to the Quds Force through one of his many companies. A more serious issue had been Zharkov's insistence on personally choosing the six-digit detonation code—a code that Zharkov had not had time to share before he died. But even that could be remedied. The general had access to Iran's finest programmers, and they could certainly find a way to decipher a six-digit code once Kardar connected them by a secure line to the submarine. If the Americans refused Tehran's demands, Kardar could explode the bomb and let Aziz be blamed. There would be no preponderance of evidence, only accusations. If America agreed to Iran's demands, he would capitalize on the threat again and again, until they located the grounded *Golden Fish* off their shoreline or killed Aziz. Even then Kardar could find another shill eager for martyrdom.

Kardar did not know who had killed Zharkov or why. But he considered his murder a favor. The Russian was no longer useful, and Kardar would have ordered him killed eventually to further cover Iran's involvement.

Kardar opened his eyes as the plane rose. A child of rape, abandoned on the streets, abused in orphanages, a throwaway Iranian. But no longer. Soon he'd be a national hero.

When his flight landed in Tehran, Kardar strutted to a waiting government car, which would take him to the Iranian president's residence to report his progress.

His private cell phone rang as he got in.

"Yes," he answered.

"You told the Jews I was in Paris."

It was the Roc.

"Zharkov told me before I killed him."

FORTY-ONE

Boris Petrov took a bite of a bologna sandwich and spit it out. The regional jail was more modern and cleaner than the Black Dolphin prison, but Russian wardens had kept prisoners better fed. There was less trouble when the bellies of condemned murderers were filled.

Petrov was walking to a trash receptacle when two inmates approached in the open pod.

"You not eating?" one asked, nodding toward his corn and green beans, applesauce, and uneaten sandwich. "Give it to me."

Petrov turned the tray upside down so its contents fell into the garbage.

"You disrespecting me?" the convict declared, fists clenched.

Petrov turned his back.

"Hey, asshole," the convict snapped.

Petrov spun and exploded upward. His open right palm hit under the convict's nose, breaking it and causing the surprised inmate to fall back. Petrov kicked the inmate's thigh just above his knee, shattering the prisoner's bone, sending him to the floor.

His jailhouse buddy backed away as guards ran toward them.

"On the floor!" an officer yelled. "Now!"

Petrov dropped to his knees and then onto his belly. The guards swarmed around him, each taught to take charge of a specific limb. They dropped in unison, pinning him to the tile floor. His wrists were handcuffed behind his back, his feet shackled. A chain was attached, connecting the restraints.

The injured prisoner's compound fracture had ripped through the leg of his dark-green pants.

"You blind and stupid?" an arriving captain asked the wounded inmate. "Didn't you see his tats? He's been down before."

Petrov was dragged to a solitary cell on the pod's ground level. Inside, it was pitch-black. The toilet was a hole in the floor. They dropped him, hog-tied, onto concrete that smelled of bleach, urine, and feces. Now out of view of the pod's cameras, the captain towered over Petrov.

"Listen, you dumb Russian son of a bitch, I don't tolerate fighting." He kicked Petrov hard in his ribs, and when Petrov didn't immediately cry out, he aimed for his head.

Petrov turned his skull just in time to avoid a blow to his face. A guard leaned down and began hammering the bound prisoner's face with his fists. When they left him, Petrov was spitting blood.

Outside the regional jail, Brett Garrett poked the intercom call button and stepped back so Valerie Mayberry could flash her FBI credentials in front of a camera.

"Who you here to see?" a voice asked.

"The Russian rescued by the Coast Guard," she answered.

They heard a loud buzz, and the electronic lock in the reinforced door opened. The lobby smelled of cleaning supplies. Mayberry went directly to the glass-enclosed control booth, which was reminiscent of a drive-through bank window. She inserted her FBI identification into a retractable drawer. Garrett tossed in an old State Department ID that he'd used when working for the CIA. The guard peered through the bullet-resistant glass at Mayberry, comparing her ID to her face. Picked up Garrett's and did the same. Retained both in a box next to him.

"You'll get 'em back when you leave. Any weapons?"

"Left them in the car," Mayberry said.

"No phones. No cameras. No recording devices."

Mayberry shook her head.

The guard nodded to a hallway directly across from the booth. "I'll have him brought to the attorney/client room—end of that hallway."

"We want a contact visit, not through the glass," Garrett said.

"That's not how we do things here," the guard answered.

"That's how we want you to do it," Mayberry insisted. "If he thinks you're recording him, he won't talk."

The guard turned off the speaker so they couldn't hear what he was saying. Raised a cell phone to his ear. When he finished, he switched the speaker back on.

"Captain has okayed it. Go through the first door on your right."

Mayberry led. They waited to hear another electronic deadbolt open, then entered a narrow room with a stainless-steel table and four stools bolted onto the floor. The hallway door behind them shut. As they heard its electronic deadbolt slide shut, a door opened in the opposite wall, and two guards brought Petrov through. An officer unlocked Petrov's leg restraints, but didn't uncuff his hands. Instead, the officer chained them to a thick steel ring on the table, preventing Petrov from lifting them more than five inches from its shiny surface.

Both guards left, but one stood watch outside the door, peering through an eye-level window at them. Mayberry couldn't see any cameras or microphones in the room.

In fluent Russian, Mayberry introduced herself and Garrett. Petrov ignored them. Stared straight ahead.

"They whipped your ass pretty good, didn't they?" Garrett noted in English, looking at the bruises and cuts on Petrov's face. "Everyone's a tough guy when they're beating a handcuffed man."

Petrov gave him a curious glance.

"Did time in Leavenworth," Garrett said. "Easy to recognize a guard ass-kicking once you've had one." He rose from the table and tapped on the glass window through which the guard was watching them.

"You already done?" the officer asked when he opened the door.

"Not even started," Garrett replied. "We need you to uncuff him, and while you're at it, we'd like three coffees. I take mine black."

"You serious? This isn't McDonald's. We don't do things your way."

"I believe that's Burger King."

The guard was about to utter an expletive when Mayberry spoke. "Unless you want the Justice Department's civil rights division coming here to investigate why this prisoner is covered with bruises, I'd suggest you comply."

"He got into a fight with another inmate. He lost."

The guard shut the door. Garrett watched him use his cell. Moments later, the captain joined them.

"You the one asking for coffee?" he said.

"It was a long drive from Washington."

The captain looked at Mayberry. "She's FBI, but why is someone from State here? Who are you, exactly?"

"I'm the one Washington sent to interview your prisoner. If you'd like, we can arrange a call from the US attorney general."

"We'd appreciate your cooperation," Mayberry added.

The captain looked at Garrett, then at Petrov and his officer. "Go ahead and uncuff him and bring them coffee." To Garrett, he added, "If he throws it in your face, that's on you."

Garrett smiled. "Yes, if he throws it, it will be on me."

The captain left, and after Petrov's hands were unshackled and the guard had retreated, Garrett offered him coffee. Petrov looked at the cup but didn't take it.

"They used to spit or worse in my drinks," Garrett said. "I've heard the KGB drugs people." He reached over and took Petrov's cup, raised it to his lips, and took a sip. "Burned my tongue, but it's okay." He placed it back before Petrov. "If you don't like that one, take mine."

He slid his cup over next to the other one.

Petrov picked up the first cup. "All prison coffee tastes like shit," he complained.

"The Coast Guard report says you jumped from the *Bella Sofia* cargo ship," Mayberry said. "Can you tell us why you were trying to enter the US illegally?"

Petrov ignored her.

Garrett nodded at the tats on Petrov's forearms. "We call your type dolphins in our navy. What do you Russians call submariners?"

Petrov grunted. "Crazy."

"At least you're used to being locked in small spaces."

Petrov smirked. "You're a funny American."

"You were wearing a deepwater submarine escape suit when you were rescued," Mayberry said.

"Let's start with your name," Garrett interrupted. "You're listed as John Doe."

"I was told in America you were allowed a phone call," Petrov said.

"Not if you're trying to enter our country illegally," Mayberry replied.

"Who do you want to call?" Garrett asked. "Your billionaire pal Taras Zharkov?"

A sudden shift in eye movement.

"Zharkov's dead," Mayberry said. "He'll not be coming to rescue you."

"I don't know this Zharkov."

"Then we're wasting our time speaking to you." Mayberry turned to Garrett. "He doesn't know anything."

"Listen," Garrett said, "it's basic. You help us. We help you. Two dead Russians wearing SEIE suits washed up on shore after you were found. Both fatally shot by someone using an underwater pistol. If you don't help us, I'm fairly certain a friendly prosecutor could be persuaded to charge you in their suspicious deaths and you will spend the rest of your life in prison drinking shitty coffee."

"This Zharkov, how did he die?" Petrov asked.

"Why would you care?" Mayberry asked.

"Murdered in the bedroom of his London mansion," Garrett said.

Petrov stared at the paper coffee cup in his hand.

"We know about Zharkov's submarine and the bomb," Garrett said. "We think you know about them too. Help us, and we'll help you get out of here."

Petrov put down his coffee. "My name is Boris Petrov. If I tell you more, I want a ticket to Moscow. No charges here."

"That depends on what you know," Mayberry said.

"Everything."

"That's what everyone says when they're trying to cut a deal," Garrett said.

"Do you know where it is?" Mayberry asked.

Petrov saw opportunity in her eagerness. "Yes, but in addition to the airplane ticket, I want a reward."

Garrett snickered. "Listen, Boris, no one is going to reward you for taking part in a nuclear attack against the United States. But I can promise you this. If there's a bomb and it goes off, you'll be executed."

"There is a bomb. I have seen it."

"We could just make you talk," Garrett threatened.

"Americans don't do such things. Tell your bosses I can take you to the exact location of the submarine in time to neutralize the bomb."

"How do you know where it is right now?" Garrett asked. "I assume it's out there, moving around."

"We need something to show you're not lying," Mayberry said. "Work with us, and we'll help you."

"You are searching for a Soviet-era Romeo-class submarine capable of traveling at twenty knots with advanced stealth technology, and it is not out there moving around. I brought it here, and it is grounded at sea in a location that you will never find."

"You brought it? You grounded it?" Garrett unfolded a map of the Virginia coastline. "Where is it grounded?"

Petrov extended his middle finger and touched the map without taking his eyes off Garrett's. "Here, or maybe here, or maybe here, or maybe there," he said, slipping his finger along the entire coast. "Five million, ten million, a hundred million—what is it worth to stop a nuclear attack?" He waved at the guard watching them. The officer opened the door. "I'm finished," Petrov said, then turned back to Garrett and Mayberry. "Don't wait too long. Tick-tock, tick-tock."

When Garrett and Mayberry reached the parking lot, both made calls.

Garrett telephoned the agency and asked to speak to Director Whittington. Mayberry the FBI.

"I can't get by the bureau's switchboard," Mayberry said moments later.

"Same here," Garrett said. "Let's drive."

"Where?"

"The White House."

FORTY-TWO

The Israeli surgeon handed Esther a glass container that resembled a tall drinking glass.

"How much time do I have?" Esther asked.

"Maximum two hours." He opened the hospital emergency-room door so Esther could enter the brightly lighted room.

Ibrahim Antar was still groggy but opened his left eye. He blinked and realized that his right eye was covered with gauze and bandages. He tried to move his arms, but they were strapped to the hospital bed. His legs too. A monitor was nearby. Heartbeat, blood pressure, respiratory. He suddenly realized he was wearing a hospital gown.

"It will take a few moments for the anesthesia to wear off from the surgery," Esther told him.

"What surgery? What have you Jews done to me?"

Esther moved next to his hospital bed. Lowered a satchel to the floor.

"Where is Fathi Aziz?"

Antar ignored her.

"Your friend Khalid Basara is dead, and so is the woman who was sleeping in his bed. No one in Gaza knows where you are. They cannot rescue you, and we can easily make you disappear."

Antar turned his head away from her.

"Ibrahim, we know you are a member of the Jihad Brigade. I will arrange for you to be executed as a terrorist, unless you tell me where Aziz is hiding."

Antar pulled on the bed restraints. Spat out a series of insults and then defiantly proclaimed: "I welcome martyrdom."

"Where is Fathi Aziz?"

More insults. More defiance.

"You welcome martyrdom," Esther repeated. "Martyrdom is too easy."

She bent and removed a photograph from her satchel. It was the picture of the Israeli solider who'd been tortured by the Roc. She cupped Antar's chin with her left hand. Forced him to stare at the gruesome photo inches from him.

"Do you see how the skin was removed while he was still alive? Imagine the pain. The suffering. Your people did this to one of our soldiers."

Antar's eyes narrowed, filled with hatred.

"His name was Avraham," she continued. "Only twenty years old. Not yet a father. Look at the floor. See his flesh? Tossed there like pieces of garbage."

"A Jew," Antar said, spitting out the words. "You torture and murder Palestinians every day. Children, mothers, old people. I only wish I had been the one cutting your friend."

Esther pinched his chin hard between her fingers. "The Jihad Brigade just murdered schoolchildren in Manhattan, children visiting a museum."

"Aziz is merely an instrument of Allah, the holy one." He spit, hitting her chin. The spittle dripped onto her olive-green military uniform. She took a cloth from a nearby medical tray and wiped her face. Tucked the photo back into her satchel.

"Where is Aziz hiding?"

"You are deaf and stupid. A Jew cow!"

Esther reached into her satchel, and when she raised her hand, she was holding the tall glass container that the surgeon had given her outside the emergency room.

"Look," she said. "Look—at yourself."

He didn't understand.

An object floated in the clear fluid. She turned the container slightly. It took him a moment. A detached human eyeball staring back at him.

"This is from your operation," Esther said.

Antar immediately tried to raise his right eyelid under the bandage. Closed his left eye and tried to see with only his right. Nothing. Only blackness.

"It's not there," Esther said calmly. "Now it belongs to me. It belongs in this bottle."

Antar unleashed a primordial scream. The numbers, beeps, and lines on his monitor went haywire. He cried again and bruised his wrists, trying to break his restraints.

"Where is Aziz?" Esther said in a menacing whisper.

"I will kill you!" he shouted. "Every one of you."

"Where is Aziz?"

Antar hollered again and tried to rip free.

Esther motioned for the surgeon, still standing behind her, to come closer.

"Ibrahim has made his choice," Esther said, standing up, stepping back from the bedside stool to make room for the doctor. "Time to remove his other eye."

The surgeon retrieved a syringe from the nearby table. He inserted its needle into a vial and pulled back its plunger.

Antar began thrashing. He twisted his head, wrestled with the restraints, jerking them back and forth helplessly.

Esther called two men. They positioned themselves on opposite sides of the bed and grabbed Antar's skull. He tried to bite one, but they immobilized him. He was breathing rapidly now, covered in sweat. Like a rabid dog.

Antar's remaining eye shifted from Esther to the surgeon, who raised the needle.

"Where is Aziz?" Esther asked.

Antar clenched his teeth. Esther nodded. The surgeon inserted his needle into Antar's cornea and injected the syringe's contents. The two men clutching his head released their grip, and Antar screamed in intense pain, lifting and dropping his head against the pillow.

"The first injection necessary for me to detach the eye," the surgeon said in a matter-of-fact voice.

"This is your last chance," Esther said. "Tell me now, before he cuts it out."

Antar again locked his teeth.

"Blind him," Esther ordered.

The surgeon inserted his hands into white latex gloves and retrieved a scalpel. Its shiny blade flashed in the overhead light. He touched the blade's tip just under Antar's eyebrow. "First, I will remove the eyelid," he explained, as if lecturing student doctors. "For easier access behind the eye, so I can sever the optic nerve, causing irreversible blindness. Then I will pull the eye from its socket."

The surgeon began to cut into Antar's flesh, drawing blood.

"No!" he screamed. "Stop! Stop!"

The surgeon hesitated.

Esther stepped forward as a droplet of blood from the incision trickled into Antar's left eye. He blinked, verifying that he still had an eyelid.

"Where is he?" Esther asked.

"Outside Dera Ghazi Khan. Punjab Province, in Pakistan." He began sobbing.

"When did you last contact him?"

"Only an hour before you kidnapped me," Antar said. "I swear it."

"If you are lying, you will lose more than your eyesight." Esther placed the tall glass that held the severed eye on a metal tray for him to see.

"The pain," he begged. "My eye is on fire."

The surgeon gave him a shot of local anesthesia. Regaining his composure, he spat out: "Allah will punish you!"

Once outside the emergency room, Esther checked the time.

"Less than two hours," she said to the surgeon.

"Perfectly played. Once the paralyzing agent wears off, he will know the eyeball in the glass next to him is not his. It will be impossible to deceive him a second time."

"If Aziz detonates a nuclear bomb," she said, "there will be no need to deceive him."

FORTY-THREE

"Saeedi," General Kardar said, hoping to disarm the Roc by using his first name, "we are brothers. Not enemies." He had no idea how the assassin had obtained his private cell number. The general was still riding in his government-issued car from the Tehran airport to the Iranian president's house.

"You betrayed my daughter and me in Paris," the Roc said. "You caused her death."

"It's a lie. Who told you this? How would I know where you were staying?"

"The sex trafficker in Claviere told you."

"A sex trafficker? I don't associate with worms. This is nonsense. Why are you bothering me with these foolish accusations?"

The next sound Kardar heard was a recording. The Roc questioning Farrokh, the hostel clerk, having used the digital recorder to memorialize their conversation. The man who had arranged for Tahira to be driven to Paris.

"Who did you tell?"

"Tehran. A nephew in Quds Force. I thought the Iranians would want to help you."

"His name?"

"The call was transferred to a general."

"Which one?"

"Kardar."

"What did you tell him? Be exact if you want to live."

"I said you were in a flat on the rue Ordener."

"Are you recording me now?" Kardar asked indignantly.

No reply.

"The sex trafficker called me," Kardar said, "but what does that prove? I refused to give him money. He must have called the French police, asking for a reward. I did not betray you and your daughter to the Jews."

Another recorded voice. Russian oligarch Taras Zharkov.

"He couldn't risk you being captured. You might talk. It was Kardar's idea to kill you and your daughter in Paris, not mine! He called the Jews."

"A weak man begging for his life," Kardar declared. "He would say anything to save himself. Why do you believe these men and not me?"

Silence.

"Did you call to threaten me?" Kardar demanded. "I am not a drunk or a frightened Russian. I am not a sex trafficker. I am the leader of the Quds Force."

The sound of another recording. Zharkov's voice.

"General Kardar delivered a nuclear bomb to me in Balaklava Bay. It came from Iran."

"How," the Roc responded, breaking his silence, "will the Americans react when they hear this?"

"Recordings can be made to say anything."

Another taped conversation.

"I paid General Kardar two million dollars . . ."

"How will your own people react to your greed?"

"Saeedi," Kardar said, "what is your purpose here? The Jews and Americans, they are our enemies. Let us resolve this between us according to the teachings of the Prophet. *Qisas* is not permissible. I did not shoot your daughter. Your loss requires *diya*."

"*Diya*? You wish to pay me blood money—fifty camels for my daughter's life?"

"Why then did you call, if not to demand payment? To ease your guilt? We are not children. I did not put a gun in your daughter's hand. I did not instruct you to take her to Bellagio to kill the Jew. You did this to her. You are to blame, not me."

"I am coming for you," the Roc said. "You will die by my hand." He ended the call.

FORTY-FOUR

A violent morning thunderstorm pelted Washington, DC, delaying Director Whittington's return flight from Azerbaijan. When his military aircraft touched down at Joint Base Andrews, southeast of the city, it was noon on a Wednesday. Fathi Aziz's deadline was Thursday at midnight.

The countdown: thirty-six hours.

Sixteen hundred Pennsylvania Avenue was fifteen miles from the military base, normally a thirty-minute trip outside of rush hour. A police escort got the CIA director there in twenty.

He found President Fitzgerald staring out the three large windows behind his Oval Office desk.

"Nothing like a good hard rain," Fitzgerald said without turning around. "Cleans the filth off this city." He touched the window with his fingers. "They don't open. Sealed for security. Too bad. I could use some fresh air."

He moved into his chair behind the Roosevelt desk while waving for Whittington to sit across from him. "You reported that General Kardar offered the Iranian Supreme Leader's help if we lift all economic, trade, scientific, and military sanctions. Is that about it?"

"Yes, Mr. President. This is exactly what Kardar proposed. He said Iran can stop Aziz."

"What do you make of this general?"

"The agency has quite a thorough file. He is cruel. Ruthless. A sexual sadist known to torture young girls, even though he claims to be deeply religious. Like all of them, he hates Israel—and us."

"Can he deliver?"

"I believe he can. Obviously, the Iranians don't want the world to know they're willing to betray Fathi Aziz and the Jihad Brigade, so it makes sense that Tehran would send its Quds Force general to meet with me privately."

"My gut tells me these bastards are behind this."

"The Israelis think the same," Whittington said. "But the Iranians are clever enough not to leave any credible evidence. They hide in the shadows, pulling strings. In a twisted way, it's better if they are. Because they can stop Aziz."

"By shaking us down to end a crisis of their making? The idea makes me sick." Fitzgerald stood, returned to the windows. "Lost some tree branches during the storm this morning." He returned to his chair. "The Navy still hasn't found a trace of this rogue submarine and bomb. The Pentagon is questioning whether there really is a submarine, regardless of what Director Levi says." He picked up an ink pen from his desk. Rolled it between his fingers. "What if I call their bluff? Tell them to go to hell?"

"You'd be a hero, sir . . . unless there *is* a bomb. If there was a nuclear attack, and the media learned we could have stopped it by meeting Iran's demands—" Whittington didn't finish the sentence.

"Let's consider what happens if I remove sanctions. How long before the Iranians come back with more demands? That's how a shakedown works."

"We could counteroffer," Whittington said. "Agree to lift the sanctions, but only if Iran provides us with evidence that the nuclear bomb has been recovered and Aziz imprisoned."

"You're missing the point. If the Israelis are correct, Iran has nuclear capabilities—and that's an entire other issue for the West to grapple with."

The president was quiet for a moment. "Why do we have to play their game?" he asked. "We're the strongest military power on this planet. We could threaten to bomb the hell out of Tehran if they don't stop Aziz. Hold them responsible, especially now that they've opened the door."

"Without evidence?"

"The Israelis would back us. Blow Tehran to hell. A nuke for a nuke." Fitzgerald chuckled. "Well, it's a nice thought. Not realistic, though, is it?"

The White House chief of staff knocked twice quickly before asking for permission to interrupt them.

"Mr. President," he said. "Valerie Mayberry and Brett Garrett are at the front gate, asking to see you. They said they've found a Russian who can take the Navy to the location of the submarine and bomb."

Fitzgerald rose from his desk. "Get them in here!"

Mayberry and Garrett were directed to the Oval Office's informal area, where two beige sofas faced each other. The president was already seated in an overstuffed chair at the end of the U-shaped configuration when they entered, and Whittington was on one of the two facing couches. Mayberry and Garrett sat on the other couch, across from him. A carpet with the Great Seal separated them from the Roosevelt desk.

"Who's this Russian," Fitzgerald asked, "and where'd you find him?"

"Boris Petrov," Garrett replied. "He's in a regional jail four hours away, near Norfolk. The US Coast Guard found him adrift off the Virginia coastline in an SEIE suit a few days ago."

"A what suit?" the president interrupted.

"A submarine escape immersion equipment suit—they're used by crews to escape from submarines stranded in deep waters. You climb into this suit, it inflates, rises to the surface, and becomes a one-man life raft."

"The Coast Guard turned Petrov over to the locals to investigate," Mayberry said. "Two more Russians washed ashore after Petrov. They were dead and both were wearing SEIE suits."

"Petrov told us he is responsible for bringing the submarine here," Garrett revealed.

Whittington rolled his eyes.

"He refused to give a specific location, but we believe it's off the Virginia coast near Norfolk," Mayberry added. "In the same general area as the map with fingerprints on it that Garrett saw in Zharkov's office."

"Tell me about these maps," Fitzgerald said.

"When we were in Zharkov's private office, there were maps on a table. The Mossad was able to get fingerprint readings off one. The maps had been touched repeatedly near Norfolk."

"I had the Navy check that area, and there was no evidence of any submarines operating in those waters. None," Whittington said. "How do you know these three Russians didn't leap off a cargo ship to enter the US illegally, wearing these survival suits? Someone on board sees them and shoots two of them for abandoning ship. This Petrov character sits in jail and watches enough news to tell you both a convincing story."

"Whittington has a point," President Fitzgerald said. "It wouldn't be the first time someone in prison tried to cut a deal by lying."

"Petrov described the submarine—Romeo-class. Soviet built. That hasn't been on the news," Mayberry said. "He also flinched when we mentioned Zharkov's name."

"Why would a cargo ship be carrying SEIE suits?" Garrett asked. "And the reason why the Navy hasn't found the submarine, Petrov told us, is because it has been grounded. It's stationary, in a spot where he says it can't be easily detected."

"You can't operate a submarine with three crew members," Whittington said. "Where's everyone else, if this submarine is grounded?"

"We'll have to ask Petrov that," Garrett said, "but my guess is they're still in that grounded submarine. Dead."

"He's willing to cut a deal," Mayberry said.

"Of course he is!" Whittington exclaimed. "This is why I don't like HUMINT. We can't trust any of this."

"What sort of deal?" Fitzgerald asked.

"Immunity and a ticket back to Moscow," Mayberry said.

"That's it?" Fitzgerald asked.

Garrett and Mayberry exchanged a nervous glance. "A cash reward too," Garrett added.

"How much?" Whittington asked.

"He didn't name a specific figure," Garrett replied.

"He hinted it would be several million," Mayberry said.

"This is ridiculous, Mr. President!" Whittington declared.

Another rap on the Oval Office door. Fitzgerald's chief of staff, again. "Mr. President, you need to watch this."

A new video uploaded by Fathi Aziz. *"Allah, in his mercy, warned you, but you have refused to listen. Was the bombing in Manhattan not sufficient?"* Aziz pointed his index finger directly at the camera. *"Let those who have ears hear my words. Americans. You and your wife, you and your daughter, you and your sons, you and your parents and grandparents, will die if your president does not meet our Lord's demands. You have seen only the first of many martyrs hiding among you."*

As soon as his video ended, the television station switched to a network reporter in Lafayette Park, directly across from the White House. Demonstrators were carrying FREE PALESTINE placards, others were on their knees, praying, under NO WAR! banners, and a third group was chanting "Nuke Palestine!"

"President Randle Fitzgerald," the reporter breathlessly announced, *"has yet to make a public statement about this nuclear bomb threat, but White House sources are trying to quiet fears. There is no credible evidence that Fathi Aziz and the Jihad Brigade have secured a nuclear bomb, these sources have told us. Despite those assurances, Homeland Security has raised the terrorism threat level to 'severe'—the highest level— because of the horrific suicide bombing in New York and additional threats by Aziz. 'Severe' means an attack is highly likely."*

"Switch it off!" the president said. He rose from his chair and stood towering over Whittington. "Contact that Iranian general and buy us more time. Tell him I'll lift the sanctions, but it can't be done by snapping my fingers. How long is a flight from Tehran?"

"Thirteen, maybe fourteen, hours," Whittington said.

"Tell him you need him to come here now. That will eat up some time. Ask him to get the Supreme Leader to convince Aziz to push back his deadline. That way we can see if Tehran really has any control over him."

"We could unfreeze Iran's bank deposits," Whittington said. "As a sign of our cooperation."

"Tell him I'm willing to do that, but only if he agrees to come here for another meeting with you."

Fitzgerald spoke to Mayberry and Garrett. "You two get back to the jail where this Petrov character is. Tell him whatever he wants to hear. I'll notify the Navy. Get him on a ship, and if he's lying, you have my permission to drop him overboard for the sharks to eat."

Turning to his chief of staff, he said, "Get my national security team here and have Homeland Security update me on its plan, in case we need to begin evacuating cities along the Virginia coast near Norfolk."

"Sir," Whittington said, "our analysts still believe New York is the actual target."

"May I make a suggestion?" Garrett asked.

"What is it?" Fitzgerald asked.

"Call Julian Levi again. When we left him, he had assigned one of his best operatives to find Fathi Aziz."

FORTY-FIVE

The day of Aziz's deadline had arrived. Thursday. The final countdown.

Under the yellowish glow of a Washington, DC, convenience store's lights, the Roc used an international calling card to dial a number on a burner phone. He checked his watch: 1:00 a.m., Thursday, on America's East Coast. That meant it was 9:30 a.m. in Tehran.

"What have you learned?" he asked when his call was answered.

"He's in the air."

"When will he arrive?"

"Two fifteen in the afternoon in America. Dulles Airport. My money?"

"Bitcoin. You'll have it in minutes."

He ended the call and tossed the burner phone into a red trash bin outside the open-all-night store. Out of the corner of his eye, he noticed movement. Instinctively he slipped his hand under his light-blue nylon rain jacket and gripped the knife hidden there.

"Hey buddy," a scraggly man called, emerging from the bushes. "Spare some change?"

The Roc ignored the beggar. He left the store's parking lot near the famed Watergate Hotel and began walking toward Georgetown, once home to JFK and Jacqueline. Multimillion-dollar Federal-style houses, cobblestone streets, late-night college bars. As he neared the K Street Bridge, he noticed encampments of more homeless. Tent cities erected under overpasses. Squatters, displaced, invisible, marginalized, only steps from many of the city's most affluent residents. He kept watch for an occasional police car on patrol, but saw none as he made his way to Georgetown's Waterfront Park, a riverside promenade of glitzy shops and gourmet restaurants. Within minutes, he'd spotted a target: a middle-aged man, clearly inebriated, emerging from a bar. The Roc shadowed him to his car, an older BMW sedan. Waited until he'd opened its door, key still in his hand.

Reaching for his blade, the Roc glided toward him.

"Hey buddy, spare any change?" he asked.

The man turned to look just as the Roc fatally stabbed him. His victim's eyes opened wide in a few moments of self-comprehension before he collapsed. A push forward, and his body fell backward against the driver's seat, feet touching the pavement, head dropping onto the center console. The Roc moved swiftly. He scooped up the car key, slipped around the sedan, and tugged the corpse into the passenger seat. It had taken him longer than he'd anticipated, but it appeared that no one had seen him.

Within minutes he was crossing the Francis Scott Key Memorial Bridge into Virginia, where he turned north on the George Washington Memorial Parkway, a twenty-five-mile scenic highway that ran along the Potomac River. When he came to a scenic overlook, he stopped, grabbed the dead man under his arms, and dragged his body to the edge of a tree-lined cliff some fifty feet above the river. A final shove, and the body tumbled down. Entangled in washed-up driftwood and branches at the water's edge, it was barely noticeable.

From there, the Roc drove to a Tysons Corner hotel, parking in its underground garage. He checked in, explaining that he was arriving late because of a delay at an airport. A believable lie. Once inside his room, he showered, dressed in fresh clothes, and focused on the next stage of his deadly plan.

That afternoon, General Firouz Kardar arrived on schedule at Dulles in a private jet that taxied to a commuter terminal away from the larger main one. The United States had severed diplomatic relations with Iran in 1980, after protestors stormed the US Embassy in Tehran and took fifty-two diplomats hostage. There was no Iranian diplomatic delegation waiting to welcome him. CIA Director Whittington had arranged for Kardar and his security team to pass through immigration and customs without being questioned and offered to provide transportation, but Kardar had declined. He didn't want to depend on the agency, nor did he trust its hospitality. To keep his trip secret from Iran's allies in Washington, he had not warned the Lebanese embassy of his arrival. Instead, he had arranged for a private limousine service to meet him and his four-man protective detail. A Mercedes-Benz S-Class luxury sedan and Cadillac Escalade SUV were waiting. As in Azerbaijan, the rendezvous with Whittington would occur at a private residence.

A black Ford sedan pulled in front and another behind Kardar's hired caravan as the Mercedes and Cadillac drove away from the private jet terminal parking lot—both CIA vehicles, unwanted by the general but sent anyway. Now four together in a line, they went east toward State Highway 28. From there, north on a toll road into Leesburg, a city established in 1740, most famous because it served as the temporary home of the federal government when invading British troops burned the White House and Capitol during the War of 1812.

Kardar had never been to the United States, nor had he ever wished to visit. He assumed Whittington was stalling for time. That is why he had immediately departed from Tehran, so he could arrive ten hours before the Jihad Brigade's midnight deadline. That would give him enough time to determine if the US was serious or playing games. He had no intention of easing the pressure off the Americans.

From his vantage point near the private jet terminal, the Roc watched the four vehicles. He knew the meeting between Whittington and

Kardar was being held inside a former plantation near Point of Rocks, Maryland, and the only road there was Highway 15, a winding two-lane stretch of narrow asphalt. Once the Roc was satisfied that he knew this was the route they would follow, he drove his stolen BMW ahead.

The highway snaked through the cookie-cutter housing developments that edged Leesburg before they yielded to lush farmlands. About seven miles north of Leesburg, it entered the tiny town of Lucketts, home to a trailer park, rural school, volunteer fire department, one-story brick motel, and a smattering of curio shops. The biggest draw was a two-story antique store that attracted a steady crowd of Washington, DC, millennials eager to duplicate HGTV designs.

A single stoplight in the center of Lucketts controlled highway traffic. The Roc reached it ten minutes before Kardar's motorcade. He crossed the intersection and immediately pulled to the side of the road, next to the antique store.

As he exited the BMW, a man hollered, "Hey, you can't park there!"

The man was in his sixties, wearing a straw hat with an American flag above its brim, large sunglasses, a plaid shirt, and overalls. He was standing with a young couple outside the building where they appeared to be examining old iron gates and wooden shutters leaning against the store's bright green painted siding.

"I work here," the man declared. "You need to park in our lot around back."

"I'll only be a few minutes," the Roc replied.

"You can't leave your car like that," the man insisted. "Your wheels are touching the highway. People have to drive around you."

Ignoring him, the Roc hurried across the road toward the town's only gas station, some fifty yards farther up from the store.

"I'm getting you towed!" the man threatened.

The first CIA escort car was approaching the stoplight.

"People nowadays," the man grumbled. "Think they can do whatever they want."

The CIA car had ventured about a half mile ahead of Kardar's Mercedes-Benz. After crossing the intersection, its driver pulled to the side of the road behind the BMW so the others could catch up.

"Don't that just take all!" the man complained. "Here's another one who thinks he can just park there." He left the couple he was helping and walked toward the Ford sedan.

"You can't park here!" he shouted, rapping his knuckles on its trunk. "I just told the other driver that. Our parking lot's around back."

The CIA officer on the passenger side lowered his window.

"How long's the BMW been parked here?"

"How long doesn't matter. You got to move."

The CIA officer who was driving checked the rearview mirror. Kardar's Mercedes-Benz was nearing the intersection. "We need to get going," he said.

"Where's the owner of that BMW?" the officer in the passenger seat asked the clerk.

"That's him, going into the gas station." He pointed toward the Roc.

"The light's about to change," the driver said. "Time to go."

"Hold it," his partner replied.

"No, we're going."

The light turned green. Kardar's Mercedes entered the intersection, but was forced to slow by the lead CIA vehicle, now pulling back onto the road.

Watching from the gas station, the Roc pressed a button on a remote hidden in his jacket pocket.

The force of the explosion from the BMW flipped the Mercedes-Benz onto its roof into the opposite lane. Steel ball bearings packed around the explosives in the BMW's trunk ripped into the other vehicles. They tore through the windshield of the Cadillac that was carrying the Iranian security team, killing its driver. Still moving forward, the Cadillac rammed into the back of the overturned Mercedes, propelling it forward into the rear of the lead CIA sedan. Sparks shot from underneath the Mercedes' roof as it skidded across the pavement, igniting the CIA car's already ruptured gas tank in another loud explosion, and killing the two CIA officers inside. An oncoming car swerved to avoid the mayhem. Its driver slammed on the brakes and was rear-ended by a car following too close behind it.

Residents from the nearby mobile trailer park dashed outside. Others came running onto the highway from the antique store and gas station. The antique store clerk and his two customers had been tossed by the blast against the side of the building and were now splayed on the road.

The only vehicle to escape harm was the second CIA car at the end of the caravan. Its two officers ran to help.

"I'm a doctor," the Roc hollered as he darted to the overturned Mercedes.

Locals stepped aside as the Roc dropped onto his belly and peered into the upside-down luxury car. The inflated front, side, and rear airbags had not saved the driver, who was dead.

"Help me!" General Kardar pleaded, held upside down by his seat belt, his head cut and bleeding.

The Roc crawled through the car's back passenger window on the other side from Kardar. Inches separated them. The hope on the general's face changed to fear.

"No!" Kardar yelled. He wasn't supposed to die this way. This couldn't be happening.

"This is for my daughter," the Roc said, thrusting his knife forward. "By my hand."

Whittington broke the news over a secure telephone line to President Fitzgerald. "General Kardar has been killed by a car bomb on the side of the highway in Lucketts, coming to meet me. A doctor at the scene tried to help him, but he was already dead—a puncture wound in his neck, apparently caused by fragments."

President Fitzgerald's temper flared. He checked the time. "What the hell are we going to do now about Aziz?"

FORTY-SIX

Esther removed the heavy bulletproof plates from her vest. It wasn't only to lighten her load. Early in her military career, a Palestinian sniper had shot an Israeli soldier standing next to her. The bullet had entered his side, passed through his chest, and become trapped by the protective vest. Instead of exiting, the slug bounced off his breastplate and reentered his abdomen, striking the soldier's back plate, where it was redirected into his midsection. When medics removed his armor, it was as if he had been struck by multiple rounds. From that day on, she'd always detached the plates.

Now Esther and a ten-member team from Kidon, Israel's most secret assassination unit, approached the farmhouse outside Dera Ghazi Khan in the Punjab Province of Pakistan in the early-morning darkness. It took an hour for them to crawl unseen through a hundred yards of furrows in the wheat fields surrounding the house.

There was no cell phone service here. Any signal to detonate a nuclear bomb seven thousand miles away would have to be done by satellite. An advanced electronic warfare system was being used to jam that signal, and prevent Aziz from carrying out his threat against the Americans.

Because Esther and her team didn't have the luxury of time to develop and practice an attack plan, Director Levi had pulled one from the past. Operation Bramble Bush had been devised to kill Saddam Hussein when he was Iraq's president. It called for firing a portable guided missile at the dictator while he was attending a relative's out-door funeral. That plan had been abandoned after five Israeli sol-diers, pretending to be Saddam and his bodyguards, were accidentally killed during a final drill exercise at the Tze'elim training base in the southern Negev. A commando had mistakenly fired an actual missile, code-named Obelisk, at the men rather than a dummy round.

Lying on her belly, Esther watched the two sentries making their rounds outside the farmhouse through night-vision goggles. The house was a two-story, rectangular building without decoration, made of bricks covered with adobe mud. Three trucks were parked near the front doorway. To the north, in the open yard, were farm machinery and a barn.

It had been difficult slithering through the knee-high wheat. Sweat matted Esther's hair under her helmet despite a cool morning breeze. Her throat was dry. She fought the urge to cough.

The team intended to kill Aziz when he came outside to lead his followers in Salat al-Fajr, the first Muslim prayer of the day. Satellite surveillance had revealed that this was the only time the terrorist left the farmhouse.

Jihadists began emerging, armed with individual prayer rugs and AK-47 assault rifles. Only after the men had formed a line facing Mecca did their leader join them. He walked forward to lead the first *rakat*—prescribed movements required in praising Allah.

Esther had split her team into groups that formed a three-pointed spear. The outer two prongs each had two soldiers, one armed with a modified Spike-SR, an Israeli-made "fire and forget" guided antiper-sonnel missile. The center prong was Esther, coordinating the attack. Directly behind her, the team's sniper and his spotter had claimed higher ground in a treed area. Esther counted eleven jihadists—one short of what intel had told her.

"You a go?" she whispered into her headset.

"Negative," her sniper reported. He didn't have a clear shot at Aziz.

"Green light," she said.

Two ground-fired missiles flew from the outer prongs of the attack spear, their fragmentation charges shattering the early-morning silence. The pellets bursting from them cut a swath through the jihadists. Miraculously, after the blast, two managed to rise to their knees. Both fired their assault rifles wildly. Both were easily dispatched by the sniper in the tree line. Esther could hear moans and cries for help from those still alive and critically wounded. She looked for Aziz but couldn't spot him from her prone position. Rising slowly from the protective wheat, she began moving toward the farmhouse, half bent over, armed with her pistol.

"We're one short," she warned through her earpiece.

"Eyes on the house," her sniper responded.

Esther had gone about twenty yards when a jihadist lying on the ground fired at her. She slid on the ground like a baseball player stealing second base while her sniper returned fire. For a moment it was quiet, and then the jihadist fired another burst, this time at the tree line where the sniper was hiding. At the same time, a gunman inside the house began firing into the wheat field, pinning down Esther and the others.

Esther spoke into her headset, and a third Spike-SR missile slammed into the upper story of the house. It blew a gaping hole, silencing the jihadist hiding there.

Although they were in a rural setting, three explosions and repeated gunfire would soon draw Pakistani police and military soldiers. "We need to clean this up!" she ordered.

She stood again and made a run toward the farm, shooting at the bodies on the ground, unsure who was alive, who was wounded, who was dead.

"Allahu akbar!" the lone surviving jihadist who'd fired at her earlier hollered, leaping to his feet, clutching a grenade. Now less than five yards away, Esther shot him, sending him face-first into the dirt.

The grenade exploded underneath him, his body shielding her from its blast and shrapnel. In that moment, she regretted removing her armor plates. She'd been lucky.

The morning became silent again. She stepped cautiously between the corpses. Human bodies proved surprisingly elastic, and even though the missile strike had torn off the right arm and severed a leg of the prayer leader, the remainder of his torso was intact. He was lying facedown, badly burned and specked with red shrapnel wounds. Esther grabbed his shoulder, turning him over to look at his face and compare it with photos of Fathi Aziz.

The dead man looked nothing like the terrorist they'd come to kill.

She moved methodically from body to body, examining each face. Most were teenagers, about half her age, who'd grown up being fed a steady diet of hatred toward Israel and those who supported it.

When she reached the last one, she realized Aziz was not there.

"He must be inside the house," she told the others.

She was the first through the ground-floor door, and she immediately heard movement coming from the second level—the sound of an object banging, bouncing down the stairs. Although she couldn't see it, she knew what was happening.

"Grenade!" she yelled, diving behind a wall. A deafening explosion and a sudden jab in her back. She cried out in pain. Dust-filled air clogged her lungs. She reached backward, trying to touch the wound, but it was impossible to reach.

One of her fellow fighters scrambled beside her while the others unleashed a flurry of automatic weapon fire up the staircase.

"Don't move!" the other fighter ordered her. He grabbed a piece of metal that had embedded itself and pulled it free. From his medical kit, he applied gauze and tape.

"You're not wearing your plates," he said.

She nodded.

They were joined by a third fighter.

"Anyone else hurt?" Esther asked.

"Only you. Where's your plates?"

She stepped to the bottom of the staircase and gingerly began climbing. At the top, she found an empty hallway. To her immediate right was the gaping hole the missile had blown through the house's wall. Through it, she could see dawn light appearing. Chunks of plaster and adobe bricks littered the hallway floor. A blood smear. She followed it with her eyes to a closed door on her left. Dropped to her knees and fished a black cable from her pack, which she slid underneath the door. Standard procedure before entering. A camera on its tip gave her an unobstructed view.

Directly across from the doorway was a half-naked man holding an AK-47. Part of his left leg was missing. He'd used his shirt as a tourniquet to slow the bleeding, but it was obvious that he was dying. He'd propped his back against a wall for support.

She checked her photo of Fathi Aziz. It was him.

Through the closed wooden door, she could hear him repeating, "Allahu akbar! Allahu akbar! Allahu akbar!"

Esther slowly pushed the door inward.

It had opened less than two inches when Aziz began firing. His rounds splintered the wooden door but failed to hit Esther and her fellow Israeli fighters, who were protected by the thick adobe walls on either side of it. Esther lobbed a flash bang inside. Its exaggerated boom and blinding light temporarily disoriented Aziz, who sprayed the area blindly until he'd emptied the rifle's magazine. Esther darted inside.

With her right foot, she kicked his right hand, causing him to yelp in pain as the AK-47 flew from his grasp. She dropped to a knee and stuck her pistol against his chest.

"Fathi Aziz," she declared.

He glared at her. Hatred. But he made no effort to fight. A strange smile appeared on his lips. She looked at his left hand and saw that it was resting on an electronic tablet. He pushed a final digit on its screen. It was obvious to Esther that he'd been told six numbers that he believed would detonate the nuclear bomb.

"Allahu akbar! Death to America!"

A satisfied look swept across his face as he lowered the tablet and stared up at Esther.

"Fathi Aziz!" Esther said in a calm voice. "You have failed. We are jamming all signals. You are impotent." She looked directly into his eyes. "Know the last words you will hear are from a Jewish woman." She fired twice into his chest before pulling back her pistol and firing a third round directly into his forehead. Quickly, holstering her weapon, she photographed him and collected a DNA sample before scrambling from the room.

"Target's eliminated," she reported to Big Jules through her headset. "No casualties, and only one minor wound."

"Can you make it to the drop site?"

"Yes. Leaving now."

It was now light enough to see a Pakistani convoy coming toward the farmhouse. Overhead, the sound of an approaching helicopter.

The Israelis slipped across the wheat field to where their sniper and spotter were waiting. By the time the Pakistani soldiers arrived, the Israelis were gone without a trace. Only the corpses of Fathi Aziz and his jihadist followers remained.

Esther used a secure satellite connection to send the photos of Fathi Aziz to Big Jules, and he in turn relayed them to Director Whittington, who immediately contacted the White House.

"It's over," Whittington said. "The Israelis have terminated Aziz."

FORTY-SEVEN

"They told us you were wounded," Valerie Mayberry said.

She'd come to the Norfolk airport to pick up Esther on a beautiful Sunday afternoon.

"A shrapnel gash in my back, but nothing serious," Esther replied. "Where's Garrett?"

"He's out on the ship, along with a Russian—Boris Petrov—the commander who piloted the submarine here."

Esther joined Mayberry in a waiting chauffeured SUV.

"A helicopter at the Naval Station will fly us to join Garrett and the others," Mayberry explained. "The station is about a fifteen-minute drive from here."

As they exited the airport, Mayberry added, "Garrett says the situation out there is dangerous and chaotic."

"Chaotic?"

Mayberry handed Esther a copy of that morning's *Washington Interceptor.*

Naval Experts to Remove Nuclear Bomb
from Sunken Submarine off Va. Coast
By Investigative Reporter Robert Calhoun

EXCLUSIVE!

Norfolk, Virginia—Naval experts will attempt to remove a nuclear bomb from a sunken former Soviet submarine today off the coast near here, the *Washington Interceptor* has learned.

The device is believed to be inside a former Romeo-class Soviet submarine lying some 270 feet below the surface in an underwater pit created centuries ago dug into the continental shelf.

A high-level intelligence source, who asked not to be identified, said a crew member from the rogue submarine is cooperating with authorities and will take government experts this morning to where it was intentionally grounded.

According to confidential sources, the submarine was able to avoid detection in US-controlled waters by traveling through an underwater canyon and using high-tech antidetection equipment recently perfected by the Russians.

"If it weren't for the former crew member," a source said, "we would have had no idea where the submarine and bomb are sitting."

The crew member assisting authorities was the only sailor to survive. The remainder of the boat's crew—still aboard the sunken submarine—are believed dead because the vessel was sabotaged shortly after it was grounded, a source disclosed. At best, the doomed crew had been left aboard with no means of escape with less than twelve hours of oxygen.

Fathi Aziz, a Palestinian terrorist, had threatened to explode a nuclear bomb on the submarine at midnight Thursday unless the United States convinced Israel to withdraw from all former Palestinian lands. Aziz took responsibility for a

Palestinian suicide bomber who murdered 40 persons outside the Metropolitan Museum of Art in Manhattan, including 26 Jewish students.

An Israeli commando team surprised Aziz at a rural farmhouse in Pakistan only hours before his threatened deadline, according to sources. The radical Islamic terrorist was killed during a firefight. After learning of Aziz's death, President Randle Fitzgerald promptly declared Aziz's submarine nuclear bomb threat averted.

Esther had read enough. She tossed the paper between them on the SUV's back seat.

"Garrett said dozens of curiosity seekers have followed the naval ships out to where the submarine is located," Mayberry said. "They're trying to get photos. The Coast Guard has been unable to turn them back."

"An Israeli newspaper never would have published such a story without government permission."

"This reporter is especially reckless. He'll print anything to get more internet hits and sell more papers. It's disgusting—'If it bleeds, it leads' journalism."

"He had so many details—someone must have given him this information," Esther said. "Find and punish that source, if you want to stop such stories."

"In Washington that's tough—especially when Garrett and I both believe the source is Director Whittington."

"Your own CIA director?"

"This reporter has printed details that could only have come from him. He has a personal grudge against both of us, but especially Garrett."

The driver slammed on the SUV's brakes and smacked his palm against the horn. They came to an abrupt stop midway in an intersection, barely avoiding a collision with a driver who'd run a red light.

The offending motorist didn't bother to slow. Instead he made an obscene gesture as he sped away.

"Sorry, ladies," their driver apologized. "No one stops when a light turns yellow anymore around here."

Neither Esther nor Mayberry had been wearing seat belts, and both had been jostled. Using her left hand, Mayberry now awkwardly snapped her belt into place. Glancing at Mayberry's frozen right fingers, Esther asked, "Has acupuncture helped your hand?"

"It has helped with the pain, but I still can't close my fingers. I never would have tried it if you hadn't called that acupuncturist in London. I need to thank you, and also I'd like to apologize."

"For what?"

"I didn't like you when we first met."

Esther shrugged and smiled. "I didn't like you either. Now tell me, what's happening between you and Garrett? It's obvious there's chemistry between you."

"He surprised me in London," Mayberry confided. "He kissed me, or more accurately, he tried and I turned away and then kissed him. It's awkward."

"You Americans play so many games when it comes to romance. If you like him, be with him."

"It's not that simple." Mayberry looked down at her hand. "I think he blames himself for what happened, and I'm not the same person I was."

The SUV passed through the Norfolk Naval Station security gate, and within moments it had reached the tarmac where a helicopter was waiting.

"Who's that?" Esther asked as they got out.

"Thomas Jefferson Kim," Mayberry said, gently covering her ears because of the noise created by the aircraft's idling engine and slowly twirling blades. "A computer genius, and Garrett's closest friend."

Kim joined them in the helicopter. After they'd been introduced, Esther asked him, "Why are you here?"

"To make certain no one detonates the bomb either accidentally or intentionally through an electronic signal. My company has developed jamming software that will stop anyone trying to reach the submarine by a satellite link. I'll also be scanning nearby boats. Garrett said there are more than a dozen out there."

"This Petrov," Esther asked Mayberry, "how credible is he?"

"So far, very," Mayberry replied. "He told us the coordinates as soon as we cut a deal."

"How much did you pay him?" Esther asked.

"Nothing. When we told him that you had killed Aziz, ending the immediate threat, and the Kremlin publicly denounced Zharkov and said it would execute anyone who'd helped him, Petrov got a grim reality check. He ended up telling us the location in return for asylum."

"You agreed to let him remain here after what he did?"

"We agreed to not execute him for mass murder in return for his full cooperation."

The helicopter was flying over the Atlantic's blue-green waters. Dozens of pleasure craft appeared as they approached a US Navy command ship. Smaller Coast Guard vessels could be seen skirting between the ship and the unwanted spectators, keeping them a safe distance away.

"Glad you're here," Garrett said, beaming, when Esther, Mayberry, and Kim exited from the helicopter onto the deck where he was waiting. "This is turning into a freak show." He looked upward at a second helicopter circling above them, also about to land.

"Reporters," Garrett said, "including Robert Calhoun, whose story is responsible for all these nuisance boats showing up. The press has been invited to observe. Let's get inside the command center before they land and begin shouting questions."

He showed them the way, complaining, "Ten minutes before you arrived, some knucklehead ran his powerboat into a sailboat, and the Coast Guard had to bring the injured here for medical care."

"Sounds more like a shit show than freak show," Esther said.

Garrett smiled at her. "Good work in Pakistan. I wasn't certain you'd find Aziz in time. I heard you got injured, and he put up quite a fight."

"Another scar. We Israelis know how to kill terrorists," she bragged. "Maybe we will teach you Americans someday."

"I'd love your help in finding and killing the Roc. He's still out there."

They entered the ship's command post above the deck. The air inside was air-conditioned cool. The room smelled of seawater. There was a greenish cast from the multiple screens in the dimly lighted area they entered.

"Meet Captain Gary Reynolds," Garrett said.

The ship's fiftysomething African American captain extended his hand. Next to him was a younger black woman wearing a major's bars. "And this," Garrett said, "is Major Brooke Grant. She's been assigned to debrief Petrov."

Esther pushed past him and hugged Grant.

"The last time I saw you," Grant happily declared, "you were being hauled away in an ambulance after being stabbed in the chest by a terrorist."

"The last time I saw you," Esther replied, "you were lying helpless on the ground with a broken leg, trying to defend yourself with a wooden plank from your exploded house."

"It did have a nail in it," Grant added. She explained to the others: "Esther saved my life, and my daughter's, that night."

"Major Grant has spent the last six hours questioning Petrov," Garrett said.

"He's shown no remorse," Grant said. "He described how he'd left his crew to suffocate in the same calm voice he'd used when asking us when he could eat his lunch."

Esther asked her, "How is your daughter?"

"Casey is wonderful. Still riding horses."

"I hate to interrupt this reunion, Major," Garrett said, "but we do have a nuclear bomb below us." He turned to Captain Reynolds. "How soon before the SRDRS launches?"

"What's an SRDRS?" Esther asked.

"Submarine Rescue Diving and Recompression System," Reynolds replied. "A two-hundred-ton submersible rescue module. Once it was determined there were no survivors aboard the submarine, I was told to wait for the reporters. We'll drop it down and attach it to the submarine's escape hatch. The team will enter the submarine and find the nuclear device. They'll disconnect the remote detonator and the bomb. We'll be able to watch the entire process here from cameras mounted on the submergible and body cams.

"You can set up over here with your equipment," Reynolds said to Kim.

"Excellent. As you are well aware, Captain," Kim replied, "there are two ways to communicate with a submerged submarine."

"Here comes a science lecture," Garrett warned.

"ELF—extremely low frequency—radio waves can reach hundreds of meters under the ocean surface. However, ELF units are so cumbersome and expensive to construct that only a few nations have built them. My company's jamming system will stop ELF satellite messages from tripping the detonation switch on the nuclear device below us. ELFs won't be the problem."

"And the second way?" Esther said.

"VLF—very low frequency—radio waves can only penetrate about twenty meters underwater, and the submarine is much deeper. But I've been told there's a floating antenna attached to the submarine."

"As long as that antenna is out there," Reynolds interjected, "we're vulnerable."

"If I understand this," Mayberry said, "someone close to the ship could send a VLF signal. The submarine antenna would pick it up and relay it to the bomb. Wouldn't they still have to know its detonation code?"

"That's right. Just to make certain there are no mishaps, my job is to ensure no VLF signals reach the antenna."

"Waves and currents keep the antenna from staying in one place," Reynolds said. "Based on the submarine's depth and the projected length of the antenna, we've drawn a circle inside which the antenna must be. Once we find and disconnect it, there will be no way for anyone to detonate the bomb, even if they know the code."

"Does Petrov know the code?" Mayberry asked.

"No, but he has given us other extremely useful information," Grant said.

Garrett jumped in. "He's confirmed the bomb was made in Iran. Which is what Nasya Radi wrote in his letter to me, when this all started." He glanced at Esther. "And what our friends the Israelis told us."

"Despite Tehran's insistence that they have not made a nuclear weapon," Major Grant added.

"How many times must you catch Iran in lies before you learn what Israel knows?" Esther said. "You are fools for believing anything they say."

"When we bring up that nuclear bomb," Garrett said, "we'll have all the evidence we need, and I'm certain President Fitzgerald and our allies will punish Iran."

An aide approached Reynolds. "Captain, sir, the reporters are all on board, and the SRDRS is ready to be lowered into the water."

"How long before it reaches the submarine?" Mayberry asked.

"Less than thirty minutes," Reynolds said, slipping on a headset. His aide handed headsets to Esther, Garrett, Mayberry, and Grant.

"The captain asked me to remind you that the White House Situation Room and Pentagon are monitoring this operation and will hear whatever you might say while wearing these headsets," the aide said.

"That include Director Whittington?" Garrett asked.

"Yes, sir."

"Now's not the time, Garrett," Mayberry warned.

All of them except Kim, who was typing on a nearby computer keyboard, were focused on the images being relayed by the various stationary and body cameras on the rescue module.

"With your permission, Captain, we will untether and start our descent," a voice in the headset coming from the SRDRS announced.

"Permission to descend granted," Reynolds replied.

As the SRDRS entered the water, curious fish could be seen darting toward it on the monitors.

"So far, so good," Garrett said. He shot the captain a thumbs-up.

"Captain!" Kim exclaimed. "Someone's trying to detonate the bomb!"

Eyes immediately darted from the monitors to Kim.

"What?" Captain Reynolds said. "How's this possible?"

"What's going on?" Director Whittington could be heard asking through the headsets. Because Kim wasn't wearing one, the CIA director couldn't hear what he was saying.

"A VLF signal is coming from a surface ship," Kim said, not taking his eyes from his computer. "I'm blocking it."

"Someone talk to me," Whittington complained through the headsets.

"Can you tell where the signal is coming from?" Mayberry asked, ignoring Whittington.

"It must be one of the boats that followed us here," Garrett said.

Kim's fingers moved lightning-fast. He split his screen in half, working on one side to disrupt the VLF signal and on the other to trace its source. "This can't be right. The signal is emanating from somewhere on this ship."

"No one on my crew would try to detonate a nuclear bomb!" Reynolds declared.

"Damn it!" Whittington could be heard uttering. "Someone tell me what is happening."

"Oh my God!" Kim stammered. "Whoever is sending the signal has locked onto the antenna. I just interrupted his signal. Disconnected him. But he's trying to worm his way through my firewall."

"Zharkov, Aziz, and Kardar are dead," Mayberry said. "Who else would know the detonation code?"

Garrett's eyes locked with Esther's. "The Roc," they said simultaneously.

Esther was the first to explain. "Our soldier and a major general were tortured by the Roc before he killed them. He cut them because he was interrogating them. He wanted information. Zharkov had the same identical cuts. The Roc interrogated him in London before he murdered him."

Garrett nodded. "That's how he got the code."

"Our theory!" Mayberry exclaimed. "I think we made a mistake. That day when Big Jules was drawing his triangle. Linking everyone. What if the Roc didn't come to London to kill Zharkov? What if he followed General Kardar to London to kill him because of what happened in Paris? He must've blamed Kardar. He's out for revenge. When he got to London, he missed his opportunity, but saw Kardar meeting with Zharkov and decided to investigate why."

Garrett said, "The reports about that car bomb attack on General Kardar said a doctor had crawled inside his limo to help him. That doctor disappeared. It must have been the Roc."

"But how would the Roc get on this ship?" Esther asked.

"The helicopter carrying reporters," Garrett said. "That's got to be how he got on board. He's posing as a reporter." Garrett called to Reynolds. "Where are the reporters?"

"In the wardroom where you and I had coffee this morning."

"I remember the way," Garrett declared, starting for an exit. "How long can you jam his signal, Kim?"

"Not long. He's good. Hurry!"

All of them except for Kim and Reynolds followed Garrett, but he stopped at the exit. "I'm sorry," he told Mayberry, gesturing to her hand. "There's going to be ladder steps."

Mayberry's face turned red. She was about to respond when Kim yelled at them: "No time to argue!"

Over the headset, Whittington said, "Captain Reynolds, I order you to tell me what is happening!"

"We have a terrorist on our ship trying to detonate the bomb."

Left behind, Mayberry started to make her way to Kim and his computer, but suddenly stopped midstep. "Where's sick bay?" she asked one of Captain Reynolds's aides.

"Are you feeling ill?"

"Garrett said there was a crash—a sailboat and powerboat. The injured were brought here."

Captain Reynolds overheard. "Marcus, get her to sick bay."

FORTY-EIGHT

A naval public information officer assigned to escort the pool reporters on the ship was showing the three men and two women a diagram
of the SRDRS module and explaining how it would be attached to
the submarine when Garrett, Esther, and Major Grant burst into the
wardroom.

"Brett Garrett," one of the reporters said, rising from his seat.
"Robert Calhoun with the *Washington Interceptor*. We finally meet."

Ignoring him, Garrett glanced at the other two male reporters'
faces. Neither bore the Roc's telltale neck scar.

"He's not here," Garrett said.

"Who's not here?" Calhoun asked. "What's this about?"

Garrett started to back out.

"Wait a minute!" Calhoun hollered. "Who are you looking for,
Garrett? What's going on?"

One deck below them, Mayberry was entering the sick bay.

"Where are the civilians injured in the boating accident?" she
asked the corpsman on duty.

"Upstairs, being put on a helicopter to go back to shore."

"How many were there?"

"Three men and three women. One man died, the others were
patched up."

"Did you see a scar on the faces of any of the men?"

She raised her left finger and ran it down her neck to illustrate. "You would have noticed it."

"You'd have to ask Corpsman Peters. I just got here and read the log. He actually treated them."

"Where's he?"

"Maybe the mess hall. He wasn't here when I came on duty."

"Has that helicopter taken off?"

The corpsman shrugged. Mayberry turned to Marcus. "We need to know. See if anyone on that helicopter has a scar."

Marcus used a wall phone in the sick bay to connect with the communications center. Had it patch him through to the helicopter, which was lifting off.

"None of the passengers have scars," Marcus reported.

"The dead man," Mayberry said. "Did they check the body bag after they loaded it on the helicopter?"

Marcus spoke into the phone. "Check the body bag. That's right, the body bag—open it up!"

After a short pause, a horrified look appeared on his face.

"Corpsman Peters is in the body bag!"

"The Roc!" Mayberry said. "He's taken his place. Must have caused the boating accident to get on board and then killed Peters. What's between here and the back of this ship?" she asked Marcus.

"The aft?"

"Whatever it's called."

"Mostly the crew berthing."

"That's too public, too open."

"A supply office, laundry, and ship repair shop."

Mayberry hurried from sick bay, with Marcus chasing after her. They entered the crew berthing area.

"Hey, you," she said, stopping the first sailor she encountered. "Did you see anyone dressed like a corpsman coming this way?"

"The dude still wearing a surgical mask and cap?"

"Where'd he go?"

"Aft—toward the repair shop, port side."

"Marcus," she said, turning to him. "We need to be armed."

"It will take time for them to reach us."

"No time. C'mon."

Marcus broke into a run, darting through the crew berthing. He slowed when he reached the repair-shop entrance. With Mayberry standing directly behind him, he pulled open its door and stepped inside.

"You!" Marcus yelled.

The Roc, less than six feet away, snatched a Glock 26 handgun from the counter, where he had placed it next to his portable computer. Marcus began to step back, but couldn't because Mayberry was behind him, blocking the doorway. She backpedaled just as the Roc fired.

The sound was deafening inside the tiny shop. Two rounds, both striking Marcus in his upper chest. Near his heart. He fell out the door, landing at Mayberry's feet.

She dropped to her knees as he gasped for air.

"Get help!" she screamed, but there was no one close to them.

Marcus stopped breathing.

Mayberry scanned the area for a weapon. She spotted a bright red fire extinguisher on the wall, next to a blueprint of the deck. She wrestled it down with her good left hand and glanced at the schematic. The shop was about eight feet long and five feet wide. Mayberry looped the extinguisher's hose around her lame right arm, positioning its nozzle between her thumb and damaged fingers. With her left arm, she lifted the extinguisher and readied herself. *One, two, three.*

She stuck the extinguisher's nozzle into the shop and unleased the pressurized container's potassium bicarbonate spray. The Purple-K powder quickly spread a whitish fog.

Blam! Blam! The Roc fired at the doorway as she stayed safely outside, only the nozzle turning the corner. One of the rounds smacked into the solid steel wall inside the chamber where it splintered into fragments, like a rock struck by a sledgehammer. The other round shattered a glass container filled with liquid on a shelf. Pieces of ricocheting metal and slivers of glass burst through the small room. Although Mayberry was squatting outside the doorway, a glass shard struck her face. She felt a splash of liquid burning her cheek. Some sort of acid-based fluid, which explained its glass receptacle. Inside the room, she heard the Roc yelp in pain.

Sucking in a deep breath, Mayberry lunged inside, staying low and aiming the spray upward to where the Roc was standing. Targeting his eyes, knowing the dry chemical spray caused instant irritation and watering.

The Roc's face had been peppered with bullet fragments, along with liquid and glass.

She aimed the last of the Purple-K powder at his eyes, and instinctively he raised both hands to protect them. Mayberry swung the now-empty extinguisher with her left hand at his skull, but he blocked it with his gun hand. The blow knocked the Glock free, sending it clattering onto the metal floor as he reared backward against the waist-high counter where he'd been typing on a portable computer.

The Roc grabbed a mallet hanging on the wall near him and swung its hard rubber tip at Mayberry, striking her near her ear. She collapsed at his feet, momentarily blacking out.

She awoke seconds later, feeling pain and tremendous pressure on her good left wrist. She was lying prone on her back, looking up at the Roc, whose foot was pinning her left arm to the floor. He was facing the counter, typing, too busy and frantic to worry about her.

She tried to free herself. He noticed and ground his foot harder against her left wrist. She screamed in pain.

"Almost," he declared, eager for her to know that he was about to detonate the bomb.

"You'll die too!" she screamed. "Don't do this! You are a doctor, a surgeon. It's wrong!"

He ignored her, focusing on his keyboard.

She bent her legs at her knees and again tried to tug her good left wrist from under his foot, but it was useless. Then she spotted the Glock. Reaching out with her crippled right hand, she swatted the handgun back against her thigh. She forced her thumb into the trigger guard and managed to twist the pistol so it was aimed upward at the Roc. She pressed her thumb against the trigger.

Nothing. The gun didn't discharge. The Glock's safe-action trigger—a blade in its center—had to be squeezed simultaneously with the trigger to fire. Try as she might, she couldn't perform the feat with only her thumb.

"I'm in," the Roc announced, without looking down at her. "Through the firewall. Now the code."

Mayberry ordered her crippled fingers to respond. Cursing herself, she concentrated harder. Her index finger bent slightly, followed by her third finger, wrapping itself around the trigger.

The Glock fired.

The first round punctured his inner thigh, punching into his intestines and lodging itself in his stomach. Caught completely by surprise, he looked bewildered. A second shot aimed higher, entering his left lung and then ripping into his heart.

The Roc stared down at her. Their eyes met. He collapsed, landing hard on top of Mayberry, his face inches from her chin. Dead.

Garrett was the first to arrive, followed by Esther and Major Grant. He pulled the Roc from her.

"I've heard stories about people lifting cars during accidents," Esther said. "You made your crippled fingers work."

"The bomb?" she asked.

Garrett grinned. "We're here, aren't we?"

A visit to sick bay confirmed that Mayberry's left wrist had been broken by the Roc standing on it. Two hours later, they said goodbye to Captain Reynolds and Major Grant. The sea was dead calm. A cloudless sky.

"Now I have two damaged hands," Mayberry commented as they crossed the deck toward a waiting helicopter.

Someone was running toward them, hoping to catch them before they boarded. Robert Calhoun had broken free from the other pool reporters and their naval escort.

"Garrett, I heard there were gunshots."

Garrett stopped so Esther, Kim, and Mayberry could move ahead and avoid the newsman.

"I'm talking to you, Garrett!" Calhoun declared as he neared him. Garrett turned his back.

"Don't you dare walk away from me." Calhoun reached out and grabbed Garrett's shoulder. "The public has a right to—"

The reporter had given Garrett exactly what he wanted. Garrett spun and clutched Calhoun by his throat with such force that the reporter's feet were momentarily lifted from the deck. He pushed him away. Calhoun tumbled backward. His legs went out from under him, and he fell awkwardly onto the deck.

"You attacked me!" Calhoun screamed. He coughed, struggling to catch a breath. "Everyone saw it. You can't assault a member of the press!"

"I didn't," Garrett said. "You're not a reporter. You're a liar."

"You attacked me first. Everyone saw it."

"You were definitely defending yourself," a nearby sailor hollered at Garrett. Several others standing on the deck agreed, and began to applaud. Their applause became cheers. Calhoun looked at the crew members, and then noticed they were not the only ones celebrating.

The other reporters in the pool were also clapping.

EPILOGUE

In a rare public appearance, Iran's Supreme Leader denied that his country had developed nuclear capabilities, claimed that the bomb retrieved from the submarine and displayed in the media was part of a CIA plot to frame Iran, and refuted accusations that Iran had assisted Aziz and the Jihad Brigade in threatening America. He accused the United States of tricking Quds Force general Firouz Kardar into coming to Virginia on a mission to peacefully resolve the crisis, only to be murdered by the CIA. The Americans and Zionists were now falsely accusing the general of participating in a "fantastical" plot conjured to justify further sanctions against the Iranian people.

Two days after the Supreme Leader's public declaration, the Israeli Air Force bombed Iran's underground nuclear facility in Natanz. The attack revealed the previously unknown existence of an Israeli-made bunker-busting bomb capable of penetrating the multiple concrete barriers that the Iranians had believed made their base safe. That same day, President Fitzgerald announced that additional punitive sanctions were being imposed by the United States and its allies on Iran to paralyze its economy and further isolate it.

In Moscow, Russian president Vyachesian Kalugin falsely announced that the Kremlin had discovered that oligarch Taras Zharkov had stolen billions of dollars from the Russian government with help from opposition party leaders. Three critics of Kalugin were tried and given lengthy prison terms. Zharkov's wife, Britt Bjorge-Zharkov, was stripped of her Russian citizenship and deported to her native Norway. Her husband's wealth, property, and businesses were confiscated by Kalugin on behalf of the state, as payment for his theft. Most went directly into the kleptocrat's personal accounts.

CIA Director Connor Whittington was forced to resign by the president after a whistle-blower revealed that Whittington had leaked information to *Washington Interceptor* reporter Robert Calhoun intended to defame Garrett and Mayberry. He retired to his Texas ranch and began work on a memoir defending himself.

Reporter Calhoun submitted his own name for a Pulitzer Prize, based on his exclusive stories, but the committee rejected his application once it was revealed that he'd allowed the CIA to edit them. He was fired and then immediately hired as a political commentator for a left-leaning cable news network.

In a private Mossad ceremony in Tel Aviv, Esther was awarded the Israeli Presidential Medal of Distinction. She left the next morning to track down a radical jihadist operating in Syria.

When Garrett returned to his condo, he telephoned the Arlington Community Services Board and requested housing and mental health services for Jacob, the homeless veteran. He was assured that Jacob's name would be added to a list, with an average wait time of five years. Garrett called the White House. The next morning Jacob was contacted by a social worker, who helped him move into a one-bedroom apartment.

Garrett insisted on driving Mayberry to her first medical checkup. He appeared outside her Reston condo on his Norton motorcycle, which she refused to ride. Reluctantly, she offered him the key fob to her Jaguar.

"I'm driving," he said, "so you don't have much choice but to have lunch with me after your appointment. I know a place in Clifton, Virginia. It's a former Texaco gas station that now serves beer and burgers."

"No expense spared, huh?"

"They make a great steak and cheese too, my favorite, served with fresh-cut fries. Can't beat it with a cold one."

"I don't really like beer."

"I'm planning on drinking yours."

"I heard the agency is considering taking you back," she said as they entered the orthopedist's waiting room. "What division?"

"If I told you, I'd have to kill—"

"Really?" she said, cutting him off. "That old joke is your answer? Not too original."

"I was told you resigned from the FBI," he said. "Why did you do that? You loved being an agent."

She raised both hands. "Would you want me as a partner backing you up? I've been offered a job as the Senate Judiciary Committee's chief investigator."

"Hunting a different kind of wolf."

She lowered her voice. Two other patients were sitting nearby in the waiting area, under a Georgia O'Keeffe knockoff painting of large flowers hanging by a rack of dog-eared magazines.

"The last time I was injured," she said, "you visited me once and then disappeared. Is this a rerun? Are you going to vanish after buying me lunch?"

Garrett stared down at his feet. "I'm embarrassed about that, Valerie. I don't want to disappear, but that's really up to you, isn't it?"

"Me? What exactly do you mean?"

"Don't make this harder for me than it is." He raised his head and looked into her eyes. "I'd like to keep seeing you. You know, on a regular basis."

"Are you saying you want to date me?"

"I think we're beyond dating."

"Garrett," she said, "you know my first husband was killed in Afghanistan, and I've not been with anyone since then. He wasn't the sit-at-home kind. He had to be chasing the action. Putting himself in danger. His death was devastating. You're not a sit-at-home kind of guy either."

"I'm not him," he said, slowly raising his arm and placing it around her shoulders in the waiting-room chair. "I'm not running off. We're a team. We work best together. I've already spoken to the agency."

"About me?"

"How's an assignment in Budapest sound?"

"For both of us? You serious?"

"Yes. The agency thinks we're a hell of a team, and yes, I've never been more serious."

"Have you checked to see if they serve steak and cheese sandwiches there?"

"If you go with me, I'll damn sure find a place that does."

A nurse appeared, holding a chart.

"Valerie Mayberry, the doctor can see you now."

A NOTE ABOUT OUR TSUNAMI PLOT

While *Shakedown* is a work of fiction, using a bomb to create a killer tsunami is a prospect that both the United States and Soviet Union have investigated. During World War II, the US military engaged in Project Seal, a top secret program formed to determine if a tsunami could be created and aimed at an enemy. At the time, US and British scientists considered their research as important as that being done to create a nuclear bomb. After seven months of testing between 1944 and 1945, scientists decided that a single TNT blast could not generate waves strong enough to cause significant damage, and Project Seal was abandoned.

In 1961 the *New York Times* revealed that the Soviet Union had undertaken its own secret program called Lavina ("Avalanche"). It called for attacking both US coasts with 100-million-ton TNT bombs. Nobel Prize–winning physicist Andrei Sakharov acknowledged working on Lavina in his 1990 autobiography *Memoirs*. After the 1961 test of the Tsar Bomba, the largest nuclear weapon ever produced, with a blast yield of fifty-eight megatons of TNT, the Soviets began looking for alternative ways of deploying nuclear bombs other than dropping them from a bomber. Sakharov wrote of Lavina that "the destruction of ports—caused by the above- and underwater explosions as a 100-megaton torpedo 'jumped' out of the water—would have resulted in mass casualties."

In a July 2019 article entitled "The Soviet Union Planned to Wipe Out the United States with a Huge Tsunami," journalist Yekaterina Sinelschikova wrote that some Soviet scientists predicted that if the Tsar Bomba were strategically detonated in the Pacific Ocean, it would create a tsunami so powerful it would flood all of California and continue roaring across the country until it reached the Rockies. Such a flood would have been pointless from a military point of view. Soviet Premier Nikita Khrushchev scuttled the project, choosing instead to focus on equipping submarines with hydrogen bombs.

Shakedown coauthor Pete Earley first learned about Lavina from Sergei Tretyakov, a high-ranking Russian intelligence officer who defected to the United States in 2000 and was the subject of Earley's bestselling book *Comrade J: The Untold Secrets of Russia's Master Spy in America after the End of the Cold War.*

ACKNOWLEDGMENTS

The authors wish to thank Joe DeSantis, who played a key role in thinking through and critiquing *Shakedown*; and Eric Nelson, our editor at Broadside Books, an imprint of HarperCollins. Their insights were invaluable.

In addition, Newt Gingrich wishes to acknowledge Herman Pirchner, an extraordinary student of both Russian and Chinese behavior whose American Foreign Policy Council also publishes a remarkable almanac of terrorism. The trips he has taken Callista and me on to both Russia and China have been eye opening. My daughter Kathy Lubbers, who has been my agent for over twenty years and helps think through the ideas that become books. My daughter Jackie Cushman, who is becoming quite a writer in her own right.

Vince Haley, Ross Worthington, and Louie Brogdon, who have all helped make me a better writer; Ambassador Randy Evans whose shrewd analysis of events constantly inspires me to think new thoughts; Bess Kelly, who has simply made everything more doable; Woody Hales, who schedules everything; Audrey Bird, who is becoming a book-launching expert par excellence; Taylor Swindle, whose money management keeps everything on track; Debbie Myers, who stepped in to grow a new and ever more interesting Gingrich 360, freeing up the time for me to think and write; Rachel Peterson, maybe the best researcher I have ever worked with; and, of course, the toughest editor I ever write with, my wife, Callista, who also makes every day worthwhile.

Pete Earley wishes to thank his literary agent, David Vigliano of AGI Vigliano Literary Associates, Dan and Karen Amato, Jose Aunon, Gloria Brown, James Brown, LeRue and Ellen Brown, Phillip Corn, Ashley Corn, Josh Corn, Donnie and Marcie Davis, Matthew Davis, Bob and Mary Donnell, William Donnell, Amanda Driscoll, George and Linda Earley, David "Gunny" Gambale, Walter and Keran Harrington, Marie Heffelfinger, Geraldine Henryhand, Scooter and Janet Holcombe, Ivania Holland, Michelle Holland, Don and Susan Infeld, Jerry and Linda Kellis, Stacey Ann Kincaid, Dennis and Lorraine King, Julian and Natalie Levine, Bella Francis Luzi, Kelly McGraw Luzi, Rosemary Luzi, Ray and Julie McGraw, Richard and Joan Miles, Dan Morton, David and Cindy Morton, Jay and Barbara Myerson, Mike Sager, Walter and Arlene Simmons, Lynn and LouAnn Smith, Dennis and Suzanne Sorensen, Kendall and Carolyn Starkweather, Jay and Elsie Strine, Stephen Tausend, and Sharon Yuras. He further wishes to memorialize William "Bill" Luzi.

He also is grateful for the love, advice, patience, and support of his wife, Patti Michele Luzi; and their children, Stephen, Tony, Kevin, Kathy, Kyle, Evan, and Traci; and granddaughters, Maribella Earley and Audrey Michele Morton.

Finally, the authors wish to thank Miranda Ottewell for copyediting our manuscript and senior production editor David Koral.

ABOUT THE AUTHORS

Newt Gingrich is a former Speaker of the House and was a 2012 presidential candidate. He is a Fox News contributor and the author of thirty-eight books, including *New York Times* bestsellers, most recently the #1 *New York Times* bestseller *Understanding Trump*.

Pete Earley is a former *Washington Post* reporter and author of sixteen books, including *New York Times* bestsellers. He was a finalist for the 2007 Pulitzer Prize.